Please Girl

A Novel

Jeannie Kraft

Jeannie.Kraft.thewriter@gmail.com

Also visit Jeannie on Instagram and Facebook,
jeannie.kraft.the writer

Dedication

For the Tina's of the world

"You never know how strong you are, until being strong
is the only choice you have."

Bob Marley

Contents

Part One

CHAPTER 1

Jorge Gabor

"**P**lease, girl... *Please pick up the phone...*" Jorge pleaded as he left another message for Tina.

He had burned so many bridges in the past years with family, friends, and clients that he doesn't remember who he can call for help anymore, but it was never a problem with Tina. He knew he could always count on her, even though it might have taken some convincing, especially these last few months.

Good job, Jorge.

Tina's stomach dropped hearing his voice again. There's no question he had another relapse. *I hate you; I hate you,* she repeatedly thought, her throat tightened as she tried to keep calm, yet her heart couldn't stop racing, being way too familiar with what was to come.

This time Jorge must have really screwed up, calling nonstop, leaving messages, or hanging up for the last hour or so.

Tina usually had a few months between relapses, but the last one was only two weeks ago. This alone was a bad sign, especially after not hearing from him in the past week, after calling and leaving messages, asking him to call back so she knew he was okay.

Tears streamed down her cheeks, burning her eyes, not having the will to wipe them away. Tina slid down the kitchen wall, crippled by the storm that was about to hit again. She desperately tried to calm her nerves, and not let the fears pull her defenses down completely, but it was always a battle with her father.

Tina always held onto the hope that he would change, like the many times he promised in the past. Just two weeks ago she gave him the money he needed to get him back on track.

He swore he would never bet again, but who knows what he thought. Jorge had a way of manipulating everything he said to be true. Many times, he convinced himself of his own lies.

She didn't ask for too much. She didn't want material things like designer clothes, high-end make-up, or anything high-end in that manner because they didn't really matter. They didn't breathe like he did.

Tina just wanted him to be a normal dad, one who had a normal job, coming home at normal times. She wanted a dad to spend normal hours together, hang out, watch TV, play tennis, or help with homework. Not one who freely gave empty promises, and disappeared at all hours of the day, and then lied about his whereabouts whenever she'd ask.

She knew the drill, but it never got easier. She hated herself for always being forgiving, giving chance after chance, still somehow always holding hope he would change.

The panic attacks started in middle school and tormented her whenever things didn't seem right at home, and that was usually often. It would come out of nowhere and escalate to Tina hiding underneath the covers for comfort, lying in a fetal position, swaying back and forth, until she felt settled again.

Jorge never thought about how all this tore her apart. This never made any sense to Tina, but during the madness with her father and the monster, she just wanted to calm the storm, and not ignite it any more than it already was. She knew its strength and she wasn't going to test it until now. Tina knew it was now or never, and she didn't even know if she could really do it this time around, even though she practiced countless times.

The dream seems so childish now, with all the broken promises and endless chances she gave him, embarrassed that she was so ridiculously gullible. She was reminded that deep down nothing had ever changed, and if anything, Jorge's condition had worsened. In the midst of it all, she had really bad daddy issues, a term she learned in therapy.

"Where is she?" Jorge asked, as he became increasingly impatient, banging on the steering wheel, riding around town having no real place to go, burning gas that would eventually leave him stranded.

He decided to pull into a gas station, hoping he had at least enough change for a cup of coffee to take the edge off his nerves and hunger, and to pass some time until calling Tina again. Jorge thought she must have gotten caught up at work and would be home soon.

Always watch your back.

Jorge looked at the dirty and cluttered floor of the car, hoping to find any change or better yet, real bills, underneath the mounds of betting tickets, reused plastic water bottles, wrappers, and other garbage, but found nothing.

He was frustrated that he couldn't even afford a cup of coffee, frustrated he couldn't live without a bet again, frustrated his life had gotten so out of control that nobody cared about him, frustrated he had really messed up again, frustrated he wasn't at the dog track, frustrated he was alive.

He leaned back against the worn leather headrest in defeat. If he could fast forward his life to his deathbed he would. He was so sick and tired of being sick and tired.

He closed his heavy eyes, feeling the sun come through the driver's window. Trying to just feel nothing and be nothing was actually a good thing now. That was until his stomach growled again, and he was back to the mess he was in. This time he didn't know if he could pull it off. He wasn't sure if Tina could either.

Don't be stupid, Jorge.

He lifted his head, looking at the car's floor again, looking for anything to eat to subdue his hunger. He saw what he thought to be mints on the passenger's side. Jorge reached over to see if it was what he hoped he saw, or if his mind was playing games with him, which has been happening to him a lot lately.

Score, he thought. Stretching as far as he could to grab them, thankful that they were mints. One rolled away under a withered picture of Tina who was about to blow out the candles on her third birthday cake. Jorge smiled, seeing how little Tina was, wearing the homemade flower dress Eva designed and sewn at night when Tina was asleep. Eva was quite the seamstress, after teaching herself to sow to save money.

He forgot about the candy and slumped back against the headrest again, soaking up the memory which still gripped his heart, one that he hadn't forgotten or wished to forget, like other memories that shamed him. It was a time when he was happy and believed in living a simple life, not wanting anything more. Maybe it was because he was 27 and Eva was 22. He didn't know the consequences of betting.

In the picture, Jorge was kneeling beside Tina, Eva next to him, Tina clapping, eyes glowing, soaking up the excitement of her birthday, wearing a smile that lit up the room, about to blow out the candles from a cake Eva had baked.

Tina couldn't stop clapping, listening to the birthday song for the third time. Jorge became teary-eyed as he remembered how she would keep saying "again" after blowing out the candles. Eva and Jorge would agree each time, adding to the excitement. Looking back, it was always the little things that mattered the most. If only he had kept living his life this way.

They were superintendents at The Windship Apartments in Queens, New York, where they lived, free in exchange for handling minor repairs in the apartment building. While Jorge attended cosmetology school at night, Eva handled the emergencies until he returned. It didn't matter because they were a team working for a better life, one where they would open their own hair salons in Florida. Things didn't happen as planned.

If only he hadn't tried his luck more than a few times than he should have and hadn't listened to its lies and empty promises of giving him and his family what they deserved - a bigger house and a nicer car. If only he had stopped when he could have, but now he did exactly what it said, and if not, he couldn't hear himself think anymore. It now lived in him, and he felt hopeless.

Maybe things would be very different now, and he wouldn't be broken and lost. Maybe he and Eva would still be married, and he would still be seeing his granddaughters.

Maybe he would still have a close relationship with Tina too, and he wouldn't have missed her last birthday because they weren't talking. Maybe he wouldn't hate himself like he did now, always calling Tina when he was in major trouble and forgetting to ask if she ever needed anything, like a father should.

A whole lot of maybes tore at his heart. He just wanted to start over. A redo with Eva and Tina.

Stop this nonsense. They don't love you anymore.

He put his car in reverse. His destination was Tina's house.

Enough of this bullshit. I should have gone there from the start.

Jorge drove his once white car, now permanently gray, through the opened community gates. As he pulled around the corner, he held his breath, hoping Christopher's pickup truck wasn't in the driveway.

If so, he would be screwed. There was no other way to get out of this mess without Tina's help. He and Christopher weren't exactly on speaking terms, but he hoped he'd come around eventually.

But as luck would have it, Tina's minivan was the only vehicle in the driveway.

"Yes!" he shouted with such joy and relief, pounding the steering wheel like he had finally won a bet.

She is playing with you. Don't be so nice! We don't have time.

Jorge called Tina again. "Hello, we are unable to answer your call. Please leave a brief message, and we will call you back as soon as we can," Tina's recorded voice played again.

Yeah, right, girl. Where are you?

This time he didn't leave a message. Time was ticking, and Gabby was on to him now. He knew he was on borrowed time because he hadn't paid up. Not by a long shot. Gabby was more than pissed. He had other people looking for him too.

Two minutes hadn't even passed when he called Tina again. It was getting down to the wire. He wouldn't hang up this time, listening to the greeting again until he heard the beep to leave a message.

"Please, girl, answer. I know you are home. I…I need you…" his voice cracked. "Please, girl. I need help… Please, girl…I love you, Tina. Please, girl…"

Tina's body trembled as she heard his voice again. Fearful that he knew that she was home, pleading for her help, she started exhaling and inhaling until she could no longer. She began counting down.

3…2….1… You got this.

He called again. The answer machine greeted him, " Hello, we are unable to answer your call. Please leave a brief message, and we will call you back as soon as we can."

"Please, girl…I need you," he begged.

Jorge called again. This time she answered on her knees. Her panicked heart could not take it anymore.

"Hello?" she stammered.

"Hi, girl. It's me, Dad. I've been calling you," he said, his voice cracking.

Tina didn't say a word. Jorge noticed this awkward silence and pressed on.

"Is everything okay?" he asked.

"No," she coldly replied.

Jorge played off her answer. "Okay, listen, I need to see you."

"No . . ."

"Please, girl, this can't wait."

"No... I'm not feeling well."

She is lying! Don't believe her! Don't be too soft!

"It will only be a second, Tina. Please let me come over . . . please."

"No."

"I'm actually outside now. It's important."

Fear gripped her, her temperature rising, the adrenaline raging in every part of her being.

"You know I'm in trouble," Jorge added.

She needed to be the one to break the generational curse. This was more than enough to give her all the strength she needed. Tina needed to save herself and her family, or they were doomed too.

"What happened to your promise?" Tina asked, mustering all the courage she had.

"I know, but you know..." he suggested.

"What excuse do you have now?" Tina cut him off. She felt rage towards her father for doing this to her again, for wanting her to feel guilty, for causing the trauma she had experienced for most of her life.

"I screwed up."

Tina exhaled again. This time, it didn't matter that he admitted to anything he did.

"Well, that's not my problem," she managed to say, feeling the sting of her bold words.

She exhaled out again, hoping to recover.

Jorge was taken by Tina's fire.

Did she just talk to you like that?

"I promise if you help me this time, I will never ask for it again. I swear to God. Please, girl," Jorge begged.

You are too weak! Push harder!

"Please, girl.... I thought you loved me."

"I don't care," Tina said, standing firm against her father's sickness, and this time there would be no looking back.

"You don't mean that, girl. I forgive you...please. You don't know what you are saying. God said to honor your father and mother."

"I do."

She slammed the phone down. This was the first time she said no and meant it, feeling it in every part of her soul. She felt a huge part of her expire, finally cutting away the pieces of the lifeline she had given her father's addiction for so many years.

The doorbell rang, and hard knocks followed. Jorge wasn't going down without a fight, even if it was his own daughter.

"Please, girl. Open the door."

Good boy, Jorge.

CHAPTER 2

Twenty Years Earlier

Jorge left the track with just a few dollars.

He was under pressure. He had less than twenty-four hours to pay Tony back. Nothing else mattered, not even the afternoon tennis game he had planned with Tina.

Jorge dared to call him earlier to see if there was a chance, he could give him another day to repay him, but this only made matters worse.

"Are you fucking joking? You know you're really pissing me off now!" Tony shouted.

"Please," Jorge pleaded.

"Don't waste my time!"

"Please, just hear me out."

That's the way to handle it, Jorge.

His phone slipped in his slick palms. He knew Tony would be pissed if he somehow hung up on him. He would think it was on purpose, and it would trigger his rage.

"It's for my daughter, Tina."

"Wow! Does she need an operation now? Maybe I should ask Eva," Tony yelled, his breathing heavy.

Jorge froze. Sweat bullets rushed down his rugged face. Fear tightened his chest harder, feeling the crunch of the situation, yet he had to think of something really quick to get money, or Eva would leave him for good this time.

"Jorge! Are you still there?

"Yes, you said I should be quiet."

"I just want my money, man. Not the bullshit you have been giving. You got me?" Tony asked.

"Sure," Jorge said, still holding the cellphone close to his flushed face.

Think! Think! Think! Who else can you borrow money from?

Driving over the Somerset Bridge, Jorge glanced at the crystal blue inter-coastal waters, the waves peacefully swaying back and forth. It dawned on him how those waves could solve his problems. He could simply drive over the bridge and let the current pull him deeper, filling his lungs until he couldn't breathe anymore. He would finally be free of the debts taunting him every second of the day.

No, that is stupid! How about Gabby?

Yes, there was always Gabby, but that was like selling one's soul to the devil. Jorge knew that Gabby would torture borrowers who didn't honor their payments, and that scared Jorge more than anything.

Your big win is around the corner. I promise.

Jorge glanced at the dashboard. The gas light was on. His heart rate rose as he knew he only had a few more miles before the car would stop dead.

"Please God, not now," he feared. "Please, Jesus! Help!"

Fear shook him again. He only had a few dollars with him. He knew the car could stop at any moment, and he could be hit from behind, adding more stress to an already stressful situation. He wasn't even sure if the car was insured anymore.

He took whatever bills Eva said needed to be paid but only paid the necessary ones, like water, electricity, and phone. He'd get to the others when he had extra money. He couldn't remember the car insurance company's name, which was a bad sign. This probably meant he hadn't paid for it in months.

"Jesus Christ, that is all I need. Please, God, have mercy."

He sees a gas station next to Walmart.

"Hallelujah!" he cried, sighing in relief.

Jorge wondered what he would tell his daughter about being late again. He couldn't remember what he said the last time, and he wasn't sure that Eva would cover for him again.

Use your smarts!

While pumping gas, he looked through his wallet to see if he had any money hidden in one of the folds. The only thing he found was a Sports Authority gift card a client gave him years ago as a Christmas gift. He tried to exchange it for cash at the track, but there weren't any takers. He looked at it now and smiled. He was finally going to use it.

Once in the sporting store, he went straight to the tennis section. He would use the gift card on a case of Penn Extra Duty tennis balls and a much-needed ball hopper. Tina was going to be overjoyed. He was sure of it.

"Thank you, Marilynn," he said, thinking back to the client who gave it to him.

He was now two hours late, but it didn't matter. He had the perfect lie and the perfect gift to back it up all nicely.

Jackpot! Now find some money!

Jorge looked at the box of tennis balls next to him, feeling vindicated as he drove home. He felt like he could walk straight into the house as if he wasn't late at all.

He was only half right.

CHAPTER 3

Eva, Mother Hen

"Tina!" Eva called, "Breakfast is ready. Hurry up."

Tina rushed to get her backpack and tried her best to get downstairs before Eva shouted again.

"Coming!" she yelled.

Eva had trouble sleeping last night, tossing and turning, desperately wanting to sleep, but her nerves and anger kept her up.

"Good morning, Mom. Something smells good," Tina said.

Eva forced a smile, looking up at Tina. She had Tina when she was just 19, just barely a child herself.

Everyone knew not to cross Eva, especially when it came to Tina.

She once called the police when another child hit Tina at the park. She was just four when a boy hit her on the head with a basketball.

When the mother came to see what was happening, Eva boldly argued, "If you would have been watching your son, none of this would have happened. I don't blame your son, but *you*."

The mother didn't know what to say, and even the police couldn't debate it.

There was no denying her love and allegiance towards Tina. Jorge knew this.

One memory that still haunted him was when he was playing guitar with Tina on his lap. Somehow the guitar accidentally tapped Tina's head, and she started to cry. When Eva asked what had happened, Jorge explained that he didn't mean for the guitar to slip on Tina. Eva immediately walked over, took the guitar from him, and banged it into pieces, leaving him speechless. Needless to say, the guitar was history and was never spoken about again. Jorge knew Eva wasn't someone to play with when it came to Tina.

"I baked you blueberry muffins."

Though money was tight, Eva did a good job hiding this from Tina, always looking for the best prices, saving whatever she could, and sewing on the side. She hid what she could from Jorge, or she was certain there would be nights they went hungry.

"Wasn't it nice of Dad to buy me a case of tennis balls yesterday?" Tina asked, hoping her mother would agree.

Eva's stomach tightened as she thought of the betting tickets, she found in Jorge's pants last night after being promised that he wouldn't bet anymore.

This time, she didn't pretend she hadn't seen them. Instead, she took every last one, appalled by the sight of each and every last one of them, and saved them. She felt nauseous knowing that each ticket was money being wasted and thrown in the garbage instead of being used for overdue bills and the family.

Eva wanted him to know she was aware of him still betting, hoping he would say something to her. She was ready to let it hit the fan. No more looking the other way. No more listening to his empty promises and lies. She shook her head, disappointed in the life she was living. She knew Jorge would never admit to betting again. He would still manipulate the truth in his favor. It became too exhausting to catch him in a lie anymore, but she did every once in a while.

Maybe she would take the whole lot she found and leave a trail all the way to the car for him to see? She couldn't, as Tina would see them. Was it really worth it?

Jorge's repeated lies and disappointments created a wedge between them. Eva couldn't help but feel abandoned by Jorge, and this created distance. She felt they were too divided, but she couldn't leave. A tiny part of her still loved him.

"Yes, it was *nice* of him," Eva answered, trying not to break Tina's spirit. "Now enjoy your food while it's still hot."

Eva went to the sink to avoid any more conversations about Jorge.

Tina nervously smiled, feeling something wasn't right, but at least Eva responded and agreed it was nice of her father to buy her a case of tennis balls and a ball hopper. Still, her stomach started to tighten. It seemed whenever she mentioned Jorge, her mom changed the subject or was short with words.

"Is everything okay?" Tina wondered.

Eva didn't answer. She had to be careful of what to say, and what not to, always feeling boxed in and guarded with what she should share. The goal was always to separate Tina from what was happening at home.

"What is it? You can tell me," Tina pressed.

Again, there was another opportunity to tell Tina the truth. Even if she wanted to, Eva didn't know where to start. Instead, she took a deep, frustrated breath.

"No…no, I was just thinking about my bank appointment later this morning. I'm fine, really. I am," Eva lied again, frustrated by how deep in the hole she was with the lies she kept from Tina.

"Are you sure? I just feel like you're upset about something." Tina stared at Eva, hoping she would share the truth if she was hiding it.

Of course, Eva wanted more than anything to tell Tina about what was really happening at home. She wanted to reveal how Jorge was financially draining them and emotionally draining her, especially now that Tina was asking. The opportunity was there for the taking, but she just couldn't.

There were many times when Eva was seconds away from exposing Jorge, but fear always took her down. She would always think it wasn't the right time, but she knew it was an excuse because she was terrified. Eva did the next best thing: tame it any way she could, even if it meant hating herself over the years to create a pseudo-family to protect Tina.

Eva was going to the bank to question the latest bank statement. It was off by thousands. Tina knew a person went to the bank for one reason only: money. This was a sore subject in her family. The lack of money was why her parents often fought at night, hearing many arguments between them when they thought Tina was asleep or got lost in the moment.

"I just have a few things on my mind. It's nothing bad, so don't you worry," Eva tried to assure her daughter, feeling trapped in a lie.

Tina would try one last time. "Are the bills still bothering you?"

"Don't worry about money. We are good. I promise you we are good. Everybody has bills. It's a fact of life."

Eva leaned over, kissed Tina, and then returned to the kitchen sink for refuge.

"I have a good idea," Eva happily proposed. Tina looked at her mother with a smile.

"I'll take you to school this morning. It's on the way to the bank."

Tina nodded, liking the idea of spending more time with Eva. Eva smiled back, feeling overwhelmed at the pure sight of Tina.

"Oh, that would be nice, Mom," Tina replied.

As Tina got up from the kitchen stool, she froze, remembering the A/C was still broken in the car.

Oh no.

She felt paralyzed by fear. What was she going to tell her mother when she'd ask why her father hadn't had it fixed?

And yet, Tina's fear didn't come true. Eva didn't say a word about the broken A/C. When it wouldn't turn on after a few attempts, Eva just rolled the window down like it wasn't a concern and smiled away.

Inside, Eva was fuming, another promise Jorge didn't follow through with. He even said the A/C was the coldest it had ever been last night. Was he that delusional?

Still, Tina felt like it was her fault for not saying anything. She also felt her father must have had his reasons. Maybe the part that was needed wasn't in stock, or he actually *did* get it fixed, but it broke again.

Never in her wildest dreams could Tina imagine or believe that his actions were the reason for the still-broken A/C.

CHAPTER 4

Missing Money

"Good morning. How can I help you today?" Gina asked. Eva had knots in her stomach, hoping she was just being paranoid about coming to the bank to check on the missing money from a savings account that Jorge promised he wouldn't touch.

For what seemed like a long moment, feeling faint. Eva was lost for words. Feeling unstable, hoping she wouldn't lose her balance, wanting out of her body, but she needed to know the truth.

Face your fear. You are stronger.

"Yes, hi there... umm...sorry, I just went blank for a moment."

Gina was sympathetic towards Eva. "No worries, I've been there. How can I help you?"

"Thank you... Gina... I actually have a question about a check I deposited a few weeks ago. I believe you assisted me then as well," Eva replied, smiling at Gina.

She looked at the young teller, maybe around twenty, thinking back to when she was around that age. She never imagined how her life would turn out. She never thought that the love of her life would be the one she shouldn't trust anymore.

Gina just looked at Eva, trying to place her because she did look familiar. She saw an average of two hundred bank customers a day, but there was something she did remember about Eva. It was her sad eyes, but it didn't come to her just yet.

"You talked about a party you were going to after work... an engagement party," Eva added, hoping this would refresh Gina's memory.

"Oh, yeah," Gina said, "That's right. That was about three weeks ago. My mind is off today too. So much going on here...Sorry. Aren't you Jorge's wife, Mrs. Gabor?"

"Yes, I'm Eva."

"What about the check?"

"Yes, the check. I'm just a little confused why the money isn't in the account anymore. I didn't take it out, write a check for that amount, or transfer it into another account. I'm certain my husband didn't either," Eva said.

Damn. Why did I just defend Jorge?

"Now, let's see. I'll look at the account in question, Mrs. Gabor. I just need your driver's license." Gina asked.

Eva looked for her wallet in her worn backpack, feeling a little ashamed. She should have cleaned it out before coming to the bank, but life was too complicated now. Reaching down, she found her matching Coach leather wallet with her driver's license inside.

Eva examined the driver's license, not remembering the last time she looked at it. It was no secret that she'd aged, but that wasn't exactly why she couldn't recognize the person she was a few years ago.

Her hair was always in a ponytail now. It had been over a year since she let Jorge cut her hair, and he didn't offer to cut it either. Eva's eyebrows hadn't been waxed in months either, and she couldn't remember the last time she even wore make-up.

What happened to that girl?

How she missed the girl who took pride in being charming and witty. She wondered if that girl was still living inside.

Gina glanced at the license, handed it back, and looked at the questioned account activity. She reviewed the balance. Eva was right; the three grand had diminished to only forty-two dollars. Gina reviewed the history of the account. Just as Eva said, the money was deposited three weeks ago, but it was withdrawn the same day by Jorge Gabor.

"It looks like the money was withdrawn by your husband. Maybe he put the money in another account in another bank, or maybe in a retirement account, and he forgot to tell you," Gina suggested with a nervous grin.

Eva felt sick again and her heart thumped painfully in her chest. She was in panic mode, but this time she didn't have the comforts of home to shake it off. Rage was taking a hold of her and she would have to internalize it until she got back to the car.

"Are you okay, Mrs. Gabor? Would you like some water?" Gina asked.

"Oh no, I'm fine. I'm just a little faint. I rushed over this morning and forgot to eat breakfast."

Eva graciously thanked Gina and left the bank, feeling utter hopelessness. She had a useless savings account, and all she wanted to do was disappear from this life.

It frightened her to know that she didn't know Jorge anymore. He was no better than a criminal, blatantly and shamelessly stealing from her and Tina. Not only did he drain the savings account, but he also didn't use the seven-hundred-dollar check to fix the car's air conditioner like he had promised.

Why are you putting up with this? You must do something, or you will die this way.

If she had a gun, she would shoot Jorge; that's how angry she was. It would be aimed straight at his heart, and she would never look back. It would serve as payback for breaking her heart repeatedly. Jorge had finally crossed the finish line.

"Enough of the lies! I hate you!" she screamed once in the car. "I have wasted my life on you! No more, you bastard! Those days are over!" she shouted as she wiped away the tears that burned her eyes.

Eva drove home fuming, thinking of her options. Though she couldn't take off on a plane, she promised herself that changes were coming.

It's time. Save yourself. Save Tina.

CHAPTER 5

Tina's New Friend

Tina was on her way to class when Alex called her name. She briefly looked at him but quickly turned away, blushing.

"Tina Gabor," Alex called again, but she kept walking.

Alex felt embarrassed too. Didn't she know that girls ached for him to look their way, let alone call out their name, and here she was, running away?

What gives? He thought.

Tina thought maybe this was a joke. Alex had friends who did pranks at school and videoed them. She didn't want to be part of some middle school game.

How did I get involved in this?

Alex called again; this time louder. He wanted to warn her, but Tina continued to ignore him. She made it to class without talking to him, but she knew if he wanted to talk to her again, he would. She was right.

Eva pulled into the driveway, devastated that it had come to this. Not so much on the edge anymore. The fresh air and the drive helped clear her mind.

So relieved that she hadn't driven to the hair salon to confront Jorge in front of coworkers and clients. Driving, she realized it wouldn't have done any good, for he would tell the perfect lie again, and she would be the one left standing looking like a fool.

Here goes crazy, Eva.

As she sat on the couch, she became emotional again. It never occurred to her, until now, that by not doing anything about Jorge's problem, it only made matters worse. Now she was willingly living, breathing, and breeding Jorge's lies, whether she wanted to believe it or not.

The phone rang.

"Hello?" Eva said.

"Hey, I'm busy here at the salon, so I won't be able to come home until later," Jorge stated.

It didn't make her hot or cold anymore. Eva was too emotionally exhausted to say much.

"Okay…just don't forget your promise to Tina."

"Oh, I forgot, I'll try my hardest, but if I get held up, I won't be able to. Could you smooth it out?"

Fuck you.

Eva's rage popped out again.

"Listen, Jorge. I'm going to call Penny to start cleaning the house again. I can't do it alone, and I'm tired," she answered, completely ignoring his request.

"Well, we'll see. Just don't call her yet. Maybe when the season starts again, and things pick up."

Seriously, fuck you.

"What? If you would stop going to the track, Penny would still be coming every Saturday."

"Okay, whatever you want, dear," Jorge uttered.

"Oh. I see. I forgot you're in the salon. Must keep your front, or maybe you're at the track," More of Eva's rage continued to boil. "Either way, I don't give a fuck."

You are going to let her talk to you like that?

Jorge continued to downplay Eva. "Okay, honey, don't worry. I'll take care of it when I get home."

He winked at Mrs. Smith, who patiently sat at his station.

Eva slammed the phone down, wishing it was Jorge's face.

"I can't live like this anymore!" Eva shouted at the top of her lungs, feeling her ears pop, surprised at how long her shouts carried on. All the pent-up frustration finally came out after fifteen minutes of screams.

You have to do something.

CHAPTER 6

Crunch Time

Jorge was a man with a hefty debt to pay.

Early in the morning, while Tina and Eva were asleep, he meticulously searched the house looking in every possible hiding place for money. He found nothing, leaving him frustrated.

At the salon, while combing Mrs. Smith's hair, the receptionist, Donna, called him over.

Donna informed him, "Jorge, you have a call on Line 1."

He looked up, not interested.

"It's Tony," Donna said, waving the phone and signaling him to take the call like she did many times before.

Shake it off. You're still good. He just wants to intimidate you, but he'll see when you win the prize tonight.

He wasn't going to take any calls from him just yet. Jorge felt he was safe as long as Tony couldn't jump through the phone.

"Donna, please let Tony know I'm busy with a client, and I'll talk to him later," Jorge responded. He smiled like he didn't have a care in the world.

As he continued to cut Mrs. Smith's hair, he thought of the money she must have in her bank account, having a rich husband and all. The thought of asking a client for a loan hadn't occurred to him until now. He assured himself he was sure to win tonight and could pay her back with interest and still walk away with enough money to settle all his debts. He felt confident that she would help him.

Ask her...she likes you!

Mrs. Smith smiled at Jorge, always appreciating the extra time he took when she flew in from Manhattan and had her hair appointments. Massaging her scalp, running his skilled, soft hands through her hair, and leaving her with a classic style that made her friends jealous. Jorge had become a dear friend, listening to her problems, and never judging.

Donna placed the call on hold and walked to Jorge's station.

"Excuse me, Mrs. Smith. I'm sorry. Can I please have a word with Jorge? It will only be a moment. I am so sorry, but this just can't wait." Donna said, with a nervous smile,

"Of course, dear. Jorge, you seem to be a wanted man today, but I can see why. Now take the call. I'm in no rush."

Donna leaned into Jorge, with her right hand covering her mouth, whispering in a shaky voice, "Tony will be on his way here if you don't take the call."

"Okay, that will be fine. Tell him I'll see him later," he answered.

Donna did a double take at Jorge. *What the hell was he talking about?* she wondered.

She tried again, this time leaning hard into Jorge, trying to knock some sense into him.

"Listen, Jorge, not sure why you aren't taking the call, but Tony will come here to tear you into pieces if you don't. Do you want that? Do you want him to tell your clients something they shouldn't know?" Donna advised in her New York accent.

Jorge still kept his stance, keeping his poker face on.

"Oh, really? I don't think so. Don't you know by now that he's all talk?" Jorge affirmed, dead serious.

Donna snapped. "Take the fucking call, or I won't cover for you when Eva calls anymore. I'm serious. I am done."

Jorge smiled and politely told Mrs. Smith that she was right and that he was going to take the call.

"Tony, how are you doing, man?" Jorge said with a smile.

"Oh, now you decide to take my call. You know I was on my way over."

Jorge turned his back, facing the receptionist's desk. "Hey man, can I call you back? I'm really busy."

"Spare me, I'm surprised people still come to see you. They'd be running to the hills if they knew the real you."

"Please, Tony. I don't want to hear this. I can't be on the phone when a client is waiting for me. I need the money, man."

He looked down at the schedule and saw that he was done by two p.m.

"I'll call you by three. I promise. I'll be done by then," Jorge assured Tony.

"You better, do you understand? I want to hear it from you!"

"I understand one hundred percent."

"Do you have my money?"

Jorge's face started to burn as he closed his eyes, tilting his head to the side, getting ready to lie again.

"Yes, I do," he responded, wishing he actually did. "It is right here."

"Good answer. I will let you return to your client, but I'll wait for your call."

"Okay, thanks, man, I appreciate it. I won't let you down."

Jorge hung up, feeling his world go to shit again. A magician, he was not. He could not create time or money, the two things he needed the most by the end of the day.

Around two o'clock, Jorge prepared himself to call Eva about not being home until later, which meant he wouldn't be around to play tennis with Tina as promised.

He didn't want to miss it but figured she'd be alright if Eva lessened the blow. He went to the empty staff room to make the call and took a deep breath before dialing home, expecting Eva to pick up. Instead, the answering machine did.

"Hello, you've reached the Gabor family. No one is available to answer your call right now, but please leave your name, number, and message. We will return your call as soon as we can," Eva's voice played.

"Hello, is anyone home?"

No answer.

"Is anyone there?" he asked again.

He expected Eva to answer this time, but she didn't.

"Girl, it's Dad. Aww... a good friend of mine from New York stopped by the salon .... and invited me to dinner.... I won't be home to play tennis with you later...sorry. I'll make it up to you with a new racket. We'll go to Sports Authority, and you can pick any racket you like. Price doesn't matter, anything for my little girl. Okay, love you two."

Another lie.

He patted his rear pant pocket, making sure the tips he made from the day were still there. He thought about Tony and knew he said he was going to call him back, but he didn't.

Screw him.

CHAPTER 7

Down to the Wire

Jorge took off to the Palm Springs Kennel Club. He calculated that he needed to win about nine grand to keep afloat: eight grand for Tony, seven hundred to get the car's air conditioner repaired, and one hundred and fifty for Tina's new racket.

Just like an unexpected heat wave, he felt overwhelmed by the task.

Can I do it? Can I turn the money into nine G's in one night? Of course, you can!

Fifteen minutes later, he arrived at the dog track with a mission.

See how good you feel? This is your home.

He parked in the VIP section, seeing familiar cars, but luckily not Tony's. Once he reached the top of the escalator, there was a bar to the left of the race pavilion where regulars greeted him.

"Hey, Jorge, good to see you," Gus shouted.

He lost his house to foreclosure weeks ago, yet one would never guess it. He was delighted as could be for a chance to be in the next race.

He inherited his grandma's house free and clear but took out a home equity line of credit when his liking for greyhounds became an obsession. He bet it all away, never able to repay it.

He told his buddies that he gave the house to his daughter and that she kicked him out. He was now living in a tent community in the woods, collecting his social security checks and living for the next bet.

Jorge smiled and waved to people who knew him, much like a movie star walking the red carpet, taking in the attention. The feeling sure beat the ones he felt most of the time. Here people liked him.

Palm Springs Kennel Club was a place where all walks of life went to try their chance at luck and for fun— lawyers, teachers, judges, postal workers, store clerks, janitors, and policemen, all for various reasons.

There were social gamblers who sought out entertainment for the day or night. Dining at fine restaurants with friends while watching the races, placing random bets just for fun, not worrying if they won. It was good either way. They just wanted to have a good time. It was a nice way to end the night, but if they lost, it wouldn't be the end of the world.

Jorge was once a social gambler. Those days were now long gone.

He arrived at his lucky seat, looking at the race schedule, his heart racing, and the adrenaline kicking in.

Concentrate!

The first race began in ten minutes. He reminded himself to stick to the plan. The one backed by data and statistics, not hunches.

Jorge looked at the roster for any past winners that pulled it in for him and was happy to see familiar Class A or Class B dogs. His heart relaxed a bit as he circled their names, feeling confident in his picks. He looked again at the ones he had just circled. All four dogs had good track records, but he saw an inconsistent favorite who could either be hot or cold.

On a very good day, she could outrun any greyhound at the track, yet she would run too fast on a bad day, then trip and fall. Others would run right past her. Jorge circled her anyway, feeling there was no harm in including her, though he knew this wasn't exactly sticking to the plan.

Jorge glanced at the clock; it was time to make his final picks. He looked at the schedule again and zeroed in on the dogs he circled: Shy Sly (2), Greta's Crown (4), Suzy Q (5), Edward Bello (7), and Madame Bovary (8).

He looked at the clock again, seeing that he only had a minute left to bet. It was getting down to the wire now. Sweat bubbles formed at his brow. He was nervous; he needed this win big time to get his life back. There was no room for any errors or fuck ups. It was a do-or-die situation, one that could bring the Gabor house together again, or divide it even more.

Jorge's first bet was a superfecta box. It was a costly bet, but he had to bet big to win big.

He especially liked Greta; she was real fast. Some compared her to the speed of light because they felt she was that fast. Jorge had a good feeling about her winning this race, believing she would pull it through for him tonight.

Nice choices, Jorge.

Jorge placed the bet at Trudy's wage window. She was his favorite cashier at the kennel club.

"Good luck, Jorge," Trudy said.

She was a young attractive English girl who started working at the track a few months ago straight from London.

"I really do hope you win big tonight."

"Thanks, appreciate it," Jorge winked back, soaking in her well wishes. He would give her a hundred-dollar tip if he won.

He returned to the viewing area and sat in his lucky seat, looking straight at the racetrack. He stayed seated until the starting bell rang. At that moment, he jumped from his lucky seat to his feet like a puppeteer had lifted him from above for showtime.

He was in a trance now, his eyes glued to the track, and hence the rush began.

The graceful dogs were neck-to-neck, not one making a break yet. Jorge was oblivious to everything else around him. A bomb could have exploded, and it wouldn't have fazed him. His eyes were laser-focused on his picks.

"Yes, yes, yes!" he shouted.

He once tried explaining his fascination with betting to a friend. The only explanation he could give was the euphoric feeling. There was no better feeling than being in a bet. The higher the stakes, the higher the rush, along with an anticipated win. It brought him a thrill that he could never really explain. Therapy books called it the zone.

"Number two, go faster! What are you doing?" he yelled at Shy Sly as he lagged to fifth place.

This was not good, as the race was about to end. He screamed louder, somehow thinking his voice would help. He needed Shy Sly to pick up the pace.

He thought about the money he needed to win. He continued to shout at number two, his fists pumping faster and faster. "Come on, Shy Sly! Show them what you got! It isn't over yet!"

However, there were four dogs ahead of Shy Sly. His voice grew louder as he jumped up and down like a child having a major meltdown. If he could, he'd run out to the track and find a way to make him run faster.

"Shy Sly, come on, boy! Come on. You can do it!" Miraculously, Shy Sly started to run faster and was making a comeback to fourth place. The other three dogs were still in the lead, but Shy Sly needed to be in the top four for him to win.

He held onto the cross around his neck, and within seconds, Shy Sly was trekking in the lead, passing those he felt dust from only moments ago.

Jorge screamed until Shy Sly ran past the finish line, leaving the others in the dust now.

See, I told you!

Jorge fell to his seat victorious, wiping the sweat from his brow. He covered his face with his warm and clammy hands in utter relief. He finally could now smile and feel good about the win turning his fate around.

It was like he had just run the race himself. He felt overjoyed and overwhelmed, closer to settling his debt to Tony. He continued to enjoy the last of the lingering high. After all, it had been a while since his last one, from the start to the end of a winning bet.

"Hallelujah!"

He looked at the prompt for the results to confirm that he'd won.

You did it, Jorge!

The prize was thirty-five hundred dollars. He was close to having all the money he needed before he could leave and be a free man again. He looked at the race schedule for his next bet, torn about whether he should press his luck. He didn't know most of the dogs but didn't want to waste a race. Time was running out for him.

He decided to play a quiniela, betting only on the first and second place, though the odds were not as good as the superfecta, and it didn't cost as much either. Regardless, it was still a bet, inching him closer to getting Tony off his back, and that was all that mattered. He wanted Eva to look at him like she used to, with loving eyes.

Good boy, Jorge. Way to go!

"Hey, hey, hey! Look who's here, the liar. I didn't know the track had a hair salon now," Tony remarked over Jorge's shoulder.

Jorge's knees weakened. Tony grabbed Jorge's shoulder and spun him around, so they were man-to-man.

"Hey, man, what's up?" Jorge said with a nervous smile, holding his hand out to shake Tony's hand.

Tony grimaced and rolled his eyes. He didn't take kind to Jorge's gestures anymore. He was past being the nice guy. It did nothing but have him run all over town looking for Jorge to get his money back.

Tony's patience was not what it once was in his twenties. He would work with his clients, but now that he was approaching forty, he didn't take lightly to anyone pulling his chain.

"Don't play me for a fool. Let's just cut the bullshit, Jorge. I just want what is mine. Where is my money?" he asked, as he leaned toward him, a snake ready to strike.

"Yes, I know."

'Well, let me have the money. You said you had it over the phone earlier, so now prove it. Times up."

Jorge smiled like a fool.

Tony once again made his demand. "So, hand it over,"

Jorge shifted from side to side. "See, I don't have all of it, but I promise I will later tonight."

Tony banged his hand on the table, almost breaking it in two, but quickly held back as people started to stare.

"So, how much do you have?" Tony asked.

You'll get it. Just get Tony off your back!

"Well, I have two grand," Jorge said, hoping this would be enough.

"What? That is not even half of what you owe. You have to do better than that, or you won't make it home tonight!"

Jorge kept quiet as he thought of what more he could do to calm Tony.

"You said you would have it all. How can you be such an asshole?" Tony took a few breaths to try and calm himself. "You know I could kill you right now with my hands."

Jorge was quiet. He knew nothing he could say would end Tony's anger. Though he was scared, he still smiled for everyone to see.

"You know what?" Tony said. "I'm just going to call Eva and let her know how her husband is back to his old ways and let her know you needed money for Tina. How's that for screwing me over again?"

Jorge's smile dropped. He was now in a major jam but had to settle this somehow. Not only would he lose his marriage this time, but he would also miss the next bet. He didn't want to end his winning streak with Tony being a thorn in his side. He had to think quickly.

"Okay, how about this? In an hour, I will have an extra grand. I'll give you two grand now, and I will get the rest to you by next week, plus an extra grand for your troubles. And... if I don't live to my word, you can tell Eva," Jorge added to sweeten the offer.

Tony looked at Jorge's desperate expression. He wanted to punch him for being annoying, but he knew Eva and Tina and felt a little sympathy for them.

"Uh, fine. I'll be back in an hour for the grand, but I want the two grand you have for now."

"Give me a minute. I have to cash a ticket."

"I'll be watching you, so no funny business, or I'm headed to see Eva."

Jorge turned away and walked up to the wage window to cash his ticket. He went to Trudy's window.

"So, you're a winner tonight," Trudy said after scanning his ticket.

"Yes, thank you. . ."

Jorge wasn't as happy as he could have been. He didn't like giving Tony the two grand, but he knew he had no other choice. At least he had more money than he came with.

Trudy slid the money under the wage window, and Jorge didn't count it this time. He took a hundred-dollar bill and slid it back to Trudy.

"Here you go. Thanks for the luck."

She smiled and responded, "Thank you. This will really help me and Joey. Thanks, Jorge."

"Don't mention it. I'm happy it will help you. Times are tough now. I know," he said as he winked at her.

He looked and counted the hundreds in his hands, pocketed fourteen hundred, and held the rest to give to Tony. It felt wrong giving Tony his winnings.

"I'll be back in an hour for the rest. Don't try any funny business. I have your home number on autodial."

Jorge just looked at Tony and shook his head. He had to start all over again. Things were starting to get stressful. He wished he could stop time and pick pocket everyone in the Kennel Club so he would have the money he needed. Giving it to Tony would allow him to have a clean slate again and not be on the verge of a breakdown. Wouldn't that be wonderful? Jorge thought of Eva and Tina at home and wanted to make everything right with his family again.

Get yourself together.

He missed the second race, which upset him. Jorge didn't even look at the teleprompt to see the winning dogs because it would have only depressed him further if the dogs he picked had won.

Instead, he focused on the race sheet in front of him now that Tony wasn't breathing down his neck.

Encouraged, he saw three dogs that he knew as top winners. Now he only had to pick one more. He settled on Tasty Cakes because he liked the name, though he knew he wasn't exactly sticking to the plan. He had a good feeling about Tasty Cakes, so he was going with his gut this time too. He rushed to place the bet at Trudy's window.

"Hello again," Jorge said, his hands slightly trembling. Yet, he managed to have a genuine smile. He needed to keep this connection with Trudy. She was his lucky charm.

"I'd like a trifecta boxed two, three, five, and six, please."

"I can do that. It will cost you six big ones," Trudy said.

Jorge used both hands to slide the money under the wage window. She counted the money before typing in the bet. Afterward, she printed a ticket and handed it to Jorge under the window.

"Here, you go, Boss."

Jorge smiled and took his ticket. He liked being called "Boss". It made him feel important.

The second Jorge moved to the side, another regular took his place.

Jorge walked slowly, waiting for Trudy to wish him luck like she had done before. She didn't, and this made him nervous. He wondered if he was jinxed now.

CHAPTER 8

Tina's Big Discovery

Tina couldn't wait for the school day to be over. It dragged on way too long. Minutes felt like hours.

The time couldn't come soon enough to play tennis with her father. Tina hoped nothing would interfere with their plans. She also hoped that the car's air conditioner would be fixed.

It would be a huge relief not to feel like she was no longer walking on eggshells around her parents. The tension was getting unbearable, but with the promise of a new racket, she felt that maybe their money troubles were actually improving.

While walking to the bus loop, she saw Alex standing in front of the bus she took home every day.

Her heart sank, wondering why he wanted to talk to her so badly. She stopped for a moment to get her bearings. She took off her backpack, placed it on the floor, then unzipped it to appear like she was looking for something.

She prayed that by the time she finished, he would be gone. When she realized most of the students were on their assigned buses by now, she got up and went to hers, relieved to see he wasn't there anymore.

As she walked up the steps, she saw him staring at her from the back row.

Calm down. He is not going to bite you.

She sat in her usual seat in the front with her friend, Macy. When the bus arrived at her stop, she rushed off, not looking back.

"Hey, why do you keep running away from me?" Alex called from behind.

Great, she thought, *what does he want from me?*

Tina stopped and turned around with a blank expression. She knew that she could not ignore him anymore.

Just see what he wants. Run if he comes too close.

"No reason," Tina said, feeling dumb.

"I just wanted to talk to you."

"What for?"

"I wanted to ask you a question."

"Okay..."

"And maybe we could even be friends," Alex suggested.

Tina looked straight at Alex, wondering what he wanted to ask her. The friend part didn't seem genuine to her.

They didn't have a class together or have any of the same friends. Tina was still thinking he was trying to prank her. She just wanted him to ask the question.

"What is it? I have to get home."

"Is your dad Jorge Gabor? I heard my dad talk about him last night."

Tina frowned, suddenly feeling defensive. "Yeah, so? A lot of people in town know him. He cuts a lot of people's hair."

"Oh, I didn't know that."

Tina didn't believe Alex.

"Come on, how else would you know him?"

"I just know my dad was mad at him for the money he borrowed, and I heard him say something like 'Tina', and I put two together," Alex said.

"What? I have no idea what you are talking about. My dad is one of the nicest people."

"They saw each other last night at the track."

This was news to Tina, and yet her dad was not home last night.

"And what track are you talking about?" she asked, wondering if Alex was going to end this in some way.

The only track that came to mind was the Ellington High School Track, which made zero sense. Her father wasn't a runner. Or maybe he recently started and was keeping it a secret.

"You know, the Palm Springs one . . ."

Tina never heard of the Palm Springs Track.

"Where is that? Are you sure you have the right Jorge Gabor?"

"Now, you're joking, right?" Alex said, feeling sorry for her.

"You know, I really have to go. My mom will worry if I'm late," Tina replied.

"Okay. Catch you later."

She walked away, wondering who Alex's father was. She also questioned why it was a big deal that both their fathers argued and why her dad was at the Palm Springs Track.

Tina wanted to know more about these questions, but it didn't give her a good feeling. For now, she was going to listen to her gut and stay away from any possible secrets. No need to know something that her father was keeping to himself. Tina believed he had his reasons, and she didn't want to stir up something that may not even be there. It was best to keep quiet and stay a happy family, or at least try her hardest to believe they were one.

Alex turned around, not knowing what to think of Tina, but he knew that he liked her.

Tina arrived home a few minutes late, but Eva didn't notice because she was struggling with breaking the news about tennis being canceled.

Here I go again, covering for you. I hate you and myself. Don't do it. It's your fault if you do.

"How was school?" Eva asked though she was still fuming over Jorge's recent message.

She had Tina's favorite chocolate chip cookies waiting for her, hoping to ease the blow.

"It was boring. Can I please take tomorrow off?" Tina asked. She smiled, hoping her mother would agree.

Eva laughed, but not at Tina's comment, but for seeing so much of herself in Tina.

As far as Eva was concerned, Tina's transition to preteen was uneventful compared to what other mothers had to handle.

She wasn't dealing with boyfriends, hormones, or defiance, but she always kept her eyes and ears open around her daughter. Eva didn't want outside forces influencing Tina.

"Well, you'll be fine. I'm not sure about missing a day of school, but maybe we can think of something fun to do over the weekend. How about going to the beach?"

Tina smiled, liking the idea.

"Why don't you sit down, and I'll get you some milk for your cookies."

Tina sat at the breakfast bar and took out her math homework while her mother prepared her snack.

"Here, you go. I'll be in the garage taking the clothes out of the dryer. I'll be right back, and then you'll tell me about your day."

"Okay. Thanks, Mom."

Tina was enjoying her second cookie when the phone rang, but her fingers had melted chocolate on them. She let the answering machine take the call.

Beep.

Tina was taking a sip of milk when an unfamiliar man spoke.

"Hey, Jorge. I just called you at work, but they said you left for the day. Are you home?"

Tina's heart elevated to suspicion as the man's voice was deep and raspy.

"All right, you must have left already. I'll see you later at the track."

Tina froze as she heard that word again.

She wanted to hear the message again to see if the caller left a name. Maybe it was Alex's father leaving the message, but her mother already walked back into the kitchen holding a basket of laundry ready to be folded.

Tina got out of her seat, washed her hands, and started her homework, taking a few deep breaths to calm the ugly she was feeling.

"Oh…Tina…, your father is going out to dinner tonight with a friend from New York," Eva stated like it was no big deal. She was too focused on folding the warm bath towels.

"Okay, but I'll still get to play tennis with him before he leaves, right?"

"I don't think so. I believe he left already."

"Oh," Tina said as she turned away from Eva. Tina did not want her mother to see she was disappointed. She could feel her emotions take over, feeling her insides burn, tears about to stream down her cheeks.

The last thing she wanted to do was cry in front of her mom because she knew Eva would let him have it whenever Jorge got home. She didn't want to be the reason why they fought, especially now when they weren't getting along.

Eva felt awful that she had to once again cover for him. She had to say something to make Tina feel better.

Here you go again, covering for him.

"But your father did say a new racket was in your future real soon, like tomorrow."

Tina just smiled, hiding her disappointment.

"Someone called earlier and left a message. I saved it for you."

Eva pushed the play button, unaware of the new message left moments ago. She waited for it to begin as she walked to the coffeemaker for a fresh cup of coffee.

Thinking too much about the coffee, Eva rewound the answering machine back to the message Jorge had left earlier. Tina listened to it and believed her father did sound genuine about breaking their tennis plans. It even looked like she was going to get a new tennis racket tomorrow. She should feel over the hills happy, but there was still an uneasiness, pondering if he could really afford to buy her a racket.

Why did her father know what to say to make up for a disappointment? And yet, she was still sad. This was something new she hadn't felt before. Jorge was never one to make her feel this way, but today he did.

Was this how her mother felt when Jorge broke a promise? Tina then thought she was being too sensitive, blowing this out of proportion. The person he went out with wasn't from the area, so he really couldn't have said no. Why did she have to make it more than it was, like Eva?

When the second message played, Tina remained still, acting like she never heard the message. At the same time, she feared her mother would ask her about it. Tina carefully listened to see if the man left his name, but he didn't. When the message ended, her mother didn't say a word, like it never played. Tina looked away and took it as a sign not to mention it.

An hour later, the phone rang. It was Jorge. Eva answered it, holding on to her anger, not wanting to lash out in front of Tina.

"It's your father," she said and handed the phone to Tina. She walked to the refrigerator with her back to Tina, rolling her eyes.

"Hi," Tina softly spoke.

She could hear loud talking in the background, like he was at a concert, trying to hear what else her father was saying.

"Where are you?" Tina asked. Her voice was louder this time.

"I'm out having dinner."

He is lying.

"Where?"

"Girl, did you hear my earlier message?" Jorge asked as he pressed the phone hard against his cheek to minimize the sound of the announcer.

"Yes," she replied, tears forming in her eyes. He had to be at the track with all the noise in the background, yet why was he saying he was at a restaurant?

"Did you hear the part about the racket?"

"Yes."

"You don't sound excited."

"I am…I just wanted to play tennis with you today."

"I know, girl, but I promise tomorrow we'll play. I couldn't say no to an old friend."

Tina kept quiet, torn between the truth and lies. Maybe she was being too hard on her father, and he was with a friend. Maybe he took his friend to the track after dinner. What was so bad about her father being at the track anyway? She still struggled with what she was feeling, going back and forth. She didn't have a grasp on what was really happening.

"I got to go. Dinner is being served…love you, girl."

Tina now believed she was the one who was making a mountain over a mole hill the entire time. Why was she letting Alex get to her?

"I love you too, Dad."

Eve felt ill knowing Jorge was now involving their daughter in his web of lies. He never called to speak to Tina when he was out, and just thinking how he thought it was acceptable now left Eva on high alert.

She wanted to rip the phone away from Tina and ask Jorge what he did with the $3,000 that he withdrew from their off-limits savings account. Eva wanted straight answers, but she didn't want it to be at the expense of Tina. Instead, she kept quiet and went along with Jorge's game, feeling trapped by her own doing.

When are you going to learn and stop doing this?

A few hours later, Eva called for Tina from the kitchen.

Eva was sitting at the kitchen bar, drinking a glass of wine. This wasn't a good sign because alcohol and her mother did not mix well. It always made Tina feel uncomfortable when her mother drank, fearing what she may say or do, remembering a few times when she cried.

"Tina, I wanted to ask you an important question," she stated as she took another sip of Chardonnay while looking intently at her daughter.

Tina's defenses were on high alert, ready to do what was needed to avoid having this conversation with her mom.

"I know you love your father, but have you ever . . ."

Instantly, she knew she had to stop this conversation from going any further. Tina felt the air being sucked from her, red lights telling her to get out as fast as she could, or she would put herself and her father in jeopardy. She did not want to answer any questions about Jorge, fearing it could be used against him.

"Mom, it's late. Can we talk tomorrow?"

It wasn't often that her mother would drink, and if she did, there was a reason for it. Why couldn't her mother accept her father as he was and let him be? Didn't she know who she married?

Eva sat on the breakfast stool and took another sip of wine, feeling depressed at how things were going at home.

She hardly had any energy anymore, spending every waking hour worrying about Jorge gambling and losing whatever money they had. Eva was also deeply afraid of how Tina was now getting unknowingly dragged into Jorge's addiction.

"Oh, I didn't realize how late it was. Just go on up and take a shower, then. Sleep well. See you in the morning. I love you, Tina. Sorry for calling you down. I'm just tired of..."

"Good night, Mom...I love you too."

Tina rushed up the stairs, went to the bathroom, and took a long shower. Then she got into her pajamas, brushed her teeth, combed her hair, took out her contacts, and finally found peace under the covers of her bed.

Around eleven o'clock, Tina was flushed, waking up to a stomachache. She quietly walked by her parent's room, not wanting to wake them up, carefully walking down the stairs to the kitchen for Tums and a cold drink.

While grabbing a cold bottle from the refrigerator, Tina heard the front door rattle. She quickly hid under the dining room table to hear Jorge curse under his breath.

Tina carefully got up from under the table, silent enough that Jorge didn't see her. Her anxiety reached dangerous levels when she saw he was beaten. The polo shirt Eva gave him for his birthday was ripped and soiled. Tina felt faint, seeing her father in such disarray.

Her instincts told her to go to him, but she didn't want to wake Eva. Instead, she tiptoed up the steps. She was thankful that Jorge was home.

"Please, God, let him be okay, and let my Mom sleep through it all."

How Tina wished this was just a bad dream, but it wasn't. It was actually happening.

CHAPTER 9

Got Ya!

Jorge foolishly thought he could pull a fast one on Tony by leaving the track without paying him. He was only a few feet away from his car when Tony spooked him.

Act stupid.

Jorge knew physically he was no match for Tony's strong, two hundred fifty-pound physique, compared to his one hundred sixty pound body frame.

All Jorge could rely on was his smarts.

"So, where the hell are you going?" Tony asked as he stepped closer to him, blocking him in

"You think I didn't see your pathetic self walk out of the track? I have been on to you, letting you hang yourself."

Jorge stood paralyzed.

"You are so fucking clueless that you didn't even look over your back once! Who do you think you are!" Tony shouted, foaming at the mouth.

When Jorge said nothing, Tony continued, "I just wanted you to think you could get away while all along I was looking to prove you wrong!"

Jorge stayed quiet as he kept his back to him.

"I thought I'd give you a taste of your own bullshit."

Jorge turned around, hoping there were a few good feet between them just in case he had to run, but there wasn't. Tony was a few inches away, breathing down his neck, the smell of cigarettes and whiskey turning Jorge's stomach.

Lie, lie, lie! What are you waiting for?

"I was just going in the car for my sweater. It's freezing inside," Jorge said.

"Enough…stop talking trash."

"No, here, look, I have my sweater on the passenger side," Jorge added.

"I swear if you open that door, I'll hurt you. Now where is my money?"

Jorge panicked.

He had won some money, but not enough to settle his debt. He did manage to win another grand, which he was planning to use for the broken air conditioner and tennis racket for Tina. Now it looked like he would have to hand it over to Tony.

"You know, you're as rotten as they come, and believe me, I have seen plenty of assholes in my life. You, Jorge, top them all."

Jorge felt chills ripple down his body.

"You steal, you lie, and you don't keep your fucking promises. I don't even know how the fuck Eva stays with you. She must be stupid too. It's not like you have anything to offer her anyway."

"No, she isn't. Don't talk about my wife that way."

"Well, let me take that back. I know why she stays with you. You're a good liar, and she doesn't know the real you. But she should. Don't you think so? Eva shouldn't be living a lie."

Jorge looked at Tony, raging at how he wanted him to shut up. He hated how Tony kept degrading him and how he involved Eva. He kept quiet. He wanted to make it out alive.

Lie, lie, lie!

"It's time that Eva knows the *real* Jorge," Tony suggested as he took his cell phone out.

Jorge became fearful. This would completely crush him.

"And how about Tina? How about I tell her that her dad would rather be at the track than at home? What do you think about that? How about we call them now?"

"No, no, please," Jorge pleaded. He couldn't take it anymore.

"I think it's a good idea."

"Please don't."

"Stop your crocodile tears because I'm ready to end them forever."

Jorge's voice started to crack. "I'm a good husband and father."

"Bullshit, look at the mess you have created."

Jorge kept silent. Tony was right about the mess part, but not about loving his girls.

"I want the other five grand now, and then maybe I won't call home."

"I don't have it. I told you this earlier. I didn't lie about it," Jorge said, his lips quivering.

"Where is it then?"

Jorge didn't want to say a word.

"Well, game over. You lost again."

"No, please!"

"Eva is finally going to know she married a loser. I'm going to say this one last time, Jorge. Hand over the money or you will wish you were never born. I know you have it. Every word you ever say is a lie."

"I told you that I don't have any."

"See, Jorge. You are the worst kind of liar. A few hours ago, you promised me a grand, which I agreed to. You also promised you would have the rest by next week, but you ran, so now all is lost."

Jorge remembered his promise but didn't think twice about it when he left the track.

"Well, when I called you at the salon, I asked if you had the money, and you said yes. Do I need to refresh your memory some more?" Tony asked.

"No," Jorge shook his head, agreeing with Tony.

"So, I want it. I want it now." Tony walked up to Jorge and squeezed his right cheek.

Jorge looked away.

"Please, Tony, I never meant to not pay you back. I needed the money for Tina."

"Spare me the lie, for god's sake, and keep your mouth shut."

Tony just smiled and finally couldn't take Jorge's lies anymore. He lunged forward and punched him as hard as he could.

Jorge fell to the hard ground. Warm, fresh blood oozed from his bottom lip. Jorge touched it, thankful none of his teeth were broken.

"Now get up," Tony demanded as he kicked Jorge in his side.

Jorge couldn't find the strength to pull himself up from the cold ground. He felt safer staying on the ground, not wanting to get punched again.

"Get up," Tony demanded again. He leaned toward Jorge, his saliva dripping over Jorge's face. He took a step closer, placed his hand on Jorge's neck, and squeezed until Jorge moaned in pain.

"How do you like that? That's how you hold a dog that doesn't listen. Are you ready to listen?"

"Yes," Jorge softly answered while covering his bloody mouth.

Beg! Beg, Beg . . .

Jorge looked at Tony with defeat. He had to fold, or he would die in the track parking lot. He reached for his back pocket to get his wallet. Before he could settle the matter with Tony, security guards were ordering them to leave.

"If either of you touch the other, you'll be leaving here with some real heavy jewelry to jail!" The rookie guard hollered as he kept his flashlight on Jorge and Tony.

Tony was startled by the bright light shining on him. He stopped, not wanting any trouble. He told his wife earlier that he was going out with a few friends for a bite to eat and some drinks, but he certainly didn't tell her the part about being at the Palm Spring Kennel Club.

He took a few steps back while keeping his eyes on Jorge. If looks could kill, Jorge would have died on the spot.

"Don't think we are done, not by a long shot. I'll look for you later, and you'll pay dearly for this. Eva will be packing by the end of the week," Tony threatened under his breath.

Jorge became frantic. He knew Tony would up the antics and live up to his word, just like the sun would shine tomorrow.

Jorge couldn't believe the guards didn't ask if he was okay after seeing Tony hovering over him. Sadly, it occurred to him that nobody really cared about guys like him.

Get your shit together!

He got in his car and wiped his lips with balled-up napkins that smelled of coffee, but he didn't care. As far as he was concerned, it was a tissue, and it would stop the blood dripping from his busted lip. It was pounding like it had a heart of its own. He wanted to see how it looked but didn't want the guards to question the holdup and then call the police.

Once out of the parking spot, he waved to the guards like they were his long-lost friends.

Jorge did leave the Kennel Club with his life and money, and yet he knew it still didn't guarantee he would be alive in the morning.

Tony was still walking to his car as Jorge crossed the exit gates of the track. He was as angry as ever.

Jorge felt like he cheated death as he drove up the street, but the light turned red. *Shit*, he thought to himself. He cautiously stopped looking over his shoulder, fearing Tony's red Mercedes would be behind him, but to his relief, there weren't any cars on either side of the intersection.

See, I got you covered.

Jorge knew he should thank God for the security guards showing up when they did, but he didn't. He was busy thinking of his next move.

As he waited for the red light to change, he leaned forward, his chest touching the steering wheel. He lifted his bottom and patted his back pocket, fearing that the money might have slipped out when Tony punched him. He didn't know what he would do if the money was gone. If it was, he might as well have turned around and jumped over Somerset Bridge, but the money was still in his pocket.

He took the money out. It was neatly secured with a green rubber band. He kissed it, then slid it back into his back pocket. He felt like a resurrected man, ready to start fresh and be the husband and father Eva and Tina deserved.

Jorge started to laugh as he thought about how the guards put Tony in his place, even though he had no part in it.

"Who is calling who an asshole now?" Jorge said, feeling vindicated.

Jorge knew it was late. The wrath of Eva popped into his mind, and decided it was best to go home, though he was really tempted to try his luck and settle his debts down south at a casino.

Jorge saw his busted lip in the rear mirror. The color drained from his face. "Shit, Eva will see this," he remarked to the mirror. His heart started to race, fearing what would happen if she did. He thought about what he would say if she saw it tonight. Otherwise, he would try to hide it until the morning and deal with it alone.

Tony lit a cigarette as he sat in his car, thinking about the evening's bizarre events.

"Ah, this is more like it."

Though he started to feel better, he still couldn't believe how Jorge once again managed to slip through his fingers.

"Asshole."

He took another long hit and looked up at the dark sky, plotting his next move. The next day he had a full day of landscaping jobs lined up, so he needed his rest.

"Should I go to Jorge's house and be done with him?" Tony grinned. "Or should I let him think it is me whenever he hears a sound?"

That same grin across his face widened, liking the latter choice for now. He thought of the two grand still in his wallet. Though it wasn't the eight grand Jorge owed. It was something. It was enough to get his wife off his back and enough for his son, Alex, to get a new computer.

"Bastard."

"Well, we all must do what we have to do. Jorge, you got lucky tonight, but tomorrow is another day."

He took his cell phone from his sports jacket; there weren't any missed calls or voice messages. As he took his last drag, Tony looked in the rearview mirror to see if he needed to comb his hair. Glad that he used extra hairspray when he left home earlier, he started the car, letting the engine warm up before driving home, feeling comfortable that he would sleep next to his wife and not in a prison cell tonight.

"I guess not all is lost."

He thought of how Jorge stiffed him again, and his insides churned. Yet, he took pride knowing that Jorge's busted lip was going to be hard to conceal and that he wasn't finished with him.

Not by a long shot.

CHAPTER 10

Walking on Pins and Needles

Tina tipped-toed up the stairwell as fast as she could, racing heart and all, afraid to be caught.

Once in her room, under the safety of the covers, she took a deep breath, but her heart still kept pounding.

"Please, Dad, just come up slowly . . ." Tina whispered.

If only she had magic powers, then she could fix this mess. Jorge would already be sleeping next to her mother, and the night would go on like nothing ever happened.

Tina wondered how he got hurt. Did he get into a car accident? Did an animal attack him? Or maybe he tripped and fell and hit his head on a rock. None of these possibilities felt right, but something did happen.

Tina's tears streamed down her cheeks as she held her hands in prayer. "Please, God. Please let him make it upstairs without waking Mom up."

Ten minutes passed, no sign of him yet. Where could he be? Hearing him would make her feel better. Even though she wanted him to be quiet, she still wanted to hear him. She started to panic, thinking he might have passed out from blood loss or collapsed because he was too weak to stand up anymore.

Irrational thoughts kept filling her mind, increasing her anxiety; she wanted to go back downstairs to check on him. A terrible thought ran through her mind. What if he was dead?

Just as she was about to get out of bed, she heard the downstairs light switch turn off.

Yes, she thought. She held her breath as she heard Jorge take baby steps up the stairs. Anxiety gripped her, as the familiar cracking sound of the landing creaked.

Shit, that was loud.

Jorge paused at the top of the stairs, holding his breath. Eva would have called him by now if she heard him, but all remained silent for now.

Almost there.

He was only seconds away from pulling this off. He carefully opened the bedroom door, ready to slide into the bed he shared with Eva.

Bingo.

Jorge couldn't wait to rest his tired body and forget about tonight's mess, if only for a few more hours.

"So, you think you can just come into bed without an explanation of where you have been, and I wouldn't notice?" Eva asked as she sat up, looking at Jorge's dark silhouette.

"Where were you? Or should I ask which track you were at?"

Jorge froze. He could hardly stand up, fearing Eva would see the tears of his shirt and his busted lip.

"Where were you?" Eva demanded.

In a panic, Tina sat up like the times before when she heard her parents argue. She ever carefully leaned against the joining wall between her room and her parents, holding her breath, listening hard, not wanting to make a sound, and not missing a word that was said.

At first, she heard a few words like "track" and "money" because Eva kept her voice low, like she usually did at the beginning of an argument. However, Tina knew that in a few minutes, she'd be able to hear her mother without having to press her ear too hard against the wall.

"So, how much money did you lose this time?"

Jorge remained still, not saying a word.

"I would think you would be sick of losing, but you go back," Eva said.

Jorge felt flushed, keeping quiet. How he wished he had slept on the couch downstairs.

Damn Eva, always butting her nose where it shouldn't be. Tell her you make the money, not her.

"It wasn't enough that you spent the car's A/C money, but to take the money from our savings account was really low, Jorge. It was all that we had. Just so you could gamble it away?" Eva raged.

Jorge still didn't respond, not caring to dispute Eva's words.

"Yeah, that's right. I went to the bank this morning to see what happened to the three grand in the savings account, only to be told you took it out the same day. Did you really think I would never find out? You must think I'm stupid. Yeah, the stupid one for being with you?" Eva said.

Tina lay down in bed and did not miss a word being said. Tears continued to stream down her cheeks, devastated that her parents' financial problems were far from over. They were actually greater than she thought, and now she felt bad about looking at the tennis magazine earlier in front of her mother. What was Jorge doing at the track that caused him to lose money?

Jorge could offer no words because he felt it was his right to spend the money as he saw fit. In his eyes, he was so close to winning it big and solving his problems.

You are doing this for your family! What does Eva know?

His silence infuriated Eva more than anything. She felt like throwing the bedside lamp at him just to get a reaction.

The three thousand dollars he took from the savings account took Eva years to save. The extra time she spent comparing food prices to feed the family while still managing to save what she could. She would even walk to stores to save on gas, cut out on simple pleasures like manicures or pedicures, and have dry cereal for lunch.

"How dare you just stand there without a word to say? Doesn't it matter to you that this family is suffering because of you? Do you not care that we can't even afford to pay the water bill? Doesn't any of this faze you, Jorge?"

Still, Jorge's split lip couldn't be seen by Eva. The darkness hid it well, and all he wanted was to get into bed before Eva could see it, but maybe this was his way out.

Leave him, Eva. Don't play his game.

Finally, Jorge said, "I didn't want to worry you or Tina."

Worry you or Tina?

Tina couldn't hold back her tears, listening to Jorge talk and feeling sorry for him. She quickly grabbed the corner of the comforter and pulled it against her mouth to muffle the sounds of her cries.

"I don't buy that. You were gambling again. Just say it."

"I'm sorry."

"Sorry for gambling? Now that's a first."

"No, I'm sorry that I worried you. I got roughed up tonight," Jorge finally confessed in his defense, though he knew he was not off the hook by a long shot.

Eva would want to know every little detail, but for now, he was going to keep his account of what happened short and believable. He was not going to mess up either with extra words or details.

"Hurt *how*?"

"I've been robbed and beaten."

"What?"

"I just want to go to bed and pretend this night never happened, embarrassed by the whole thing," Jorge said.

"Please, when have you ever been embarrassed? You are standing, aren't you? I don't believe you."

Come on, Dad, please speak up and end this, Tina thought. She saw him with her own eyes.

"I could have died tonight. There was a gun pointed at my head," Jorge cried as he fell to the ground.

He went for it like a risky bet; he didn't care about the odds. He really had nothing to lose anymore. Eva was about to boot him out of the bedroom and the house.

Tina wasn't sure if she could listen anymore. The suspense was gut-wrenching. She was just happy that he was home now, safe. *Just forgive him, Mom,* she thought.

"It's a miracle that I'm alive," Jorge said, lying on the foot of the bed crying.

He froze as he thought about Tony again. Thinking of what he was brewing in his calculated mind at this very moment, fearing he would call Eva, looking around to see if the wireless phone was in the bedroom.

Eva just sat on the bed, debating whether to cry or laugh. Jorge had never pulled a stunt like this before. Just hearing him say that he could have died was almost comical.

He is lying!

"Have you heard a word I said?" Jorge asked.

Eva stared at him, still not sure what to believe. She turned on the lamp, expecting to see maybe a scratch or bruise.

But to her shock, Jorge was roughed up with a busted lip. The bottom lip was swollen, split in the middle, and caked with blood. He certainly did look like he was harmed, appearing distorted and lost.

Don't be fooled!

"My God, what happened? Who did this to you? When and where did this happen?" Eva was shooting questions left and right, wanting answers just as fast.

Jorge kept quiet. His wounds, he believed, spoke better than he could.

"Was it someone you know? Why aren't you talking? Did you call the police?"

"No, they took off."

"Did you get a good look at any of them? Did you recognize any of their faces?"

"No, they were wearing ski masks."

Tina thanked God for her father's safety, and Eva had forgotten about the lost money in the savings account.

Jorge felt safe avoiding Eva's questions for now and hoped she would forget about them all together. She was pretty shook up seeing his damaged face.

Eva got out of bed to get a better look at him. She feared he might need stitches, but she wanted to wait until after his shower. No use scaring him yet.

Jorge's face and body were dirty. Patches of dried blood napped in his hair. Seeing this upset Eva, thinking whoever did this was still walking the streets.

She wanted to call the cops, but Jorge didn't want to involve them. Yet—even though she didn't know it, she actually knew the person responsible. About a week ago, Eva left Tony a message about a quote for trimming the two front palm trees close to the house, and she was still awaiting his call back.

As she stared at Jorge's face, she saw a man she hardly knew anymore. As the years passed, he became more of a stranger than a husband.

What has happened to the man I once loved?

She was torn between a rock and a hard place, believing she hated him more than she loved him. Earlier today, Eva was consumed with anger and rage, ready to pack up and leave him.. But for tonight she decided to be his wife

She gently helped him remove his shirt, softly touching his body with her warm, shaky hands, going up and down his chest, shoulders, and arms, careful not to miss a spot.

Jorge was getting aroused. He couldn't remember the last time Eva had touched him or even really looked at him. Even as they slept, Eva slept on the edge of the bed, not wanting any physical touch.

As far as Eva could tell, his busted lip was the only injury. "Take a shower. When you're cleaned up, I'll look at your lip again, and we'll talk more too."

Jorge thought back to when they first met at a soccer game. He smiled as he remembered Eva's shyness when he asked her name. She had a hard time looking at him without blushing, and he believed then that she was the girl for him. It was the beginning of their life together, but now, Eva was different. She no longer blushed around him, no longer spruced herself up anymore. Their marriage was in trouble, and he had to think of a way to turn it around.

He knew his life was not his, debts tugging at him every which way they could. Jorge never seemed to have a peaceful moment anymore.

As he got up, he kissed Eva on the cheek and walked to the bathroom for a long, hot shower. The fear of Tony played in his mind, wondering what his next move would be.

He just hoped Tony wouldn't show up at his house. Jorge's heart raced as he thought about the money he needed to repay Tony. Where was he going to come up with it in such a short time? He realized he had been stringing Tony along for months now. If the tables were turned, he would have started to apply pressure too.

Jorge couldn't fault Tony. However, the problem was still the same, he didn't have the money to repay him. He only wanted more time to do so. Jorge wondered if he could tell Eva the truth about being at the track.

Maybe she would forgive him for being honest. It might even be his only chance to get out of this mess. He believed there was still a little bit of money in Eva's retirement account from when she worked at the brokerage firm.

He stood in the shower, thinking of other options, but kept returning to Eva's account. He knew it would be a huge gamble if he asked if she could help eliminate his debt for good. Maybe if he came clean and promised not to ever gamble again, she would agree to help him.

Or would it be the last straw?

Finally, the shower turned off, and Eva felt uneasy about seeing Jorge, afraid of what she would feel when he would be back in the bedroom. Throughout the years, she had come to realize that her intuition was ninety-nine-point nine percent right, regardless of how she might have wished it wasn't.

Please, God. Help me.

She saw Jorge's pants on the floor in the corner of the room. *I'll look at them later,* she thought, but Jorge already emptied them. Jorge walked out of the bathroom half-naked, wearing only a towel around his waist. He winked at Eva, trying to flirt a little.

Why not? She is still my wife. We used to have sex.

Eva hated it when Jorge tried to use his charm to avoid uncomfortable conversations like he was doing now. It was the same story every time, but things were different tonight. Her emotions went all over the place, uneasy about how she could have gone to bed a widow, never seeing Jorge again, and Tina fatherless.

The reality brought chills. Eva didn't know what to think of Jorge's gambling problem anymore. She questioned if she should just accept it. Was it really that bad? Maybe if she stopped focusing on the gambling part, she wouldn't be so hurt and upset. Maybe she didn't try enough to understand it. Also, deep down, she really didn't want to lose Jorge, though she would often catch him in his lies. She just wanted to lose the gambler in him. Was that even possible? Was there any type of medication he could take to end the gambling? Would he even take it?

Why are you always going back and forth?

Then she thought about Tina, only a few feet away sleeping, feeling a wave of emotions, knowing how much Tina loved Jorge, but would that be enough? However, the reality of Jorge's gambling could not be ignored. Would Tina think what was happening at home was normal? Her worst fear was that one day, Tina would follow her steps, look the other way, and deal with Jorge's lies.

Eva struggled with what she felt and what she wanted to feel. She still wanted to love Jorge but wasn't so sure anymore. He wasn't the same Jorge she fell in love with many years ago. That version was long gone, never spending quality time with her anymore, always having an excuse about being late, or having to go somewhere important.

It seemed the only time he was affectionate to her was when he was caught in a lie, and was deeply sorry, which saddened her. The truth was they were living two very different lives now. Was this really the life she wanted?

There were days when she felt she could leave with Tina for a new life, away from the chaos and lies, but her emotions always got the better of her. It wasn't so easy to just walk away and leave everything behind.

And yet, she knew that his gambling was the thorn in their marriage, keeping them apart. It was the mistress who wouldn't go away, always calling the shots and taking what little money they had. Eva knew she could never compete against it.

Tears overwhelmed her as she brushed them away, letting her hair hide her face, feeling so tormented at what was real right now.

Jorge sat next to his wife. He looked at Eva's deep blue eyes, hoping she was done being upset, and was ready to love him. They stared at each other like teenagers trying to figure out what the other was thinking and who would make the first move. They were dangerously close—the sexual tension could be cut by a knife— and neither of them knew the last time they were intimate.

How can you forget what he did?

Jorge pulled Eva close to him and passionately kissed her. He hoped she would kiss him back, but she didn't. He got up from the side of the bed, took his towel off, and walked to his side of the bed. Jorge smiled, ready for Eva to go underneath the covers with him, but she stayed still, deep in thought. He patiently waited, ready to make love to his wife, but Eva couldn't.

She turned to Jorge and said, "I want to know the truth."

And suddenly, Jorge felt soft inside and out.

CHAPTER 11

The Morning After

The alarm clock awoke Tina from a deep sleep. The light coming from under the door broke the darkness in the room.

She felt uneasy about last night.

Now she had to go downstairs and pretend she didn't know what happened, not wanting to cause any suspicion.

"Okay, Tina, let's get on with it," Tina said, getting ready for school. "Just don't look Mom in the eyes, and you'll be okay."

She walked by her parent's room, feeling uneasy. It brought all uncomfortable feelings, like anxiety, anger, embarrassment, but mostly sadness.

Eva had a plate with eggs, hash browns, and bacon in the warm oven for Tina. She hoped the breakfast would keep Tina from asking questions about what she may have heard last night. Her only regret was being too loud, but not her words.

Eva looked through the real estate section of the Yellow Pages for a realtor, though she was tempted to look for a divorce attorney. Jorge admitted last night that he was at the track gambling, only after Eva threatened to go to the track with his photo and ask everyone if he was there earlier.

He finally came clean, fearing that she would talk to Trudy. He told her that he was at the Palm Springs Kennel Club but left out the part about being punched by Tony because he didn't pay a debt.

Moving out won't do anything. Divorce will!

"Good morning, Tina. How did you sleep?" Eva asked. Tina didn't respond yet, fearing her voice would crack. "Still half asleep, I see."

Tina nodded. Eva placed the plate of food in front of Tina. "I hope you like it."

Tina pulled the plate closer and took a bite. "Yum, thanks, Mom."

"How did you sleep?"

"Okay."

"Did your father and I keep you up?" Eva asked, turning away to refill her coffee cup.

"No," Tina replied.

If Eva could see Tina's insides, she would see her daughter's heart in distress about where the conversation might go. Scared that her mother was going to say something about her father that she wasn't ready to know.

"I am just tired," she lied.

"Is everything okay at school?" Eva asked, feeling restless herself.

"Yes, I'm just burnt out from testing all the time. I fell asleep last night once my head touched the pillow. There could have been a storm, and I wouldn't have heard anything. I was so tired," Tina lied again, hoping her mother would stop with the questions.

"Yes, I know the feeling."

Eva felt relieved.

"I love you, Tina. Please always remember this because life is hard," Eva said as she looked straight at Tina's chestnut eyes.

"Always."

Eva felt a bit settled now that all seemed well with Tina.

When her mother turned away, Tina looked around to see if there were any signs of her father. She would feel better if she saw something of his, anything, like his work bag. Relief overcame her when she saw his black jacket hanging over the dining room chair. She thought he was probably still sleeping upstairs. As far as she could see, everything looked the same, but she knew that things weren't always what they appeared to be.

"If you're too tired, maybe you should stay home today."

"No, I have a quiz. I just wish . . ."

Eva turned around, wanting to hear the rest of the sentence, but Jorge walked in from the garage with a suitcase. This surprised both of them, causing Tina to not finish her thought. Eva looked away and tidied up the kitchen, wiping the counters and organizing the plates.

Tina looked at her father, saddened by his appearance. She forgot he had broken their tennis plans yesterday and was just happy to see him alive. He sat beside her and leaned in to kiss her on the cheek.

"Good morning, Tina, my little girl. How did you sleep?" Jorge asked.

"Good, I'm just a little tired from studying."

"I remember those days."

How was your night? Did you have a nice dinner with your friend?" Tina asked.

Jorge didn't know how to answer with Eva around. "Fine, sorry about missing tennis yesterday, but I couldn't turn down an old friend. I promise I'll be home later today."

Eva stayed preoccupied in the kitchen, avoiding any contact with Jorge. Tina noticed this, hoping there would be a few words exchanged between them, but not a word was said.

Are they getting a divorce now? Tina thought, taking a deep breath.

"Are we playing tennis later?" Jorge asked.

Tina felt uneasy about the question. "Sure, if you can make it."

"Of course, I'll make it. Nothing will stop me."

Jorge's promise made the tiny hairs on Eva's neck stand up.

"I hope so," Eva said, though she didn't want to be part of the conversation. She just wanted to make sure Jorge lived up to his word this time and not come up with another reason why he couldn't make it again.

Tina finally saw her father's busted lip feeling her temperature rise. She wondered if her father had seen her last night.

"Dad, your lip, what happened?

Jorge took a sip of coffee to sort his thoughts, then laughed, and answered, "It is a long and silly story, but I'm all right. The important thing is that I'm here with you and your mother. It was just a dumb misunderstanding. Who knew I had a twin walking around with enemies?"

How could a busted lip be silly? How dumb of him!

She continued to clean the kitchen, pretending she didn't hear a word he said.

"Do you want a ride to school?" Jorge asked.

"Sure, let me get my things upstairs. What's with the suitcase, Dad? Are you going somewhere?" Tina wondered.

"Not sure yet."

Tina rushed up the stairs to her room. She wanted a few moments to reflect, and her thoughts went to Alex. She was certain Alex would have the answers she needed to know more about her father and the track.

She headed down the stairs feeling anxious but determined. Jorge looked up at Tina, ready to go with the keys in his hand, but she had other plans.

"Dad, I forgot that I promised a friend I would study with them on the bus this morning. Sorry."

"Oh, okay," Jorge said.

Eva's heart dropped; she wanted Jorge to leave the house too. She didn't want to be alone with him just yet.

"Oh, Mom, thanks for the poetry tip last night."

Eva looked at Tina, startled, as they didn't talk about poetry last night. Was her daughter talking in code?

"Mom, how about if you walk with me so we can review it again?"

"Well, okay . . ." Eva walked past Jorge, acting like he wasn't there.

"Eva, before you leave, do you have a twenty until later?" Jorge asked.

She walked past Jorge like she didn't hear him.

Eva and Tina started to walk to the bus stop in silence, but that was only until they turned the corner.

CHAPTER 12

Deeper in the Hole

"**M**om, I heard you and Dad fighting last night." Eva kept quiet.

Tell Tina the truth.

"Are you getting a divorce?" Tina softly asked, feeling like her troubled heart was just ripped out as she struggled with each word.

Eva stopped, looking at Tina, careful not to say the wrong thing. She learned the hard way that words can never really be taken back.

"It's just…. we don't see eye-to-eye on a few things, but we'll work it out."

Why are you doing this to yourself?

"Really?"

"Marriage is never perfect."

Tina's heart suddenly became calm, and she could finally breathe at a normal pace. Her worst fears were just that; there was no need to worry anymore. Parents fought and disagreed. It didn't mean they were going to get divorced.

Tina hugged her mom and was relieved she could put last night in the past.

"Oh, my! The person I have been wanting to get a quote from is at the bus stop," Eva said.

Anxiety filled Tina, seeing Alex standing beside the man her mom wanted to talk to.

"Hey, I didn't know you moved into the area?" Eva asked Tony.

Tina thought she might faint seeing this Tony person talk to Alex. He had to be related to Alex somehow.

Tony turned to look at Eva and said, "Hello, Eva."

He wondered if she knew he was responsible for Jorge's busted lip, but after a few minutes of small talk, he was pretty certain she didn't.

"We actually just moved to the new apartments across the street. I needed an extra room for my business. And there is also a pool at the development for Alex and the wife to swim in. It was a win for all of us."

Eva smiled, "How nice. I would love to have a pool to go to."

"Yes, Alex and Jane swim almost every day."

"Nice…do you think you could come by the house and give us a quote for trimming the two palms in the front?"

Tony couldn't believe his luck.

"I actually have an opening today."

"Great. Jorge should be home now. It's been a moment since you last saw each other."

Yeah, only eight hours ago, thought Tony.

Seeing the school bus approach caused Eva to stop talking and focus on Tina. She checked to see if her backpack was closed, making sure it was zipped all the way.

Eva affectionately patted Tina's back because she felt a goodbye kiss may be too much for a middle school girl, and she didn't want to embarrass her. Surprisingly, Tina turned around and hugged her tightly, mostly because she was so thankful that her parents were staying together. Then she went on the bus.

"Goodbye, son. Have a good day," Tony said.

Alex said goodbye and followed Tina on the bus. He then sat next to her.

"I'm surprised you aren't trying to get out of the seat."

Tina smiled. "Not really. I'm just a private person if you haven't noticed."

"I have." Alex smiled back, liking Tina more. He liked that she wasn't like the other starstruck girls.

"What do you mean you have noticed?"

"I've been trying to talk to you for about a month now, duh."

"So, you have been stalking me?" she asked jokingly.

"What?"

"Stalking—it's when you are watching and following someone. People go to jail for it, duh. After all, it is against the law. Didn't you know that?"

"You're crazy, you know that, right?"

"Really?"

"So, do you want to be friends?"

"Okay, you seem harmless for now." Tina grinned.

"Listen, my dad tells me your dad likes to bet," Alex said.

Tina leaned back, feeling uneasy again. "Well, that's your father's opinion. I don't want to talk about this right now."

"Okay, we won't."

It became quiet and remained so until the bus pulled up outside school. Tina was anxious to get off the bus. However, she wanted to keep the lines open with Alex. The curious part within her wanted to know what Alex knew about her father, even though it may open a door that could never be closed again. She wondered why she was hesitant to know anything private about Jorge and why her father didn't want to share it.

Why are you afraid?

Here it was, her instinct talking again, desperate to get her attention. It only wanted her to see the truth, but she wasn't sure if she wanted to.

While walking to class, Tina realized she had the key to open the door to her father's so-called secret. The hard part was done. She knew Alex would tell her what she wanted to know about Jorge. Now all she had to do was ask. It couldn't get any easier, but she feared the consequences.

CHAPTER 13

Saved by the Skin of His Teeth

Eva kept waving goodbye as the bus drove off until it disappeared. She felt a headache come on after promising Tina that things between Jorge and her were normal marriage problems.

When was this madness going to end?

Tony stood a few feet away. She had no idea his injured hand was responsible for Jorge's busted lip. Eva also hadn't a clue that he was the one who supplied her husband with criminally high interest-rate loans to gamble. He had been Jorge's gambling pimp for the past few years and occasional landscaper, mostly for coverup purposes. Tony was far from innocent, though he appeared to be a hard-working family man.

"Nice seeing you. Please say hello to Jane," Eva said.

"I will, thank you," Tony said.

Eva just smiled. "So, I'll see you later, right?"

"Yes, just do me a favor. Don't tell Jorge I'm coming. I want to surprise him."

"I won't."

After saying their goodbyes, Tony walked back to the apartment complex, elated, not believing his luck. It couldn't have worked out better, even if he had plotted it all night.

Finally, the bastard is going to get his own.

Eva took the long way home. She thought about Tina's question and how tormented she was, fearful her parents were getting divorced.

But now, after promising everything was fine, she figuratively had made her bed and herself a prisoner in her marriage to Jorge.

She loves me no matter what. Even if she knew I gambled, so what! It's not against the law; nothing will change if she knows unless you make a big deal about it.

Eva kept replaying what Jorge had said last night about Tina.

Bastard!

Eva hated that he used their daughter to downplay his gambling. Even when she said Tina knew about their financial problems, he would say, "Well, she has a roof over her head, doesn't she? What more could she want? She's not starving."

This infuriated Eva because she and Tina deserved more than just a roof over their heads, and the not starving part wasn't true. If Eva hadn't been the one saving what little money she could and being creative with meals, they would be starving.

How low can he get?

She returned home to see Tony's landscaping truck parked in the front and couldn't be happier. Maybe a little maintenance around the house would motivate Jorge to stay home more. Tony was still in the front seat smoking a cigarette, like he didn't have a care in the world. Then she saw the car was missing.

"Sorry, Jorge isn't here."

"Oh, I saw him. He just left."

Eva found that strange, but she didn't think much of it.

"Oh, did he say where he was going?" Eva asked.

"No, I actually didn't get to talk to him. I just saw him leave down the street while I was driving up."

Tony couldn't believe Jorge managed to elude him again, but he knew Jorge's breaks were soon coming to an end. He had Eva in the mix now.

"Oh, he didn't stop when he saw you?"

"No, I was coming from the opposite end of the street. I just saw the back of the car. He didn't see me."

"Oh, okay…he should be back soon. He probably went to the grocery store."

Eva didn't think Tony would come by this early, but now she could plan the rest of the day. Deciding she would not call a realtor just yet; she took a deep breath after thinking of her promise to Tina.

If you can't leave him, don't cover for him anymore.

"Well, here are the two giant palms I mentioned earlier."

She pointed to the two overgrown Queen Palms with spent fronds that needed removing. They also needed to be trimmed before hurricane season.

"We actually got a notice from the homeowner's association saying we have until next week for them to be trimmed, or we'll have to pay a fine," Eva said.

Tony looked at the big palms. They were overgrown and unkept. He then took out a pocket-sized notebook and started adding numbers.

"Well, to trim both would be a hundred dollars."

"Each?" asked Eva.

"No, for both. I usually charge $100 for each, but I'm feeling generous this morning."

"When can you start?" Eva asked.

"How about early tomorrow morning?"

"Great, we are always up early, so no worries."

"Oh, and tell Jorge I'll do it for fifty dollars if he helps me."

Eva's eyes smiled; a fifty-dollar savings was huge.

"He'll help, even if I have to drag him out of bed myself."

Tony grinned, wanting to kiss Eva for another set up. He waved goodbye as he left. He knew he had Jorge cornered now, but he was still up for getting his money sooner if he had the chance.

However, the idea of having Jorge help him tomorrow for half off was brilliant. Jorge would either have to pay him back, or he would tell Eva that he was going to place a lien on their house for the amount Jorge owed. He had Jorge sign a mechanic's lien a few months ago to secure payment. Either way, he was going to get his money.

Eva walked into the house to coffee brewing. Next to the coffeemaker was her favorite Picasso's sunflowers coffee mug, ready to be used. Jorge must have done this to make amends with Eva. This didn't impress her as he had hoped. If anything, it irritated her to think he could inch his way back to her good side by brewing coffee.

She took the coffee pot, poured the coffee down the sink, and made her own pot. Then she exchanged coffee mugs, picking a new favorite beach scenery one.

"Who does he think he is? Always believing he can charm his way out of the shit he pulls. No, Jorge, not anymore. I'm finished. There is not enough coffee in the world to forget about last night."

Eva was livid at Jorge for gambling. It tore and broke her like nothing else, especially when he promised the last time, he was done betting, begging for her to stay, and he was a changed man. It was too painful to even try to explain anymore. The only thing she could do was just feel the anger and let it pass.

She heard the front door rattle. It was Jorge. Her instinct was to run, feeling vulnerable, not wanting to be cornered with no way out.

Relax. He can only hurt you if you allow him to.

Eva stayed in the kitchen, waiting for her coffee to brew. Her insides now churned from disgust and bitterness for him, but she would no longer allow him to intimidate her. She kept her back to the door, like she didn't hear it open.

"Hi," Jorge said.

Eva remained silent, her back still turned, hoping he would get the hint and leave her in peace. She had nothing to say to him.

"Is this it? You're going to ignore me forever?"

She didn't say a word.

"So, are you?" Jorge walked closer to Eva.

In the corner of Eva's eye, she saw the steak knives on the counter. She turned away, feeling the urge to get one and strike Jorge.

"Not a bad idea," Eva finally said, still keeping her back to him. She couldn't help the response after he said something so dumb.

"Well, I'm sorry," he responded, taking closer steps to Eva.

He placed his hands on her shoulders, but she quickly shrugged them off and walked away to the kitchen bar and sat down. Her hands were shaking as she held her coffee mug, hoping the warmth of the cup would radiate throughout her body.

"Sure, you're sorry. How many more times will you say this when you keep doing the same thing?

Jorge said nothing.

"I'm immune to that word because you don't know what the word really means. You're going to have to come up with something else to say. 'Sorry' means nothing to me anymore. If anything, it angers and reminds me that you have lied again."

Jorge didn't know what to say. He knew it wasn't his first, second, third, fourth, or hundredth time saying sorry, but still. He didn't think there was a set number of times he could say it until he couldn't. He didn't think he was doing anything wrong. He was just having a dry spell of good luck and that was about to change.

Eva doesn't understand!

"Have you figured out how you're going to return our savings by next week?" Eva asked as she remembered Jorge's promise from the night before.

"Don't worry about it, and stop mentioning it."

Eva took a step back. "I am worried about it. Do you have another account I don't know about? If not, then where is this money coming from when you can't pay the fifty-dollar water bill?" she questioned.

Jorge thought of something quick.

"My brother owes me money."

Eva noticed Jorge's demeanor change. His smile disappeared as if he remembered something unsettling. Maybe he was thinking about being attacked last night. This was the only part of last night's conversation that Eva separated his gambling from, believing this had nothing to do with him betting.

"Where did you go earlier?" Eva asked.

"Oh, I just went to the store to buy something for my lip and some coffee creamer since there's hardly any left."

"Listen, before I forget. While you were at the store, Tony Deluca stopped by."

Jorge felt sidewinded. He couldn't move. His chest tightened like the worst heartburn, shooting pain to the chest.

Shit. You better get yourself together.

"What did he want?"

"He stopped by to give a quote for trimming the palm trees in the front. Remember, the ones I have been begging you to trim? I actually called him last week after getting a second notice from the HOA, but as luck would have it, he was at the bus stop this morning. I asked him to come over."

"Wow," was all Jorge could say.

"His son rides the bus with Tina. They may even be friends. Anyway, he's going to do the job for fifty dollars."

"Really? That's cheap." Even Jorge knew this.

"Yes, it is, but the catch is you have to help him, or the price goes up," she said with a smile. "I told him you would, of course. It will be good for you to get your hands dirty. Hey, maybe you can get a side job with him. Extra money would be good right now."

Jorge couldn't think straight, not really listening to Eva. Tony wasn't only coming to trim the palms. He was coming for his money or to ruin his life if he didn't have it.

You know what you have to do, or you're a dead man.

Eva sipped her coffee, noticing the time on the kitchen clock. "You better get ready for work. Just don't go to the track today."

Jorge rushed up the stairs, brainstorming how to make the best use of his time to settle his debt by tomorrow morning. Who else could he call for money? Who hasn't he called yet? He couldn't think of anyone.

How about Fernando?

After getting ready, he went into Tina's room, looking for money. He saw a piggy bank on her desk. He studied how it was positioned so he could return it the same way. Finally, he held it in his hand, his heart pounding, fearing Eva would catch him. It was heavy. Tina took pride in saving every penny, nickel, dime, and quarter for a trip to New York City to one day watch the U.S. Open.

Take it!

He told himself that he would only borrow the bills from the piggy bank. He carefully turned it upside, not wanting to make a sound. Jorge still worried any moment Eva would walk up the stairs and catch him in the act. Yet he felt he had no other choice. He quickly pulled the black rubber plug, reached in, and pulled the neatly rolled bills out.

There you go, always thinking.

He placed the money in his back pocket, plugged the piggy bank back, and put it exactly where he found it on Tina's desk.

Good boy, Jorge, well done.

CHAPTER 14

A Secret Revealed

"**I** want to show you what I found in my dad's office. It has something to do with your father," Alex mentioned.

"What is it?" Tina asked.

"I needed a notebook for school, so I borrowed one from his desk. When I opened it, I saw your father's name written inside. I flipped through the pages, and it looks like your father owes my father money...a lot... unless I'm reading it wrong."

This was enough for Tina not to finish her lunch. She couldn't figure out why her father would have to borrow money from Alex's father, or anyone for that matter. He worked, and Eva was frugal. There were no big purchases in the last couple of years she could remember. Nothing made sense, yet Alex had evidence that her father owed money.

"I'll see you later."

Throughout the day, Tina began to fit the pieces of what her father really did at the track, and so far, she didn't like what she was putting together.

CHAPTER 15

The Salon

Jorge arrived at the salon distracted, plotting how he would leave and try his luck at the track. He now had eighty dollars to change his situation.

"Good morning, Donna," Jorge said, walking by the receptionist's desk.

Donna didn't even flinch. He then backtracked and tapped the desk three times for her attention.

Donna looked straight at him, still not saying a word. Maybe she was on her period, or something bad had happened. He just hoped that whatever it was she would get over it.

"What do you want?" Donna snapped.

"Is Mrs. Friedman in?"

"Yes, she is in the back getting her hair washed and conditioned," Donna said coldly as she kept looking down at the schedule.

"Why the sad face?" Jorge asked, hoping Donna would at least crack a smile. Instead, she fluttered her eyelashes annoyed. "Sorry, it looks like you are having a bad day."

The comment upset Donna. She wondered if Jorge was that clueless about his past actions.

"If Eva happens to call looking for you, and you're out, oh well," Donna said. "And if you don't understand what I just said, it means you better think twice before leaving the shop for a few hours."

He felt flushed, understanding exactly what she was saying. There was no need to read between the lines. It was simple. Donna was not going to cover for him anymore, yet he kept his poker face on, not letting her see that he was bothered by her threat.

"Oh good, I'll be in the staff room if you need me," Jorge said, still being friendly.

Bitch!

On his way back to the staff room, Mary, a stylist, gave him the evil eye too. It wasn't anything new, but it still cut Jorge's insides each time, reminding him what he still needed to do.

A few weeks ago, she had loaned Jorge sixty dollars. She really couldn't afford to, but she felt sorry for him being in a bind. Jorge promised his life he would return the money the very next day, but he didn't.

Jorge passed the shampoo station on his way back, not wanting to be seen just yet. He wanted a cup of coffee before getting to work.

Keep your eyes open!

Mrs. Friedman was a loyal client for over twenty years, flying down from New York during the off-season. During the winter months, she lived part-time in Palm Beach. Her husband was a successful businessman who owned office buildings around the United States. He was well respected and generous in the community, giving to various charities.

Once in the staff room, John, another veteran stylist, was pouring coffee into a mug. Jorge sat down, waiting his turn. "Sorry, I just took the last of the coffee, but I can pour you half if you like. I don't have cooties," John said with a playful laugh, trying to lighten the mood.

Jorge laughed back. "Oh, no thanks, I'll be fine. I'll just make a cup of tea."

"Umm…there are no tea bags left either."

"Are you serious?" Jorge asked.

"Here, take mine if you don't want to share. You're gonna need some energy for Mrs. Friedman."

Jorge finally broke out with a real smile.

"Honey, the whole salon knows this. Please. She *is* the definition of a chatterbox."

Jorge blushed at John's humor.

John and Jorge had known each other for over a decade, not only as fellow stylists but as good friends, though they didn't see or speak to each other outside the walls of the salon.

"So, how have you been?" John asked. He knew about Jorge's gambling habit, as Jorge knew about his occasional cocaine habit, but John thought Jorge had control over his betting, but maybe not.

Two years ago, Jorge had tried to convince John to go on a bet with him, but he wasn't interested in watching greyhounds racing or betting, and from that day, Jorge kept his distance from John and vice versa.

"I'm good."

"Are you really? John asked, hoping Jorge would open up.

"To be honest, you look like you just came back from hell and back, man. What's up with your lip too?" John questioned, just noticing the welt on Jorge's bottom lip.

Jorge kept quiet, sipping his coffee.

John can't solve your problems. Only I can.

"Is it true that you still owe Mary sixty bucks? You know, she needs the money …being a single mom and all."

Jorge felt threatened by the questions, fearing they wouldn't stop.

"Nah, I am fine. I look like hell because I got punched last night while leaving a restaurant. Someone thought I was someone else. A funny story, actually. Otherwise, I couldn't be better. Seriously."

Jorge didn't say anything about Mary, though it bothered him she told John about the money he owed her. How many times did he give her rides home and now she was telling John that he owed her money? In his eyes, she was the one owing him.

What a bitch!

He wondered if Mary had told anyone else about the money he borrowed. If she just told John, he was still okay. Now he had two problems to fix before he could leave the salon. He also had to give Donna a tip or something to change her mood and return the money he owed Mary.

"It was nice chatting with you, Jorge. I hope you feel better soon. And remember to pay back Mary. She needs the money. Do the right thing."

Jorge just smiled like he usually did when he had nothing to say. His life was getting more stressful, always jumping hoops trying to pay back his debts while hiding them too.

In the next twenty-four hours, he needed to pay Donna, and Mary, replace the money he took out of Tina's piggy bank, repay Tony, replace the three grand he took out of the family savings account, and still needed around two hundred dollars for Tina's new tennis racket. If not, there was no telling what would become of him.

"So, how are you, Mrs. Friedman? It's been too long," Jorge said.

He gently patted the warm towel around her head to lift as much water as possible. Though Mrs. Friedman was twenty years older than Jorge, many younger ladies had nothing on her. She was still very beautiful and sophisticated.

"And it's so good to see you, my Jorge. You look a little tired. Is everything okay, my dear? I hope you are not working too hard," she said with a sincere smile. Jorge just smiled at her reflection as he started to comb her wet and silky hair.

"What happened to your lip?"

"I'm just getting over a cold. But seeing you now, I feel a hundred percent better, and you look lovely as ever. What have you been doing?"

"Jorge, you always know how to get a girl to smile."

"So, tell me. How has it been? It has been a few months."

Mrs. Friedman loved how Jorge took the time to ask how her life was going. This was one of the reasons why she continued to come to him for haircuts after all these years. He knew her past, and she never had to worry that he would gossip behind her back.

"I've been good, darling, but guess what?" Mrs. Friedman said excitedly as she smiled into the wall mirror, staring back at Jorge.

"Just tell me. I can't wait a second longer." He leaned into her back as he waited to hear what she was so happy about, still combing her fine blonde hair.

"I'm finally going to be a grandmother. Isn't that the best news you have heard in a while? I started to believe being a grandmother was not in the cards for me, but I was wrong. Thank God! I'm so happy! I can't wait." Mrs. Friedman giggled and continued, "Now I'm busy planning my daughter's baby shower, and I'm just beside myself. I seriously never thought this day would happen. This is a wonderful thing for our family, Jorge."

"Amen! See now. God has his own plan. Now you can be the best grandmother in the world."

Mrs. Friedman's smile stretched. She was going to lavish her grandchild with not only the best money could buy, but with time.

"So, how far along is Kate?" Do you know if you will be having a granddaughter or grandson?"

"She's six months along but looks like eight months already. If you ask me, I think she enjoys too many chocolate éclairs. She looks like an éclair with a big cream bump in the middle. Now don't tell her I said that. You know how sensitive she is about her weight."

"Oh, that is okay. Let her enjoy being pregnant after what she has been through all these years. I can't believe little Kate is about to have a baby. I remember when I cut her hair for the first time. She was six."

"I know, and guess what? She is having a little girl. Isn't that just precious? She will be my forever princess. I just can't wait to hold her and spoil her. Isn't it just wonderful, Jorge? I'm just beside myself."

"Oh, you'll love having a granddaughter. Little girls are gifts from God wrapped in love. It is a favorite quote of mine because they are."

"I know, darling, and you have so much experience in that department with your little Tina. A dear friend from the community tennis courts told me that she is no longer a little girl anymore. I hear she plays tennis like no one else's business. You know she is the talk around the tennis center. My friend Janice tells me that Tina's backhand isn't to be reckoned with."

Jorge smiled, thinking of Tina.

Mrs. Friedman added, "She is quite the player."

"She actually just started playing not too long ago."

He started to feel guilty about the money he took from her piggy bank, even though he only borrowed it.

Don't. You are doing this for her.

"I see you have let your sides grow out. It looks good on you, very chic. Maybe we could go for a new look now?" Jorge asked while combing her hair.

"I don't know. I miss my short hair. It's sort of my signature look. Many say they can recognize me from a mile away, and you know how I love that."

"Yes, you do wear it so well. Nobody wears it as well as you. You have the perfect cheekbones for the cut."

"Well, after all, you're the master of the cut. No one does it better than you, and I mean no one," Mrs. Friedman said with a wink.

It took him forty-five minutes to cut her hair. It would be perfect for the vacation she was going on. She and Mr. Friedman were heading to Barbados the next week.

She was pleased as ever with the time she spent with Jorge. He was a dear friend, and a fabulous hair stylist rolled into one. Mrs. Friedman completely loved her haircut and doubled his usual tip of fifty dollars. It was enough for Jorge to clear the air in the shop.

"Jorge, I promise I will be back in six weeks. Also, darling, if you need me for anything, you call me, and I mean anything. You have always been so good to me. You know I am always here for you."

Ask.

"Here is my new phone number. Don't lose it." She handed him her business card. "And I mean anything." She gave him another kiss and couldn't stop admiring her haircut in the mirror.

It was now close to eleven, and Jorge's next appointment was minutes away. He grabbed the *Post* and sat in his stylist chair, waiting.

He pulled out the sports section and looked back to the race schedule. He skimmed through the race schedule at Palm Springs Track to see if he recognized any of the greyhounds. There were a few he knew that made it happen for him in the past. He circled their names, feeling a surge of excitement spark within. Their names were Ace the Great, Curious George, and Bertha Saint Clare.

There you go! Getting what's yours.

There was a sixteen thousand jackpot at the track today. It would be offered at the fifth race and would overlap with the next race if no one won. The track had to give it away. Seeing this gave Jorge heart palpitations. He knew winning this jackpot would solve all of his problems. This was the jump start he needed to get in gear, move to leave the salon, and plan his bets.

He pushed off the black, sleek, Italian stylist chair and walked to Donna, who was labeling the shelves behind the receptionist's desk.

"Donna, what does my schedule look like for the rest of the day?"

"Let me see . . ." She looked down at the schedule book. "You're booked until three this afternoon."

"I just hope I make it."

Donna just looked at Jorge. He didn't look very well. In fact, he looked flushed. "What do you mean that you hope you'll make it?

"My stomach…it isn't feeling that great. It's starting to make these strange sounds and starting to hurt. I think it's from the coffee I had earlier. It tasted a little different, but I thought it was just me. "

Donna's heart raced because she felt she was responsible. "Shit, I hope you didn't use the spoiled coffee creamer. I thought I threw it away this morning."

Jorge saw the window of opportunity and ran with it.

Go for it! It is now or never.

"You know, now that I think about it, I did. Now I feel like I am going to throw up."

"See if you can make it through your 11 o'clock appointment, and I'll call the rest of your clients to reschedule."

Jorge turned away from the receptionist's desk, trying to hide his smile. He knew he would be walking out of the salon shortly. Dr. Reynolds walked in just as Jorge returned to his station, and he was relieved he was on time.

However, he just remembered that he still owed the doctor money. He couldn't remember the exact amount, but it was around two hundred dollars. Jorge patted his pocket, feeling safe as he had the money to give Dr. Reynolds. He didn't want to, but he really didn't have a choice, or he would have another person upset at him.

Your luck is about to change. Believe it.

Jorge was very polite and admirable to Dr. Reynolds. He told him how his stomach hurt from spoiled creamer. The doctor told him it would take twenty-four hours for the sour milk to pass through his system and that he should expect to go to the bathroom regularly before he got better.

"The good news is that sour milk doesn't like to stay in the system. It flushes well."

As Dr. Reynolds got out of the stylist chair, Jorge said, "Dr. Reynolds, this is the money I owe you. I'm grateful for your help. It was used for Tina's school trip to St. Augustine. She was able to go because of you, and I must add she had a wonderful time. It was really important for her to go, and you made that possible. Thank you."

The doctor smiled, feeling good about his good deed.

"I even had pictures to show you from the trip. I must have left them at the house as I was rushing to work this morning. I'll have them next time you come. I promise," Jorge said.

"Thanks, Jorge, I knew you were a man of your word. Just keep the money and save it for the next time Tina needs it, or just deposit it in her savings account."

"Are you serious? I am humbly thankful."

"Tina is worth every cent. Goodbye, Jorge. Please don't mention it again." The doctor then walked out of the salon feeling good.

Now Jorge could easily repay Mary and Donna and still have enough money to go to the track. He never actually forgot about paying Mary back. The truth was he never had extra cash and thought she might forget.

He walked up to Mary as she was busy organizing her workstation for her next client.

"Here you go, and there's an extra twenty for your boy, sorry," Jorge said.

"It's about time."

Jorge just smiled as if she thanked him. He calmly walked back to his station and started to pack his sears, combs, and brushes.

"Oh, Jorge, could you come here before you leave?" Donna asked from behind the receptionist's desk.

"I managed to get in touch with your clients, and they have all been rescheduled for tomorrow and Thursday."

Thank God.

He wrapped his arms around his waist, bending over, faking sickness to gain more sympathy from Donna.

"I'm so sorry, Jorge," Donna said, feeling responsible.

"It's okay. It happens, but I need to go."

"Of course, just go. You're covered here," Donna said.

"Oh, here is a little something for you. I hope you didn't think I forgot."

Jorge slipped her a twenty he borrowed from her last week.

"I was a little upset, but we are good now. If you need anything, please call."

"I will. Now let me get home before I make a mess here."

He turned away and left the salon with the sports section under his right arm. Though Donna felt they were on better terms, she was still upset that she was careless about leaving the coffee creamer out to spoil, hoping no one else would get sick.

Donna covered her eyes in distress. John noticed from his workstation and walked over to see if he could help. He lightly tapped her on the shoulder. She looked up, her eyeliner smeared and her cheeks wet.

"What's wrong? Did Jorge say something?"

"No, I did something really stupid."

"What did you do? It can't be serious, Miss Goody Two Shoes."

"Well, you know the coffee creamer I left out yesterday afternoon? The one I showed you?"

"Yes, but you threw it out before anyone could use it. Don't you remember? I saw you."

"Are you sure? I must be losing it because Jorge said he poured some in his coffee this morning and just left the salon with a severe stomachache."

Liar, thought John.

"He is just pulling your leg. I made his coffee, and he drank it black, but you know where he probably went."

Bastard, she thought. Jorge was probably halfway to the track.

"John, you just made my day. How about I get you lunch today? You just saved my sanity."

"I could go for Chinese."

"It's Chinese, then."

John walked back to his workstation, let down by Jorge. He didn't like how Jorge was playing people in the salon now, realizing that he wouldn't be surprised if Jorge already pulled something over him, and he didn't know it. He knew from now on, he would be prepared.

Donna picked up the phone and dialed Jorge's number. She wasn't going to let him get away with it. If anyone was going to get the last laugh, it would be her.

"Hello, you have reached . . ."

Donna's heart started to race, wondering if Eva would pick up. It was too late to hang up because the caller ID would show the call was coming from the salon.

"Please leave a message after the beep."

"Oh, hi. This is Donna . . ."

CHAPTER 16

A Warning Ignored

As Jorge opened the back door of the salon, he was greeted by a gust of wind. It felt like he was being pushed back inside. Noticeable dark clouds were forming and in the distance, thunder could be heard. Was a thunderstorm brewing, or was it something else?

Boom!

Jorge jumped into the car terrified of the lightning. He quickly rolled up the window to avoid any harm. The sudden bad weather was a surprise. He somehow felt that the storm was somehow warning him.

Be careful, Jorge. You're about to course in dangerous waters.

His heart quickly reacted, his heart rate rising steadily, feeling out of breath, sweat streaming down his body. He began to wonder if he was really hearing the sounds of a storm or was he going mad. He laid back on the headrest, closing his eyes, just wanting refuge from what may or may not be real.

Maybe he was losing his mind. After all, he was under tremendous financial pressure, something may have just clicked, and his mind was no longer his own.

Jorge felt that he just needed a moment to collect himself. If only he could erase the worries that were haunting him. Jorge knew people were starting to doubt him, and this pained him, seeing and feeling people lose their trust in him by avoiding and brushing him off.

Screw them, Jorge.

He looked up to see the gray clouds again, but they were gone. It was his cue to get on with his plans.

He thought about what he heard just moments ago. *Be careful, Jorge. You're about to course in dangerous waters.*

What is there to be careful of? Why are you being paranoid?

The storm was somehow gone now. Only blue skies appeared, causing Jorge to believe that what he saw and heard earlier was just from his imagination. He did not see the importance of the message anymore,

Jorge headed toward the track. This time he was going to win, feeling it in his bones. He knew Tony would be at the house early tomorrow morning expecting his money, and Jorge knew of the consequences if he didn't pay him. It would be far worse than a busted lip because he would lose Eva this time. The stakes were too high for him not to go to the track. No one was going to bail him this time. It was his responsibility to get out of this mess.

"Please, God. Help me!" Jorge pleaded; his voice stricken with anxiety as he feverishly drove to the track.

"Please, please, please."

The silence only made him worry more. Then he heard it again, *Be careful, Jorge. You are about to course into dangerous waters.* Jorge shook his head, desperate to shake the voice away, fearing it, feeling delusional. This time it felt like the voice was warning him against going to the track.

"I'm a son of God. Your son. Please help me."

There was nothing but the sound of newspapers flapping on the car floor.

"Don't you care that my life will be over if you don't help me?"

Tears ran down his troubled face, desperation settling in, fearing his life was about to end if he didn't win the $16,000 prize.

Jorge thought of how he had no one else to blame but himself. He couldn't even remember how or when the loan even started. It was like he erased it from his memory, foolishly thinking that Tony would do the same. However, it now was this great, giant snowball, getting larger and larger by the minute, when at one time, it was just a snowflake.

A sane part of him wanted to turn the car around and drive back home to Eva, confess everything, and beg for forgiveness. Maybe this would repair their marriage and bring them closer, and he would never gamble again.

What, are you crazy? She will divorce you.

Deep down, Jorge knew the voice was right. What was he thinking? He lied to her last night when she allowed him to tell the truth. It was then when he should have told her the real story, not just the part that he only went to the track, but also the part that he owed a lot of money. He forgot that important detail. He knew now it was too late to turn back time and change any of this. Now his only option was to go to the track and win his life back.

Now you're thinking straight.

He thought about Tina, believing she still didn't know the gambler in him, but he knew one day she would. It would all catch up to him. She would eventually put two and two together and leave him too.

Tina would eventually think back to when he was late or didn't come home and make connections that he was actually at the track. He wondered if she would still love him if she knew he was a gambler.

In his desperation, he couldn't even call his brother, Fernando, because his brother promised his wife he wouldn't help him anymore.

It seemed anyone good to him was now turning their backs, no longer wanting to help a sinking ship, and that was Jorge. He was a bloody, sinking sink with no hope of ever sailing again. This depressed him even more, but he was trapped between a rock and a hard place.

"Please, please, I can't live like this anymore! I want to kill myself!"

He continued to plead to God. He was waiting for a response, like he did to anyone else when he made desperate pleas, but there was only silence.

"Come on, say something. I need a sign! Let me know if everything is going to be okay! I am sorry! I'll never gamble again," Jorge cried, trying to say the right words to make things right again.

"What about, 'Ask and you shall receive?' I am asking, and I need to receive money. I need to win!" Jorge said, again expecting to hear God speak.

"Please, I need to win! I need this to happen more than anything else in my life. I'm at your mercy. I need you, and my family needs you."

Tears gushed down his cheeks, feeling flushed and confused, not seeing clearly as he drove. He felt anxious, he knew his days were numbered now, and it was a do-or-die situation at the track. Sweat bullets fogged his vision and what was left of his fate.

You're going to win the jackpot!

He knew this voice was not from God. Deep down he knew God wouldn't want him to gamble.

You can only win if you bet. How else are you going to get out of this mess you created? You will lose your family if you don't.

Jorge continued driving, but he had a couple of stops to make before going to the track.

Good boy, Jorge. Now man up!

CHAPTER 17

Pandora's Box

Tina glanced at Alex as they walked to the bus. She thought he was cool, a boy she could be friends with, who just happened to be popular. His popularity was something she really couldn't fault him for.

"Here's our bus," Alex said, moving to the side so Tina could walk up first. Tina blushed. She walked to an empty row in the middle of the bus, and he followed, sitting next to her.

"So, do you still want to know what I found in the notebook?" Alex leaned in, talking low so only she could hear.

"Sure, why not," she answered, acting like it was no big deal, though her heart was now racing.

"Well, as you know, my father and yours are friends."

"Sort of, but go on." Tina just wanted Alex to get to the point so her heart could stop pounding and return to normal beats.

"Do you know what my father does for a living?"

"Yeah, he does outside work, lawns, and stuff."

"Yes, he does. He has a landscaping business, which your mom knows about, but he has a second business, a secret one, where he makes bank-on. My mom doesn't know about it, and I don't think your mom knows either. So, this has to stay between you and me."

Dang, thought Tina. That was certainly a mouth load of information. She didn't see anything wrong with the first part, but the second part didn't sit well with her.

"My father's second job is kind of shady, but that's where he makes most of his money from," Alex said.

"Okay, what is it?" Tina wondered.

"So, I found this page in my notebook. My dad must have thought he was writing in his notebook or something like that."

He handed the paper to Tina. In one sentence, it said in big, bold writing: **JORGE GABOR OWES $8,000 PAST DUE...20 % interest...BASTARD!**

This shocked Tina. Why in the world did he need to borrow that kind of money? No repairs or new improvements were made to the house, and the car's air conditioner was still broken.

Nothing she could think of would require that kind of money, but the truth was staring her straight in the face. It showed he owed Alex's father lots of money. This didn't settle well with her. No wonder her mother was upset at her father last night.

Tina's head started to tighten. A splitting headache was on its way, and she was glad she was on the bus and not in the classroom to experience it.

"Do you know why he needed the money?" Alex asked.

"No, I have no idea," Tina answered.

"I'm just going to say it. He gambles."

This word gamble came up again. Her mother had said it last night, and now Alex just repeated it. It must be a bad word, she thought.

"I know he goes to the track, but that is all I know," Tina said.

"The first time I went to the track. I thought it was where people went to watch dog races for fun, you know? But it's not just that. They go to win money."

"Win money? How? I don't get it."

"About a month ago, I went with my dad to Palm Springs Kennel Club."

Alex took a deep breath before continuing, believing Tina would forever feel differently about her father when he told her what he saw.

"I followed him to a glass window where a pretty lady stood. She had an English accent, and she knew my father's name, which I thought was strange, but I didn't say anything. Anyway, my dad said four numbers to her, then slid some money under a little opening at the bottom of the window. As soon as her hands touched the money, she counted it, then pressed on a keyboard that looked like a smaller version of the cash registers at Winn Dixie. Afterward, she slid a small ticket under the glass window. It was the size of a lottery ticket if you have ever seen one. My father took it, and suddenly his eyes became large. He quickly walked to the sitting area, and he couldn't keep still. He just kept on looking out to the racetrack. It was like he forgot that I was even there."

Tina was fascinated with the story so far.

"You know what I realized about my father?"

"What?"

"I realized it wasn't his first time at the track."

"You're right. How else did the English lady know his name?" Tina was starting to get a better picture of betting and gambling, but she was anxious to hear the rest of the story.

"I followed him to the viewing area where we sat and waited for the race to begin. There were a lot of people sitting all around talking, but once the race started, everyone went into an uproar, jumping out of their seats, shouting at the dogs and themselves. I wanted to see what was happening, but I was too short, and my dad was too busy watching the race. He wouldn't look at me. I was scared. Finally, when the race ended, people were either happy or really upset, throwing their tickets to the floor. Some people looked like they were punched. My dad won that race. I followed him again to the window with the pretty lady, and she congratulated him. He gave her the ticket, and she ran it through the same machine that printed it out, confirming it was a winning ticket. She kept the ticket and gave him the money he won."

"Wow, it sounds like a crazy place to me. Still not sure what is so great about it."

"I have something else to tell you . . . I saw your father at the track that day."

Tina held her breath. She didn't know what to think.

"He was sitting alone, staring at the track after the race. My father pointed to him and said how sad it was that he was chasing his losses like I would know what that meant."

Of course, this was not what Tina wanted to hear. It saddened her, thinking that her father was chasing his losses and trying to win back the money he'd spent. This was what she believed Alex's father was saying. This gave her a sad image of her father staring out to the track with a troubled face. No wonder he was moody. He was hooked on gambling.

She felt like she had just opened Pandora's box with this new information about her father. Now she knew she would always think differently of him. The evil within the box would always try to taunt her.

She just didn't know how far it would go and how it would try to destroy her.

CHAPTER 18

Twisted Tim

Jorge had to rebuild his funds before he could go to the track. First, he'd stop at Tim's slummy apartment across town because Tim owed him money. Then he'd go by Fernando to see if he could spare him a few hundred.

For the last few days, he had been trying to get in touch with Tim, but with no luck. Jorge left voicemail after voicemail, and still nothing. His last resort was going to his apartment in the sketchy part of town.

Jorge felt like a target as he approached the Grandview Lakes Apartment Complex. The eight-foot chain link fence around the building gave it a prison vibe. The complex was dated, gray, and lacking landscaping.

He noticed Tim's sky-blue Honda scooter chained around a massive oak tree next to the parking lot. Two boys were pretending to ride it. The boy in the front held the handlebars, while the boy in the back clutched his friend's waist screaming that he wanted to go faster.

Jorge quietly walked to the stairwell; no one was around. Walking up the dirt-packed black steps, he covered his mouth and nose to minimize the stench of urine that started to burn his nostrils.

He continued to walk, alert of what may come his way, keeping his eyes and ears open. He reached for the cross around his neck, praying, "Please, let me make it out of here." He then placed the necklace back underneath his shirt.

He stopped at the third floor. Tim's apartment was to the left of the stairwell. To his surprise, the front door was opened. This alarmed

Jorge because Tim was paranoid, always thinking someone was out to get him and always hiding from people he owed money or favors to.

Jorge thought the worst. Maybe one of Tim's bookies had it with him and left him for dead. This was enough for him to turn away and get the hell out of there, but he had come too far to turn back just yet. He needed the money he loaned Tim.

Come on, don't be a baby, Jorge.

Jorge lightly knocked on the door, expecting to hear a noise from Tim. He was greeted with silence. He knocked a little harder, his heart picking up a notch, fearing the next-door neighbor might hear it too.

He was faced with a dilemma. If he went in, would he possibly walk into a trap, or worse, a crime scene?

"Tim, are you in there?" Jorge asked.

Finally, he heard Tim's voice. He carefully stepped into the living room, though he couldn't see him. He stopped when he heard moans, not sure what to think.

He waited for a moment; his stomach turned to mush. A wave of anxiety panicked him. The last thing he wanted was to walk in on Tim in a compromised position.

"Yes, again, yes, yes . . ."

Jorge stayed frozen in his tracks. He realized Tim was far from hurt.

Instantly, the moans stopped, and he heard rushed movements. Jorge stepped further inside the living room. A winded Tim approached Jorge.

'What are you doing here?" Tim asked.

"I'm here for my money," Jorge said softly, barely hearing his own words.

"I don't have it. Can't you see I am busy?" Tim shouted.

Jorge collected his thoughts.

"I know you won last night. I just want my money back, not the interest. Just give my money or I'll . . ."

Jorge knew he was taking a chance by playing a tough guy at Twisted Tim.

"Or you will *what*? Tim asked.

Jorge kept quiet and clenched his fists.

Tim looked up at him, and then he started to laugh.

"Jorge, man, you are too soft, and that's putting it mildly. Everyone knows that. What are you bluffing about? Now shut the fuck up."

At the track, Jorge witnessed Tim go off on a man when the man asked him to move so he could bet. Tim took off his worn Velcro belt and wrapped it around the man's neck. It almost suffocated him, but he stopped when he saw security guards come his way.

Tim glanced at the clock. In less than two minutes his lady friend would be calling again.

"You know you came at the worst possible fucking time, you lucky son of a bitch," Tim said, smiling at Jorge.

Tim got up from the withered couch, wrapped the stained beach towel around his beer gut, and walked straight to the kitchen. He opened the narrow cabinet to the right of the stove and reached for the Great Western coffee mug hidden in the back behind the sugar jar. Inside the jar was a roll of money. Jorge was salivating at the cash, feeling his luck change. He couldn't wait to get his hands on the money and get the hell out of the apartment.

See, he has money.

"This is all I have. It's seven hundred and fifty dollars. I'll give you the rest later. Now shoo. I'm expecting my lady caller." Tim winked and smiled and was ready to push Jorge out the door if he didn't leave.

Jorge knew Tim well enough to know he still had money stashed in some other place in the apartment, but he wasn't going to tempt his luck.

"See you later, man," Jorge said.

This time Tim deadbolted the front door.

Jorge rushed downstairs. As he took each step, he couldn't help feeling dirty. If anyone would tell him one day he would be begging Tim to sleep on the couch for a place to stay, he would have told them to get lost.

He pulled out of the parking lot with the money he needed. Jorge looked at the dashboard's clock, seeing he still had time to spare before the big jackpot payoff began. He decided he would stop by Fernando.

At least at his brother's place, he could relax, have a cold drink, and not worry about Tony just yet.

"Hey, brother," Fernando said as he opened the front door.

Jorge and his brother were close, but their relationship was strained because Fernando's wife didn't think Jorge was a good influence.

"Hey, man," Jorge said, embracing him. "Can we talk in the back?"

Fernando knew that was code for 'I want to talk to you in private', not wanting Sara to hear their conversation.

"Sure, but I'm not sure what I can do for you," Fernando replied.

Jorge ignored the last part of Fernando's response.

Once by the pool, Jorge felt comfortable talking again.

"Listen, brother. I'm in big trouble, and I need your help."

Fernando looked down, avoiding eye contact with Jorge. Realizing whenever he looked at his brother, he had a hard time saying no because brotherly love always got in the way.

"Eva talked to Tony this morning."

"What? How did that happen?" Fernando asked, looking up now. He was fearful of what else he was about to hear.

"He was at Tina's bus stop," Jorge added.

"That is messed up. Do you think he said anything to Eva?"

"I don't think so…but he's up to something."

"And you are sure he didn't tell Eva you owe him money?"

"I am because Eva wouldn't have been able to contain her anger if he did."

Fernando didn't want to say that she actually could if she had a plan of her own, but he didn't want to stress out his brother any more than he did.

"Yet, this isn't even my real problem."

"What do you mean?" Fernando asked.

"At the bus stop, Tina asked Tony for a quote to trim the two overgrown palm trees in our front yard."

"Unbelievable."

"Yeah, the asshole came to the house while I was at Winn Dixie and told Eva he would trim the trees for half price if I helped him," Jorge said, feeling weak.

"What? He has some nerve."

"Of course, she agreed."

Fernando now saw the problem. Jorge needed the cash by tomorrow, or Tony would tell Eva about the money Jorge still owed him.

"How much do you owe?"

"Eight G's,"

"What? I don't have that kind of money," Fernando stated.

Jorge looked at Fernando as he lit up another cigarette.

"Jorge, you swore on Mom's life that you weren't going to gamble anymore, and here you are twenty years later."

"Please don't involve Mom in this mess, and I never said that. Stop putting words in my mouth."

"I can tell you if she could reach down from heaven and shake some sense into you, she would for your own good. What the hell were you thinking to borrow from Tony?" Fernando asked.

"I know I'm a failure, but that won't help."

Jorge touched his forehead, hating himself. It didn't look like his brother was going to help him. He looked at his wristwatch; he had to leave in five minutes to make it in time for the jackpot races.

"What are you going to do?" Fernando wondered, hoping he would do the right thing. He always worried about his younger brother. When they were kids, their mom told him to watch Jorge and ensure nothing bad ever happened to him. Her wishes always stayed with him, even long after Jorge was an adult.

"What else? I'm going to the track. I have about two thousand dollars, and I'm going to win the sixteen-thousand-dollar jackpot. I will make everything right again. You'll see."

"No, you go home, stay away from the track and tell Eva everything. I'm telling you; you'll have a better chance of saving your marriage if you do this. Fuck the jackpot. Fuck the track. Fuck gambling. Save your life," Fernando said.

Hoping to talk sense to his brother, Fernando could see it was just going in a deaf ear. Jorge was going to the track, and there was nothing he could do about it.

"Brother, listen, don't worry about me. I'm going to win that jackpot, and you'll be asking me for money, and guess what I will say?"

Good boy, Jorge, that's how you stick it to him

CHAPTER 19

Jackpot

Jorge felt stopping at his brother's house was just a huge waste of time. Not only was Fernando unwilling to help him, but he had to involve their dead mother in the conversation, trying to make him feel guilty.

Bullshit, he thought. Fernando was the one who should be ashamed for not helping him.

He's just jealous he can't do what you can. Brush it off. Now go to the track and win before someone else does.

His thoughts were calming, like a faithful friend, knowing what to say. Pulling out of Fernando's driveway, he decided to put his feelings aside and move on with his plans.

Hurry up!

Jorge arrived at the track parking lot, pulling into the VIP section. Walking to the entrance, he gave himself a pep talk, "Okay, Jorge, this time, you are going to be smart. Stick with the plan, and don't get sidetracked!"

"Jorge!" Mike, a friend from church, called out. "Why don't you come join us amateurs for a drink? Maybe you can give us a few pointers on how to bet. The first round is on me."

Jorge smiled and waved back, but he declined. There was no time to waste; he had to get situated for the big race. "Maybe later, sorry.

I'm meeting a friend, and I'm late but thank you. If we don't meet up later, I'll see you at Sunday mass."

You're going to win tonight.

He looked at the scoreboard and was pleased to see that Race 4 hadn't started yet. Race 5 was when the jackpot was offered for the first time. Jorge went to his lucky seat and looked at the sports section of the newspaper he took from the salon.

It was already marked for Race 5, and all he had to do was place the bet at the wage window. He felt confident in his picks.

Don't second-guess yourself. Keep to the plan.

Jorge cautiously looked around the pavilion, hoping Tony wasn't around.

He looked at the wall clock, elated to see it was time to place his first bet. He just knew he was going to win. He rushed to his favorite window, smiling when he saw his good luck charm, Trudy. She had a special way of making him feel good about being Jorge Gabor. It was hard not to blush like a little schoolboy around her when she would smile at him.

"Well, hello, Jorge. Nice seeing you, my friend. I had a feeling I'd see you today," Trudy said, feeling a kinship towards him.

He reminded her so much of her sweet, soft-spoken father who lived over the pond. She was grateful for Jorge's generous tips.

"Hello, Trudy, and nice seeing you too. I hope the winners tonight treat you right," Jorge said.

"What bet are you going to start tonight? You know tonight's jackpot is sixteen grand."

Jorge just smiled and looked down at the sports section and the names he circled. He had exactly four, and not five, which would only confuse him if there was an extra, he'd have to pick from.

"I'd like the winning ticket, *please*. Any which way you like. I'm fine with it," Jorge joked.

Trudy giggled and shook her head.

"I really wish I could give you the winning ticket, Jorge, but it's in fate's hands."

She's right, Jorge. What are you waiting for?

"Come on, Trudy. You know I'm only joking, but it's nice to know you would if you could."

"I would print myself one too while at it," Trudy added.

"Our problems would be gone," Jorge said, having too many to count.

Trudy understood what he meant. "Yes, it would be nice. So, what's it going to be, Jorge? There's a line behind you."

"Oh, yeah, let me see." He looked down at the newspaper again, trying to find Race 5. "Okay, here it is. I like a superfecta boxed on Daisy Duke, Maxwell the Great, Speedy Reni, and Fast Sandy."

"What are the numbers?" Trudy asked.

"Sorry, they are four, three, one, and five, and when I win, I'll be back," Jorge answered with a wink.

He knew of Trudy's dreams of going to college to become an English teacher like her mom. He thought how nice it would be if he could help her get close to her dreams. Jorge would hate for her to be working at the track forever unless she wanted to.

He took the cash from his front pocket. It was all the money to his name. It was a combination of money from Tina's piggy bank, Dr. Reynolds, Tim's repayment from the funds Jorge had taken from the joint savings account with Eva, and the grand he kept from last night. None of it was extra money, making it much more valuable.

He held the money tight until he knew how much the bet was. He calculated it would be around a hundred fifty to two hundred dollars. He didn't usually bet superfectas, but he knew desperate situations required taking desperate measures. His usual quinella box wouldn't win him enough money to be a free man.

"It will cost you one hundred and sixty big ones, Jorge."

Jorge felt the sting of the bet but went with it.

As Jorge was counting his money, Trudy noticed Jorge's swollen lip. She didn't notice it yesterday and wondered if it happened later in the night when a few security guards were talking about breaking up a fight in the parking lot.

He counted his money carefully, making sure the bills weren't sticking together. He didn't want to give her any extra money just yet.

"What happened to your lip?" Trudy asked.

Suddenly, he began to shake. The question returned him to the reality he may lose everything tonight if things don't work out. He thought of Tony again and just wanted out of his body.

"Did it have anything to do with you running out yesterday?" Trudy continued.

"It's nothing," Jorge said coldly. He did not want to feel like he had to explain himself. "I just don't want to talk about it right now. It's nothing. Really."

"Okay."

The change in Jorge's mood didn't go unnoticed by Trudy. The unspoken words of Jorge pulled at Trudy's heartstrings. She heard the stories about Jorge and his problem, but she didn't want to believe them. Yet, a part of her couldn't help but believe in them now.

"Well, here is your ticket. Hope you hit the jackpot tonight, and *please* remember me if you do," Trudy said, trying to change Jorge's somber mood.

He finally cracked a smile. "I hope so too, and I won't forget you either, Trudy," he said.

On his way to the viewing area, he bumped into a few more acquaintances. Everyone was excited about the jackpot race. It was like Christmas time. People were happy, ready to take their chance at the jackpot.

Jorge was surprised to see a few more church choir members; maybe they took a bus over, hoping to win for the church.

You need the money for yourself!

Jorge then wondered if any of them were closet gamblers like him, but he dismissed the thought.

There is no such thing as a closet gambler. There are only real gamblers like you.

He sat in his lucky seat again. He couldn't help but smile and wait for the perfect moment to begin. A lady was sitting alone a few seats down, holding a betting ticket and a bag of popcorn. When their eyes met, she asked Jorge if he would like some popcorn, and he accepted. He hadn't eaten all day.

"Thank you."

"You're welcome."

And that was as far as the conversation went, both munching on warm, buttery popcorn. He noticed people getting to their seats, not yet sitting, holding their tickets in a trance-like state, looking out to the racetrack for Race 5 to start.

Winning this race was what they wanted. Their eyes were fixed between the wall clock and the racetrack, excitedly seeing the dog handlers near the dog boxes below, starting to feel the euphoria build up.

Jorge saw little kids with their parents and grandparents. This was a family event for many patrons. There were children also holding tickets in anticipation. One would never think gambling was involved.

He then thought of Tina and how he took the money she had saved for years from her piggy bank. Jorge knew what he did was wrong, but he promised to return the money.

He also thought about the tennis racket he promised she'd get today, but the likelihood of that happening was close to none. He feared that she would turn her back on him like the others if he kept breaking his promises.

Don't worry about her.

Please, God. Help me, he whispered. Jorge saw more unfamiliar faces occupying the pavilion for the jackpot race.

Jorge focused on the racetrack. The moment of truth was approaching. He took a final look at the clock; it was now a matter of seconds before the shot would be fired, the dogs would be off, and he'd win the sixteen-thousand-dollar jackpot.

He imagined the glory he would feel. The joy of victory was moments away. He leaned forward to get a better look at the raceway. Though he knew the track by heart, he looked at it like it was his first time. It was the only place he could change his financial situation within moments, which hooked him. He tightly held the betting ticket. He wouldn't let go of it for anything because it was the winning ticket. A wager ticket was one of a kind and could never be replaced.

Bang!

The whole world was now numb as he stood watching the race. Nothing could pull him away. Race 5 was now in play. Jorge shot up from his seat like a rocket being launched, his heart exhilarating, watching the greyhounds sprint through the starting gates, running for dear life. The euphoria was building for many. It could not be imitated or compared as it got stronger, tense, and pleasurable.

The dogs were neck to neck, but eventually, they broke, reaching ahead of each other. People were shouting, either praising or cursing. What only a few seconds ago was a friendly place was now a madhouse.

People were on the edge of their seats, some looking down in shame staring at their losing ticket. Jorge was happy to see the dogs he picked were still in the lead but became nervous when other dogs started to edge up from behind. Then, Speedy Reni pushed into the lead.

"Oh, good boy, Speedy Reni! Just keep running, boy!"

He saw the other three dogs sandwiched in between two other dogs. Jorge screamed louder. He knew it could go either way. It was too close to call it a victory yet. Anything and everything could happen until the race was over. Sweat streamed down his brow.

"Come on, Daisy Girl. Come on, Maxwell. Show me what you got, boy. Don't let them boss you around. Come on, Fast Sandy. Go, girl, go!"

His heart dropped as he watched Maxwell trip over his feet, lying on the ground, unable to move. Jorge fell to his seat. He couldn't believe the luck he was dealt with when he was so close to winning. If Maxwell hadn't fallen, he was certain he would have won.

Damn dog, he thought.

Panic set in for Jorge, afraid to look at the scoreboard to see if the jackpot had been won. He thought he had it all figured out. He placed the perfect bet, but by a fluke the prize dog was hurt. Jorge thought about the money he still had. He could pay Tony just about half of what he owed him if he left the track now.

Speedy Reni came in first, Daisy Girl was second, but Maxwell and Sandy didn't make the top four. Sandy came in sixth, and Maxwell didn't even make it to the finish line.

Dammit, Jorge thought.

Try again. Now dust yourself off. You'll make it up in this race. Move on!

Yet he thought about the message he heard when he left the shop earlier. *Be careful Jorge. You are about to course in dangerous waters.*

He shook his head, thinking he was going mad.

I won't win if I don't try, he assured himself. He had ten minutes until the next race. He sat back down and closed his eyes for a breather. After a few moments, he looked at the sports section again and reviewed the sixth race roster. He circled three dogs he knew with excellent handicaps and instinctively picked the last dog based on its handicap.

As he walked to the betting windows, he started to feel better. Trudy's window line was so long that he was tempted to bet at another one but stayed, fearing bad luck.

"Hey, Jorge, consider this your lucky day," a voice said only a few feet away.

Jorge didn't even have to turn around to know it was Benny, the asshole. He was the last person he ever wanted to see. Benny was an ex-gambling friend who cheated him on a bet, and he never forgot about it.

Jorge gave Benny money for a bet because he couldn't leave the salon. Later during a break, Jorge called the track results line and was ecstatic to hear the numbers he had given Benny to bet on came in. The winnings were going to get him out of a jam. He waited for Benny to come by the salon later to give him the cash, but Benny never showed. The next day, Jorge called him, wondering why he hadn't come by, aware he had won. Benny said he arrived at the track after the race and didn't actually place the bet.

Jorge always remembered how those words felt like a punch in the gut because he knew Benny never missed a race. H

"Get lost, Benny. Can't you see I'm busy?" Jorge gave Benny a fleeting look, then turned away.

"Listen, Jorge. I want to make it up to you," Benny suggested.

Jorge looked back, this time having a good look at him, and was taken at how much he aged. He had deeper wrinkles than he thought possible for a man in his early sixties. His hair was mostly gone now, and his glossy eyes indicated he had a few too many drinks.

"Make it fast."

"I know the winning dogs for the next race. I'd even bet my life on it if I could." Benny said.

"What are you smoking? Just leave."

Jorge became frustrated and turned away, hoping Benny would get the message and go away. He didn't. Three people were still ahead of him. He couldn't simply walk away, or he would lose his place in line and miss his chance at the jackpot.

"I'm telling you. This is a sure thing, man. I studied this, and I know the odds." Benny said.

If Jorge had a quarter for each time, he heard this song and dance, he'd be a millionaire by now. He decided to see what else Benny had to say. It's not like he could leave, either.

"So, why are you really here?" Jorge asked.

"Well, there are two things I want to say. First, I lied to you about not placing the bet you asked for. I did, and it was a winning bet, but I needed the money to pay the bills, or Stella was going to divorce me. I didn't tell anyone, but she already filed divorce papers, and I didn't want to lose her. I'm sorry. I always wanted to tell you the truth, but I was so ashamed."

Jorge became red, his blood boiling.

"I don't blame you for hating me. I actually hate myself. If it is any consolation to you, they lost respect for me after you told most of our friends what happened. Even after I lied, saying I didn't place the bet, they wouldn't believe me," Benny said.

Jorge's face showed his anger, ready to strike. Benny edged back, feeling the heat from Jorge.

Now there was only one person ahead of him in line, and he wasn't going to ruin his chance to place a winning bet.

"So, what is the second reason? I really don't have time for this bullshit. I'd kick your ass right now if I weren't a nice guy."

"No, I see we don't have much time. The truth is I don't have any money to bet with. I'm offering my tip for your money."

"Um, I see. So, you play me for a fool again?" Jorge asked.

"No, it is not like that. I have been looking for you. I want you to win too. I want this awful feeling in my stomach to go away. This bet will erase the past between us. I promise."

"What happens if I pay for the bet and it's a winner?" Jorge asked.

"No one won the jackpot last race, so the sixteen grand is still on the table. I'd say we split it."

Jorge didn't respond immediately. He wanted Benny to sweat. In his mind, he wanted at least sixty percent. He knew he could call the shots because he had money, not Benny. Before Jorge could say a word, he was finally facing Trudy at the wage window.

"Hi again. The good news is no one won the jackpot in the last race," Trudy smiled.

"Hallelujah!"

Jorge then placed his bet. Afterwards, he looked at Benny and gave him an offer.

"I'll fund your bet for a cost of sixty percent of the winnings."

"It's a deal, man!" Benny said, shaking Jorge's hand to make it official.

"Trudy, Benny, and I are on a bet together. He'll tell you the details, and I'll pay."

"Okay, boss. Whatever you say," Trudy said.

She looked at Jorge, knowing Benny all too well. He was the track's runt, but she wasn't going to say anything.

"A hundred and eighty dollars, please," Trudy said from behind the wage window.

Jorge slid the money under the window. Trudy counted it, printed the betting ticket, and slid it under for Jorge.

"Benny, I don't like company. So, get lost."

Benny shook his head but knew to keep a close watch on Jorge. He heard how Jorge bailed on Tony yesterday and found a seat a few rows up from Jorge, having a clear view of him, ready to charge if necessary.

Race 6 started, and sure enough, people were on their feet cheering, screaming, cursing, and some even crying. Jorge was no different. He was desperate to win too. *It had to happen*, he thought. The place looked like a circus, no one caring how silly they looked, only caring for the euphoria of betting. Jorge's tired eyes were glued to the track. While he shouted at the top of his lungs, he felt the thrill take over his body.

"Go, Charlie! Run, boy! Good boy . . .Go, Bertha! Come on! Go, Johnny! Run your heart out!"

Finally, the race was over as quickly as it started. He lost again. This time the underdog greyhounds won. None of the dogs he picked won. The betting slips fell from his hands, and this time he felt faint. Time was ticking, and he started to feel like he was in line for the guillotine. He had forgotten about the wage ticket he had with Benny.

Come on, Jorge! Make another bet. You will win this time.

From the corner of his eye, he saw Benny rushing down the pavilion with his fists clenched together, up in the air claiming victory. Jorge quickly bent down and collected the betting tickets he carelessly dropped before the worker on the pavilion floor could sweep them away. His heart felt like it was about to jump from his chest.

"Could we have really won?" Jorge asked.

"See, I told you. Now we are even."

He held the ticket as he looked at the scoreboard. He saw the winning numbers 5-2-1-4. Jorge looked at the ticket, and it was a perfect match. His hands started to shake. He almost fell to the ground but got his bearings. He then hugged Benny before rushing to the wage window to collect the jackpot with Benny on his tail.

Jorge could have walked away with nine thousand five hundred dollars and a clean slate, but he didn't.

Why leave now? Have some fun. You deserve it, Jorge.

CHAPTER 20

Plans Broken Again

"Our stop is coming," Alex said, sitting next to Tina on the bus ride home.

Tina shook her head, lost in thought, watching the changing skies. It looked like a storm was headed their way. It was getting alarmingly darker and darker.

"Maybe I should have kept quiet about your dad," Alex said.

"Oh, no, it's not that. I was just looking at the sky. It looks like a storm is coming," Tina replied, her attention now on Alex.

Alex leaned towards her to look out the window, "Yeah, you're right."

The bus arrived at their stop.

Alex got out of the aisle seat. Tina followed behind, relieved to see neither of their parents was waiting at the bus stop. Tina really didn't want to see Alex's father after knowing how their fathers knew each other.

"I could walk you home," Alex hinted, hoping Tina would agree.

"No, I don't think it's a good idea."

"Is it because of my father?" Alex questioned.

"No, it's not that," Tina said, "I have things to do."

Alex was disappointed, but he knew she had her reasons and wanted to respect them.

"Well, have a good weekend then. I'll catch you on Monday." Alex said with a playful grin.

"Okay, maybe we can hang out next week."

"Yeah..." Alex let out a smile.

Alex and Tina looked at the sky again, surprised to see the once gray clouds were now smaller and further away as if they were being sucked into an invisible vacuum.

"Well, that was strange," Alex said, still looking up at the sky.

"Yes, it was. Now I can hardly see the gray clouds. Where did they go?" Tina wondered.

"Well, it looks like the clouds are over the Palm Spring Kennel Club," Alex answered as he pointed to where the gray clouds were faintly hovering around.

"Oh, I am sorry. I shouldn't have said that."

"It's fine, really."

"I wasn't supposed to see that paper about your dad," Alex said.

"It is okay. You did nothing wrong," Tina said.

"If he knew I showed you, he'd wring my neck. And I'm serious about that. He has a wicked temper and . . ." Alex stopped himself, watching his words, feeling like he had already said too much.

"I won't say a word to anyone because I don't know what you're talking about," Tina bluffed.

Alex smiled, looking at Tina's brown eyes.

"Thanks. When I get home, I'm going to return the notebook to my father's office, and it will be like I never took it."

"Good plan. Also, don't tell anyone about our talks about my father."

"What talks?" Alex said with a smile, keeping his gaze on Tina.

"Catch you on Monday," Tina said with a grin.

"Yes, catch you Monday then. Looking forward to that hangout."

"Me too."

How could she really forget what Alex said? It didn't make sense why her father was gambling, losing, and borrowing money to gamble again. Tina walked home, debating how she could talk to Jorge and hear his side of the story. Maybe she was missing something, without revealing what she already knew.

Be careful.

Tina arrived home disappointed that the family car wasn't in the driveway. This was not a good sign. Jorge should have been home already, as it was close to five. She rang the doorbell like normal, ready to smile when Eva opened the door.

Eva answered, happy to see her daughter home from school.

"Mom, did you see the gray clouds? It looked like a storm was about to hit us."

"No, I didn't, but let me see." Eva looked out. The empty driveway triggered her heart rate, not wanting Jorge to disappoint Tina again. She kept her doubts in and said, "Well, it looks safe now. Come inside. I missed you."

"I missed you too. Let me change, and I'll be right down."

Tina went to her room and changed into a tennis skirt and shirt, though she had a sinking feeling that Jorge wouldn't show again. She looked at the tennis magazine on the desk, still open to the page with the tennis racket she wanted, wanting to close it now. She believed she wouldn't get the racket after all and regretted leaving it on her desk to see.

Tina didn't like that she was starting to doubt her father, because she never wanted to, now and never did in the past. She stayed in her room, going underneath the covers, hoping to calm her nerves and reject any doubts she had about Jorge.

Come on, Dad, where are you? Tina thought, hoping somehow her words would reach him and bring him home. How she wished her father didn't gamble and instead was home with her and Eva. Tina got out from under the covers and headed downstairs to the living room, seeing her mother keep busy as she organized the entertainment center.

Eva was aware of the time, fuming inside that Jorge was now late. "Oh, hi. Why don't you eat something?"

"No, I'm not hungry, but I'll take a fruit bar for the tennis courts if I need a snack. I'll wait."

This crushed Eva, for the odds of Jorge coming home now were slim, but she didn't want to break Tina's heart.

Don't you dare cover for him! You're only making things worse by covering for him. She has to know.

It was now eight o'clock, and Eva and Tina were watching the news. It was pitch black outside. Neither spoke about Jorge, though he occupied both of their minds. After being two hours late, Tina felt like a fool, believing her father would actually pull up in the driveway to play tennis with her now.

The pathetic thing was that even if he did, she would have jumped off the couch to greet him like he wasn't even late. She had this tendency and ability to forget about the bad or disappointment that would come her way. Though Tina was only inches away from Eva, the one person she could always talk to when she needed a shoulder to cry on, she knew it was not the case this time.

"Well, it looks like something came up," Eva lied. She got up from the sofa, trying not to show her anger.

Don't you dare cover up for him!

Tina looked at her mother despairingly. Eva saw this instantly and was ready to comfort her daughter any way she could.

"Where is he?" Tina asked.

Don't you dare cover up for him!

But before Eva could answer, Tina answered her own question. "Is he at the dog track?"

Eva froze, not expecting to hear those words coming from Tina.

"Mom, last night I heard you ask Dad if he was at the track."

Eva's heart dropped further down. No, her mind wasn't playing tricks. She had heard exactly what she thought she did, and she was starting to feel nervous, wanting out of her skin, wondering where the conversation with Tina was going. Was this actually happening now?

Don't you dare cover up for him!

Eva sighed, took a deep breath, and said, "Well, it's a high possibility."

Those few honest words brought Jorge's addiction to life for Eva and Tina.

Tina rushed to her room, took her tennis clothes off, threw them in the garbage, and cried herself to sleep.

CHAPTER 21

The Last Straw

Jorge left the track with nothing. He didn't have a penny to his name.

You can do it again.

While driving in the darkness of the night, he racked his brain, thinking of what he could do in the little time he had left. Tony was going to be at the house in less than five hours. There was no time to waste. Then, he smiled as he thought of his way out. He knew it would work, but just for this one time.

Your plan is foolproof.

When he arrived home, the front lights were off, and the house could hardly be seen. He already knew Eva was upset. This gave him time to fine-tune his plan. He was going to increase the fear factor of it more. He didn't care if Eva's had the worst scare of her life.

Go for the tears.

He tiptoed up the stairs, and to his surprise, Eva had locked the bedroom door. This upset him, but he knew this could be easily solved.

Above the door frame there was a small key for emergencies. Being so tired, Eva forgot to take it down. He grabbed it and carefully unlocked the bedroom door. Eva was breathing hard, very much in a deep sleep.

Jorge slowly walked to the walk-in closet, not to make a sound at the opposite side of the room. He turned on the soft lights and closed the pocket door behind him, looking for the black file cabinet. At first, he didn't see it, but when he moved Eva's dresses, he knew he was at the home stretch. All he had to do now was find the file he needed. As he passed the letter O, his heart sank. The Oppenheimer file was gone. He wondered if Eva had taken it.

Dammit, he thought.

Chill!

He decided to look again, this time going slower as he carefully looked through the files. His hands were shaking, sweat forming on his brow. Thankfully, he could still hear Eva breathing hard, giving him time to look through the files again. He started at A again, knowing Eva didn't always file alphabetically when she was in a rush, especially when Tina called for her.

Just as he approached O for the second time, he held his breath. His heart started to elevate, fearing the do-or-die moment. To his absolute joy, he saw the Oppenheimer file hidden in another file.

He took the file, quickly opened it, and scanned the last statement of Eva's retirement account. It didn't look good—there was less than five hundred dollars in the account, way less than he was expecting. But before he could get angry, he saw something else.

Bingo, he thought. There in front of his eyes was his new lease on life. He took the file, kissed it, and rushed to Eva's side of the bed.

"Eva, wake up."

Eva groaned as Jorge called for her.

"Eva, Eva, wake up," he said again, jerking her left side until she woke up.

Eva finally opened her eyes, feeling off-balanced and confused.

"What is it? Why are you here?"

"No, listen. It's an emergency. It's for Tina."

Eva quickly sat up, fearing the worst, getting out of bed.

"Where is she?"

"Stay quiet, or you will wake her up," he said.

Jorge felt lost for words. His plan of what he was going to say was quickly forgotten.

"What is happening?"

"I'm in trouble…"

"What trouble?"

Eva's worry shifted to anger, seeing this was a setup. She now saw through him more than she ever did.

"We need eight thousand dollars by tomorrow, or our family will be in danger. Tina will be in danger."

"What?"

"If I don't have the money, we will be targeted. Think of Tina and our family.

"Targeted…by who?"

"The guys who beat me up the other night."

'What? Why would they attack you again?"

Jorge wouldn't answer.

"Answer me! Why would they attack you again? Did you do something stupid?"

Jorge took the Oppenheimer file from behind him and said, "You are approved for a ten-thousand-dollar personal loan. Just sign this, and all will disappear."

Eva grabbed the file, got out of bed, and reached for her robe and slippers. She knew this was another lie to cover up a gambling debt he had. Now things were starting to come together. The busted lip Jorge got the other night was probably from a bookie, and the same bookie was coming after him again.

Eva looked at him hard for one last time before going downstairs and said, "I'm done with you and your gambling mistress. It's over… you made your choice…now live with it."

From that moment, there was nothing left between them. The marriage was more than over. Whatever little piece she felt for him died that night, never to be found again. She now had to plan for the future, which would not include Jorge. Yet, she was good with it. She was actually looking forward to making a life for her and Tina and letting Jorge go forever.

Jorge was now to suffer a fate worse than death. As Eva said her final words, he saw the light in her eyes vanish. Their relationship was irrevocably broken. He now would have to be careful not to lose Tina the same way.

Tina will be your forever girl.

Eva was restless as she tried to sleep on the couch, holding the Oppenheimer file she ripped. She was now free of Jorge, but she didn't realize Tina would now take her place.

Part Two

CHAPTER 22

Nine Years Later

"I'm so proud of you," Eva said, on the verge of tears, Tina stood before her, now a college graduate. It was Tina's college graduation day.

Jorge was just a few steps away. They had been divorced for about four years now, and the only connection they had was Tina. The day after Tina's high school graduation, Eva served Jorge divorce papers she had drawn years ago but was reluctant to give them to Jorge. She wanted to wait until Tina finished high school.

At first, Jorge didn't want to sign them, believing, in time, she would cool off and change her mind like the other times when she was upset. But not this time.

When he came home seeing boxes piled high to the ceiling, he knew she wouldn't back down. The next day the boxes were gone, and so was Eva, the love of his life. Somehow, he still believed she would return, but she didn't.

"My going to the track has nothing to do with it. Just come out and say you have met some rich guy, and that's why you want a divorce. Why don't you just say it!" Jorge demanded, finally signing the papers, slamming the door when he walked out, seeking refuge at the track.

Tina glanced at her father heavy-heartedly. He smiled when their eyes met, feeling sad he wasn't part of the mother and daughter embrace. Yet, she was still happy to take whatever time she had with her parents together again, even if making memories was for a short time.

Jorge still felt like he was married to Eva, and in his confused mind, he felt Eva still loved him too. He often thought of the song "You Were Always on My Mind" by Willie Nelson whenever he saw her.

Every line summed up how he felt about her, especially the one, "Little things I should have said and done / I just never took the time / You were always on my mind". There would be times when the song would play while Jorge was driving, and he couldn't stop the tears from falling, thinking how stupid he was for not being there for Eva when he had the chance, but once the song was over, he would quickly recover. He'd just wipe what was left of the tears and move on with his day like he never suffered the loss of his marriage, almost like a losing bet.

"So, where am I taking you two for dinner tonight?" Jorge asked, thinking along the lines of something casual, but Eva had higher expectations.

Tina was surprised that he even asked, thinking they would grab a pizza or burger. Nothing out of the ordinary.

"Are you paying?" Eva asked.

"Come on, Eva, give me a little credit. I may not be a Rockefeller, but I do work."

"I don't know. I never said you don't work, but you have a hard time keeping your money from the track," Eva said.

Jorge pretended that he didn't hear Eva's condescending remark and turned to Tina and said, "Anywhere Tina would like to eat tonight is good with me. After all, it's not every day that our girl graduates from college, and money is no object this time."

Jorge turned to look at Eva with hard eyes.

That's the way to handle her.

"I'll believe it when I see it," Eva lashed.

Tina looked at her mom, giving her the please be quiet look, not wanting a fight to erupt between them.

Eva backed down for Tina's sake. Otherwise, she would have continued. It was hard for Eva to be quiet when dealing with the past lies Jorge told throughout their long marriage of over twenty years. It was like she was making up for all the times she kept quiet to keep the peace within the family whenever he would blatantly lie. But for now, she would hold the reins of her battered emotions—after all, it was Tina's day, not hers.

"Well, that's really nice of you, Jorge, considering you really don't have any bills," Eva said, starting out kind but ending spiteful.

"Mom, please," Tina finally said.

"Sorry, I was joking again," Eva said with a forced grin. She apologized again for extra measure, "I really didn't mean it. It just slipped out. Sorry, Tina. I really am. Let's enjoy the time here together."

Eva knew she had to back down for Tina's sake, yet she couldn't help but still be angry at Jorge for all the years of hurt he caused her and Tina.

"It's okay, Eva, I have the money, so you don't worry about anything. I have it covered. I promise. As I said, money is no object anymore."

Eva faked a smile, hiding the disguise of hearing the same lines he used many times in their marriage when he didn't have two pennies to rub together.

Jorge asked Tina, "Have you thought about where you would like to have dinner tonight? Any restaurant is fine."

Tina thought of what was around that wasn't too expensive, but before she could answer Jorge, her mother already had a place in mind.

"How about the restaurant you always talked about?" Eva asked as she snapped her fingers, hoping to recall its name, knowing it was somewhere in her memory.

Tina's heart dropped, feeling like her own words were coming to spite her. She knew the name all right, but she wasn't going to say it.

"No, I don't remember the name," Tina said.

"You said it had a great view of the Charles River, and it's a five-star restaurant," Eva said. "Tina, can you remember any part of the name? Try, honey…you said it many times."

"No, I can't, but no worries, there are other places we can go to," Tina said, hoping her mother would consider a more affordable place to eat. She knew the meal at The Hill for the three of them would cost a few hundred dollars, or more, which she felt deep down her father couldn't really afford, even though he was saying he had it covered.

"Tina, I bet if we both just forget about it for a moment, the name will come to one of us. I know it will. Let's try," Eva pleaded.

"Okay, sounds good, Mom. But we could just go to TGI Fridays on Beacon Street. I actually could go for their loaded potato skins, a cheeseburger, and fries," Tina said.

Jorge liked the idea of going to Fridays too. He had close to a hundred dollars in his pocket. He left another hundred in the car, so he wouldn't be tempted to spend it on lottery tickets. It was meant for gas money to drive back to West Palm Beach, or he would be stranded in Boston.

He knew the money in his pocket wouldn't cover a round of drinks and appetizers at the fancy restaurant Eva wanted to take Tina to let alone dinner. He last had a credit card eight years ago, so he knew he couldn't spend over a hundred tonight.

"It's called The Hill!" Eva shouted at the top of her lungs.

"Is it?" Tina asked. "I don't think so." Tina saw the dread in her father's eyes, the one she saw many times when she was a middle school student. He was lying about having the money.

"Yes, I am certain of it. Let me call and see if I can make a reservation for us tonight," Eva said as she rushed off to the recreation hall to make the call.

Tina's heart raced, feeling anxious like her father, yet she still had hope that there was a good chance there wouldn't be any available dinner reservations this late in the game, with over twenty colleges and universities in the greater Boston area having graduations all week long.

"So, we have a moment to ourselves," Jorge said.

He wasn't really good at expressing himself with words, and Tina didn't fault him for this either. However, she was incredibly good at reading body language and could see that Jorge was stressed about the dinner situation and needed some reassurance.

"Dad, I'm glad you made it to my college graduation. I wasn't sure you would. It meant everything, and dinner is dinner," Tina said, feeling teary-eyed.

If there was anything she knew about her father, he always had money problems. It was no secret that he liked to bet at the dog track, but he had promised Tina that he had it under control, and she believed him.

Though there were moments of doubt when he wouldn't answer Tina's calls at night or when she would call the hair salon during the day to be told that he went out for a moment. Her heart would race, thinking he was at the track again, but then she thought of his promise not to gamble, and her heart would settle a bit, though not completely.

"Well, I wasn't going to disappoint my girl," he said, = sighing. "I knew I would make it here, even if I had to drive, which I did. And if I couldn't drive, I would have hitchhiked to be at my girl's graduation," Jorge said with a smile.

Tina still felt bad that he drove through nine states for her graduation, but she would have felt worse if he hadn't made it.

"Tina . . . Jorge . . ." Eva shouted, as she ran towards them. They both turned to look, smiling as she had difficulty running in her heels, her black Chanel purse barely staying on her shoulder.

"I did it! We have reservations at The Hill at 8:30 pm tonight. Can you believe it? See Tina, if you want something bad, you must go for it, and nothing will stop you! I'm so excited for you. Now you can say that you had your graduation dinner at the most exclusive restaurant in Boston."

Tina smiled. "Really, what did you do? Who did you have to bribe?" she said, knowing her mother too well.

"No one. I just said I would keep on calling until they gave us a reservation."

"Really, Mom?" Tina questioned.

"Yes, and they didn't think I was serious until I kept calling, saying it was your special night. The hostess said he would arrange an extra table so we could all squeeze in and celebrate your college graduation."

"I have to hand it to you, Eva, you always get what you want," Jorge said.

"Why thank you, Jorge. Sadly, that wasn't always true, as you know, but that's the past, and life goes on. Let's just be happy for now and this happy occasion," Eva said, which was something that all of them could agree on.

Tina was actually getting excited for the night. It was true; she had always wanted to go to The Hill in the four years of being in college, but something always came up each time she planned to go. She wasn't going to order anything too expensive, maybe a salad, so it wouldn't cost Jorge too much.

"So, be ready to pay up tonight, Jorge. After all, it's our daughter's graduation, and she deserves to be wined and dined for her accomplishments and being the best daughter to both of us. Don't you agree? I'll even pay the tip if that helps any," Eva said.

Jorge just smiled. Eva was right. It was a special day, and Tina did deserve a night to remember, even though he didn't have the money to pay for it yet. He would have to think of how he was actually going to pull this off before 8:30 pm arrived.

"Isn't this exciting, Tina?" Eva asked.

Tina nodded, "I can't wait."

"Now, that makes us very happy, right Jorge?"

"Yes, Eva, it makes me very happy to see the two of you very happy," Jorge said, feeling like they were a family again.

"Do you want to come back to the hotel with us?" Eva asked Tina, hoping she would.

She really didn't like alone time with Jorge, feeling apprehensive. Eva really didn't know him anymore, but she wanted to have a cordial relationship with him as he was Tina's father.

Tina thought it was considerate that her mother was including Jorge in the same sentence. "No, I have more packing to do. I also wanted to say goodbye to a few friends at the dorm," Tina said.

"Sure, just don't overwork yourself. If you like, we could stay and help," Eva said, hoping Tina would accept the offer. Though Tina would like the help, she would rather go back to the dorm alone and enjoy the last bits of college life.

"Okay, then, your father and I will just go back to the hotel and rest before dinner tonight. If you need us, call us anytime at the Chestnut Hill Marriott. I'm in Room 201. Jorge, what's your room number?" Eva asked.

"Oh, I don't remember."

Eva just looked at him; he hadn't changed much. He could never remember anything when he needed to. "Well, you know my room number, and that is where I will be, and I'll know your dad's when we get to the hotel."

"Dad, are you sure you will be okay to drive back to the hotel? Do you need me to go? I can always take the T back," Tina said.

"Oh no, you just do what you need to do. I'll have your mother next to me; believe me, she knows how to get back to the hotel."

Eva just smiled, knowing Jorge was only trying to be nice, yet he was also right.

Tina gave both her parents a kiss goodbye. Jorge walked to his car, and Eva followed. It was the same car he got from the divorce settlement, and the air conditioning still wasn't working.

She wondered how he survived a road trip to Boston without A/C, but it wasn't her concern anymore. Eva decided that she would keep quiet and got in the car. Eva was thankful the hotel wasn't that far away. Soon she would be in the comforts of the hotel room and away from Jorge.

As Jorge pulled out of the parking lot, Eva looked around the car. He felt uncomfortable thinking she might find a betting slip or race schedule, even though he believed there weren't any left after he cleaned the car last week.

"Our little girl isn't so little anymore," Jorge said. He didn't like the silence between them. It made him feel like they were strangers, instead of once lovers and husband and wife.

Eva just looked at Jorge and smiled as she rolled the passenger window down. "The car's air conditioner broke last week," Jorge said. Eva just smiled; she wasn't going to debate that overused lie.

"Yes, Tina has grown up a lot in four years. Boston was good for her," Eva agreed.

"The years are going by too fast; don't you think?" Jorge asked.

"Yes, the years are going faster," Eva said, though she was not one for small talk, especially with the man who had deeply hurt her more than anyone in her life. He repeatedly broke her heart with lies on top of lies, and here she was in the same car with him.

"Eva, when I look at her, I see a lot of you," Jorge said, hoping to soften Eva.

Eva remained quiet as she admired the estate homes as they drove by. He'd try again, hoping to snap Eva out of her daydream.

"The little things she does, like the stares she makes when she wants us to be quiet. You still do that, don't think I didn't notice the look you gave me about taking Tina to the fancy restaurant," Jorge said, trying to soften Eva more.

Eva smiled at Jorge as he drove, though she still wasn't certain if he was being honest. Yet she hoped he was. She kept her gaze on him, feeling like the clock had gone back twenty years somehow. It was a shame that gambling took their marriage away because there was a time when they were really in love and happy together.

However, all she had left was a mix of bad and good memories and their daughter. If it weren't for Tina, she wouldn't have kept any sort of relationship with Jorge. She knew he was still gambling and didn't want any part of it. It was a self-centered being that took anything good in the man she once loved. The addiction did everything to sustain its unending hunger by sucking its victims for dead.

Jorge drove up to the hotel without getting lost.

"Well, thanks for the ride, though to be honest, I feel like I just came out of a sauna," Eva said as she shut the passenger door. Jorge dropped Eva at the hotel, saying he had to get a few things for the dinner.

Jorge took a turn back to Beacon Street, venturing how he was going to pay for dinner. He had two hours to make it happen. Eva went to her room, took a shower, and then a nap.

Eva heard a faint knock on the door an hour and a half later. It became louder and louder, pulling her from a deep sleep. She got out of bed, put her rope on, and walked to the door feeling drowsy.

"Yes, who is it?" Eva called, thinking it may be room service.

"It's your husband," Jorge teased.

"Then you must have the wrong room," Eva said. She was not in the mood for his games.

"Come on, Eva, can't you take a joke?" Jorge said.

She slightly opened the door, hiding behind it. "You're a little early. Why don't you go to your room and we'll meet later. I'm not ready yet."

"You're right, but there seems to be a problem with my room. Could I just stay here while you get ready? I'll just watch some television to pass the time. I already told the front desk they could reach me here. They even said it wouldn't be much longer until my room was ready," Jorge said.

"Okay, sure," Eva agreed.

Jorge rested on the spare bed. On the drive up from West Palm Beach, sleeping at rest stops. Lying on the bed was heaven to him with the soft comforter. And he could finally spread his legs.

"Wow, you look even more beautiful than the first day we met. I hate to say this, but divorce has done you well," Jorge said.

Eva blushed. She was surprised that Jorge even mentioned their divorce, knowing it was a sore subject matter between them, and he was right. Divorce did her well, or rather being divorced from him did her well.

But then she thought about Tony and the whole fiasco attached to that awful memory. For today, she just wanted to block it from her memories, as it only took her to a very dark place that ended their marriage for good, feeling the urge to throw Jorge out of the hotel room. But she promised Tina that she wouldn't get in a fight with Jorge on her graduation day.

"Well, let's get out of this room and take a stroll to the restaurant. I can't imagine when I'll be back in Boston again now that Tina has graduated," Eva said.

Jorge knew this was true because he wouldn't even be in Boston if it wasn't for Tina's graduation. "Is there enough time? I thought we were going to pick Tina up from the dorm," Jorge asked, really wanting to stay in the room for a little longer.

"Didn't you get Tina's call?" Eva asked.

"No, like I said, there was a problem with my room," Jorge said.

"She called and said she was getting a ride from a friend who is having dinner at the restaurant next door."

"I must have just missed the call," Jorge said.

Eva looked at him funny, like she didn't believe there was a problem with his room anymore.

"Anyway, let's go for that stroll," Jorge said to avoid any further questions about the room. He was still tired from the car drive, and his mind was really in shambles.

"Yes, it will be nice to walk through the Commons again. I also would like to talk to you about Tina's future. I hope you'll continue to help her with any expenses she has now as a college graduate, at least until she gets settled with a job. After all, you don't have anyone else to take care of other than yourself," Eva said.

Help, he thought. How was he going to help when he could hardly take care of himself? He was dreading going back to West Palm because many angry people were waiting for him to pay them back.

"So, what do you say, Jorge?" Eva asked.

She wanted a commitment from him.

"Of course, I will do what I can," Jorge said.

"Can you do a little bit better?" Eva asked.

"Let's just go," Jorge said, feeling frustrated by Eva's subtle commands.

She's not your wife anymore! Don't listen to her.

Tina arrived at The Hill, surprised to see her parents sitting close in the corner of the restaurant, laughing and drinking wine. She would have thought they were on a date if she didn't know better.

Eva looked up once she saw Tina.

"Here's our college graduate," Eva said, cupping both hands over her lips.

"It looks like you and Dad are having fun. I hope this doesn't change now that I'm here," Tina said.

"Why would it? You're the reason why we are so happy," Eva said.

"Okay, Mom," Tina said, embarrassed now.

"And your father took me down memory lane when we first got married. I must say I'm a little surprised that he even remembered after all these years," Eva looked at Jorge.

She is taking the bait.

"Honestly, I just couldn't stop laughing . . ."

Tina was surprised to see her mother drinking with her tendency to go overboard, but she seemed fine for now. Eva still had half a wine glass. Tina hoped it was the last glass for the night.

"So, how is the packing going?" Eva asked, taking another sip of wine.

"It's just about done. I can't believe how much stuff I have accumulated in the past four years," Tina answered.

"Well, that's expected. We can come by later to help you finish, and then you could come back to the hotel and stay the night," Eva offered.

"No, thank you. I'd like to stay in my dorm room for one last night."

"I understand. I'd feel the same way," Jorge said.

He was relieved that Tina decided not to go back to the hotel to stay the night. He knew he would have a hard time explaining how he didn't have a room by now. He planned to crash in Eva's room, pretending he fell asleep on the spare bed.

He was certain he could get away with it. Otherwise, he would have to sleep in the car again. Then another idea came to him: maybe he could sleep in Tina's dorm room if he ran out of options. He was just thankful it wasn't wintertime.

"Excuse me, Mademoiselle Tina, I'm Henry, and I'll be your server tonight. What would you like to drink?" Henry asked, with a sexy French accent.

Tina blushed. The handsome waiter was in his mid-twenties and looked like he jumped out of *Vogue* magazine. Henry kept his gaze on Tina, attracted to her innocence. She glanced at him, torn between ordering a glass of red wine, like her parents, or just a glass of iced tea.

"I'll have an iced tea," Tina said.

"Are you sure?" Eva asked.

"An iced tea will be fine. I'm actually thirsty," Tina said.

"Very good then," Henry said with a smile, wiping his blond, overgrown wisps from his brow.

"I still have some packing to do, and I don't want to be sleepy later. If I had one more day to pack, I would have wine too."

"Yes, it must be something you inherited from me because I get the same way." Eva smiled. "I know when I get back to the hotel. I'll fall asleep the second my head touches the pillow."

Jorge smiled, hoping this was going to be true. He discreetly placed his hand in his front pants pocket to check that the credit card was still there, the one he'd stolen earlier from a tourist, and it was. Thankfully, the evening was going as planned. He wasn't too far from the finish line.

Good job!

He almost felt like asking Eva if she wanted another glass of wine to show that money was no object and to soften her for his plan later, but he knew Tina would get upset.

Eva couldn't wait to give Tina her graduation gift. She thought long and hard and believed it to be the perfect gift for a young, intelligent, aspiring college graduate starting a new chapter in her life.

And, of course, it had to be over the top, and it was. If anything, it was a little too over the top, but that was how Eva rolled. Nothing was too good for Tina.

"Let's look at the menus and have ourselves a good meal," Jorge said.

Tina opened hers, floored at the prices, but she didn't mention the double-digit items. "I heard that anything chicken is amazing," Tina said, trying to influence Eva.

"I also heard the filet mignon is to die for," Eva interjected. Tina looked over her menu and gave her mother a look.

"No, I am serious. Earlier, we asked Henry what he recommended. And, of course, he said in his French accent that the filet mignon was a house favorite, and they're flown from Colorado."

"Your mother is right; that's what Henry said," Jorge said.

Tina knew she didn't have to look at the menu to know the steak was super expensive. However, when she opened the menu again to see what it came with. It was way more than she expected. It was in the triple digits, enough for her to want a glass of wine to calm her nerves. It would take her a month's salary working at the library to pay for one filet.

She looked up at her parents in awe, feeling relaxed seeing them amicable with each other. It was a nice change of pace. Tina turned the menu page, still undecided. She knew her parents were going to order the choice filets.

"Dammit," Eva shouted as she jumped from the seat. She somehow spilled red wine on her new dress.

"I'll be right back. I better go and get some club soda, or the stain will set in, and the dress will be ruined." Eva said as she rushed off.

"If Henry comes by, please order the filet mignon, medium, with the vegetable of the day," Eva said.

Then she rushed off, disappearing to the bar for club soda, hoping she would be able to salvage her designer dress.

Tina made sure her mother was far enough away, so she could talk openly with her father.

"Dad, have you looked at the prices?" Tina asked.

"Not really. Why?" Jorge asked.

"Well, you should because the prices here are not like Outback's. We could eat there five times for the cost of one meal here. Are you sure you can afford this, Dad?" Tina asked, literally on the edge of her seat.

"Girl, please don't worry. I'll manage. Just order away because I now have a credit card. I was actually going to surprise you with this later," Jorge said.

"Wow, really? That's good news, Dad…sounds like you've really built your credit back. I'm so proud of you, Dad," Tina said, feeling like her father was on the road to recovery.

Jorge smiled, taking his daughter's praises, though it wasn't deserving.

"Hush, Mom is walking back," Tina said.

Jorge knew they had to change the subject fast.

"I like how long your hair has gotten. It looks good on you. Are you going to keep it long, or do you want a Jorge cut when you're back home?" Jorge asked, with a genuine smile, admiring Tina's natural beauty.

"Not sure yet, maybe. I like it longer, too," Tina said.

Eva sat back down at the table.

"Thank God, I went when I did. I was able to get rid of the spill before it had a chance to set in and ruin my dress," Eva said.

Everyone at the table smiled and agreed too.

"I'm glad the club soda did the trick, too," Jorge said, playing into Eva's happiness.

"Thank you, Jorge."

"Now it's like it was never there," Tina said.

Eva just smiled and agreed.

"Oh, did Henry come by for our order because I'm famished?" Eva asked.

"No, but he's on his way. He was probably waiting for you to return to the table, Mom," Tina said.

Tina had to turn away when her eyes met Henry's again, feeling like her heart was about to explode. There was no denying that he was a babe. She wondered how many hearts he already broke in his short life, yet she also imagined how much fun the ex's had with him.

"Oh, that's true. Not only is Henry considerate, but a professional waiter. How did I get so lucky to have such a loving daughter like you to point this out? I must have been an angel in my last life to deserve you," Eva said.

Tina smiled, always appreciating her mom's sweet words.

The Gabors all ordered the filet mignon. Jorge ordered it rare, Eva ordered medium, and Tina ordered hers medium rare, resulting in a perfect combination of her parents. Eva made arrangements to surprise Tina with a decadent white raspberry cake from a little French bakery on Beacon Street to end the night.

When they arrived at The Hill, she gave the cake to the hostess, giving specific instructions to bring it to the table at the end of the meal. Eva even found tall, thin, red sparkly candles in the specialty shop next to the bakery, which matched the cake perfectly. When the candles were lit, the cake would look like a fountain of fireworks.

"You know, I'm so grateful to come here with you both. This is a dream come true, one that I will always remember on my college graduation day," Tina said.

"Oh, Tina, we feel the same way," Eva said.

Tina went on to say, "It's extra special because the two of you are here together, us like a family again, even if it's just for one day." She took a deep breath, wiping her moist eyes, feeling her insides start to burn. Not wanting to break down.

"Honey, we love you so," Eva said, teary-eyed.

Eva and Jorge looked at each other for a moment, then turned to look at Tina. Both knew they had to keep any ill feelings towards each other at bay, at least for the night. Here their little girl was pouring her heart out to them.

"We will always be family," Eva said.

Bingo! Use this tonight.

Then, from the corner of her eye, Tina saw Henry holding a gorgeous white cake. The candles lit up the room, and for a second, time stood still as everyone admired Henry and the cake. Patrons at the restaurant wondered who would get the spectacular cake and watched until Henry stopped before Tina's table. They all smiled when they saw it was for a beautiful young lady.

Henry placed the cake in front of Tina and said, "Congratulations on your college graduation, beautiful. Your beauty lights up the place."

Tina blushed as she looked up at Henry as he winked at her. The cake was divine, just like dinner. The Gabors talked about their plans for tomorrow, and as they finished their last bits of the cake, Henry walked over with the check.

Jorge didn't even look at the bill; he reached in his front pant pocket, took out the American Express card, and placed it in the leather billfold made in Italy.

Eva looked at Tina, surprised that Jorge actually had a credit card now.

"It was a wonderful night," Jorge proudly said.

"Yes, it is and was," Eva said.

Henry took the billfold and Jorge didn't flinch, but Tina was worried whether her father's card had enough credit.

"So, should we take one last walk on Beacon Street for the road?" Jorge asked.

"Yes, in a moment," Eva said.

Eva reached into her Chanel purse and took out the graduation card and present for Tina. She thought long and hard about giving Tina the perfect gift for her little girl.

"Here, honey, this is your graduation gift. Please take care of it. It is from my heart. *Don't lose it or let anyone take it away from you*," Eva said.

"Thank you, Mom, and I won't," Tina said.

"May it bring you success and be the start of having more," Eva said.

Eva looked to Jorge to see if he had anything for Tina, but he didn't. Henry walked back with the printed credit card receipt for his signature. Jorge saw the dinner cost $580.00. Tina was right—they could go a handful of times to Outback, but it wouldn't have been as special.

He was relieved that the credit card went through. He didn't think the person he'd stolen from would miss it just yet. However, he knew there still could have been a chance that they did, and this whole evening could have ended ugly.

See? Everything worked out.

"So, are we ready to walk some calories off?" Jorge asked.

However, as they were walking out of the restaurant, Henry called to them.

"Wait, wait!"

"You two stay here. I'll be right back," Jorge said.

Stay calm. Don't admit to anything.

Tina got a little nervous but stayed behind with her mother.

"What do you think of my gift to you?" Eva asked.

"I'm waiting to open it later. Your cards always make me cry," Tina said.

"Oh, honey, just open it. You can read the card later. Look what's in the card," Eva said.

Tina opened the card, thinking it would be money, but within the card was a folded sheet of paper.

"What is it?" Tina asked.

"Unfold it," Eva said with a smile.

She did as her mother said, and was a little puzzled. She never saw anything like it until now.

"Read it."

Her eyes popped out as she saw the deed to a lakefront villa in her name as the new owner, and it was in West Palm Beach, her hometown.

CHAPTER 23

Tina's Return Home

Jorge returned to Tina and Eva, waiting for him under a light post. "What was that about?" Eva asked. Her pessimistic side felt there might have been a problem with Jorge's credit card.

"Oh, it was nothing, really," Jorge said, downplaying Eva's question.

"Oh, is that so?"

"Yes, it's so," Jorge said, annoyed at Eva.

"I just find it strange that he would call you back unless something was wrong."

Jorge already knew what Eva was initiating, and he didn't like it.

Here she goes. It's a good thing she left!

"Well, he just wanted to thank me for the tip I left him, that's all," Jorge said, feeling his stomach churn, feeling in the spotlight.

Tina looked disinterested in the conversation but wasn't buying what her father said either.

"Please, Jorge, if anything, you didn't leave a tip," Eva said. "Let's be real here."

"No, I'm serious, Eva." Jorge stuck with his story, though he was lying. He purposely didn't sign the bill, thinking he found a loophole.

Eva still didn't believe him, seeing how he tried to make himself look good. She never heard of a waiter running out to say thank you for a tip. It would be suspicious to anyone.

Jorge looked around him and said, "Do you see anyone after me now? I'm here, aren't I? If you like, we can go back to the restaurant, and you can ask Henry yourself." Jorge said, wearing a poker face, waiting for Eva's answer.

"Oh, no I am not about to make a fool of myself. If Henry did as you said, that was nice of him and you."

"Yes, it was. See, your father knows how to treat a person right, even if I'm not a millionaire," Jorge said, staring right at Eva with hard eyes.

He was chiding Eva, though Tina didn't notice.

The familiar dark eyes immediately gave Eva the chills, taking her back to when they used to argue years ago about his gambling. Feeling the old, sick feeling of air being sucked from her insides, she was afraid to take a breath, even a small one, or risk Jorge being even angrier. It was Jorge's perfect *I fooled you* look. The evil look that said, "Ha, ha, I got away with it, and there's nothing you can do about it."

After they took Tina to the dorm for one last night, Jorge and Eva returned to the hotel.

"Well, thanks for the dinner and the ride" Eva said, just wanting to go back to her room, be alone, and call it a night, but Jorge had other plans.

"Eva, you're welcome. You know, today was like the old days. You, me, and Tina, a family again. It was nice."

Jorge hoped that Eva would want to go out for a nightcap.

"Well, it was, but I'm tired. I'll see you in the morning, sleep well," Eva said.

"You know Eva ... I still love you," Jorge said as he looked at Eva, hoping to rekindle any love she still had for him.

"Yes, it was, but we are only family because of Tina and no other reason. Our relationship ended years ago, and I don't want to get into it . . . it's late, and it's in the past," Eva said.

"Well, I just wish things could have been different between us. Actually, I don't like being...divorced. I miss you," Jorge said.

"Jorge, I'd like to chat, but I'm so tired. The bed is calling me. I'll see you in the morning. If you like, we could even have breakfast before you go to Tina's," Eva said.

Eva waited for Jorge to say goodnight, but he just stood there. Without really having to think, she knew why Jorge wasn't on his way to his room.

"Oh, my God, you don't have a room, do you?" Eva asked.

Jorge cringed as he shrugged his shoulders and shook his head from side to side.

"How did I know? Here I was, trying to believe that you had changed. I gave you the benefit of the doubt. How stupid I was to think you were finally responsible with your new credit card, but it seems like you are still the same. How could you not have a room?" Eva asked.

Lie, make up a story.

"Well, I did, but after the problems I had with it, I told them they could keep it. You know how hard I work. I don't have that kind of money to burn. Maybe you do, but I don't," Jorge said.

"Yes, you do, at the track," Eva rebutted.

"What I do is my business."

"Oh, I see, yet you just thought I'd feel sorry for you, and what? Offer you to stay in my room tonight? I don't think so," Eva said, feeling rage overwhelm her.

"Well, I'll just go to Tina's and stay with her. She won't turn her back on me like you."

This was what Eva wanted to avoid at all costs.

"Why would you want to bother Tina tonight? Tonight, of all nights too, when all she wants to do is be like a normal girl, enjoying her last night in Boston. Why would you want to embarrass her?" Eva said.

"She wouldn't see it that way."

"No, she would see it as something way worse. You know how she stresses about the littlest things, always believing something is wrong when something out of the ordinary happens. You should know this about Tina. Why would you want to stress her?" Eva asked.

"So, let me stay with you for the night. Tina will never have to know, and I'll pay for half of the room," Jorge said.

Eva kept quiet, feeling pinned to a wall.

"And don't worry, I'm not going to touch you. I ran out of Viagra last week anyway," Jorge said.

That's my boy, Jorge.

Eva wished she could tell Jorge to screw off, but she had to think about Tina. She didn't want him to ruin her last night in Boston. What an asshole, she thought.

"Humor me, what sort of problems were you having with the room that couldn't be solved? Or do you want me to go to the front desk and see if I can get you a better room? You know I am good at that," Eva said.

She's still a bitch.

Jorge had it. He wasn't going to play Eva's game anymore.

"Forget it. I'm off to Tina's."

"Wait . . ." Eva said.

Jorge turned around, staring at Eva.

"You know I'm tired, and I don't care anymore because every word from your mouth is a lie, covering up another lie."

"So, can I stay?"

Eva caved in, resenting her decision, doing it only for Tina. Yet hating herself for allowing Jorge to call the shots again.

"You can stay for Tina's sake. Otherwise, I really don't care where you sleep tonight. It can be at a park bench if that is all you can do."

Jorge wore that stupid smile again, which she wanted to rip off for good.

"And you better keep your hands to yourself," Eva demanded.

See, she still loves you.

Eva turned and walked to her room, depressed. Jorge once again manipulated her, using Tina as a pawn to get what he wanted. The same old nauseated feeling she thought would never be felt again after they divorced was back, and this time it felt a thousand times worse.

Once in the hotel room, Eva kept quiet, only speaking, when necessary, which were conditions he would have to follow if he were to stay in the room for the night.

"First, you're to stay on that bed over there." Eva pointed to the one closest to the window. "I don't want you on my bed or my side for any reason."

Jorge smiled, not really caring which bed he'd sleep on. "No, problem, as long as it's firm," he said, trying to get Eva to laugh.

Eva wasn't amused.

"And instead of paying me half of the room you promised, give it to Tina tomorrow morning as a graduation gift. I still can't believe you didn't get her something. Are we clear?" Eva asked.

Jorge didn't answer because he didn't like the part about giving Tina a hundred dollars. But he knew he would have to keep it to himself or be out.

"I said, are we clear?" Eva asked again.

"Why are you so uptight? Remember, not so long ago, we used to be married," Jorge said.

"Yes, we *used* to be married, but not now."

This wasn't the reaction he was hoping for, though he wasn't completely surprised.

"You still haven't answered my question?" Eva said.

"Yes, you have my word. I'll give Tina a hundred dollars if that's what you want," Jorge said.

Jorge was getting annoyed with Eva. He couldn't believe his charm didn't work even for a little, and now he was out a hundred dollars.

Jorge fell asleep as he watched *Law & Order*. The hotel room had more comforts than his place. He was finally sleeping on a clean bed, where his pillows didn't smell and weren't yellow like the ones at home.

He couldn't remember the last time he held a remote control, effortlessly surfing the cable channels instead of having to get off the couch to change the channels like at home. Jorge also couldn't remember the last time he had cable, either. He was blacklisted at all the cable companies for nonpayment. If he ever wanted cable again, he would have to pay what he owed, plus all the extra fees.

Eva woke up at six a.m. to go to the bathroom. She forgot that Jorge was in the room sleeping and became startled when she saw him on the bed next to hers. She quickly grabbed her robe.

On the way to the bathroom, Eva looked at Jorge sleeping on his side, seeing the man she once loved long ago. Realizing it was the inside part of him that she disliked, which was the selfish, manipulating, and lying part. The gambler part, the one that took everything away from her and Tina.

Once in the bathroom, Jorge's khaki pants hung behind the door. She was curious to know what was in his pockets.

No, she thought. *It is not worth looking at. Nothing he has would interest me.*

However, while brushing her teeth, her eyes remain fixated on Jorge's pants, reflecting in the mirror.

Go on, just take a look, she thought.

Eva decided there would be no harm in looking. Nothing would really surprise her anymore.

Remember, you are also doing this for Tina, too, she thought.

Eva found an American Express credit card, which he used to pay at The Hill. She had missed that it didn't have Jorge's name as she placed it back in the pocket. When she saw the receipt of The Hill, she wanted to flee from Jorge, not because of the charges, but because of the unknown name Jorge signed as his own.

Eva wanted to jump out of her body as she stared at her reflection, feeling trapped by Jorge's criminal activity. Feeling now that she was somehow part of Jorge's ploy, and couldn't help but be afraid that the police were after them. Believing any moment, there would be hard knocks on the door. Eva left the bathroom wanting answers from Jorge, to prepare if the police arrived because she wasn't going to go down for him.

"Who is Jeff Collins?" Eva asked.

Jorge was surfing the cable channels when Eva walked out of the bathroom, ready to confront him.

"What did you say?" Jorge asked.

"Who is Jeff Collins?" I said.

"Who are you talking about?" Jorge asked. He hadn't a clue why Eva was asking him about this person.

"You know, Jeff Collins?"

"I don't know. I never heard of the name before. Why do you keep asking so many times?" Jorge asked, getting quite annoyed.

"Well, you should know who he is because you signed his name on the credit card bill you used last night for dinner," Eva said.

Jorge felt himself becoming smaller and smaller, wanting Eva to shut up.

"Oh, him, yes, he's a friend, sorry I forgot," Jorge said, trying to retract what he said and not look like a liar.

"Really, he's a friend whose name you didn't know after I said it about three times. You're a liar, just admit it," Eva said.

"I'm telling you he's my friend," Jorge protested.

She laughed. "Now, why would a friend give you his credit card to use at an expensive restaurant in another state, or maybe you stole it," Eva said, feeling disgusted.

"He owed me money, saying he didn't have any cash, so he said I could use his card instead. I just forgot," Jorge said. He believed this reason would clear any suspicion Eva had.

"I really did pay for the dinner because he owed me the money. I could have charged something else with it, but I didn't. I just forgot. Why are you always thinking the worst of me?" Jorge asked.

"Because you haven't given any good reason not to for a very long time. Not since you gave yourself to the track. All I know is that you could have stolen the card. How stupid I was to think we could've had one last nice morning together until we left," Eva said.

"I'm telling you the truth," Jorge pleaded.

"You know, Jorge, I really don't care what you do, but if you put our daughter in danger again like you did years ago . . . I'm just saying you better be careful. I'll turn you to the police in a heartbeat," Eva said.

"Is that a threat?"

It's good that you are rid of her.

"No, those days are over. I don't threaten anymore. I do. We all could have been arrested last night, but you don't care. That's actually normal for you, isn't it? But not for Tina or me," Eva said.

"No, we couldn't. It was mine to use. How many times do I have to say it? Don't always think the worst," Jorge said again.

Eva turned away, appalled, as Jorge got out of bed, wearing only underwear.

Eva shook her head, hoping Jorge would just get dressed and leave, but he didn't. He decided to take a long hot shower, and to add more annoyance to the situation, he sang. And Eva especially hated when he sang like he had no cares in the world.

Eva called Tina as soon as Jorge left.

"Good morning, Tina. How did you sleep?" Eva asked.

"Pretty good, once I got to bed around three this morning," Tina said.

"What? We should have gone back with you and helped," Eva said.

"No, Mom, it was fine. I wasn't packing all night…the girls in the dorm had a last hurrah."

"Oh, I see. Glad you had one last night of fun in the dorm with friends," Eva said.

"And you? How was your night?" Tina asked.

"Uh, okay," Eva said halfheartedly, not wanting to worry Tina, but her tone said otherwise.

"What's wrong, Mom?"

"Nothing, I'm still tired from all of yesterday's excitement," Eva said.

"Did you and Dad get into a fight?" Tina asked, feeling knots in her stomach.

"Not exactly, but don't worry, nothing bad happened. I just realized that your father hasn't changed much, and I'll leave it to that," Eva said.

Tina's heart dropped, feeling tense and out of place, knowing there was much more that her mother wasn't sharing. Why would she make such a statement if nothing happened? It was the undertones that Tina read well when her mom spoke.

"How so?" Tina asked.

"I just don't think it is a good idea that you move back home with him. How about moving into the villa when the tenants move out in a few months?" Eva asked.

This wasn't what Tina wanted to hear because she wanted to go back home to her old room and not feel the pressure of getting a real job until after the summer.

"Oh, I got to go. Dad is at the door," Tina said.

"Okay, see you soon. He should have coffee and a bagel for you," Eva said.

"Thanks, see you soon, and love you," Tina said.

"Love you, too and see you at the airport soon," Eva said, still on edge from when Jorge left, trying to shake off the ill feelings.

Tina wished her mother had come along with her father, but she knew there wouldn't be enough space for all her things, as he was driving them back home, but she'd see Eva soon enough at the airport, the two of them flying back to West Palm.

Jorge walked in empty-handed. He figured he'd get Tina breakfast if she hadn't eaten and possibly save money.

"So, girl, how did you sleep?" Jorge asked.

"Good, and you?" Tina asked.

"I can't complain. You should have seen the room I got. It had a better view than your mother's, but don't tell her. You know how she gets upset about the littlest things, but I did offer it to her," Jorge said.

"I won't," Tina said.

"Looks like this is it for you?" Jorge said, looking around her empty dorm room.

"Yes, it is."

"I bet you are going to miss this place," Jorge said.

Tina looked at her father, thinking how in tune he was with her feelings. "Yes, I'll miss this place. It's been my home for four years, and it's hard to believe that I won't be here anymore."

Jorge realized there wouldn't be hundreds of miles separating them anymore. And he wasn't sure that was a good thing because he had promised Tina last summer that he would stop going to the track.

"Maybe you should stay in Boston. You know you still can. Isn't there more opportunity here than in West Palm Beach?" Jorge asked.

"No, I can't. I don't have a job here or the money to stay without one," Tina said.

"I just thought you could stay with friends until you found a job. You must have a few friends around that you can stay with."

Tina shook her head, wondering why he was suddenly pushing for her to stay.

"Here are five boxes that can hopefully fit in your car," Tina said.

Tina looked at her empty room, feeling emotional. It was hard leaving, but she was ready to return home, even though Jorge wasn't feeling the same. Christopher, her long-distance boyfriend, was also on her mind. She couldn't wait to get back to him and start their lives together.

"Here, take my car keys and open the car," Jorge said.

Tina walked ahead of him, looking around the lush grounds for one last time, admiring the massive oak trees she often would study beneath, grateful for the time in Boston. She thought of the many times she walked on the winding paths to classes, the library, and the dining hall. Tina nervously opened the trunk; her father's clothes were everywhere.

"Oh, I meant to take them to the dry cleaners."

"Even your underwear?" Tina said, feeling uneasy.

Jorge placed the first box in the trunk as he pushed the dirty clothes to the side like it was no big deal.

"Why don't you stay here while I get the other boxes?" Jorge said.

"Okay," Tina said.

Tina sat in the car, hoping to calm the wave of anxiety she felt. She saw the sports section of *The Palm Beach Post* open. This wasn't good.

Is he gambling again? She wondered.

"Do you want to stop by Dunkin Donuts before going to the airport?" Jorge asked.

Tina almost said no but knew Eva would ask if Jorge brought her anything from Dunkin Donuts, and she didn't want to lie.

"Yes, I'm a bit hungry, thanks," Tina answered.

Jorge hoped Tina would only get a donut as he had to make the last hundred-dollar stretch until West Palm Beach. He was tempted to use the credit card again, but he didn't. Instead, he threw it in the wastepaper basket of the dorm bathroom, making it seem like a college student stole it. He didn't want to press his luck.

CHAPTER 24

911

Tina arrived home, surprised to see how rundown it was. It was just last summer when she was home for break, but it felt like years the way it looked now.

Family items were missing, like her sister's antique highchair, which carried the most sentimental value. Tina looked around to see if it had been moved to another area, but it was gone. She wondered if her father had sold it to pay a bill.

The place did not feel like home anymore, feeling more like an old dingy hotel room without any air circulation. She was afraid to see if the A/C was broken. This would make living at home unbearable, especially now in the summer months.

Maybe this was his backup plan. Maybe he wanted Tina to run back to Boston or find another place to live, or maybe he did clean it before she arrived. Now that was a scary thought, but she thought possible. Tina couldn't imagine the house looking any worse than it did.

Walking up the steps to her room, the smell of stale air was nauseating. Tina took a deep breath as she opened her bedroom door, fearing what she might find. It seemed like the house was full of unpleasant surprises. Tina was taken back as her room was empty now. Not one piece of anything she owned was visible.

She looked to see the closet open, with only cheap dry cleaner hangers and a pair of men's black dress slacks. Yet all her clothes, shoes, and belts were missing, along with her keepsakes.

What the hell happened here? She thought.

"Tina, are you here?" Jorge called from below.

"Yes, I'm in my room!" Tina shouted.

"I bought us lunch. Come down and eat with your dad."

Tina took a deep breath and rushed down the stairwell, feeling out of place.

"Dad, where are my things?" Tina asked.

"Oh, yeah, I'm sorry. I didn't want to tell you this while you were at school because I didn't want to stress you, but I was having a difficult time paying bills. I rented your room to a buddy of mine, but he's gone now," Jorge said.

Tina didn't like the betrayal of not telling her about someone else living in her room, leaving that important piece of information hidden during their weekly phone calls. There was no reason to hide it, making her uncomfortable, wondering what else he was hiding from her.

"But, where are my things?" Tina questioned. "I hope you didn't get rid of them or sell them."

"Oh no, they're in a box in the garage," Jorge said.

"A box? How could all of my things just fit in a box?" Tina questioned.

Tina was now on the verge of tears, fearing her father was lying, and got rid of the things that mattered to her, like the journals she had hidden in the closet. There was no possible way her books and photo albums could fit in a box.

"Tina, it's in a big box. Please, do not panic like your mother. What's the big deal anyway? You weren't living here, and I needed the money, especially with you in college. I thought you would understand. Please don't be like your mother," Jorge said, sighing heavily.

"I'm not. I just hope you packed everything because they can't be replaced," Tina said.

"I did, and please don't tell your mother because you know how she is. She wouldn't understand and blow this out of proportion, and it's none of her damn business anyway. And I don't want her calling me either," Jorge demanded.

This episode motivated Tina to get a job as soon as possible, then move to the villa she was gifted by Eva, and never have to walk on pins and needles around her father again. She just wanted to live alone, in her own place, because this was no longer home.

"How is it living back with your dad?" Christopher asked.

"Fine, we hardly see each other."

"Is he going to the track again?" Christopher asked, looking at Tina.

He knew *fine* didn't really mean *fine* when Tina said it to answer any question. There was always something behind it that wasn't, but he wasn't going to push to know what just yet.

"No, he said he hasn't anymore," Tina said, though she felt he was, wanting to just avoid the possible truth.

Tina had been home for two weeks, scanning the classifieds for a writing job.

"Oh, I saw a job opening for a staff writer at *Dice Magazine*," Christopher said. "It was in the classifieds this morning. Not sure if you have seen it yet."

"No, I haven't. What magazine? I've never heard of it," Tina said.

"It's supposedly a new, alternative magazine in the area," Christopher responded.

"Uh, sounds cool, like you," Tina said, flirting with him.

Tina smiled and walked over to him, kissing him on the cheek, loving every part of him.

"Thank you for always looking out for me," Tina said.

Christopher smiled, looking at her like she was his everything. Grateful that she returned back to West Palm to start her adult life with him. He knew she was the one when he first met her in high school.

"You know, I'm going to stop by this *Dice Magazine* tomorrow and apply for the job," Tina said.

"You should. You're a good writer."

"You're just saying that because I'm your girlfriend."

"No, I'm saying it because you are and also because you're my girlfriend," Christopher said.

Tina kissed Christopher.

He was her rock and the person Tina knew who would always be there for her, and that meant more than anything. They spent the rest of the day at the beach, relaxing, swimming, and having lunch at Sea Sides. It was just what Tina needed to get ready for a night of resume writing.

"Thank you for today. I'm so glad that I'm home now with you. But I need to leave and work on my resume for *Dice Magazine* tomorrow morning." Tina said.

Tina spent the rest of the day in her room, busy tightening her resume. She also went through her writing portfolio, seeing which article had an alternative modern edge.

It wasn't until eleven at night that she realized how late it was, nervous that Jorge wasn't home yet. The awful sinking feeling she was familiar with living in this room years ago as a young girl was getting the better of her, thinking the worst. Fearing that Jorge was hurt somewhere by someone he owed money to.

Tina locked the bedroom door and turned on the television, looking for a distraction. As she lay down, she kept thinking of Jorge, looking out the window every five minutes to see if his car was in the driveway.

It was past midnight now, and no sign of Jorge. Tina was exhausted and restless, but she couldn't fall asleep. Tina feared he got in an accident which seemed possible with the rain.

She had become so fearful for her father's safety that she broke down and called the police.

"This is 911. What's your emergency?"

Tina found it hard to speak when the operator asked the question.

"It's my father," she said softly. Tears building in her eyes, feeling vulnerable.

"Is he hurt? Should I send an ambulance?"

"No, no, it's not that. It's just . . . I'm sorry. I shouldn't have called," Tina said.

"Don't be sorry. What is it? I want to help you," the operator asked.

"It's late, and he hasn't come home yet. I think something bad happened to him," Tina said, feeling faint, feeling like a worried sick fourteen-year-old and not the twenty-one-year-old she was.

"How old are you?" the emergency operator asked, thinking she was talking to a minor with Tina's soft voice.

"Twenty-one," Tina answered.

"Are you sure?" asked the operator.

"Yes, I'm twenty-one. Sorry...this was a dumb idea, but I worry about my dad...," Tina said.

"No need to apologize. What's your full name?"

"Tina Gabor."

"Maybe your dad had plans he didn't tell you about, like a date. After all, you're an adult, and everyone is so busy now. He must have forgotten to call you," the dispatcher said, hoping to calm Tina's nerves.

"No, he knows I worry. He would have said he was going on a date. I still think something bad happened to him. He would have called," Tina said.

The operator felt sorry for Tina, believing more and more that Tina experienced something awful that made her as fearful as she was.

"Well, how about calling the area hospitals? They'd be able to check and see if he's there."

"I hadn't thought of that...thank you," Tina said, feeling slightly better.

"Anytime, and if you ever want to talk to someone, call us again. My name is Julia if you would like to talk to me. I mostly work during the night."

"Really? That's so nice of you, Julia, and I will call again if I need to," Tina said.

"Take care, Tina. I'm here for you."

"Thank you, Julia."

She called three hospitals in the area, but none had Jorge Gabor listed as a patient, which Tina took as a good sign. Exhaustion eventually dragged Tina into a deep sleep, waking up the next morning with a migraine. Worrying all night caused her brain to hurt.

Tina went downstairs, hoping to see evidence that Jorge came home last night, like dirty dishes in the sink or a half-full coffee cup left on the kitchen counter, but there was nothing. Tina then looked at the answering machine, and there weren't any messages. Before calling the hospitals again, Tina would call the hair salon to see if he was there.

"Hi, Donna, it's Tina."

"Oh, hi, honey. How are you?"

"Good, thanks. Is my dad there?" Tina asked, feeling the air being sucked out of her.

"Yup, just a few feet away cutting a client's hair. Do you want to talk to him?" Donna asked.

Tina's heart dropped as she felt disappointed by Jorge. She couldn't believe he didn't at least call and let her know he wouldn't be home for the night.

"No, it's fine. I'll call him later. There's actually someone at the door. Thanks, and have a great day."

"Okay, I'll let him know you called," Donna said, thinking how kind Tina was.

Tina hung up the phone, upset and relieved at the same time. The Palm Springs Kennel Club sprang to her mind. She hoped he didn't go back on his word after promising last summer that he was done with betting. Tina bailed him out of a gambling debt with the money she saved, and he still has yet to return it.

Tina rushed up to her room to get ready for the impromptu interview. She was determined more than ever to get the staff writer job at *Dice Magazine*. Tina wanted to move out and live on her own with Christopher. She was done worrying about her father, believing as long as she lived at home, this would be the case, and she didn't want to become like her mother.

Tina wore a pair of black Gap slacks she got on sale, a white Ralph Lauren oxford shirt and black flats. It was her signature classic look.

The lease at the villa was ending in two months. The tenants weren't going to renew because they were moving out of the state. The villa didn't have a mortgage. The only bills would be the water, electricity, cable, property taxes, and homeowners insurance. This was an investment property her mother had purchased years ago at a good price. The plan was for the property to pay for itself, and afterward it would officially be an income property.

Tina rushed to Rosie's Cafe, where she was meeting Eva. She called to see if she could borrow her gold hoop earrings for the so-called interview at *Dice Magazine*.

As Tina walked in, Eva was enjoying her coffee. It wasn't even a minute until her mother asked about her father.

"So, how is it living with your father?" Eva asked as she took a sip of her cappuccino.

"Fine."

"What do you mean by fine?" Eva asked.

"Mom, why do you always have to read into everything I say?" Tina asked.

Tina already had it with Jorge, and she didn't want to feel the same way about her mother.

"Well, I'm your mother, and I want to know. You can tell me anything. Remember? What's gotten into you?"

Tina knew she should have known better than to answer her mother with a word.

"Nothing has gotten into me," Tina said.

"I just love you, and I want to make sure you are taken care of, that's all. Please don't shut me out," Eva said.

"No, everything is fine at home. Dad has his life, and I have mine. He's actually the perfect roommate," Tina said.

"And how is that?" Eva asked.

"He is never around, Mom, that's how. Again, I don't want to get into it," Tina pleaded.

"Oh, I see," Eva said.

They sat in silence for a few moments, looking away.

"I'll be right back. I don't think the waitress saw me. I need some coffee; I hardly slept last night," Tina said, almost biting her tongue, wishing she could take the words back. She knew Eva's radar must have gone off by now.

"Oh, I already ordered you a cappuccino. It's being made now."

"Oh, thanks," Tina said, letting out a sigh.

"So, your father is not home much?" Eva said, looking at Tina.

"It's not what you think. He doesn't gamble anymore," Tina said.

"You know, he still goes to the kennel club. A friend of mine just saw him the other day," Eva said.

"Really, Mom, who saw him? What's the person's name?" Tina shook her head, becoming defensive, not believing her mother.

'Why are you protecting him? I'm just trying to warn you to be careful at home. Don't fall into the same trap I did," Eva said.

This wasn't how Tina wanted to spend time with her mother. Why was it that their conversations always had to involve Jorge and not just be about what was happening in their lives? She just wanted to enjoy normal conversations with Eva, like what shows they were watching and sharing favorite recipes.

"You know, Mom, he has a girlfriend now," Tina said.

This took Eva by surprise as Jorge never had time for anyone other than going to the track, and it was a little hurtful. Maybe what Tina said was true, maybe he stopped gambling, but she still had doubts. Eva's friend didn't say that she saw Jorge, but that she saw someone that looked like him.

Eva decided it was best to change the conversation away from Jorge as it was igniting anger and causing tension between her and Tina. Which she honestly did not want to happen around Tina. Eva knew talking bad about Jorge would never erase what he did to her, but she still struggled with keeping the past the past.

"Here are the earrings. They will look perfect on you," Eva said as she passed them to Tina.

"Oh, they're perfect and beautiful," Tina said as she held them.

"I'm impressed that you got an interview at *Dice Magazine* just being home for a short time," Eva said.

"I don't actually have an interview. I'm just going to stop by and sort of have one."

"Wow, I like that even better." Eva smiled.

"Another trait I got from you," Tina said.

Eva smiled, appreciating the compliment. "I'm sure they'll hire you on the spot, seeing what a beautiful, intelligent, and excellent writer you are."

"I hope so." Tina grinned as her mother always knew the right words.

Tina decided she would keep her plans about moving out of Jorge's place and into the villa until she got a job. She knew if she mentioned the move, Eva would become suspicious, which would trigger her to pry more. Tina left the cafe feeling overwhelmed and exhausted by her parents.

"I see you know how to write a byline. That's more than I can say for a lot of the applicants these days."

"Um, great storyline, too. I like your Hemingway style. It's direct and honest. People appreciate that these days, not wanting to think too much as they read, especially when they just want the writer to get to the point like you," Mr. Jackson said.

Tina liked everything she heard, even if it wasn't a formal interview.

"Well, you're everything we're looking for at Dice Magazine and more."

Tina felt she was about to be hired.

"But I already hired someone this morning," Mr. Jackson said.

Tina was crushed. She could not believe her luck.

"Well, not all is lost, Tina. I do have another job if you are interested."

Tina's smile reappeared again, beaming with glee, wanting to hug this man, waiting to hear what the job was.

Mr. Jackson admired her willful eyes and said, "Don't get too excited. It's not exactly being a staff writer, which you are more than qualified to be, but it will get you in the door. I'm not sure you will even want it, but it is yours."

"I'll take it," Tina said. The only thing that mattered was getting her foot in the door of a major news publication.

"Let's go to the copy room, and I'll explain the job duties. You can also meet the staff, too. Can you start today?" Mr. Jackson asked.

"Of course…yes…thank you," Tina said.

Mr. Jackson walked beside Tina with his right hand over her right shoulder, telling the ropes of the office and what her job would involve. She was relieved that she would be working closely with writers and editors as an assistant.

"Why don't you leave a little early today, and I'll see you early tomorrow morning at seven. The news never sleeps, so there will be much to do assisting around the office," Mr. Jackson said.

"Thank you, Mr. Jackson."

"No, thank you, Tina, for coming by today. You're like a breath of fresh air in this office of old-timers. I know you will do well here," Mr. Jackson said, hoping to make Tina feel welcome.

Tina left *Dice Magazine* happy and excited, feeling like her dreams were coming true. As she walked to her Volkswagen Bug, she called Christopher.

"Where have you been?"

"Working!" Tina screamed.

"You got the job! If there's a world record for getting hired the fastest, you would win, hands down. You never cease to amaze me, Tina," Christopher said.

"Yes, I did, even though it wasn't the one I went for. It's still good," Tina said.

"Oh, so what's the job?" Christopher asked.

"I'll tell you later."

"When will that be?"

"I should be at your door in about ten minutes," Tina said.

"I can't wait."

They had dinner at Ciao Bello, a little, cozy romantic Italian restaurant in Palm Beach. It wasn't part of a national chain; an Italian couple ran it from Parma, Italy. It was the perfect place to celebrate Tina's new job and new life.

Christopher also had good news. He had been called for two interviews. One in Boca Raton and the other in Lake Worth. Tina went back to Christopher's place for a little while, but she had to get back home, as tomorrow would be her first full day at work.

"Okay, Chris, I have to go. I'm a working woman now," Tina said.

"Yes, you are, and I hope to follow in your steps soon," Christopher said.

"I know you will, and then we can move in together."

As Tina drove home, she felt relieved that she was closer to moving out of what seemed like Jorge's place and not her home anymore. She thought getting a job would be the hardest part, but it was the easiest.

It was ten o'clock, and not a single star could be seen, looking like black ink. Driving home, she started to get an unsettling feeling in the pit of her stomach. Eva wondered if her father would be home. Her thoughts drifted to her mother and how she said, "I know he still gambles," fearing she was right. Tina knew it was not normal to feel as panicked as she did, but that was part of living with a father like Jorge.

Tina's heart started to race as she took a turn to her street. In a few seconds, she would know if he was home or not. It seemed like her day couldn't get any better because his car was there.

Thank you, God, she thought, pulling into the driveway. The outside lights were on, and the front gate was opened for her to walk through. She wondered if he would be up watching television or if he was already asleep. Walking by his car, she dared to touch the hood, and it was cold. *This is a good sign,* she thought.

Tina walked in to find Jorge sleeping on the couch with the sports section of the newspaper on his lap. She didn't see that underneath were betting tickets he'd bought earlier.

Donna told him about Tina's call earlier. He had forgotten that she was living home again and went straight to work earlier in the morning after going to the track last night and then down south to the casino. He decided that he would play it safe tonight and went to the track after his last client to make bets and then return home.

On her way up to her room, she stopped to kiss him on the cheek, and thought what a good father he was. Maybe she was all wrong, and she was just being too paranoid.

CHAPTER 25

Hook, Line, and Sinker

Tina had been working at *Dice Magazine* for six months when she started to feel uncomfortable around Mr. Jackson.

"So, how is the job treating you?" Mr. Jackson asked.

"Great, thank you!" Tina said.

"I'm happy to hear this."

"Is there something you'd like?" she asked when he continued to stand there.

"No, I just like the view."

Great, she thought. There was no doubt that he was coming on to her, but she wasn't going to show Mr. Jackson that it bothered her.

Tina just smiled, but she felt anything but happy about Mr. Jackson's advances.

The last thing she wanted was an older man lusting after her. She wasn't going to tell Christopher about Mr. Jackson acting inappropriately, or she would have another problem on her hands. Tina knew he would march into the office and tell Mr. Jackson where he could go, and her career at Dice Magazine would be over.

"Tina, call on line two."

It was Christopher. After just working at his new job at the local cable company for a little over four months, they promoted him to one of the top engineers in the firm. This also included a five thousand dollar raise, which would come in handy now with the bathroom renovations at the villa. Three months had passed since Tina and Christopher moved into the villa.

"Tina, line two again."

"Hi, what more good news do you have to tell me?" Tina said, expecting to hear Christopher's voice.

"Hi, girl, it's Dad," Jorge said.

Tina's heart sank as she sensed something was wrong because Jorge never called her at work.

"Oh, hi, Dad, is everything okay?" Tina asked.

"Yeah, I just need a favor, girl."

"I'm working, so it will have to be later," Tina said, her heart skipping a beat. She didn't like the sound of a favor.

"When is your lunch break then?" Jorge asked.

"In an hour . . ."

"Good, then meet me at the Denny's on Belvedere Road. It is not that far away."

"Remember, I only have an hour break."

"It won't take too long. I need you to do something for me. Please, girl," Jorge said.

Bingo. She will be there.

"What is it? You know I don't like not knowing," Tina said.

"I'll tell you when I see you. I'm just finishing up with a client. I'll see you at Denny's then." Jorge said, then hung up without saying goodbye.

After forty-five minutes, she rushed to Denny's, not having a good feeling. Tina saw Jorge parked in the parking lot instead of inside the restaurant.

"Why are you still in your car?" Tina asked.

"Hi, girl," Jorge said, ignoring her question.

"Dad, I don't have much time. What is it?"

"It shouldn't take that long," Jorge said.

"What shouldn't take that long? Why couldn't this wait?"

Jorge's eyes sparkled as he showed Tina a wage ticket.

"See this ticket?" Jorge asked.

"Yes," Tina said, as she rolled her eyes, not liking the sight of it, as it confirmed that he was still going to the track trying his luck.

"I thought you weren't going to the track anymore," Tina said, disappointed by her father's disregard for his promises of not betting again.

"Well, it is a winning ticket. It's worth eight thousand dollars, more money than you and Christopher make in a few months. See, I did it," Jorge said, pleased with himself.

Yes, Jorge, you did. Way to go.

Jorge was beside himself, feeling on top of the world, boasting about the ticket.

Tina imagined the money he lost to finally have a winning ticket.

"I need you to take this ticket and cash it at the Palm Springs Kennel Club across the street," Jorge directed.

"Why can't you? It's your ticket." Tina said.

She didn't like the sounds of his plan and was suspicious of why he was asking her to cash the ticket and not cash it himself.

Jorge looked away for a moment. He did not want to tell her he didn't want to report the earnings to the IRS. He still owed them five thousand dollars and other fees and interest.

"I just don't want the attention," Jorge lied.

"And I do?" Tina asked.

"Well, nobody knows you there. You'll be fine. If I go, I'll have a trail of people wanting money from me. I just want to get my life on track again. Please, girl, believe me. It's been hard without your mother," Jorge pleaded.

Jackpot.

"You lied. You said you stopped gambling, but you haven't. I can't believe how I believed you ever stopped," Tina said, seconds away from leaving Jorge alone in the parking lot.

"Well, I did, but I still come once a week for the big races. Look at the ticket; it was from last Friday for the jackpot. I wasn't really lying," Jorge said.

Tina looked at the ticket, and it was from last Friday. Maybe he was telling the truth. If he was, then she was making a big deal about nothing again. She took a deep breath, feeling that maybe going to the track once a week was an improvement, and was better than him going every day.

Great save, Jorge.

"Here is the ticket. Just go to any wage window and cash the ticket. Just make sure you have your driver's license. They just need to see that the person collecting the prize is the person on the driver's license. It's nothing to worry about," Jorge said.

She rolled her eyes, still not wanting to do this favor.

"Now go before I have to be back at work," Jorge demanded.

Tina grabbed the ticket, annoyed, and left Dennys feeling the urge to rip it up.

Jorge went inside and ordered a cheeseburger and Coke, though he had no money. He would eat slowly until Tina returned with the money. He didn't bother to ask Tina what she wanted for lunch or even if she was hungry. He just wanted her to cash his ticket.

Once she arrived at the kennel club, she felt like she was doing something illegal. It just didn't feel right to cash a ticket that wasn't hers. It would have been different if he had given it to her as a gift, but he just wanted her to cash it and return the money to him. Later she would know that other gamblers did the same thing when winning. They would ask someone else to cash in their ticket, and in return, they would give them some money. It was common practice at the track to avoid paying taxes.

Tina nervously walked up to a wage window and was greeted by an attractive English woman in her late thirties.

"I have a ticket that I would like to cash."

"Okay, just slide it under," said Truly, "and my computer here will say how much you've won."

Tina did as she was told and waited to hear what was next. She leaned against the window feeling out of place.

"It looks like you won last week's jackpot. Well, congratulations."

Tina broke out a smile, not saying a word. She just wanted the money, so she could get out. She saw enough gamblers to last a lifetime in the short time she waited in line. Some with children, not even watching them as they keep their eyes on the track. Not caring if they got hurt or worse encouraged them to bet too.

"I need your driver's license, honey."

Tina's heart raced, feeling like she was on the verge of being arrested. She nervously opened her wallet, took out her license, and passed it under the glass wage window.

The woman looked at it and then at Tina again. "You look about sixteen in this photo."

Tina just shook her head, feeling lightheaded and warm.

'I was," Tina said.

"Tina Gabor," the woman said.

Tina looked at her, worried she was about to say something bad about the ticket.

"Oh, my, this can't be."

Tina leaned on the counter for support. She tried to think what the problem could be. Could it be that her license has expired?

"I just have to ask. Are you Jorge Gabor's daughter?"

Tina turned beet red as she shook her head to say yes, not thinking this was a good thing to admit.

"Yes, I am," Tina said.

"I see you have followed in your father's footsteps. I'm Trudy, by the way."

Tina was relieved for a moment, then upset that the wage window lady knew her father so well. This meant that her father was still a regular at the track. She began to doubt if her father was ever being truthful about coming to the track only once a week. It had to be a lie. There were just too many people at the track for Trudy to remember him unless he was a regular.

"First sign this. It is for the IRS saying you won."

Her father said nothing about signing a form, especially not one for the IRS.

"Why do I have to sign it?" Tina asked.

"Well, you have to pay taxes on this win," Trudy said.

"Oh, can't you just take it out now?" Tina asked.

"No, we don't do that here. Ask your father. He knows how to file," Trudy said.

Tina reluctantly signed the IRS form and felt cheated again.

"Here's the winnings," Trudy said.

"Great."

"Oh, and John over there will walk you to your car. I wouldn't want you to get jumped in the parking lot. There are eyes everywhere watching, desperate for money," Trudy said.

John looked like Rocky from the Rocky movies. He was a young Italian bodybuilder in the police academy.

"It looks like you know a thing or two about picking dogs?" John asked.

Tina looked at him and said, "Not really, it was just luck."

John chuckled and said, "Yeah, that's what they all say."

He walked Tina to the car and waited until she exited the parking lot. She sat in the car collecting her thoughts and was now famished. And her lunch break was just about over too.

She pulled into the Denny's parking lot and saw her father sitting inside. She was livid but felt it was better to be quiet than to let her emotions get the better of her before returning to work. How was it that she always had a way of just brushing things off?

"Here is the money," Tina said.

Jorge grabbed the thick white envelope, and opened it, salivating as he saw the crisp hundred-dollar bills. He just wanted to run across the street to the track again and try his luck.

"Oh, I saw a lady friend of yours," Tina said.

"What friend?" Jorge asked, surprised.

"Trudy, she asked if I was following your footsteps. I guess she assumed I'm a gambler like you."

"Ah, Trudy, she is a nice girl. She wants to be a teacher," Jorge said.

"You know, Dad, you didn't tell me that I would have to pay taxes on this win," Tina said, looking straight at Jorge.

"No, you won't because you don't work," Jorge said.

"What are you talking about? I work. Remember? You called me at work."

"Oh, that's right. I forgot; I thought you were still in college."

"Oh, how could you forget? I have been working for a few months now, and you just said this win was more than Christopher and I make in months. This doesn't make sense," Tina said.

"Well, don't worry. If you have to pay the IRS anything, I'll have the money by then."

"I have to go," Tina said.

She left before he could kiss her goodbye and was so frustrated with Jorge. Moments later, she returned to the office, ate the rest of the bagel she hadn't finished for breakfast, and had pieces of the leftover cheese and salami platter in the staff room.

Around midafternoon she started to feel wheezy. *You're fine*, she thought. *You're still upset about Dad.* Thinking about what happened earlier, how Jorge would say the same words he would tell Eva, "Don't worry about it," when she was concerned about signing IRS papers. She felt like this would end up being her responsibility. *Why do I keep falling for his favors? She wondered.*

Later at home, she felt extra tired and just wanted to sleep.

"I'm not feeling right," Tina said.

"How?" Christopher asked.

"I just feel off. I have no energy, and my boobs are super sore. When I went to the supermarket earlier, I couldn't stand to be in the fruit section. The smells of peaches were so nauseating that I had to leave, and that's why I couldn't get you bananas. Sorry.

Christopher looked at Tina, saying the first thing that came to mind. "Are you pregnant?"

"No, I don't think so," Tina said.

"You know sore boobs are a pregnancy symptom."

"I'm not pregnant," Tina said, feeling scared of the possibility. However, the thought did cross her mind. It just wasn't one she was ready for. After she looked at the calendar, she calculated that her period was a week late. This was enough to take the possibility of being pregnant seriously.

"I'm going to get a test," Tina said, as she had her purse over her shoulder with car keys in hand to get a pregnancy test.

"Do you want me to go with you?" Christopher asked.

"No, I'll be fine. I'll be back soon enough."

A half-hour later, Tina returned with two pregnancy tests.

"Are you okay?" Christopher asked. He noticed how pale and worried Tina looked.

"Sort of. I'm just disappointed in myself," Tina said.

"Why? You know it took two of us to get pregnant. If that is what you are talking about."

"Oh, no, it's not that. It's my father. He is gambling again, and I really thought he stopped. I'm sure now that he never did."

"Oh, Tina, don't worry about him. We have something very important to find out. No?"

"Yes, we do."

She wanted to tell him how she went to the track earlier to cash her father's betting ticket but decided to keep it a secret for now. It wasn't important with the possibility of being pregnant. Confiding in Christopher wouldn't change what she did and the guilt she felt.

Tina went to the bathroom, carrying the plastic bag with the tests. She sat on the covered toilet and read the pregnancy test instructions.

"Okay, this is pretty simple," Tina said.

The moment of truth was upon Tina as she stood up, undid her pants, and followed the instructions exactly. She started to shake as she thought of what was happening. Tina could never have imagined she would end the day taking a pregnancy test and possibly be expecting.

After two minutes, she glanced at the test on the white-tiled vanity beside her, though she knew it wasn't five minutes yet. There was already a pink line in the testing circle, and it got darker as she kept staring. There was no denying there were now two dark lines on the test; it could have easily been seen from across the room. The test line was now darker than the control line, which meant that Tina was pregnant.

Christopher was in the living room, anxious for Tina's return. He kept glancing at the bedroom door, waiting for Tina to open it. Suddenly, the door opened, and he saw Tina smiling, and he knew he was going to be a dad.

"Come here, hot Mama."

Tina went over to Christopher, and they hugged. Tina cried tears of happiness for the child that was growing inside of her that Christopher and her created. She already loved this baby more than anything.

"You always manage to surprise me," Christopher said.

Staring at Christopher, she knew this was the perfect time to start a family of their own.

CHAPTER 26

Another Save

Jorge paid back two loan sharks from the winnings, fearing they were closing in on him.

One was Tony, who he still borrowed from time to time. He still had the lowest rates, even though they were still high. Then there was David, a newbie in the area who was suggested to him by a gambler friend who loaned larger amounts, but his interest rates were even higher. David also had a cruel edge to him.

The only thing the money did for Jorge was give him a clean slate to borrow more money from these guys. It was such a vicious cycle. He didn't keep up with the household bills: electricity, water, cable, property taxes, or homeowners' insurance, which were all overdue. He would figure out how to pay them when receiving the final notices before services were shut off. He was also behind in his mortgage payments, yet Jorge saw no way out but to gamble.

In the same week, Jorge's gambler friend, who moved into Tina's room a few months ago, stopped paying him rent.

He promised Jorge, he would pay him when he'd receive his paycheck. He sweetened the promise by saying he would also pay last month's water and cable bill. Jorge believed Zach, feeling his chances of getting the money were greater if he just let him stay than kicking him out this late in the game.

But this was all a lie. Zach was just buying himself more time until he could find another place to live for free. He had no intention of paying Jorge because he was fired from his last job. But Jorge couldn't be told otherwise by his track friends, warning him about Zach, the freeloader.

It was like Jorge was banking on a hopeless bet. These were the types of friends that Jorge was making at the track—con artists that he vowed he would never associate with. Now he was surrounded by the likes of them, learning their tricks as they financially sucked him dry. And he eventually transformed to their low moral standards too.

Jorge came home to find that Zach had moved out. He left Tina's room a mess. The water and cables were shut off, too, for nonpayment. He wasn't as upset as disappointed. He even called Zach thinking there was a good reason why he left, but all he ever reached was his voicemail.

He saw the mail on the table with the letter from Chase Bank on top. He didn't need to open it to know they were writing about his mortgage. Jorge wasn't too worried, as it was not yet a certified letter.

"Screw them. They screwed me on the interest rate," Jorge said.

He now owed more on the house than it was worth and decided to let it go into foreclosure, but he would be smart about it. He would live in the house as long as he could. He just had to find out how to stay for another year or two without being foreclosed. He knew there had to be a way to delay the process, some loophole in the system that he could ride for a few months or years.

He decided to talk to an attorney that a few of his gambling buddies used from the dog track when they were in the same situation.

He asked later, now he had to go to work.

"Good morning, Donna. How is my day looking?" Jorge asked.

"I'd say a full one. John Smith, Sara Parker, June Diaz, Mr. Jim, and Barbara Turner are scheduled for haircuts today."

"Oh great, I thought Mr. Jim was coming in next Thursday. Can you call to reschedule him?"

Donna looked up at Jorge oddly; she never heard him complain about Mr. Jim. He was a nice older man who always gave him a good tip. She was always under the impression that he was one of Jorge's favorite clients. They would get into these deep conversations about God and the importance of being true to one's word because Mr. Jim was also a pastor.

"I thought you liked Pastor Jim. Also, company policy is you can't reschedule unless you're basically about to die, and even then," Donna said.

"I do like him, but . . ."

The phone rang, breaking the conversation between Donna and Jorge. Phew, Jorge thought as he didn't know what else to say. He walked out the back door to his car to phone Tina.

"Hi, girl. How are you feeling?"

"Good, just a little tired, but I hear that's a good sign. I'll take it any day for this little bean."

"Oh, is that right? Just make sure you are drinking enough water. I can't just believe that my little girl is going to be a mommy, and I'm going to be a grandpa."

"I'm still getting used to it too." Tina laughed.

"Have you been to the doctor yet?" Jorge asked.

"Yes, yesterday was my first prenatal appointment. I tried calling you afterward, but you didn't answer. Where were you?"

"I was playing soccer. So don't worry. I need to lose this little gut I have." Jorge laughed, as he knew he was exaggerating, for his tummy was quite trim for his age.

"Okay, Dad, I have to go. I have a call on the other line. I'll call you later. I'm glad we got to talk. Hey, why don't you come by for dinner tonight?" Tina asked.

Jorge needed Tina's help before Pastor Jim arrived for his appointment. Though Pastor Jim was the kindest man, he was quite the pistol when he felt he was being had, especially when money was involved. Jorge could still hear his last words, "Jorge, don't double cross a holy man. God doesn't think too kindly of it."

Pastor Jim loaned him two hundred dollars out of good faith that it would be repaid as agreed. Jorge had said he needed the money to help pay his property taxes, or the county would auction his home.

"Sounds good, but listen, before you go . . . I have a small favor to ask."

Tina's heart dropped. His favors always seemed like a bail out, somehow connected to gambling. How she wished she never knew the word. It triggered her fears like no other word in the English language.

"You see, I borrowed money from a client for car repairs."

"Car repairs?" Tina questioned. Here we go again, she thinks.

"Yes, I didn't want to ask you for money because you just moved into the villa and were making repairs. When my radiator went bad, I borrowed part of the money to fix it. I was short around two hundred dollars. Otherwise, I wouldn't be able to get to work. I needed the money for a good reason," Jorge said.

Tina didn't say a word. She listened hard to see any inconsistencies in his story, but so far, there weren't any.

"So, now the client I borrowed money from is coming to the shop today for a haircut and expecting to be repaid. The problem is that I won't have the money until Friday, and he is leaving tomorrow morning for a trip," Jorge said, taking a deep breath before finishing his story.

"I just need two hundred dollars until tomorrow. I'm embarrassed to even ask you. If anything, you should be the one telling the story."

Tina didn't say anything, though she knew where he was going. He wanted to borrow money. Something she always felt uncomfortable doing but had a hard time saying no to.

"Girl, it was for my car, not what you think. I borrowed the money from Pastor Jim. He sometimes helps Father Michael at church. You may remember him; he's short and looks like Spock from *Star Trek*."

Tina stayed quiet, still carefully listening to Jorge.

"If you like, you can talk to Pastor Jim, and he will tell you that he loaned me the money for my car. I don't want you to think I blew it at the track. I don't do that anymore."

She thought about what her father said and believed him. She felt that there was no harm in helping him until he got paid. After all, family should help family, and she did remember Pastor Jim as he described him to her.

"All right, you're lucky because I still have money in my bank account. I just need the money back by Friday. Are you sure you'll be able to do that?" Tina asked.

"Of course, I would never let you down, girl. I only borrowed the money for my car, otherwise, I wouldn't have. It was a do-or-die situation," Jorge said.

Tina wouldn't go far to say that he never let her down. However, it actually looked like he borrowed the money for the radiator. Still, she wasn't sure if that was a good thing or not.

"I can come by the shop during my lunch break and give you a check."

"Thank you, Tina girl. See you then."

"See you," Tina said.

You know how to play them.

Tina came into the shop around 11:30 a.m., and they went for lunch next door at a Greek restaurant.

"Have you had any cravings? How about chocolates? Oh, your mother would eat two or three Hershey bars a day. But don't tell her I told you, or she will call me upset about why I told you. You know how sensitive she gets about things, even though she was a toothpick back then," Jorge said.

Jorge leaned forward, touching the table as he tried to get closer to Tina. He remembered when Eva was pregnant, how she loved it when he'd come home with goodies like cookies, Hershey kisses, pizza, and dill pickles.

Eva never told Tina that Jorge wasn't in the delivery room when she was born. It was never really established where he was. Instead, Eva let it go. Feeling the truth would only rip her apart and eventually Tina. It was better not knowing.

Tina now radiated as she spoke. Jorge saw his daughter, a woman now with a child on the way. As the years passed, she became stronger and tougher like her mother but was happy that she always had a heart for him.

"Not yet, but now that you mention it, I could go for a slice of chocolate cake after lunch. How about if we split a piece? Then I won't feel so bad," Tina said.

"Let's do it," said Jorge. "How's your mother? She must be doing well because I haven't heard from her for a while."

Tina didn't like it when her father asked about her mother, especially since they still had years of bad feelings between them. Jorge and Eva were like oil and vinegar; they never mixed well together.

"Mom is doing well, busy with real estate. But how are you?" Tina asked, switching the subject. "It is not often that we get to see each other and talk."

"Good. Divorce has done me well. We should have done it years ago. No offense to your mother, of course."

Tina wasn't buying it completely but smiled as she ate her Greek salad. Then she asked about his gambling.

"What about the dog track? Are you still going on Fridays, or have you stopped?" Tina asked, looking straight at him, hoping he'd be honest, though she wasn't sure if she could handle the truth.

He was expecting she would ask, as she did every few months. Jorge wasn't going to let on that the question still bothered him. He wasn't going to say that he was still gambling almost every night, especially now that Tina was expecting.

What you do is your own business.

"I go Fridays for a chance to win the jackpot, but I only bet with my tips. Not like I did before. I have it under control. I know my limits now, so please don't worry, Tina. Let the past be the past, please," Jorge said.

Tina took a bite of her salad to gather a bit of courage.

"I really hope so, Dad. I worry when you gamble, and I don't want to bring up what happened last year because I said I wouldn't. I just don't know what I would do if it happened again. I just can't go through it again, and sometimes I feel like you have forgotten about it…like it never happened," Tina said.

Tina found herself burning up, feeling a panic overwhelm her as she felt boxed in a cage. Sweat rolled down her back and legs.

She is overexaggerating like Eva. Just don't take what she said seriously.

Jorge didn't respond, not wanting to acknowledge what had happened that night. As far as he was concerned, it was in the past, and there was no need to rehash it because he really couldn't remember what lies he told. He just knew there wasn't any real danger towards him or Tina, but he would never admit to any of it. The only thing he remembered was that he was about to be caught for his lies, but instead, Tina rescued him.

"Here is the check made out to Mr. Jim. I wrote your name on the bottom left as a record of you paying him back. Listen, Dad, soon Christopher and I will be sharing a checking account, and I won't be able to help you anymore."

Jorge smiled, as the check would now buy him time and credibility.

"Just don't forget I need the money back by Friday. Our cable bill and water bill are due."

"No, problem, I'll give you another twenty for your help."

"It is not necessary. I just need the money back."

"You got it. Don't worry, girl."

Tina smiled, "You know I'm always here to help when I can. Just don't let me down, Dad."

Jorge just smiled, and pretended he didn't hear the latter part of Tina's words.

She's so dramatic.

Tina got up from the table and kissed Jorge goodbye. She was happy that she could see him for lunch, though she still had reservations about his gambling. It was the way he looked away when she said the word. Jorge was hesitant to answer her questions and acted like he didn't hear them.

Of course, Tina still loved him; after all, he was and always would be her father. The hopeful part of her believed Jorge knew better than to let another slip-up happen again and felt Jorge learned his lesson, promising it would never happen again. The terror in his eyes tore her, and she felt if she didn't help, he would have been killed. And it would be her fault for not helping when she had the means to.

She tried keeping that awful night way back in her memory, but every so often, she would think when Jorge woke her up in the middle of the night in a complete panic. He had said that he owed the wrong type of people and that if he didn't pay them back by the next day, they would come after him and get rid of him. Tina believed his cries as he promised that he would never gamble again.

Out of fear and love for her father's life, she gave him all of the money she had earned for the summer, which was meant for college. He had promised down on his knees that he would repay the two thousand dollars in the next few months, but he didn't. Tina had no choice but to get a weekend job at the library to replace the funds. She never dared to tell Eva, who questioned her why she got the job at the library in the first place. Asking her time and time again, "What happened to the money you saved over the summer?" Making her look like she was the irresponsible one.

This was the start of harboring Jorge's secrets.

CHAPTER 27

Changes

"Honey, the dinner is awesome," Tina said, savoring each bite. "I'm glad you like it."

"Listen, I wanted to talk to you about something."

Christopher looked at Tina and waited to hear what was on Tina's mind.

"A coworker of mine, who I am friendly with, is selling her house. She just got hired at *The New York Times* working in the editorial department and is looking to move fast."

Christopher looked confused as he took a bite of the spaghetti he had made, wondering why she was bringing this up. They just moved into the villa, and here she was talking about another house.

"Well, I was thinking we could look at it," Tina said.

Christopher didn't seem too interested when he just finished updating the bathrooms with his brother Matthew. He was looking forward to enjoying the new bathrooms for at least a few years.

"I like this place."

"I do, too, but I was thinking we would eventually need a bigger place with the baby coming, and what better time to move than before the baby arrives," Tina said.

"Tracy is also asking $50,000 less than what it's appraised for. Did I mention the house is on a half-acre tree lot overlooking a canal on Old Country Road?" Tina said.

"Really, keep talking. You've sparked my interest," Christopher said.

"The appraisal came in at $300,000, but she would sell it for $250,000."

Christopher liked what he was hearing, but he wasn't so sure about moving again.

"It sounds great, but we just moved here."

"I know, but let's just see it anyway, please."

Christopher looked at Tina with his *I know what is up your sleeve* look and said. "Well, okay, just don't fall in love with it, or I might just have to buy it for you."

Tina smiled, feeling it was already too late because the way Tracy described the house, she was already sold. It was the house she always wanted as a child, and now she could have it with her family.

"We can see it tonight. Tracy said that if she doesn't sell it in the next few days she will list it with a realtor, and then this opportunity will be lost. I'm telling you; it will sell fast."

Christopher smiled and said, "I already know how this is going to end, but I'm not going to lie. It sounds like the perfect house for us."

"I think you may want to bring the checkbook just in case," Tina said.

"So, what do you think? "Tina asked, hoping Christopher loved the house as much as she did.

"It does have a nice big yard, which would give the baby plenty of room to run when the time comes," Christopher said, already seeing their lives at the ranch-style house.

"What else do you like?" Tina asked.

"I like the fact that it has four bedrooms. A huge master bedroom for us, and a good size room for the baby, an office, and another nice size room for baby two down the road," Christopher said, smiling. "It really does have everything we discussed we'd want."

"Do you like the house enough to put an offer on?" Tina asked.

"I like it a lot. Yet, the timing is not ideal."

Tina felt disappointed in Christopher's response.

"Well, not everything can be planned, as we know. But this place is perfect for us. We'll never have to move again, and who knows if the opportunity will happen again."

Christopher knew Tina was right and thought it over again. "Okay, let's go for it."

Tina smiled, feeling that having the house of her dreams was now a possibility.

"So, what should we offer?" Tina asked.

"I thought your friend was asking $250,000."

"Yes, but I was thinking we could offer a little less if we can close in a month."

"Is that even possible?" Christopher asked, surprised that one could buy a house so fast.

"It is. Once you're pre-approved, it can take as little as two weeks to close on a property."

"All right, Ms. Real Estate expert, are you sure you don't have a real estate license hidden under your sleeve?"

"No, I just learned by listening to my mom talking on the phone when she had a real estate deal pending."

"I can see that. So, I'll let you handle this."

Tina smiled, got a yellow pad of paper, and constructed an offer. Afterward, she reviewed it with Christopher, and he agreed to all the terms and found himself excited about a house he didn't even know existed until today.

She phoned Tracy and said she would have an offer for her in the morning. Tracy was happy to move on with her life in New York, as she felt this home would be in good hands with Tina and Christopher.

Tracy accepted the offer of $240,000. Both parties were thrilled, but Tina was a bit nervous as she never imagined she'd be buying a house with Christopher so soon. But unexpected surprises seemed to be the theme in her life now, and she was going to trust that everything would be okay.

By 10:00 am, Tina got loan approval from Chase, and now all that was left was the appraisal, home inspection, survey, and seller repairs if needed.

They would have the interior and exterior of the house painted. The carpets would only have to be steamed, because they were just a year old. A few tiles in the kitchen needed to be replaced as they had cracks.

The room she was most excited about decorating was the little being growing inside her. Though she didn't know the gender yet, Tina's gut feeling was that she was having a girl. In a month, she would know, that's if the little bean cooperates during the sonogram.

Earlier in the morning, there was a memo in Tina's mailbox from Mr. Jackson. It was about a required pre-evaluation conference about her upcoming work performance evaluation. They would discuss Tina's goals at *Dice Magazine*. Tina hoped he would stick to business and forgo the flirting this time. Tina still felt she owed it to him to be nice after hiring her, but she was tired of his borderline inappropriate comments.

Might as well get this over with, Tina thought, mindful that stress was not good for her or the baby. Maybe he would notice she gained weight, and he wouldn't be attracted to her anymore.

When she got up from her chair, she felt a gush of wetness between her legs. Tina hoped it wasn't what she thought it could be. Was she bleeding? Could she be miscarrying? Her heart raced as she felt panic cripple her. She wanted this baby more than anything now that it was a part of her, and now she wasn't sure if the baby was alive.

Tina pressed her legs together. Tina thought the worst, thinking it could be blood. She had to walk by Mr. Jackson's office to get to the bathroom. She was relieved to see that he was on the phone, engaged in conversation, laughing and doodling on a piece of paper on his desk that he wasn't aware that she even walked by.

In the bathroom, she sat down to see what the wetness could be. Her heart couldn't stop racing, pounding hard against her chest. She looked down and saw blood. Tina was too afraid to wipe, thinking she might see the baby or parts of a baby. She rolled up enough toilet paper to make a pad. She cried, believing she had lost the baby. How could this have happened? Did she do something wrong?

Tina was eleven weeks pregnant, just a few days shy of the second trimester. She left the bathroom heartbroken, not having much faith in a happy ending due to the bleeding. She left the office telling the secretary that she wasn't feeling well. Tina called Christopher on the way to the car crying.

"Hey, Tina. I was just thinking about you. How's your day going?"

"I'm bleeding…I may have lost the baby," Tina said, crying too hard to even see through the tears.

"Oh, no…don't say that. We don't know for sure. Please call the doctor."

"I'm scared too. Why is this happening?"

"I'm on my way. I'll take you."

"No, no, I'll call the doctor. I'll go alone."

"Are you sure? I can leave now," Christopher pleaded.

"Yes, I'm sure."

Tina started to cry again as she thought about losing the baby. Once in the car, she called the Women's Comprehensive Center, her hands shaking, afraid that the phone would slip and the call would hang up.

"Hi, I'd like to come in today," Tina said.

"How can I help you?"

"I was just in the other day for a prenatal appointment."

"Okay, is everything okay?"

"Not really. I'm bleeding," Tina said in a sad, weak voice.

"What do you mean by bleeding? Are you bleeding like a period, or are you spotting?"

"No, not a flow, but there is blood on my underwear."

"Well, light bleeding or spotting can be normal in early pregnancy, but it can also be the start of a miscarriage."

"Is there any way I can find out for sure?"

"An ultrasound would confirm if the pregnancy is viable or not," the nurse said.

"How soon can I have one?"

"Can you come by four this afternoon? The technician just had a cancellation."

"Yes, I'll be there."

Tina called Christopher and repeated what the nurse said and how she would have an ultrasound at four. Christopher didn't like these do-or-die situations either but kept his fear at bay, not wanting Tina to stress any more than she was.

"Please pray that our little bean is okay," Tina asked.

"I will," Christopher said as he wiped away the tears.

Jorge's addiction to gambling grew hungrier as the days passed. It wanted more from him, asking money from clients. This used to be taboo for him, but now it was second natured.

He would first listen to their stories, being supportive as he could, waiting patiently to be asked how he was doing, and then he would make his move. Jorge would say, "Oh, I'm afraid not so good," setting the tone for clients to feel sorry for him.

Then he would take the opportunity to say that he was about to lose his house if he didn't catch up with his mortgage payments. "How could that be?" They'd ask, surprised, not expecting him to have money problems. He seemed so normal, so level-headed.

"Well, I refinanced my home last year to pay for Tina's college, not thinking the rate would change to as high as it is now. My payments are doubled now, and I can't afford the mortgage anymore. I just feel like a failure," Jorge always said, to seek enablement. He lied, as Tina had a college fund from birth, started by Eva.

Clients rushed to his aid, helping their dearest hairdresser, who had been a friend for years, giving him hundreds and thousands of dollars. They never knew he gambled it away, as he told himself that he was using the money to win the mortgage amount back. However, he never did.

Eventually he conned everyone, and when clients came back for a haircut, he told them that he could refinance his mortgage and save his house, thanks to them.

Jorge mentioned his mortgage problem to a track friend, who said he should see Mr. Baldwin. He was a regular at the track too. He decided to speak to him now.

"Hey, how is it going?" Jorge asked.

"Hey, Jorge, I heard you missed the big one yesterday," Mr. Baldwin said.

"Yeah, I know. I was so close to winning," Jorge said.

"I was too."

"Yeah, the best thing is to come back and try again. The big one is bound to happen. I have a feeling that today is my lucky day," Jorge said, with despairing eyes.

He noticed how sharply Mr. Baldwin was dressed, wearing a navy suit. He reminded him of Tony.

"I hope you do. It would be nice if at least one of us won. I have been having a mean losing streak. I have to beat it, or I'm going to be in trouble with the wife," Mr. Baldwin said.

"I know what you mean, minus the wife part. I hear you're a lawyer. I didn't know that," Jorge said.

"Shhh, not so loud, or I'll have everyone asking for free advice," Mr. Baldwin said softly.

"No kidding, I can't believe I didn't know, but now that I do, I can see you being a lawyer. You have a smartness about you," Jorge said, taking a deep breath before continuing, "Tim told me I should talk to you".

Mr. Baldwin smiled, not wanting to mix business with pleasure.

"I'm behind on my mortgage payments," Jorge said.

"Isn't everyone here?" He chuckled. Mr. Baldwin was also having difficulty paying his mortgage, but the difference was that he still made them with the late fees.

"I need advice. I don't want to be kicked out of my home."

"I see. Well, I know how to play the mortgage game if that's what you want to know, but it will cost you," Mr. Baldwin said with a grin.

"How much will it cost? "Jorge asked.

"Well, as long as you don't blow my cover, I'll charge you half my usual rate," Mr. Baldwin asked.

"So, will you help?"

"When you receive the foreclosure papers, come and see me, and we'll talk."

"Okay, man, I appreciate it. You know your secret's safe with me. How much time would you say I can live in the house until I have to leave?" Jorge asked.

"I'd say if you are two months behind, like you said, you'd have another month before hearing from the lender. The banks are backed up and are trying to work with their borrowers to avoid foreclosing."

"Good, good…that's good news." Jorge was happy to hear this and thought he could still win the mortgage amount back before foreclosure.

"However, if we play our cards right, this could drag up to a year, and you wouldn't have to pay a cent," Mr. Baldwin said.

"No kidding," Jorge said.

Jorge was now over the moon. He had more time to win the mortgage amount.

No worries, you got this.

"Of course, but you'll have to keep up with your payments to me, or I'll stop representing you. You know I can't work for free."

Jorge now didn't have to worry about not having a place to live. The knowledge he just learned was in his favor. All he had to worry about was paying the electric and water bills.

"Here's my business card. Call me when you get those papers."

"I will, but I'm sure we'll see each other before then."

Mr. Baldwin smiled and walked away.

Jorge won a hundred dollars, but he still needed another hundred by tomorrow to repay Tina. He decided to try his luck again as he walked to Trudy's wage window.

"Hey, Boss, are you feeling lucky tonight?"

"I do. I feel this race is going to be the one," Jorge said.

Trudy smiled, hearing this familiar delusional phrase.

"I'd like to box 2, 4, 6, and 8," Jorge said.

"Are those your lucky dogs? The ones who won for you?" Trudy asked.

"You know I didn't even look to see who the dogs were this time. This time, I'm going with numbers."

Trudy forced a smile, noticing a different Jorge than the one she first met years ago. These days, he looked rougher around the edges, unshaven, and wore the same couple of shirts and black pants every couple of days.

"Really? Is that your new strategy to make it big now?" Trudy chuckled, hoping he was joking.

Jorge felt she was being a little too sassy for his liking. He just couldn't wait until the end of the race when he would march up to her window, give her the winning ticket, and see who had the last laugh.

"Oh, I've been meaning to ask you, why did you send your daughter to cash your ticket? When you could have cashed it yourself," Trudy asked.

Jorge was dumbfounded as he looked at Trudy, not expecting to hear this.

"What are you talking about?" Jorge asked.

"Your daughter was here not too long ago. She cashed the jackpot ticket and didn't even give me a tip."

"I couldn't have known about this, or I would have told her to give you something."

"Well, here is your ticket."

Trudy didn't believe Jorge as she knew damn well that he brought the ticket from her. She hated to be lied to.

Jorge walked away, and this time Trudy kept quiet and didn't wish him "good luck," nor would she anymore.

CHAPTER 28

The Addiction Laughs

Tina arrived at the doctor's office at three forty-five.
After speaking with Christopher, she went back to work to
see if there was any blood on the makeshift pad. It was upsetting to
see that there was, though it couldn't be more than a teaspoon. Tina
couldn't shake the awful feeling that she was miscarrying.

"Tina Gabor," the nurse called as she waited at the door, separating
the waiting room and the exam rooms.

The office was mostly of pregnant women in different stages of their
pregnancies. Some hardly had a noticeable baby bump, while others had
ones that were. And then some looked like they were close to delivering.
Tina hoped she would be one of those lucky ladies in the next five months.
Tina was also excited to wear maternity clothes if the time came.

She calmly got up, leaving behind the magazine she really wasn't
reading and followed the nurse into the examination room. Tina
hoped the nurse wouldn't take her blood pressure, as she knew it
would be too high and only cause more alarm and panic. Maybe even
rushing her to the hospital.

"So, you've had some bleeding?" the nurse asked.

"Yes, but now it seems to have stopped."

"Well, let's take a look and see what's happening."

The nurse told Tina to lie back on the exam table and raise her
shirt. Tina did as she was told, and she knew in a few short moments
she would know if the baby was alright.

"Well, you are measuring at twelve weeks, and according to your
chart, that's where you should be."

"That's good, right? Isn't it?" Tina said, trying to keep calm.

"Yes, it is, but let's see if we have a heartbeat," the nurse said.

Tina felt like she was on trial. Seconds away from knowing if the baby was viable. There was no in-between. Tina looked at the computer screen and saw her "little bean," as she called the baby the moment, she saw the two pink lines on the pregnancy test.

The technician smiled and turned the volume up. The little bean was thumping away. Its heartbeat was strong and steady.

"Your baby is just fine. I don't see a medical reason why you were bleeding, but Dr. Sanchez would like to run some blood tests to check your progesterone levels, which could be the reason for the spotting."

Tina was elated, feeling now more than ever that she was meant to have this little bean and to be a mom.

She called Christopher, who picked up on the first ring.

"Honey, the baby is all right. Thank God!" Tina said.

"Aww…that's the best news. See, things don't always have to end badly," Christopher said.

"Yes, you're right. I seriously need to keep that in mind and not always think the worst. I also saw the baby as the nurse was doing the ultrasound. She has one strong heartbeat."

"Oh, so you know the baby is a girl?" Christopher asked.

"No, no, I don't. Sorry, not sure why I said girl because it is still too early to tell," Tina said.

"But if you feel the baby is a girl, maybe she is."

Tina smiled, having the typical girl symptoms like severe morning sickness and craving sweets.

"I'm so relieved our little bean is well. I just want to go home and relax. Today was a stressful day," Tina said.

Tina called her mother and told her what happened. Eva was horrified.

"Why didn't you call me earlier? I would have gone with you," Eva asked.

"I know, but I just felt if anything was wrong with the baby, I wanted to be alone. Christopher wasn't even there with me. You know how I am. I like to face problems alone."

Eva knew this to be true ever since Tina was a child. She wondered if it had anything to do with hearing her fights with Jorge.

"Did you tell your father yet?" Eva asked.

"No."

"I think you should, so he knows how hard pregnancy is. He should be coming around more, helping you, and not gambling like he's been doing. He is going to have a grandchild soon, for God's sake."

"I'll call him later. I don't think he would know how to handle it, and I don't want to relive it all over again. I also don't want to jinx myself from it happening again. I actually want to forget about it," Tina said.

"All right, but I still think he should know; he's your father. Just tell him the short version."

"Okay, I will. I just need rest," Tina said.

"If you need anything, please call. I'll come right over," Eva said.

"Thank you. I'll call you later."

"Okay, love you."

"Love you too, Mom. Please don't worry about me because I worry when you worry."

"Well, I'll try, but you're my little girl. You've had enough stress to last the end of your pregnancy."

"Bye, Mom."

Tina called the salon, but her father wasn't there. It was 4:45 pm, near closing time. She was tempted to ask Donna when his last client was, but she didn't want her to think she was checking up on her father. Part of her didn't want to know either, especially if he left early.

She wondered if he would have the two hundred dollars by tomorrow so she could mail in the cable and water bills without being late. Tina went to bed early, thankful that she still had her little bean safe in her belly, and only wished she could shake off the feeling that her father was gambling more than he was letting on.

"Hi, girl. Last night, your mother called."

Tina's heart sank as she feared what her mother told him. She didn't need any unnecessary stress, especially with her parents.

"She told me what happened. I'm sorry. How are you feeling?"

"Good."

"At first, I thought your mother was calling about the money I borrowed. I didn't think you would tell her, but still."

Tina wondered when her mother got in touch with Jorge, as she had tried a few times without any luck.

"I have the money I owe you."

"Great, I'm home today resting. Come by anytime."

"Good. How about now?"

Thirty minutes later, Jorge was at Tina's house with the money. When Tina asked if he wanted anything to drink or eat, he jumped at the chance to have breakfast. As she watched him eat, she couldn't believe how fast he was consuming food. Looking like he hadn't eaten for a while, hardly speaking. He quickly left after his last bite, saying he needed to go to work.

Later that afternoon, Jorge received the foreclosure papers, which said that the bank wanted the mortgage to be paid in full, along with other costs and fees. He had thirty days, or the bank would take possession of the house and auction it off.

He immediately called Mr. Baldwin, but the office was closed. Though it was just after five, Jorge felt he would still be at the law office. Jorge got in his car and drove to the track, believing he had a better chance of catching up with him there than any other place.

As he expected, Mr. Baldwin was there. He was with a client and couldn't speak with Jorge for too long. But he said that he would contact the bank on his behalf and let him know the next steps.

"Jorge, you need to start saving your winnings for my service, which includes court appearances. I don't work for free."

"How much will it cost?"

"I need five hundred to start."

Jorge wasn't sure he could do that, but he said he would. Though he knew the cost was probably reasonable, he had other loans to pay first. He was actually hoping Mr. Baldwin wouldn't charge him anything or at least work a payment plan with him, but he said he was already doing him a favor by slashing his normal hourly rate.

"Okay, just forward me any other mail you get from the bank."

"Okay, thank you."

Jorge started to weigh other options. He felt there had to be a better one that wouldn't cut into his funds.

In the next six months, Tina was getting ready for the baby. Tina's intuition was right, as an ultrasound confirmed that she and Christopher were going to have a girl.

Little was left to do at the house, as Tina was at the end of the pregnancy. They had it all ready for the new chapter in their lives. Kate's nursery was finally done, awaiting her arrival.

Jorge lost his house and most of his clients, losing the respect of many. However, he still had Tina. He already convinced her to let him move into the villa until he could find another place to live, and that was just the beginning of Tina's struggle.

Another perk of being pregnant was that Mr. Jackson lost interest in Tina and focused his attention on a new intern in the office.

"So, you are about to be a mother?" Mr. Jackson asked.

"Yes, I have about three months left before the baby comes," Tina said. Her baby bump was clearly noticeable now.

"Ah, I hear you're having a girl. Is that true?"

"Yes, I am. Don't you have a daughter as well?"

"Yes, she can be a little pain in the you know where sometimes, but she's a lot like me. And she's actually about to graduate from college next semester. I still remember when she was just born."

Mr. Jackson thought about his daughter Jill, who wanted to follow in his footsteps and be a journalist, as he once was when he first started working for a newspaper. Now he was the managing editor.

"She's a good writer like you. Her name is Jill. She's planning to work here as well. Maybe you two can be friends if you come back."

"I will be coming back if that is what you're asking, and I look forward to working with Jill too," Tina said with a smile.

"Good. I'd hate to see you leave, especially when I see a great future for you."

CHAPTER 29

Tina Under Pressure

Tina was awoken by Kate's cries from across the house. She got up half asleep, pushing through the tiredness, reaching over for her glasses on the nightstand, but they weren't there.

She rushed across the dark, cold living room to Kate's room as her cries became louder and louder. *Where can my glasses be?* She wondered.

"Waaaaahhhhh!"

"Oh, Kate, Mommy is here. No worries, little one. Food is on its way."

Tina went to the kitchen, holding Kate close to her, and warmed up a bottle of formula.

Tina settled into the lush, oversized, blue rocking chair Eva bought. She took the plastic top off the warm bottle and nestled Kate securely within her left arm against her chest. Tina then took a fresh burp cloth from the right armrest, always using a fresh one after each feeding, and placed it under Kate's chin, to prevent formula from streaming down Kate's neck.

"In a few moments, you will be full and happy again."

Kate spit out the pacifier, as she knew the routine well, her tiny lips working hard for a little formula at a time, but she never complained. Tina was taken at how determined her little girl was, and this comforted her, feeling Kate would be strong-willed.

Tina thought of the fight she had with Jorge yesterday afternoon. She still couldn't shake the disgusted feeling, still tormenting her sanity, wondering if he would follow through with his threat.

What he wanted Tina to do felt wrong, yet he didn't think so. Jorge actually made her feel that if she didn't go through with it, she wasn't a good daughter and was stealing from him.

Fear, guilt, and hopelessness possessed her as they never did before. She felt caught between a rock and a hard place.

Jorge wanted her to take out a home equity line of credit from her villa. "No," she had told him, but he told her it was his right because Eva had no right to give her the villa in the first place, saying it was communal property.

"I will take her to court if you don't."

When she kept quiet, he confessed that he needed the money to pay off his new car. If not, the bank would repossess it because he couldn't afford the payments, and if it got repossessed, he wouldn't be able to get to work.

Still Tina kept quiet, feeling like he was asking the impossible.

"What is it going to be?" Jorge said in an adversarial way.

"Why is it that you can't manage your money?" Tina asked.

"Bad luck," Jorge explained.

Tina found this hard to believe, as she didn't think bad luck was responsible for every hardship Jorge had.

"What about the house? You lost our home," Tina said, on the verge of tears. Feeling emotional, knowing so much was already lost because of Jorge's so-called bad luck. Why wasn't he seeing that his actions were the cause of the bad luck he was complaining about?

Jorge didn't answer. Instead, he became defensive, changing the subject.

"I've already spoken with a lawyer. He said I have a good case against your mother, and he has the papers ready to be filed."

Tina took a deep breath as she felt the pressure of his words. She saw this was getting ugly and saw no way out than to give him hope.

"Well, I'll have to see, but I'm not saying yes either," Tina said.

"Okay, girl, thanks. I would do the same for you. I'm not asking to keep the money. I'm just asking to borrow it, and I plan to pay it back in a year anyway. I'm working more these days, more clients are referring clients, and I should be able to pay this loan sooner."

Jorge was saying everything he could think of for Tina to say yes.

"And you don't even have to tell your mother because it will be like I never took it. She doesn't even need to know, and I won't take her to court," Jorge said.

Tina knew then that her father wasn't as nice as she thought.

Jorge wrapped up his visit with a hug. Tina cried as Jorge embraced her, still believing taking a home equity loan was wrong, but she felt that she still had to at least consider it. After all, he was her father, and she didn't want to involve her mother in a court case either.

Tina cried as she held Kate, reliving yesterday's trauma with her father, one she wished never happened. She got up exhausted from the rocking chair holding Kate against her chest, who was still asleep. Tina carefully placed Kate in the crib, turned on the baby camera as she left, and slept a few hours, hoping a little sleep would give her a fresh perspective of what she should do.

However, Jorge went to Bank of America a few hours later, who advertised the lowest home equity interest rates. He wanted to talk to a loan officer about the timeframe of the loan.

"How long does it take to get the money?" Jorge asked.

"Two weeks, with good credit," Jane said.

Jorge's eyes beamed, "Really, that's good news."

Jane said, "A home equity line of credit isn't like a traditional loan with all the charges and inspections. The person already owns the house, so those costs are spared. If your daughter has good credit and a job, she should qualify. As the home is at stake."

Jorge couldn't contain his excitement.

"My daughter will be happy to hear this. Just between us, she has high credit card debt, and this will take care of them in a mortgage she can manage. Otherwise, she will spend the next ten years living hand to mouth. Isn't that terrible? I'm just helping her out with the information since she's a bit embarrassed about her situation."

"I know. I have a son who likes to spend a little too much, too. I guess it's the generation of wanting it now and not saving for it," Jane said.

"I guess so. It's not like when we were growing up. It was save, save, save until you could afford it," Jorge said. This was how he and Eva bought their first car. They saved for years before buying a used Ford.

"Oh, but your daughter must know this rate is not fixed. It can go up each month. This may not be what she is looking for. Maybe she should refinance at a fixed rate which would take thirty days to finalize."

"No, she wants a home equity loan. The rate isn't a problem because she's planning to pay it off this year."

"Okay, here is my card. Why don't you give it to her? I'll wait for her call."

"I will, thanks, but I think it would be better if I give you her phone number because my daughter easily loses things being a new mom now. And I wouldn't want you to lose the business."

"Why, thank you, Jorge."

Jorge sat back down and wrote Tina's phone number and address just in case Jane wanted to do a scratch title search.

"Her name is Tina Gabor. Call her tomorrow morning. This is when she has a little extra time."

Jorge shook Jane's hand goodbye.

"Bye, Mr. Gabor."

Jorge was on his way to Tina's house.

Tina heard the bell ring. She hurried to the door as Kate just fell asleep for a morning nap. The last thing she wanted was for her to wake up after she rocked her to sleep for thirty minutes.

Looking through the peephole, she saw her father smiling like he didn't have a care in the world. She opened the door, noticing that he was carrying a red-and-blue folder.

"Hi, girl. I stopped by Bank of America this morning and got this for you," Jorge said.

He handed her a Bank of America folder.

She took it, though she wasn't interested. It was obvious that Jorge was pushing real hard for this home equity loan.

"Girl, the rates are really low now. I think about 3%. Way lower than my car payment of 12%."

He was acting like the money was free.

"However, the rates are due to go up next month. So you have to act fast, and I'm behind with my car payments. This would make everything alright again. I'll then start paying the loan," Jorge said.

"Okay, I'll look over it when I'm not so tired. I haven't slept a full night for months. And I'm having a hard time keeping my eyes open," Tina said, hoping Jorge took the hint that she didn't want to be pushed to do anything right now.

"Does okay mean that you'll do it?" Jorge asked.

"No, I didn't say okay to the loan yet. Didn't you hear what I just said?"

Jorge's misdemeanor changed as he looked like he had been had.

"I can't think straight right now. I just need sleep, Dad. Please let this loan fascination go," Tina said.

"When will you know then?"

"I don't know. Maybe a few weeks or so. Please respect that."

Don't accept that kind of an answer.

"Tina, you are playing with my life. I stopped paying for the car, and I can't afford to get it taken away. I have been more than nice. Don't you think so? Do you want me to involve your mom?"

"I am tired . . . I'll let you know soon," Tina said.

Push harder!

"How soon is soon?" Jorge asked.

"A couple of days."

"So, two, right?

A day later, she still felt sick to her stomach. Her mind was racing as she thought of what she should do. This was serious; placing a bank loan on the property wasn't like helping her father with a past due electrical, or water bill. It was so much more, the villa could be lost. Yet, Jorge was pressing for it like it was no big deal and that it was owed to him.

Tina also feared that he would take Eva to court and she started to doubt if her mother had the right to give her the villa in the first place. And she didn't want to ask her mom either because then Tina would have to tell her about Jorge wanting to take money out. She was wedged between a rock and a hard place as she still heard a voice say, *"Don't do it."* If she did go through with the loan, she was jeopardizing the villa, a gift from her mother. Though it was deeded to her, she still felt it wasn't hers to take money from for Jorge.

"I will pay it back. Didn't I say that? "Jorge aggressively said. "There is nothing to worry about."

The next morning, Jane called, ready to give Tina the sales pitch. "Hi, is this Mrs. Gabor?"

"Yes, this is Tina."

"Good morning. This is Jane from Bank of America."

Tina's heart dropped as she couldn't believe how her father would go to such great lengths for her to go through with the loan. Her instinct was to hang up, yet she knew the calls wouldn't stop if she did.

"Mrs. Gabor, are you there? Can you hear me?"

"Yes, I am. I just have to talk low, so I don't wake up my newborn daughter."

"Oh, that's right, your father did mention you're a new mom. Congratulations."

"Yes, I am, and thank you."

"Your father stopped by our branch saying you were interested in a home equity line of credit."

Tina's heart dropped hearing the word home equity.

"I'm just thinking about it. I still haven't looked at the folder you gave my father yesterday. It's on my list, though."

"Well, I took the liberty to look at the title of your property, and from what I can see, there is nothing preventing you from getting the loan in that regard. There are no other liens on the property either."

Tina kept quiet as she started to tear up, feeling like she had no choice in the matter anymore. It seemed like her father was setting her up. Kate started to cry in the background, like she was in tune with Tina's distress.

"I hear your little girl," Jane said.

"Yes, I think the neighbors do, too," Tina said, trying to remain pleasant to Jane.

"Alright then, I'll call later. It was nice talking with you. If you give me your social security number, I can do a quick credit check."

"Sorry, I gotta go..."

"Oh wait, actually, I already have your social security number. Your father wrote it down yesterday when he gave me your phone number. I just need your permission to do a credit check. Do I have it?" Jane asked.

"Sure."

Tina felt defeated now and knew all she could do at the moment was be the mommy Kate needed and deserved and not worry about her father and the loan. She just couldn't help but think that his gambling was the reason for everything wrong in his life.

Jorge came to the house a few hours later while Christopher was still at work.

"Isn't Jane nice? She said everything is ready for you to sign. Remember, I'm just borrowing the money...I'll pay it back in a few months."

"Ok, I'll do it, but under a few conditions, and I'm serious about them."

Jorge smiled like he just conquered the world. He couldn't be any happier; his begging, whining, and bullying got him what he wanted.

"You have to promise you will pay the loan on time each month."

"I swear to God."

"I mean it, Dad because you are not just playing with my financial wellbeing but my family's."

"I swear to God, girl. I will send out the money on the first of every month. You don't need to worry about anything."

Jorge looked at Tina's worrisome eyes. He was only saying what she wanted to hear because Jorge didn't know how to keep a promise. However, he was good at making promises all day long if he had to.

If he had to pay the monthly payment now, he couldn't.

Two weeks later, Tina signed the home equity line of credit.

"So, girl, I heard you signed the papers today."

"Yes, I did."

The ink was hardly dried on the loan papers, yet Jorge already plotted how he would double the fifty thousand at the track.

"I can still cancel the loan. Dad, I just don't feel right about this. You should be able to pay for your car, or you shouldn't have gotten it."

Calm down, Jorge, take it easy. Don't blow it now. Sympathize with your daughter.

"I understand your fears. There is nothing to worry about. I already have it."

"Dad, let's be real. You never pay anything on time. You have a hard time paying the phone bill. I don't want to lose the villa because the loan payment is too much, like the car payment you can't afford."

"You won't lose the villa… and remember the car loan is high because of the interest rate. Otherwise, I could handle it." Jorge was fuming inside.

Calm down. Just think about what you can do with that check. Breathe in and breathe out.

"How are you going to handle the payments and the expenses at the villa? You still haven't paid the hundred you owe from last month."

"Oh, I forgot, but here I have it." Jorge reached into his pocket and proudly gave Tina the money. "Come here, girl." He reached for her hand and pulled her into an embrace.

Tina started to cry like a little girl, hoping her father would see her distress and tell her to cancel the loan and he'd find another way to fix his financial problems, but he didn't.

Jorge deposited the fifty-thousand-dollar check in his checking account the next morning. Three months later, as Tina was driving back from Kate's nine-month wellness check, she received a call from Bank of America that almost caused her to crash.

"Hi, is Tina Gabor available?"

"Yes, this is Tina."

"I'm calling because we haven't received last month's home equity payment."

"What? That can't be. There must be a mistake."

"Are you saying you sent the payment?"

"No, actually, my father is the one who does."

"Well, we haven't received a payment since late January."

"No, that can't be right. It is mid-March now. There must be a mistake with your computer system. Can you call my father? His number is—"

"No, that won't be necessary, as the loan is in your name, not his."

Tina realized the sickening truth to this. The loan was in her name. Suddenly, she needed to stop the car as she felt faint and in utter disgust for Jorge.

Her chest felt tight, her heart racing as it wanted out. Tina took long, deep breaths, inhaling and exhaling to keep from having a panic attack. Then Kate started to cry. Tina couldn't even turn around to comfort Kate because the pain in her chest wouldn't let her move.

Tina smiled as she looked in the rearview mirror, hoping Kate was looking at it too.

"It is okay, honey. Mommy is okay."

Kate still cried as she saw the fear in her mother's eyes.

"What have I done, Kate? What have I done? I'm so sorry," Tina said, as if Kate knew what was happening.

In all her life, Tina never could imagine that her father would go back on his word to his own daughter and not have a care that she was going down a dark hole with his lies. She called Jorge at work once she got settled, but he wasn't there.

"Do you know when he will be back?" Tina asked Donna.

"He left before lunch, and he's not expected back."

"Oh," this surprised Tina, as Thursdays were always his busiest workdays. How was it that he was not busy? *Another bad sign,* she thought.

Donna noticed the disappointment in Tina's voice that she tried to cover for Jorge just to make Tina feel better.

"You know your father. He makes house calls, too, since many of his clients are older now. I'm not supposed to tell anyone this. It isn't exactly allowed when working in the salon. Why don't you call him on his cell phone?" Donna said.

Tina wished this was the case, but she felt let down, believing his only house call was at the track. Why should she call him on his cell phone when he should be at work?

"Is there anything I can do?" Donna asked.

"Oh, no, but thank you, I'll catch up with him later," Tina said.

Uncontrollable tears rushed down her cheeks, thinking what a fool she was ever to believe a word Jorge said. She was starting to hate him as Jorge crossed the line affecting her family's well-being.

A small part of her hoped there was a legitimate reason why the bank payments were late, then this reality wouldn't be, and she could forget about what was really happening. Something she was really good at, something that wouldn't have to affect her family. Tina would know, but they wouldn't have to, and she was fine with the consequence.

She had swept the secrets of Jorge under the carpet so many times that Tina believed she could continue to do so for the sake of keeping peace, yet she would learn it was what was preventing Jorge from hitting rock bottom.

Hearing Tina's distressed voice brought back unpleasant memories for Donna, remembering back to when Eva used to call looking for Jorge years ago. It was unsettling that Tina was doing the same thing, and there was nothing she could do or say to help her.

Jorge was now running away from his daughter.

CHAPTER 30

Tina in a Panic

Tina hung up the phone, furious and terrified. Feeling the safe world, she was building crumbling apart.

"This just can't be!" She said as she shook her head in despair, wanting to turn back time, never signing the home equity papers.

A river of inconsolable tears streamed down her cheeks. Her eyes started to burn like they were mixed with Clorox. She felt trapped in a situation she could have prevented if she hadn't listened to Jorge.

Tina quickly turned the radio on, switching the channels until she found a classical station playing Chopin. Next, she closed her burning eyes seeking refuge, taking deep, long breaths, counting to ten until exhaling.

"Please, let this not be happening."

If Kate weren't in the car, she would have driven to the Palm Springs Kennel to find Jorge and confront him about the missed payments.

"Why did I ever believe you, Dad?" she asked, as if he were in the car sitting next to her, feeling the ultimate betrayal.

How irresponsible, she thought, visualizing him placing bet after bet at the wage window like an alcoholic, drinking another drink. It sickened her to think he was one of the desperate gamblers she saw at the track when she cashed his ticket. Tina wondered now if maybe he had stolen it. Tina couldn't believe how blind sighted she was to the signs that were all around her. When did this denial of not seeing the truth take such a hard hold of her senses?

Tina decided to pull in the driveway to look around the villa to see if anything was out of the ordinary.

Tina got emotional again as she thought of the home equity loan now on it. She opened the mailbox to see if there was any mail for her or Christopher. When she opened the mailbox, she was surprised to see how full it was. It was like it hadn't been touched for weeks.

So far, all of it was for Jorge. She noticed a letter from a collection agency, which was unsettling because she thought he was paying his bills. There was also an overdue electrical and water bill. Then she saw a letter for a person called Tim Soto, which she found strange, as no one had ever lived in the villa with that name. As she continued to look through the mail, she saw Tim Soto's name again on a letter from the Department of Motor and Vehicle.

"Who is this person?" She wondered.

Then she saw another letter addressed to Tim Soto from the District Attorney Office. He must have had a roommate he didn't tell her about. From the looks of it, this person was establishing the villa as his residence.

Tina left, leaving the mail at the foot of the front door. Feeling her heart race again, she decided to wait until tomorrow to do anything, for there was so much her heart could take. It was like a tornado just hit out of nowhere, and only she could clean up Jorge's messes, or all would be lost.

Five hours later, Eva went to Tina's house for dinner.

"Hi, honey, I wanted to come by and bring you a home-cooked meal for my little girl. You must be tired of take-out by now. I know I would."

Tina couldn't break a smile because she felt guilty about the home equity line of credit and feared Eva would find out.

"What's wrong? You look drained. Are you okay?" Eva asked.

Tina just shook her head, trying to keep the tears in.

"Aww...my baby, come over here. What's wrong? You can tell me," Eva said, concerned about how thin Tina looked.

"No, I'm fine. I'm just tired," Tina said.

Eva walked over to Tina, feeling her daughter was hiding something, and decided to do a little investigating on the low.

"I think you should see the doctor again to check your hormone levels. I'm sure something can be done to regulate them."

"I just had a checkup last month, and my blood results were normal. I'm just tired."

"Come here, honey, just know this will pass as difficult things do. It's going to be okay. I promise. Soon you will be sleeping through the night again," Eva said, thinking of everything she could say for Tina to feel better.

Tina went over to her mother, wishing she could tell her the truth. How she wanted to turn back and rip up those loan papers, but sadly, she knew that wasn't even possible, and neither could her mother. There was no point in including Eva in the mess she created by signing the loan papers. She would have to somehow figure it out on her own.

"So, when is your father going to move out of the villa? I'm a little surprised that you are letting him stay there for free for this long." Eva asked.

"He is paying for water and electricity, and he said he's putting money away for the property taxes and insurance when they come due."

"Really, come on, that's nothing. You should be charging him rent, too," Eva said.

"I don't know."

"Forget it. The last thing I want is for you to get upset, just try to get more rest. So where is my little granddaughter?"

"She is still sleeping."

"Oh, why don't you do the same? Don't worry about the house. No one is expecting you to be a superwoman."

Eva kissed Tina goodbye and left for home.

The next morning, Tina called Jorge, not wanting to miss him later in the day.

He was still at the shop, and her heart raced as she waited for him to answer.

"Hi, girl. I just got off the phone with your mother. She tells me she worries about you because you're not sleeping."

"Oh listen, I got a very upsetting phone call yesterday from the bank," Tina said, not wasting any time.

Jorge stayed quiet.

"Dad, why haven't you paid last month or this month's home equity payment?" Tina asked.

Jorge stayed quiet like he didn't hear the question.

"You promised that you would always pay on time. It's not just one month late, but two! How could you let this happen? I trusted you."

Tina shook uncontrollably, feeling her temperature rise as she waited to hear Jorge's response.

Tina could hear her father excuse himself from his client, hearing footsteps as he went outside to speak freely.

"Listen, girl, whoever is calling you is not from Bank of America. It's a fraud. I'm telling you, the next time they call, hang up. I have to go. A client is waiting for me," Jorge said, hanging up before Tina could say a word edgewise.

Tina was now speechless. Tears started to stream down her cheeks.

A few moments later, Kate woke up from a mid-morning nap. This time she wasn't crying. Tina could hear her cooing in her room. She was getting bigger with each day. It broke Tina's heart to think that she wasn't embracing the time with Kate as much as she could because she was too preoccupied dealing with Jorge's lies.

As Tina walked closer to the crib, Kate cried, moving her arms and legs in excitement to be taken out and held. How she loved her mommy. Whenever she would see her, Kate would smile, wanting to be with Tina.

"Ah, Kate, we're going to have a good day. How about going to the pool and having some mommy and daughter time?"

It was like Kate understood; she excitedly clapped her hand. Tina dressed Kate in her new Hello Kitty swimsuit with matching coverup. Tina also took many pictures at the pool, wanting to remember these precious moments.

Around six thirty in the evening, there was a knock at the door. Tina was busy feeding Kate to hear it, but Christopher did. He opened the door to find Jorge holding two big bags of food from Giovanni's Pizzeria, an Italian eatery that just opened in town.

"Grandpa is here with dinner! I hope everyone is hungry," Jorge said. He lifted the bags for Tina to see, expecting her to be all smiles, but she wasn't. All she could muster up was a half-smile, and that was pushing it. Her motivation was not wanting Christopher to think something was wrong between her and Jorge.

However, Jorge noticed her coldness. He walked over and dared to kiss her on the cheek, which almost landed on her lips as she turned around.

"Hi, girl."

"Hi," Tina said, with no feeling.

Don't worry. She will come around.

"Oh, hi Kate, it's Grandpa." He turned his attention to his granddaughter, as he was not getting the response he wanted from Tina.

Christopher walked over to Jorge and took the bags. "Thank you, Jorge. What a nice surprise. Isn't it Tina?"

"There is nothing I wouldn't do for my family, especially my little Kate," Jorge said.

"How nice, and we feel the same about you, right Tina?" Christopher said.

See, you can always get to Tina.

"Thank you, I appreciate it," Jorge said.

Jorge ignored Tina and started to play peekaboo with Kate. She couldn't stop smiling as he covered and uncovered his face.

Tina finally broke a smile, as it was funny seeing Jorge doing everything, he could to make Kate laugh. It reminded her of when she was a little girl, and he'd do the same thing to her. It was a nice change of pace to actually see Jorge be the grandfather she wanted him to be with Kate.

Jorge decided to try and talk to Tina again, "She has gotten so big." "Yes, she has," Tina said, as she finally broke a full smile.

See, you did it again. My man.

While Christopher was setting the dining room table, Jorge sat on the couch next to Tina. She hoped she could now speak to him about the call from Bank of America, with Christopher not being so close to hear. Yet, when she turns to start the conversation, he's asleep, drained by the day's unsuccessful events.

Not only was he called on the loan not being paid by Tina. He rushed to the track with the pressures of having to win, yet losing everything, even with the best intentions, and being in a worse financial situation than he was in the morning. Tina stared at him, breathing hard like he was knocked out by exhaustion or medication, and she decided there was no use in trying to talk to him now.

"Dinner is now served," Christopher said with a laugh, trying to lighten the mood as he walked in the living room.

Christopher noticed Jorge asleep on the couch, "Should we wake him up?"

"No, just let him be."

But Kate had other plans as she started to make loud sounds, attempting to speak, eventually pulling Jorge from a deep sleep. Jorge started to move and soon was up.

"Sorry, I didn't realize I drifted off, but now I'm up. I am hungry."

"Well, let's all go and eat," Tina said.

Jorge got up and followed Tina. Unknown to Eva, this was one of the last evenings she would enjoy family time with Jorge as they laughed, told funny stories, and watched tv.

Jorge only stayed for an hour.

Tina walked him to the door as she carried Kate, who was smitten with Jorge.

"Oh girl, I went by the bank today and took care of everything," he said.

Tina stood there speechless, but before she could ask what he meant, Christopher was behind her, and she didn't want to continue the conversation.

"Okay, I'll talk to you later," Tina said.

"Girl, could you come by car?" Jorge asked.

"Sure," Tina handed Kate to Christopher.

As she walked behind her father, she wondered what he was going to say.

"I don't want you to worry. I paid last month's payment."

"So, you lied to me. Bank of America really did call, after all." Tina said, feeling angry.

"Don't worry. I got it covered."

If anything, Jorge's last words made her worry even more, and she knew he wasn't being honest.

"I didn't expect Jorge to come by tonight with dinner. That was nice of him," Christopher said as Tina walked back in. Kate leaned forward, so Tina could take her back.

"Yes, I suppose," Tina said.

"Why are you so glum lately?"

"Nothing. I'm just tired."

Later that evening, as Tina was looking under the bathroom vanity for soap, she saw a pregnancy test and decided to take it. Her breasts were unusually sore, but she didn't really think she was pregnant. Yet, she was wrong.

"Guess what?"

"You're pregnant!"

"Yes."

CHAPTER 31

Bank Calls Again

Two months later, the bank calls again.
When Tina saw the one eight hundred number on the caller ID, her heart dropped. She took a deep breath before answering the call to prepare for the worst.

"Hello?"

"Hi, is this Ms. Gabor?"

"Yes." Tina was now in panic mode, still hoping the lady was calling on behalf of the police benevolence, looking for donations instead.

"Good afternoon. This is Josie from Bank of America."

"Hi." Suddenly Tina's stomach took a nosedive, and her heart started racing. Her t-shirt could be seen going back and forth with each stressed beat.

"Our records show that we called you two months ago about not receiving February and March's payments," Josie said.

"Yes, I remember, but the payments were paid, either that same day or the very next," Tina said, repeating what Jorge had told her.

"I see that, but that's not what I'm calling about. We actually haven't received April or May payments, and the bank is concerned. There seems to be a pattern here."

Tina closed her eyes in disappointment, leaning against the kitchen wall. Here we go again, she thinks.

"Oh, I thought they were sent."

Tina's voice tapered off. She slid down to the floor, hating her father.

"Ms. Gabor, if you are suffering financially. The bank should know."

Tina couldn't even find the words to say, nor would any words come from her. The shock kept her quiet and locked in fear of what was about to come.

"If you are, we can help. Just let us know. You are not the only one," Josie said, trying to reach Tina.

"No, I'm just speechless that my father did this to me again. I'm sure you can see from the last notes that I said that my father is the one who is supposed to pay the monthly payments. The bill gets sent to him."

Tina hoped Josie would confirm this, but she just kept quiet.

"I'll just call him and see what he did with the payments. Maybe he sent them to the wrong address. Can I call you back?" Tina asked.

"Ah, why don't you just pay in the meantime and we can work something out if the payments somehow got lost? I see you just turned thirty, so you don't want to tarnish your good credit now. Paying now would stop you from any further credit damage," Josie said.

"I'm not sure if I can."

"Well, unfortunately, because of the late payments, the bank has frozen the account from further usage," Josie said.

"What does that mean?"

"It means you cannot use any of what is left of the home equity line of credit, and there isn't a chance that you'll ever be allowed to ask for more credit."

Tina didn't think that was bad; there was now thirty grand her father couldn't use, believing he only used twenty grand for his car. She thought this might be a good thing until she heard the balance and was shocked again.

"How much is left?"

"Four hundred dollars."

This didn't seem right to Tina. "So, what would the loan balance be if I were to pay it back today?"

"Forty-nine thousand and six hundred dollars."

"What? That is basically the entire fifty thousand dollars. This is awful. How could he do this?" Tina said.

She could only imagine what he did with the rest of the thirty grand. It was gambled at the Palm Springs Kennel Club.

"Ms. Gabor, I can take the payment over the phone and waive the late fees this one time. But the payments need to be made today. Otherwise, the bank may demand the full loan amount per your loan papers."

"Can I just pay for one month?" Tina said, fearing the repercussions.

"You can, but then we would have to report the late payment to the credit bureau, and I wouldn't be able to waive the late fees."

"Can I use a credit card?"

"Yes, you can. I'm ready when you are."

Tina didn't want her credit ruined, but she didn't want to start racking up her credit card either. Tina didn't know what she would do about Jorge's debts, but she knew this time she wasn't going to pretend that any of this was alright and that his gambling wasn't the reason behind this mess.

"Okay, let me get my purse."

She would use a credit card that was only in her name. Tina paid the two-month payments, feeling like a fool paying for a loan she didn't use.

After getting off the phone with Josie, she went to the bathroom and showered. Tina hoped the water would calm her rage and anger. Now she had to be careful not to get too worked up because she was pregnant.

Luckily, Christopher had taken Kate to his parents so she could sleep. It was like God had known it would be best if Kate wasn't around. Tina needed this time to cry, regroup, and think of the best way to get out of this nightmare, even if it meant cutting him off. Tina couldn't even call her father because she already knew he would just deny what the bank had said and create the perfect lie. She knew she needed evidence, and the only way she would get this would be to go to the bank, and that was exactly what she did.

When she finally had everything in front of her, she called Jorge ready for battle. She was prepared to give dates and totals if he started disputing what she was saying.

"I got another call from Bank of America. I've never felt so betrayed in my life after you promised me everything would be alright. How is this all right?

"What?" Jorge acted like what Tina was saying was so far-fetched.

"Bank of America called saying you haven't paid the last two months again! What don't you get? Did you really think they wouldn't call and somehow the loan balance would disappear? Tina said.

Jorge held his breath, fearing what more Tina could say.

"Come on, Dad. Are you trying to destroy me and my family?" Tina shouted.

Jorge was fuming, not liking the tone of this conversation, reminding him of the fights he would have with Eva.

Tina doesn't understand.

"I'll pay it when I get my social security check. So, stop nagging me like your mother," Jorge said, hoping that would shut her up.

"What? How dare you! I'm not nagging you! You should have paid the loan each month it was due, as you promised. And your social security check doesn't arrive for another two weeks. And it still wouldn't be enough to pay what you owe," Tina shouted.

"Well, that's the best I can do. Take it or leave it. I don't have any money now," Jorge said.

"What! How could you do this to me?" Tina started to cry as she spoke through her misery. She hated how Jorge had no shame in himself.

Jorge kept silent as if he wasn't even on the line anymore. He was going to let Tina get her frustrations out and hoped she'd calm down to where she had nothing to say anymore.

"Not only could I lose the villa, but my credit rating is dropping daily because of these late payments," Tina said, nowhere near being calm.

"You won't lose the villa. A few months won't do anything. So there is still time. Stop worrying so much."

"Oh, I forgot you should know. How about my credit? Have you thought about that? What about my family? How can I buy anything with bad credit?" Tina asked.

"What are you worrying about? You already own your dream home. You have newer cars. You don't need good credit anymore. Don't you know half of Americans have bad credit? And they still have credit cards. You're being so ungrateful." Jorge lashed.

"Have you completely lost it? Do you even know what you're talking about? Are you going mad? Where is my real father? Can you please bring him back?"

"Don't talk to me like that!" Jorge snapped.

"I should have listened to Mom. You don't care about anyone else but your precious gambling."

There she said it, letting the cat out of the bag.

Jorge's breaths became labored, and he couldn't take the heated exchange any longer. He just wanted out of the conversation but knew if he hung up, Tina would call back and wouldn't stop until the discussion was over.

"You don't know what you are talking about. You know you should stop listening to your mother. She's why we're in this mess," Jorge said.

You better tell her to shut up!

"I know exactly what I am talking about. I heard the fights when I was little. You and gambling, that is what it has always been. I shouldn't have let you bully me into signing the loan for you. I"m so sickened by your irresponsibility and careless attitude. I never would have thought in a million years you would screw your own daughter— but you did."

Jorge hung up the phone furious, and at that same time, Tina dropped the phone as stomach cramps overtook her. A gush of blood rushed down her legs. She hurried to the bathroom to see the heavy flow had already penetrated her jeans.

"No," she shouted, as she feared she lost the baby.

Tina called Eva, who rushed over to take her to the emergency room, where an ultrasound confirmed Tina's fear of a miscarriage. The news was devastating; she just saw the baby alive and kicking last week at her first ultrasound. She couldn't help but think about her fight with Jorge and how it had something to do with losing the baby.

A few hours later, Tina had a dilation and curettage procedure at the hospital. It sucked all the joy she had, mourning the loss of her unborn child until she passed out.

The next day Jorge called. Eva had told him about the miscarriage. Though Tina had told him, he acted as if he didn't know about the pregnancy.

"Hi, girl. I'm really sorry."

"I don't want to talk."

"I just wanted to call and say sorry," Jorge said.

"Sorry for what?" She wanted to hear what he was sorry for since he never seemed to remember anything bad he did.

"You know."

"No, I don't. Listen, you always want money help, but you couldn't care less about how I feel and what I go through every day. Do you ever wonder if I need any help? I lost a baby yesterday," Tina said.

"Wait, wait, I am sorry for yesterday. I am really sorry about that."

"What?"

"I'm sorry about being late with the payments."

"Is that all you can say? It's more than about the late payments. It's way more. You love gambling more than anything else in your life. You love it more than me or you."

Though Jorge knew Tina was upset, he didn't realize how much.

"I've been thinking about this mess and this awful situation you have suckered me in. I just can't continue to live life worrying about you and whether you will pay the loan or not."

Jorge was about to hang up again, but he didn't.

"I haven't been able to sleep since losing the baby. There is only one solution."

Let her speak, don't blow it now!

"I told you I was sorry."

Tina took a deep breath and said, "That is not enough anymore. I just think you should move out of the villa."

"What?"

"I see how letting you live there for nothing was a mistake too. All it has done has allowed you to gamble more. Remember you were only going to stay for a few months, but it's been nearly a year. The villa was a gift from Mom and not to you," Tina said.

"Tina, please let me make it up to you. From now on, I'll pay on time. I swear to God," Jorge said.

"You know what? That's what you always say, but never do. You have not only been playing with my emotions but my family's. I've been so stressed with you not paying the mortgage that I can't think straight. I'm always worried that the bank will call, or you will call frantically because you need money. I hate it when the phone rings because I automatically think its bad news involving you. I just can't handle it anymore. I can't live like this," Tina said.

Sweet-talk her! You cannot let this happen.

"Well, this time, I will never be late again. I swear to God. Please, I have nowhere else to go. Please, girl. I'll be homeless," Jorge pleaded.

"Dad, I didn't even tell you everything the teller told me. The account is closed because of the late payments, and I had to pay the last two months on my credit card. I just don't understand why it's so hard for you to do what you say."

"Please give me one more chance," Jorge pleaded.

"I just can't."

"Please, girl, I swear on my life. May God strike me if I'm not telling the truth."

"I can't afford to. I shouldn't have given you the chance I did because you didn't take it seriously. I'm out of giving chances," Tina said.

"You are alone, like a grown man should be."

"Yes, just give me another chance. I'm begging you, please, girl. I will be the responsible father you want. I promise."

Kate started whimpering in the playpen as she was starting to get hungry.

"Please," Jorge pleaded.

"I have to go," Tina said and hung up.

It wasn't even ten minutes until she heard the knocks on the front door. She didn't have to guess who it was. Tina opened the door, not sure if she had enough energy to handle another round with Jorge.

"Dad, you acted like nothing happened yesterday. I had a D&C. Do you even know what that involves? It's when the doctor uses a machine that sucks everything behind from a miscarriage. Yesterday was one of the hardest days of my life. What happened can't be brushed aside, and here you are, pressuring me until you get what you want. I just can't do this anymore. I have to protect myself and my family," Tina said.

Jorge just stood there thinking about what Tina said, taken by her strong will, yet he wasn't going to back down.

"You know what I want?" Tina said.

"No, tell me."

"I want you to pay the $50,000 back! That's what I want. I don't want to live this nightmare anymore. I want it to be over like it never happened."

"Tina, if I had the money, I would. You know this. However, I will do what I can now," Jorge said as he thought of a good idea. Not perfect, but good enough to show his seriousness.

"I will give you my Social Security checks."

"I don't want them."

"Look, girl, I am sorry. I am sorry you lost the baby. Don't forget, it was my grandchild, too," Jorge said, his eyes watering.

Tina started to tear up as she saw her father get emotional, but she still didn't budge.

"I feel responsible. Can you forgive me? You know, you're right. I don't deserve another chance," Jorge said.

Tina was surprised by his candor. Did she really hear what she thought she did? Her father was now begging her for forgiveness and agreeing with her.

"I am sorry that I have caused you so much pain; that is the last thing I ever wanted. My Tina girl," Jorge said, wiping away a tear.

Tina's mood changed. She felt maybe she had crossed the line in making her father feel bad.

"You know you are right. I should move out. If I have to sleep under a bridge for the rest of my life, let it be. I don't deserve to be your father anymore," Jorge said.

Jorge just took the biggest gamble. He upped the stakes. He was going for the ultimate guilt trip. He just hoped it would work or he'd really be up the creek without a paddle, sleeping under a bridge. He started to panic but he stuck it out.

Wait for it, wait for it.

Jorge turned away. He was counting the seconds in his mind as he believed Tina would call after him and she did.

"Dad, please don't go."

Bingo!

Once again, Jorge had Tina fooled, and the sick part was he took pride in it. He turned around, and walked back, trying his hardest not to smile. Immediately hugging Tina so he could let his smile out while Tina cried in his arms.

Jorge, I have to hand it to you. You are the man. Way to go!

He smiled again as he felt it to be true too.

He managed to change Tina's mind by changing his strategy. It was a lot like planning for his next bet.

"I only wanted you to be responsible and stop gambling," Tina said.

"Ok."

Tina wasn't sure if he included gambling in his response, but she was happy Jorge acknowledged his shortcomings and took it as a good sign. She hoped to God that her father meant what he said.

"Why don't you come inside? Kate should be up in a few moments, and I can also make you a snack until then."

Jorge calmly smiled, still trying to portray the hurt father, yet inside, he was dancing, only wanting to jump up and down. However, if he did, he would blow his cover.

CHAPTER 32

Nothing Will Stop Jorge

A few days later, Jorge called. "Hi, girl, how are you? Hope you are feeling better."

"A little . . ."

"You're not going to like what I'm about to say. The last thing I wanted to do was come to you again after giving me another chance, but I have no one else to turn to. It's serious…please, girl," Jorge said.

Tina's shoulders dropped.

"What is it?" Tina said, fearing the worst, as she was about to find out what serious was.

"I could go to jail, and it isn't even my fault. It's a big mix-up in the salon, and I'm being blamed for something I didn't do. I'm telling you someone is out to get me," Jorge said.

Tina shook her head as she sat on the kitchen stool, her heart racing just hearing the word *jail*. She wondered what he did now.

"See, two weeks ago, I borrowed two hundred dollars from the cash drawer, so you don't think this just happened. Anyway, I returned the money yesterday, but it went missing. Donna is under pressure from the salon owners, saying if I don't return the money by tomorrow, they are going to call the cops, and I'll be arrested for stealing and will be fired," Jorge said in a panic.

Jorge took a deep breath before continuing his story, hoping Tina would run to his rescue. "I can't let that happen. If this gets out, my reputation will be lost, and I won't be able to pay any bills."

Tina took a deep breath. He was saying that if he didn't get the money from her, he would lose his job and wouldn't be able to pay for the home equity.

"Are you sure that you placed the money back?" Tina asked.

"Yes, I did."

"Did anyone else see you? Isn't Donna always at the front desk? There has to be someone who saw you," Tina asked.

"She went to the restroom, and the only person around was Mary, but she was too busy reading the newspaper. And she said she didn't see me because she doesn't like me."

"Why didn't you wait to give it to Donna? It doesn't make sense why you would return the money when she wasn't around."

"I don't know, but I do know that I don't want to go to jail."

"I don't have any more money to give you. I paid the last two months of the home equity payments on my credit card."

"You must have something? I'll take whatever you have. Please, girl. Do you want everyone to know that I got arrested for stealing? When I didn't do it? Think of you, Christopher and Kate."

Tina took another deep breath as she felt like her father was back to his old ways.

"If you tell me what you have, Uncle Fernando will help with the rest," Jorge said.

Tina wanted to say zero but knew he wouldn't accept it as true.

"How can you ask for money when you still haven't paid back what I have paid on the home equity," Tina asked.

"If I go to jail, you can forget about me ever paying you or it back to the bank. It's your choice."

"How soon you forget about your promises," Tina said. She was again stuck between a rock and a hard place. There was nothing left but to give in. She was too tired to do anything else.

"So, how much do you have, Tina?" Jorge asked.

"Wait a second, let me get my purse," she said, feeling like a servant.

Good job, Jorge.

"Okay, I have sixty dollars."

"Thank you, girl. I'll get the rest from Uncle Fernando," Jorge said, relieved that Tina had come to the rescue again.

"I was going to use it for formula," Tina said, hoping her father would say to keep the money, but he didn't.

Jorge acted like he didn't hear the last part. He was a professional at tuning out what he didn't like hearing. It had no effect or barring on his wants.

"Thanks," Jorge said.

"Oh, Dad?"

"Yes?"

"This will be the last time I will help you ever. The help and favors end today."

She is bluffing!

Jorge just let it go in one ear and out the other. What he cared about was going to the track. He had made the whole story up, like the ones before. He never stole from the desk drawer, though the idea did cross his mind, Donna would never leave the desk as Tina said, and if she did, she locked the drawer.

The following year flew. Tina returned to working full-time at Dice Magazine and kept busy running around with a toddler. Kate was now close to eighteen months, getting into everything, and Tina was pregnant again, in the second trimester. Life was good. Jorge was up to date paying the home equity, and there weren't any more calls from Bank of America.

However, a relentless hurricane tore through South Florida, which caused roof damage to the villa. After the insurance adjusters came to the property, they were only willing to give a grand towards repairs. This wasn't enough to cover any of the quotes she received, so Jorge said he would do the repairs with a friend of his.

"Don't worry. I've already talked to a roofer friend who does side jobs. I got this," Jorge said.

Tina knew Jorge had friends in the business and didn't give it much thought.

Jorge spent the grand at the track and didn't think twice about the roof repairs until Tina asked a few weeks later.

"How are the roof repairs going?" Tina asked.

Jorge was back to coming over every Friday night. It became a regular date again, where Tina, Jorge, Kate, and Christopher had family dinners together. Kate looked forward to Fridays, asking Tina during the week if it was Friday yet.

"Good, almost done," he said, avoiding eye contact with Tina.

Christopher was still outside mowing the lawn. Jorge came by earlier because he had a date later. He was dressed nicely in navy slacks and a white oxford shirt. He also had a sports jacket, which he kept neatly hung in the back of his car.

Ever since dating Lisa, he seemed happier and cared more about his appearance. Tina had met her once, and from what she could tell, Lisa seemed like a pleasant, down-to-earth lady. Someone ideal for her father.

"So, where are you and Lisa going out tonight? Anywhere exciting?" Tina asked.

"The dog track."

Tina's eyes strained, questioning what she had just heard, shocked that Jorge admitted to this.

"Oh, I'm not sure if I like Lisa anymore," Tina said.

"Don't worry. Tonight, is a special night—it's the 70th year celebration. We're meeting another couple. It will be fun. I have fifty dollars to bet with and not a cent more. Maybe I'll get lucky."

"Oh, just be careful. I don't want to remind you how hard it is for you to walk away. I just don't know what I would do if you started…" Tina said.

"Don't worry."

"Was the thousand dollars enough to cover the supplies and cots for the roof repair?" Tina asked, changing the subject.

"Yes, it was. My friend Tim helped me. I paid him three hundred dollars."

Tina knew that name. *Oh my,* she thought, *that is the name of the guy who was, or maybe still was, getting mail at the villa.*

"Why is he getting mail at the villa? Tina asked.

Jorge felt like the carpet was ripped from under him.

"Ah, mail sometimes comes for him because his wife threw him out. It's just until he finds a new place. He's a good person."

"Are you sure he isn't living there now?"

"He isn't, but he stays over sometimes when he can't find a sofa to crash on. He doesn't do it often."

"I told you I didn't want anyone staying at the villa."

Jorge turned his attention to Kate, who was busy entertaining herself with dinner.

Tina wouldn't let this slide but knew the time wasn't now to pursue it.

"Hi, honey, I'm hungry. I hope you both left some ziti left," Christopher said as he walked in from the backyard.

"There's plenty left. Dad said the roof repairs are just about done."

"Nice, see your father has real connections," Christopher said, hoping to brighten the mood as Tina looked upset.

"'ll come by Monday to check on the repairs," Tina said.

Pushy, just like her mother!

Jorge had allowed his friend Fabio to stay in the villa, under the condition that he would help with the roof repairs in exchange for a place to stay. But Fabio didn't even begin the repairs, and it wasn't until a month later that Jorge said anything about it.

"Come on. My daughter is coming over Monday to check on the roof. I told her it would be done by then, but you haven't even started. You said the repairs would be done within the first week you moved in. If you don't get them done, we both won't have a place to live," Jorge said.

Jorge was nervous as Monday was only two days away. He had been busy going to the track, thinking Fabio would have done the repairs without him having to remind him. He told Jorge not to worry and that he would take care of the roof, but he never did.

"Well, where are the supplies? I can't even start the repairs with no tools or materials," Fabio said, blaming Jorge.

"What? You said you were getting the supplies from your job. Remember that was part of the agreement," Jorge said.

"I lost my job," Fabio said, but the truth was he lost it before he moved in and promised to do the repairs. Now he had no incentive to look for another job, as he was collecting unemployment and living rent-free, though he didn't tell Jorge this.

"Well, find the materials elsewhere. You must have buddies who can help you. I'm sure you can ask a favor."

"I can't."

"Just forget about it. Just start paying me for rent or get out."

"I don't have the money now. I'm going to the unemployment office later today. I should get my first check in about two weeks. I'll give you all of it if you will let me stay."

"Okay, but if you don't, you'll have to leave," Jorge said.

He felt like he had to let Fabio stay for another two weeks. Fabio smiled as he managed to pull another one over Jorge. He now had two weeks to live rent-free and find another place to stay because he had no intention of paying Jorge.

Jorge knew somehow, he had to get the roof repairs done fast or Tina would never believe him again.

He went to the next best person for help, Fernando. He knew his brother had a shed full of materials and tools.

"Hey, brother, I haven't seen you for a while. How are you?" Fernando asked.

"Good, good. I'm hoping you can help me," Jorge said.

"What sort of help?"

"Well, Tina's villa has roof leaks from the last hurricane, and I told her I would take care of them."

"But you didn't," Fernando said as he gave his brother a hard look.

"No, I didn't. I forgot, been busy at the salon, but the problem is that she is coming by the villa Monday expecting them to be done, and if she sees that nothing has, she will throw me out," Jorge said.

"I don't think she would do that."

"Yes, she would."

"If you say so, what do you need, brother?" Fernando asked.

"I need supplies, like plywood, soffit siding, shingles, nails, and I will do the repairs myself," Jorge said.

"Well, why don't I go back with you and look at the roof? In the meantime, let's go and look in the shed and see what I have."

"Thanks, brother. How is it that I always get myself in these messes, trying to help someone else, and then I'm the one who gets screwed?"

Fernando followed Jorge to the villa, thinking the roof repairs were minor. As Jorge wasn't that good at home repairs. Yet, it was a big job. He didn't even think he could help Jorge.

"What happened here?"

"Well, the hurricane ripped off the singles, tarp, and now there is now a big hole in the roof."

"I see that, but the hurricane was months ago. Why wasn't it fixed, then? Didn't Tina call the insurance company? Her homeowner's insurance would have covered it," Fernando said.

"She didn't want to involve the insurance company because she was afraid, they'd drop her. I told her I would fix it and not to bother with them."

"Well, this is a bigger job than I expected," Fernando said.

"It needs to be fixed by Monday."

"Why don't you just tell Tina the truth, and then I can see if I can get some guys, I know from work to come by next weekend and get it done properly."

"No, I need to get it done by Monday, or I will be sleeping under a bridge unless I can stay in your spare bedroom."

Fernando looked at Jorge like he was crazy. He knew that was not possible.

"Jorge, a patch-up job will not do." Fernando said.

His brother's words gave Jorge an idea he hadn't thought about. "So, I could patch this up?"

"Yes, that wouldn't be too hard, just slap on a few shingles, and it will look like new, but the roof leaks will eventually continue. It would only solve the problem for a little. Otherwise, the roof will collapse."

"I'm only doing this to buy some time. See if you can get a few guys over for next weekend."

"How about we go to Home Depot and get the supplies? It won't cost that much."

Suddenly Jorge had this panic-stricken look that Fernando knew all too well as he'd seen it over a thousand times. It said, "I don't have money." He looked lost.

"Don't worry, brother, I'll cover it today. What are brothers for after all?" Fernando said.

"Thanks, brother, you saved my life."

Fernando smiled and patted his brother on the back as they walked back to his car and drove off to Home Depot.

Tina went by the villa as she said she would. She was happy to see that the roof was repaired, and Jorge followed through with his promise.

Tina just wanted to do a quick walk-through before leaving. She had to know if anyone else was living in the villa other than her father.

She looked at her cell phone, seeing Christopher called. Her heart started beating faster and harder, as she felt overwhelmed by anxiety, which wasn't good for her or the baby. All she needed was for the doctor to insist she should be induced because of her high blood pressure, but she had to know if someone else was living in the villa. She had to know if her father was lying or not. Tina started to take deep breaths.

"Calm down. You'll be fine," Tina said. "Lana, you and Mommy are going to be detectives today," she said, looking down at her tummy.

She nervously walked back up the narrow path to the front door, keeping quiet as she stopped next to the kitchen window, feeling weak.

Just open the door, she thought. Tina had the villa key in her hand, but it wouldn't work. First, she thought she had picked the wrong key from the key chain. The key would go in, but it wouldn't turn and open the door. She tried a few times, and it still wouldn't budge. Then she started banging on the door in frustration.

How could I be locked out of my own place?

"Open the door!"

Tina was prepared to go around the house to see if the sliding glass door was open by chance, but she knew her time had run out.

Fabio snapped out of sleep, awoken by banging and jerking movements from the front door's knob. He was terrified. He quickly got off the sofa and got dressed. He hid in the master bedroom closet. Jorge warned him that Tina might come by and for him to hide if he heard the door open.

Tina only had six minutes to make it to her doctor's appointment, so she left without getting into the villa. She was beyond frustrated, feeling like Jorge was hiding something or someone from her again.

It didn't help that she had to run up the stairs to the office to avoid being late. Her blood pressure was 180/100, which was dangerously high and worried the doctor. She told the doctor she had received bad news, but he said, "Your blood pressure still should not be so high."

Tina was admitted to the hospital and hooked up to machines for three hours. All tests came back normal, her blood pressure stabilized, and a few hours later, Tina was able to leave the hospital, but her blood pressure went right back up as she drove home, thinking of Jorge.

CHAPTER 33

Tina Narrows In

Tina was home for a good hour before she could even call Jorge. Kate had fallen asleep while watching *Snow White* for the fourth time, giving *her* the perfect opportunity to talk to him about the villa key not working.

"Oh girl, I can only talk for a few minutes. My client is just about done getting shampooed," Jorge said, as the only client getting their hair washed was Mary's.

He was just sitting in his station chair looking at the Palm Springs Kennel Club race schedule, still waiting for his three o'clock client to arrive, who was now fifteen minutes late. Jorge started to get restless; as he needed cash to bet, it wasn't looking good so far. He was now hoping for a walk-in as he was the only available stylist.

"Dad, I went by the villa earlier today, and I discovered something upsetting. So much that when I arrived at my doctor's appointment, I was rushed to the hospital," Tina said.

"Well, doctors are always looking to make money. You should know this, Tina," Jorge said, downplaying the hospital visit.

"Not really, there was a medical reason," Tina responded.

"Oh," Jorge said, yet not asking why, as he kept looking at the race schedule.

"It was because my blood pressure was dangerously high."

"Did you see the roof repairs?" Jorge asked, ignoring her.

"I did, but I wasn't able to get inside the villa, and why is that?"

There was still no response from Jorge.

"I really wanted to see if the master bedroom ceiling were replaced like you said it would be," Tina said, feeling like she was talking to the wall.

Tina did not like how Jorge was being so insensitive, as if she didn't mean anything to him.

"Do you know why I couldn't get in?" Tina asked.

"I did a pretty good job, if I say so myself. The roof is basically new now. No problems for you for a while. I did you a favor." Jorge boasted, soaking up his praise and somehow believing his own lies.

Tina kept quiet, disappointed that her father wasn't concerned about her being in the hospital. It was like she didn't even tell him.

"Girl, you know your uncle helped me. He even took time off from work so the job would be done properly," Jorge said, trying to keep Tina on his good side.

"That was nice of him. Please tell him I said thank you."

"Yes, it was. I have an idea, why don't you thank Uncle Fernando yourself? I know he would love to hear from you," Jorge said, lying again as he continued to dance around the reason for the call.

He was waving to Donna, hoping she would walk over so he could hand her the phone, but she just brushed him off.

Jorge was holding out until he couldn't any longer, just like when he lost at the track. He always had a hard time leaving. It was his specialty to avoid reality and problems, even if they were staring him straight in the face. He felt if he ignored them, the problem wasn't there.

"You still haven't answered why my key doesn't open the front door? How can it even be possible?" Tina asked.

"I told you I lost my keychain, which had the house key on," Jorge lied.

"Yes, but I gave you another key."

Jorge was silent as he tried to remember what happened that evening.

"Don't you remember? I saw you place the new key on your keychain. So there is no reason for you to change the front door lock unless you want me out," Tina lashed.

Jorge turned around, facing his back to the others, his signature pose when he didn't want anyone to hear him or read his expression. This time he felt like he was fucked. His daughter was getting a little too street-smart for his liking. He figured it was the influence of Eva.

Set her straight!

"I know that something fishy is going on at the villa, and I'm going to find out whether you tell me or not," Tina said.

"Stop worrying. I forgot because I already bought a new lock before I told you about losing my key. I went ahead and changed the lock, feeling it was a good idea as I often worry about floating keys getting in the wrong hands. I was going to give you the new key, but I forgot. I didn't mean anything by it."

Good save.

Sure, Tina thought. "You should have told me then. I was so upset that I almost knocked down the door and had a heart attack."

"I know," Jorge said. How he wished he could suck back his words. "I mean, I know how you can get upset. Sometimes you can blow up like your mother. You should try to be more like me, calm and carefree," Jorge said.

Tina was still brewing, believing now that Tim or someone else was in the villa when she tried to get in.

"I need that key now!"

"Okay, girl, let me go. A client is waiting for me. I'll call you later," Jorge said, as his blood pressure rose. He then hung up before Tina could say another word.

He wouldn't fight with her, especially now that she was about to have a baby. Jorge was smart enough to know to keep his distance.

Tina became upset again, feeling that her father was lying. He was hiding something or someone in the villa, and she was going to find out whether she had the key or not.

Hours later, Tina went into labor, delivering sweet Lana. Jorge was happy to know he had a few months of freedom. He knew Tina would be too tired to check on him now with a newborn.

Yeah, she won't be bothering us!

During this time, Jorge gambled daily. He was down to working only twice a week. Clients were tired of his bad luck stories and being asked for financial help. They stopped going to him because they didn't want to be bothered by his problems anymore when they had their own. Soon they asked around and went to other hairstylists.

Jorge was now involved with hardcore gamblers. They didn't care about their children, spouses, parents, brothers, sisters, friends, jobs, and homes. All they lived for was the next bet, and without remorse, many even cashed in their retirement funds and children's college funds to gamble. They believed it was their right to do so, and if anyone told them otherwise, they'd tell them to "fuck off."

These hardcore gamblers used Jorge for his car to go to other gambling venues. They slept at the villa, taking showers every couple of days when they were bothered by their body odor. They were even happy sleeping on the tile floor, which was better than sleeping under a bridge, or the park in a makeshift tent at record high temps and vulnerable to violence. They didn't have a permanent address as they were transients, many having criminal records of some kind, mostly petty crimes like trespassing, or disorderly conduct and a few had felony charges.

However, they praised Jorge because they did not want to lose what his friendship provided, a place to stay, yet they laughed at him when he wasn't around.

For the next couple of months, Tina hardly slept, worrying about Jorge. The sickly worrying feeling couldn't be shaken off, as it kept denying her any peace. Always thinking about him. Tina lived in fear that the carpet would be pulled from under Jorge, and she would be the one that would have to save him, and she didn't know if she could anymore.

There were too many signs she couldn't avoid. They were haunting her like a bad dream, and she felt it was just a matter of time until Jorge would come out of the woodwork and demand every last piece of her. Tina felt that she would be called and told that he was either dead or arrested. The question was not will it happen, but when it will happen, and whether she could handle it.

Jorge had become too secretive. He could never give a straight answer anymore. Jorge was masterful as he knew how to avoid questions he didn't like and only answer ones he could with a yes or no. He always had the perfect exit when he was about to be cornered.

It had gotten to the point where his eyes would avoid any contact with Tina. His weekly Friday visits were infrequent. Her gut kept saying that he was gambling, but she hoped it was the hormones making her paranoid. What terrified Tina the most was how she downplayed Jorge's gambling for so long that her mother and husband thought he had it under control. And in the process, she had somehow convinced herself to believe it too.

On a muggy, wet morning, Tina was in a panic; she had not heard from Jorge for over forty-eight hours. Jorge would normally return her calls within a day. She believed something really bad happened to him. Maybe he was in a car crash. The bad weather, mixed with his speeding tendencies, seemed like a real possibility. She paced around the house full of worry, nursing her sour stomach.

Jorge was now two hours late. Tina even called the salon hoping he would be there, saying that he had forgotten about watching Kate and Lana for her doctor's appointment, but he wasn't there either.

Six days ago, he agreed to watch Kate and Lana, so she could go to a doctor's appointment alone. Tina could still remember his exact words, "Girl, don't worry, I will be there no matter what."

"Who else can I call?" Tina wondered.

A few seconds later, she thought of Lisa. Maybe he was with her.

"Hi, Lisa."

"Oh, hi," she said coldly.

"This is Tina, Jorge's daughter. How are you?" Tina said cheerfully.

"I know…. I've had better days."

"I'm sorry."

"It is not your fault. It is your father's."

"Oh? I was actually calling to see if he was with you. He was supposed to watch the girls today so I could go to my doctor's appointment, but it seems like he is nowhere to be found. I'm worried that something may have happened to him. Is he there?" Tina asked.

Lisa shook her head, knowing the feeling too well when Jorge didn't return her calls or be at the apartment when he promised.

"Your father and I haven't seen each other for over a month now. We broke up," Lisa said.

Tina was confused, as she remembered Jorge saying last Friday that they were good, even hinting that things were getting serious between them. Tina wondered why her father wanted her to believe they were still together. Was it another lie he was covering up? She wondered.

"Are you still there?" Lisa asked.

"Yes, I'm just surprised. My father didn't say anything about you two splitting. He actually said things were good between you two. I'm confused by this and don't know what to think."

"Well, that's because your father is a compulsive liar and gambler. He doesn't care about anyone but himself. I'm sorry, but it's about time you know this, Tina. I learned the hard way and—"

Tina felt sick listening to the word *gambler*.

"Your father scammed me out of ten grand, which I took from my retirement account. I'll admit, I was stupid to believe him, and I thought he loved me. He promised he could double my money on a sure bet, so we could use the winnings to travel to Europe. He even said he would return the money if he didn't win. He was that sure, and I went along with the biggest mistake of my life. How dumb I was and to think I'm a college graduate," Lisa said.

Tina kept quiet, not knowing what to say; she felt sorry for Lisa.

"Tell your father I'm going to take him to court if he doesn't pay me back. He signed a promissory note saying he would pay me back, and I intend to pursue this until he does. I will not let this go. He needs to pay."

"I wouldn't either," Tina said, feeling anxious. The day was becoming more unbearable than Tina could imagine.

"If you want to know where he is, take a drive by the Palm Springs Kennel Club. He'll be there with his new girlfriend, Sheri. She's a gambler like him. He told me that she understood him like no other person, but something tells me she is just with him for the ride."

"I thought he only went to the track on jackpot nights."

"That was what he wanted you to believe. I'd say he goes to the track at least five times a week, if not more."

Now Tina started to tremble as she heard her deepest fear as true. Her father was lying the entire time.

"This is just awful. I can't stop shaking . . ."

"Your father had me fooled, too. I thought he was just a social gambler. Yet, this was far from the truth. Now I can't even think about the kennel club without my blood pressure going up. It's sickening how he blew my ten grand away and thought it was no big deal."

"I feel sick for you."

"Well, what I'm about to tell you will really upset you, so please sit down. I feel nauseated just thinking about it. I struggled with telling you, but now that you called, I'll take it as a sign to tell you," Lisa said.

Tina could feel it in her tone that what Lisa was about to say was really bad. She hoped her heart could take it.

"I know about the home equity loan you took, so your father could pay his high-interest car loan."

"Yes, that is true. I did this to help him, and I regret it."

"Are you sitting down?"

"Yes," Tina said, thinking the worst as she held her breath.

"Well, your father never paid the car loan. He still owes twenty thousand dollars on it."

"What? That can't be. He said he paid it off," Tina said.

"He didn't, honey. I know this because I loaned him five hundred dollars to pay January's payment."

"What? This just can't be. How could he?"

"Instead, your father gambled the fifty thousand in one month. He was having a hard time paying the home equity because of the car payments. When he told me this, I couldn't look at him. I even told him how wrong it was of him, and he just laughed, saying he was entitled to the money because your mother should've never given you the villa. I asked what he would do if he couldn't pay the home equity, and he said that he wasn't worried since the loan was in your name. I realized then that your father was sick. Unfortunately, his only life ambition is to bet. Of course, this was after he lost my money."

"I just can't believe this!" Tina shouted, tears streaming down her face.

"I wasn't really working on the day of your baby shower. I just couldn't face you knowing what I did, how your father scammed his own daughter. I told him I would be a hypocrite if I went to your shower. He thought I would be a hypocrite if I didn't go. I hated how he could just laugh about it like it was one big joke," Lisa said.

"Oh my God, oh my God . . ."

Suddenly, Tina felt a deeper pain than she had ever felt in her chest and fell to the ground. At that second, she was served the ultimate betrayal that ripped her into a thousand pieces, one she could no longer ignore.

After taking the girls to her in-laws, she drove to the Palm Springs Kennel Club, the last place she ever wanted to be. Just the thought of walking through its hand-smudged doors of lies overwhelmed her, but she just needed confirmation of what Lisa had said and wanted to see Jorge in action.

"Calm down, Tina, it will be okay," Tina said, struggling with the raging anxiety within.

Tina rushed to the wage windows. There were six, and all had long lines with ten or more people standing like soldiers waiting their turn at luck. She quickly scanned to see by chance if her father was standing in one of the lines, but he wasn't. Tina then went to the pavilion overlooking the racetrack but still didn't see Jorge. Tina tied her long, brown hair under one of Christopher's baseball caps, hoping not to be recognized by anyone, especially not by her father yet.

He is here, just look harder. You are not leaving until you find him, she thought. Again she changed her search direction, walking down the steps of the veranda in front of the racetrack. Looking at the clock, she saw that a new race was about to begin as patrons rushed to their seats, almost tripping over each other. This helped as she methodically scanned the rows, starting from the bottom, looking from left to right like a typewriter.

It wasn't until she got to the tenth row that she finally saw her father, and he was not alone. He was with his new girlfriend, Sheri.

"He is using her, too," Tina whispered.

Jorge's right arm was around Sheri's waist like she was a prize. They sat facing the racetrack, anxious for the race to begin. Jorge was pointing to the dogs like he had some insider news. Sheri smiled too, feeding on Jorge's energy, laying kiss after kiss on his scruffy face like he was the president, dignified and important. Then the announcer came on.

Tina kept her eyes fixed on Jorge, holding his ticket close to his mouth, talking to it like it was alive. Tina used every bit of restraint, not to storm to him and let him have it because her rational side said it was pointless to do anything. After all, she was in his territory and especially did not want to meet Sheri, his betting sidekick.

Bang!

CHAPTER 34

Intervention

Jorge jumped up from his seat like it was just set on fire.
He smiled, his fists up, rocking back and forth, hysterically shouting, watching the greyhounds sprinting from their pens. He didn't see them for their beauty or strength, only pawns in his addicted mind.

Well done, Jorge.

He kept his gaze on 2, 4, 5, 7. They were his picks, believing they'd win. All were in the lead, running their hearts out. He didn't care how they came in, as he boxed them, just as long as all four placed in the top four. He kept shouting their numbers, sweat streaming down his brow, very much in his feelings.

Watching Jorge so absorbed by the race caused Tina to move closer like a magnet. She wanted to know the fascination of the bet. Maybe then she could help Jorge.

It was easy to see that he was oblivious to his surroundings with the race happening. He paid no notice to Sheri tugging on his left arm, though he was very much lopsided. Somehow he was immune to any physical touch. Nothing could pull him away from the race.

Suddenly, his mood changed when he saw his four picks were no longer in the lead. Number 1, 3, and 6 ran right past them. The only dog that placed was number 4. He needed all four to come in to win. Now he was in a panic, feeling his life slip away as the race was over, and he lost.

He buried his head deep within his lap in defeat. He could have stayed this way for the rest of the night, as he had no more money to bet with, but Sheri had other plans. She wasn't going to let him off the hook as she was livid. He lost her money, too.

Jorge looked up with defeated eyes. The monster was now hiding within Jorge. He stood up and placed his hands in his pant pockets, looking for money that wasn't there. Even pulling the insides out, hoping somehow money would appear, but nothing, absolutely nothing. They were shamefully empty.

"What the fuck! Sure bet, my ass!" Sheri shouted.

"It was going to plan until dog five tripped. You saw that. I can't be blamed for it." Jorge pleaded with her.

"Really?" Sheri answered.

"Calm the fuck down!" Jorge demanded.

You tell her.

This was the first time Tina heard her father curse, which scared her.

"Well, it wasn't exactly a trip, and either way, you said it was a sure bet. Trip or not, you lied!"

"Let's go and find Nick. He's good with a few trainers here. They already plotted who is going to win the next race. You know these races are fixed, yet there are times when even the best plans are broken," Jorge said, hoping to calm Sheri from making a bigger scene.

"Are you sure?" Sheri said as she took the bait.

"Yes, and I see Tim by the snack bar, and he owes me a hundred, so we are good for another bet or two. Just trust me."

Sheri just looked at Jorge not sure if she should believe him, though the better side of her wanted to.

"All I know is that if we don't win the next race, there will be hell for you to pay."

Tears ran down Tina's cheeks as she felt the ultimate betrayal after seeing Jorge gamble from the beginning to the end. Seeing how hooked he was to the thrill of the bet was too much to see and handle. Tina now saw how easy it was for him to gamble the home equity away.

Sheri followed Jorge as he walked up toward the wage windows. She was very close, almost touching him. If he'd stop for any reason, she would have plowed into him. Tina took this as her opportunity to leave as she could not bear being in such a toxic place for another minute.

Once out of the racetrack, she looked up at the sky, thankful she was out. What an awful place, she thought. Once in the car, Tina cried, feeling the walls crumble around her as she now knew the truth. Jorge was a compulsive gambler. He lied to her all these years, never really stopping like he let on.

This day would be fixed in her memory as one that she would look back to whenever she started to feel sorry for him. As she dried her tears, she thought about her next steps. There was so much to think about, and he could not be trusted.

"How could you do this to your own daughter?" Tina said in anger, starting to separate her feelings of love for Jorge.

Tina picked up Kate and Lana from her in-laws and decided she would not think about Jorge for the rest of the day. Yet, that was all she thought about it.

The next day before lunch, Tina called Jorge at work.

"Oh, hi, girl . . ."

"Where were you yesterday? Tina asked.

Jorge was silent.

"You know you were supposed to watch Kate and Lana so I could attend my doctor's appointment. What happened?" she asked again.

"Oh, I thought your appointment was next Thursday."

"No, it was yesterday. Now I have to wait another month."

"Well, I thought it was next Thursday," Jorge said.

"Kate is playing, and Lana is sleeping. Could you stop by Eckerd's and pick up my prescription when you have a break? It is already paid for. I also finished making tuna if you haven't had lunch yet."

"Sure, I'll be over in about an hour after I cut Ms. Dawson's hair."

"Great, see you then," Tina said.

Tina sat down feeling jittery and restless. In an hour, she would confront Jorge about his gambling.

Jorge rushed to Tina's. He hoped Tina already had his sandwich prepared with his favorite Cape Cod potato chips.

"Hi, Dad," Tina said, feeling intimidated, not sure if she could go through with it. Jorge leaned forward to kiss her, but Kate ran to him before he could. He picked her up, holding Kate like all the times before.

"Grandpa came by to see you and your sister."

Another lie, Tina thought, as she was the one who called him over for lunch.

Kate wasn't hungry for lunch yet, so only Tina and Jorge were at the kitchen table. Kate was playing mommy with her baby dolls in the living room.

"I'm glad you called when you did. I was about to get a sandwich at Subway," Jorge lied.

Tina got up from the table to get ice tea for the two of them, not sure if she could go through with her plans. She felt overwhelmed, the fear was taking her breath away, but she also knew she couldn't live like this anymore.

Just take it easy, start slow, she thought.

"So, how have you been?" Tina asked as she looked straight at Jorge. Their eyes met for a second, but he quickly looked away.

"Fine, couldn't be better."

"Well, I don't believe you," Tina said, feeling some anxiety leave her.

Jorge just glanced up at Tina.

"I had an interesting conversation with your ex yesterday," Tina said, setting up the mood.

Jorge continued to eat.

"Don't you want to know why it was interesting?" Tina asked.

"No, why should I? There is nothing to say other than this tuna sandwich is delicious," Jorge said.

"Is that all you are going to say?"

"You probably know that Lisa and I aren't together anymore."

"Why didn't you tell me?"

Jorge kept eating his sandwich.

"I'm still having a hard time understanding how you betted her retirement money and—"

"It doesn't surprise me that she would try to fill your mind with lies. It was why I broke up with her," Jorge interrupted.

Jorge thought the conversation was over, but Tina was on a roll.

"Yesterday, when you were supposed to be here, I went looking for you. I thought something bad happened to you, and guess where I found you? Tina said.

Jorge just smiled at Tina, not wanting to answer.

"You were having a blast with your new girlfriend. Do you want to take a guess where?" Tina asked, feeling the anger in her temperature rise.

"The dog track, I could hardly stomach watching you."

"Why are you checking up on me? I can go and do whatever I want. Stick to watching your children, not me."

"Sorry for caring. I was worried because you didn't show up and you weren't answering your calls," Tina said as she got up.

Tina couldn't stand being so close to Jorge anymore.

"Well, stop caring so much. I don't go between you and Christopher."

"Dad, you have a gambling problem. You have betted Lisa's money away and the home equity loan. You lied about paying the car loan because you are still paying it, and it's the reason why you are late with the bank payments. What happened to you? Do you not see this is serious? That you could lose everything?"

"I am done," Jorge said, as he got up from the chair and rushed to the front door, wanting out of Tina's house.

Good boy, Jorge! Tina doesn't understand like Eva.

"You have to stop. Can't you see what it's doing to you and me? It is destroying you and our family," Tina said as she started to cry.

"Come on, Tina, you don't know what you're talking about. I'll watch the girls tomorrow if you want to get some help. I don't need any."

"I do know what I'm talking about. I saw you yesterday and am still having difficulty erasing the memory. How come you lied about the car loan being paid?"

"Don't worry. I will pay you back."

"It's not just that. You are twisting everything I'm saying and ignoring the truth."

"No, you are. I will call Lisa and give her a piece of my mind. After how nice I was to her, and this is the thanks I get. She should be ashamed of herself. My problem was that I was too nice to her."

Kate ran up to the door to see why Jorge was screaming.

"Quiet Grandpa, baby sleeping," Kate said as she put her finger to her lips.

Jorge leaned down to Kate and placed his index finger to his lips. "Shh, I am sorry. Grandpa has to go back to work, but I will see you tomorrow."

"Okay, then we'll play races."

"What races?" Tina asked.

He left, acting like he was the victim, but he knew he was buying himself time.

Tina was stunned again by the lies and denial. There were no words to describe Jorge's manipulating ways. It was heartbreaking how he would turn against her, his own daughter, whenever his betting was mentioned.

Later that evening, Tina went for a jog around the neighborhood, hoping to clear her troubled mind, but she couldn't stop thinking about Jorge with each stride.

She then decided to drive to the villa and talk with him.

When she arrived, Jorge's car was there. She pulled behind, feeling anxious after their earlier heated conversation.

She walked up the dark, narrow pathway leading up to the front door, feeling like something would jump at her. When she tried to open the screen door, it didn't budge. Tina thought it could be jammed, but after trying a few times, she realized the handle had been replaced with a locked one. Anger swirled through her, then rang the doorbell a few times, but no one answered.

Don't leave yet, she thought. *Calm down.*

Tina went back to her car and looked in the trunk for a flashlight. Thankfully, the black one she remembered having was there. She then walked to the back of the villa. The patio door was wide open, and Tina could see through the sliding glass doors.

She knocked three times, and still no answer. She then turned the flashlight on and saw the inside. Horror overwhelmed her. There were sleeping bags out and open, lanterns, candles, and duffle bags opened with clothes, food wrappers, ashtrays, and beer cans littering the floor.

This is unbelievable, she thought, as she stared at the deplorable mess, feeling an adrenaline rush come on.

Tina jerked the sliding glass handle, and to her amazement, it opened. *Thank you,* she thought.

"Hello, is anyone there?" Tina called as she used the flashlight to see in the great room. Going up and down the ceiling and floors, making sure she covered all parts of the room before going in

"Dad! Are you here?"

"Dad," Tina called again.

She stayed on the threshold, still afraid, waiting to see if anyone or anything. Like a feral cat was still in the villa.

"Is anyone there?" she called again, concerned that she may not be alone. Tina pretended to call Christopher, hoping if someone was hiding, they'd come out and show themselves.

"Oh, hi, I'm at the villa. I need you to come by. This place is a mess, and I'm about to call the police."

It is now or never, Tina thought.

She took a deep breath and went inside, leaving the sliding door open just in case she wanted to run out.

The smell of cigarette smoke and mold permeated the villa as there wasn't any circulation. Tina checked the a/c, and the temperature was

92. She tried turning it on, but it wouldn't click on. She then reached for the light switch to see what was wrong, but the lights wouldn't turn on either. Tina then realized why there were candles and lanterns scattered throughout the villa. There was no electricity.

How could he think this is okay?

How can he live like this?

Why can't he see what his gambling is doing to him?

"He is out!!" Tina couldn't contain her rage anymore.

Tina called Jorge, but he didn't answer. The call went to voicemail. She hung up frustrated, seeing enough to know that her father was living in denial. Her eyes were burning from the mildew, and it started to hurt just to breathe. Walking through the great room, she tripped, and the flashlight fell to the floor, rolling to the master bedroom door.

Why is there an orange towel rolled up against the door?

What could he be hiding?

She tried opening the door, but it was locked. She recognized the handle. It was originally on the front door. Tina thought he must have switched the locks. It still had a deep scratch on the bottom of the keyhole she made when she first moved into the villa. Quickly she grabbed the keys from her jean pocket and looked for the matching key.

What awaited her was utter horror. The walls were dark and black. There was toxic mold everywhere. She then took out her phone and snapped photos. Then she ran out in tears and was as mad as ever.

CHAPTER 35

Alex

Jorge couldn't be reached for the next month.

It was like he had disappeared in thin air, but actually, he was hiding.

His cell phone calls went straight to voicemail, and he no longer worked at the salon.

Donna said, "The owners fired him for losing too many clients." This didn't surprise Tina, yet it was saddening to hear that Jorge could no longer handle a job. Tina even drove by the villa a few times during the day to check on him, but his car was never there.

Tina couldn't stand worrying about him anymore. As a last resort, she went to the track to see if he was there, and he was. Seeing him alone, looking out to the track, both angered and broke her heart. But she couldn't go to him. Seeing him alive was enough to calm Tina's heart for now. Anger and frustration overwhelmed Tina again as she drove home.

"Is your father all right? He hasn't been by for a while?" Christopher asked.

"Oh, he's fine."

"Oh, then why hasn't he been by the house?"

Tina couldn't take it anymore and broke down.

"He's actually living his best life at the track. Haven't you heard? He even parks at the VIP lot."

"What?" Christopher said, confused. "What are you talking about? I thought he stopped going."

"Nope, it was all a lie, he never stopped, and he managed to con his own daughter again," Tina said with a heavy heart.

"I thought he stopped after you helped him pay the property taxes years ago," Christopher said.

"I recently discovered that he kept gambling. Also, I never told you, but he never paid me back for the property taxes either," Tina said.

Christopher became quiet; he always thought Jorge paid Tina back. Now he felt lied to.

The awful conditions of the villa would cost thousands of dollars to repair, and the outstanding home equity loan was enough for Tina to have a nervous breakdown. She also had a bad feeling that Jorge was late on the payments or worse wasn't paying them again. There were a few 1-800 voicemails she hadn't listened to yet, and even if she wanted to rent the villa, it was not rentable.

"It's not your fault Tina. You trusted your father like any daughter would have. Unfortunately, it's your father who lied about his gambling, and that's on him, not you," Christopher said.

"I know, but I did something I'm afraid will ruin us. If only I could rewind time and take it back," Tina said, crying again.

"Don't be so hard on yourself. I know you too well to ever think or believe that. Tell me, what is it? It can't be that bad."

"My father..." Tina started to say.

"What did he do?"

Tina bawled as she told Christopher about the home equity loan she took out on the villa to pay Jorge's car loan off because it had such a high interest rate, never thinking he would go back on his word and not pay.

She told him how the villa was falling apart and how the roof was never really fixed, just patched up. How black mold was growing on its walls, and the electricity and water were shut off for nonpayment.

"I'm speechless. How could he?" Christopher asked.

"He seems to be perfectly fine with it as long as he can..." Tina said, not wanting to say the word gamble.

Christopher couldn't believe what he was hearing. He never thought Jorge would be capable of doing the unimaginable things Tina said, placing her and their family in harm's way. He once aspired to be like Jorge. How he was fooled into thinking he was a good man. A man he wanted to be for Tina, Kate, and Lana. Now he was ready to punch him.

"Don't be so hard on yourself. It is not your fault."

"It's hard not to when your own father has played you. I don't know if I'll ever get over this," Tina said.

"You will…"

"I have to call him again…this can't be ignored."

"I'm here if you need me to talk to him," Christopher said.

"No, I have to end this myself," Tina said.

Tina went out to the backyard and called Jorge, but the call went to voicemail again.

The nerve of him, she thought.

He really doesn't care.

What to do? Tina thought as she knew she couldn't just sit around and do nothing like the times before. This did nothing but create a bigger hole for her to fall into Jorge's mess.

She spent the rest of the morning at the park with Kate and Lana. The girls ran and tired themselves out. Tina soaked up every moment, watching her daughters enjoying life and laughing with one another. Their different personalities were a combination of herself and Christopher. Minutes before leaving, the ice cream truck arrived, and the girls enjoyed the last minutes of the park eating snow cones.

When Tina and the girls arrived home, she saw a letter from Bank of America in the mailbox. She quickly took it and hid it in her purse as the girls ran to say hello to Christopher.

What is this? Tina wondered, believing it was bad news, hoping she was wrong, but her gut was painfully right.

The letter said the loan was now two months past due, and the statement also included the current month's payment along with the late fees. Tina was left with the hardship of coming up with three months of payments and extra fees or would lose the villa. How could Jorge even think this was okay?

Now she knew exactly what she was going to do. She was going to write him a letter.

Dear Dad,

It is unfortunate it has come to this, but you have given me no other choice. You just ignore anything I say when it comes to your gambling. I'm in disbelief how you chose it, when it took everything from you.

It has turned you into an irresponsible person who doesn't care about anything but your next bet. I can no longer watch you go downhill. It's too hurtful to see you this way. Your gambling has destroyed the villa. It's in poor condition and getting worse. I know about the roof leak. I saw the black mold. Just today, I received a letter from Bank of America for past-due payments.

I am giving you and your gambling buddies two weeks to get out. If you do not, I will have you evicted. I think back to all the times I helped you when I was struggling, but I did so because you were my father. I realized you just used me, never thinking about how I was doing. I was only good to you when I gave you money. Remember, God helps those who help themselves. It is time that you help yourself.

Love,
Tina

She was in tears as she tried to find the box of envelopes in her closet. Tina never could have ever imagined she would have to take extreme measures as she was doing. The thought of evicting Jorge never entered her thoughts before and was scary because she did not want to.

Tina hoped the letter would scare him to stop gambling. It was mind-blowing to think Jorge still believed his actions were right. How he could still gamble when his life was at such a low point. Yet, he found ways to bet at the Palm Springs Kennel Club every day.

"What is that?" Christopher asked.

"It's a letter I wrote to my dad."

"I'm sure it wasn't easy to write."

"Actually, it was. My feelings just poured out on the paper. It's the sending part that's going to be hard. I know when it's sent, it can't be taken back."

"You could always wait to send it until you are ready. There is no rush."

"I thought about that too, but then I realized I could not wait. I feel like I have waited my whole life to say something, and he hasn't given me any reason not to send it. If you'd have seen the villa, you'd say to send it by express mail," Tina said, as she tried to make light of the situation.

Tina gathered her belongings and left with the letter. She still couldn't believe this was all happening. Tina would call her mother later and tell her everything. She hoped Eva wouldn't be upset and instead be understanding, even after warning Tina about Jorge's gambling. How she still wished she could rewind the hand of time. The only thing she could do now was to move forward and not let her father's gambling call the shots anymore. It did enough damage to last a lifetime.

She cried to the post office, thinking about when she was around six, living in New York. It was snowing as she stared out of the apartment window, thinking how magical it was, telling her parents how it looked like a Winter Wonderland.

Not too long afterward, Jorge had a surprise. He went to the neighbors and borrowed their sleigh and took Tina out for a ride as he ran as fast as he could while pulling the sleigh. Tina always remembers that day as one of the happiest ones.

"When should this letter arrive?" Tina asked the postmaster.

"Tomorrow."

"Great, so he doesn't even have to sign anything?"

"No, not a thing. The postmaster will swipe the letter when it's delivered to the mailbox. This service was established for people who don't like to sign or can't sign because of their job."

"What a smart idea."

Tina left the post office feeling liberated yet nervous. The wheels were now in motion, and the real test would be when her father received the letter. Rosie's Cafe was in the same plaza, so she decided to stop in and get a coffee, feeling a headache brewing.

While pouring creamer into the coffee cup, she heard a familiar voice call her name.

"Tina Gabor, is that you?"

Tina turned around, surprised to see Alex.

"Alex, is that you?"

"Yes, how have you been? I can't believe it is you."

"Well, to be honest, not too good, and I'm sure you can guess why," Tina said.

"Your father, he's still gambling," Alex responded quickly.

"Yes, he is and probably never stopped. I can't even tell you what a nightmare it's been. And I don't want to get into it either; otherwise, I'll start crying, and I can't stop when I start. I just don't know what to do anymore," Tina said.

"I know how you feel. Can you stay a little and talk?" Tony asked.

"For a little."

They sat at the corner table.

"What do you mean you know how I feel? I thought your father mostly loaned money and just gambled a little."

"Nah, I think he gambled more than he let on, but he knew when to stop back then. He always had my mother checking up on him, and when he'd lose, he would somehow win it back. But once I left for college, his luck ran out, and so did my mother," Tony said.

"It always does."

"I just know that he gambled whatever my parents had in savings and then convinced my mom to take a hundred thousand home equity line of credit on top of refinancing the property when the housing prices were high. He promised her his landscaping business was going so well that he needed to expand. Of course, he was lying at the time and gambled the money away. Eventually, he lost everything and couldn't pay it back, and my mother left him. I feel bad for my mom as she had to move in with my aunt, her sister. Otherwise, she would be homeless," Alex said.

Tina felt like Alex and her were singing the same themes, except with different lines. Gambling destroyed their families.

"Do you still see him?" Tina asked.

"Rarely, he makes it hard to have a relationship because he always wants something."

"I can see that. I have that happening now."

"It's also hard to see him. He's a different person now, full of anger and blaming others for his situation. He lost his landscaping business, lives in a beat-up car, and still gambles. And if that wasn't bad enough, he works for Gabriel now."

"Who is he? "Tina asked.

"Let's just say you don't want any ties to him. He is the cruelest loan shark around. When my father lost his business, he went to Gabby. And he took pity on my father, giving him a cut if a sucker borrowed from him."

Christopher stopped to look around to make sure no one was listening.

"If he had to, he would bite the head off his child if he felt he was being played. I don't even like to say his name. You never know who could be listening. I just hope your father hasn't gotten involved with him, especially since he isn't good at paying people back."

Tina's stomach sank as she thought about Jorge. She knew it could be a possibility that her father was involved with this evil man.

"Last year, I had a huge falling out with my father," Alex said.

"At first, I was beyond scared, but I realized that it was what set me free."

Tina leaned forward; she wanted to know more, as this could help with her situation.

"Last summer, when my grandfather died, he left me a hundred thousand dollars. In the will, it said to use the money wisely. Of course, my father knew his father's wishes."

Tina already knew where the story was headed but had no idea how cruel Alex's father was until the end.

"One day, my father called me. He said that he needed money to pay off the mortgage."

"Was it your parent's house?" Tina asked.

"Actually, no, this was a condo they still had left. My mother was not interested in moving in with my father after what happened."

"Oh."

"Anyway, he wanted me to buy the unit from him, let him live there for free, and rent one of the rooms to pay the mortgage."

Tina just shook her head.

"He said if I didn't, he would lose the property and would live on the streets. Then he went on to say that if I didn't help him, I wasn't good enough to be his son and was abandoning him. I actually started to cry, thinking maybe he was right, but then I realized he was using emotional blackmail."

"He said that? Making you feel like it was your fault after he got himself in this mess by betting. I'm afraid to hear the end," Tina said.

"Oh yeah, and hold on, because it gets worse, but I will admit, a part of me still thought about helping him."

"Don't feel bad about it. I would have thought about it, too. We are good people and their children."

"That always seems to get in the way, especially being blood related." Alex said as he paused to collect his thoughts. "But the more I thought about it, the more I knew it would only be a big mistake. If I bailed him out again, he'd only gamble more, and the vicious cycle would start again. So, I said no," Alex said.

"You did?" Tina said, taking a deep breath.

"I did… no is a simple but powerful word," Alex said.

"How true. I wish I used it more than I did."

"In the end, I realized that I wouldn't help him gamble more by saving him. So, I detached myself from him…and that was the hardest part."

"I'm going through a similar situation, though mine is just starting."

Tina felt hopeful that, eventually, she could be as strong as Alex.

"I'm so grateful we happened to be at the same place at the same time. What's been your secret?" Tina asked.

"No secret, really, other than to know you are not responsible for your father's gambling and that you are not here to clean his messes. That's for him to do," Alex said.

"I know, but it is so hard," Tina said, her eyes burning.

"At first, it is, but it gets easier. I promise you are being treated this way all these years by allowing him to treat you this way. You can change this."

Tina smiled at Alex's uplifting words, feeling now that she had a better handle on the troubling situation and was determined not to give in anymore.

"It was so nice seeing you, Tina. Just remember that you aren't responsible for your father's actions."

"Same here, Alex."

"Oh, also, there is this great website for friends and family of gamblers. Let me write it down for you. When you have a chance, go and check it out. It will change your life."

"I will and thank you again. You have been a Godsend."

"Actually, Tina, you have been. Oh, my screen name is Swagger."

"Okay, Swagger, I like it, though I am unsure what it means."

"Google it."

Tina walked back to the car happily, and couldn't wait to check out the website, and thought about what screen name she would use.

After dinner, while the girls were playing with the Little Tikes kitchen, Tina went on the website Alex recommended. She spent two hours reading hundreds of posts of family and friends dealing with their compulsive gambler.

Many were on the edge, as their compulsive gambler continued to gamble, even after promising they'd stop. Reading post after post was a huge wake-up call, realizing that compulsive gambling was far worse than she thought imaginable. It was a dark, ugly disease she never knew existed, as she learned for the first time that it was an addiction many battled.

Tina especially liked the "Starlight" posts, feeling like she could have written them herself. Her posts made her laugh, and they didn't beat around the bush about the addiction. Tina then noticed a chat group scheduled for tomorrow night, and she wasn't going to miss it for anything in the world.

CHAPTER 36

Denial at its greatest

The next day Jorge received Tina's letter. It was in an official white envelope, the same kind he received many times from the bank. Jorge didn't blame Tina, as he had been avoiding her for the past month, yet he was upset that she wouldn't let him be.

He didn't see any fault in the condition of the house. It was his right to do what he saw fit.

Sometimes Tina wished her mother never gave her the villa for all the trouble she endured, but she still knew if she had not let Jorge move into the villa, none of this would be happening.

Jorge knew Tina had been in the villa, as the neighbor mentioned seeing her leave upset. He then went to the backyard patio to read the letter. The electricity was still off, and now with the weather getting hotter, it was unbearable to be inside during the day. But at night, when the temperature cooled down and the windows were down, it wasn't that bad.

He looked out to the dark lake, feeling depressed. Jorge also hadn't gambled for two days, not because he didn't want to, but because he was broke. However, the addiction would still taunt him, and he could only get a break by sleeping or watching sports.

Call Fernando!

Two of his gambling buddies already moved out because they were frustrated with Jorge and the living conditions. He promised he would have the water and electricity up and running again, but he still couldn't get the money to make it happen.

Jorge even called Tim to see if he wanted to move in again, allowing him to sublet his place for more gambling money and give him a cut too, but he wasn't interested. Things were looking grim for Jorge, but he still didn't think there was anything wrong with his gambling.

The last time he ate was a day ago, and it wasn't much more than expired cereal left in the kitchen pantry.

He finally opened the letter, hoping for the best, yet the first sentence set a serious tone. He shook his head as he read it, tempted to throw it out before he got to the end.

"She is crazy."

Throw it out!

Jorge folded the letter and placed it in his rear jeans pocket. He was taken by what Tina wrote. He knew he had a problem, and it wasn't gambling but her. He walked back to the villa, grabbed his keys, though he had less than a quarter tank of gas, got in his car, and drove to the track. He didn't care that he didn't have any money. He'd worry about it once he got there.

First, he would stop by Fernando to see if he could spot him a few twenties; if not, he knew he still had one option. A dangerous one, a suicidal one, but at this point, he didn't care as it was an option. It was Gabby. He would look for Tony at the track and see if he could put a good word in for him.

Now you are thinking, my good man.

Tina spent the day with the girls at the pool, trying not to think about Jorge. She wondered if he would rush over, upset by the letter. Tina didn't want to be home if he decided to come over. Christopher didn't think Jorge would come by, as Jorge wasn't one for confrontations, and he loved the girls, but Tina wanted Christopher to be prepared if he did. So, they came up with a plan just in case.

Hours later, when Tina came back with Kate and Lana from the pool tired. She was relieved that Jorge didn't go by the house. Maybe he didn't receive the letter yet, she thought, believing he would have called or gone by the house. But then she realized her way of thinking and her father's were not alike.

She spent the evening reading all of Starlight's posts. Their stories were very much alike. The biggest difference was that Starlight was now two years estranged from her father. She had no idea where her father was and stopped checking up on him as it only hurt to know he was still gambling.

Starlight: Welcome Palm Beach
Palm Beach: Thank you.
Victoria: Welcome PB
Palm Beach: Hi Victoria & Starlight
Victoria: What brings you here tonight?
Palm Beach: My father
Victoria: How long has he been gambling?
Palm Beach: 30 years or more
Victoria: My husband gambled for 15 years before he stopped.
Starlight: My father is also a cg. We don't speak anymore.
Palm Beach: Sadly, I think we're headed in that direction.
Victoria: I'm sorry… things must have gotten really bad.
Palm Beach: Yes, V. I'm still numb by the lies he fed me for so many years. It is hard to believe that I didn't see through them. How stupid I feel.
Victoria: CGs are masters of manipulation. They will say or do ANYTHING TO GAMBLE! You're not stupid.
Palm Beach: I'm beginning to see this and thank you.
Victoria: Yes, they are.
Victoria: PB, chat is about over. Why don't you post a thread? I will leave you ladies with one last thought. It is important to focus

on your recovery. We cannot control what the CG does, but we can control what we do XXXXX.

Palm Beach: Thank You, Starlight and Victoria, I hope to chat again soon.

Starlight: I'll be looking for your thread.

Victoria: Me, too

Palm Beach: LOL

Tina logged off, feeling hopeful to know others were suffering like her. There seemed to be a whole world of people like her that she never knew existed.

She thought of Victoria's final words: "It is important to focus on your recovery." Tina never thought about her recovery, believing her father needed to recover. This became her light bulb moment, realizing that she was the one that needed support for the hurt and pain she endured as a child of a compulsive gambler.

Before logging off the site, she read the gambler's section of those in recovery. Tina was in awe of their stories. Some had been in prison for various crimes powered by the voice to gamble, some just admitted to themselves and others powerless over gambling, and some had been living gamble-free lives for years, others just had a slip, yet all of them were not in denial about their gambling.

Tina went to bed thinking about her recovery and how that would look, feeling peaceful and calm.

Yet, this calmness did not spill to the next morning because it was Friday. Though Jorge had stopped coming by, Tina still had this nervous feeling he would show up, and he did.

He came knocking on the door like nothing happened between them. He was holding an extra-large pizza box from Nino's Pizzeria.

She did not want to open the door, but that plan was ruined when he kept shouting, "Kate, it's Grandpa. Open the door."

What a bastard, she thought. Here he was trying to get Kate's attention over hers knowing his chances were greater.

"Mommy, it's Grandpa." Kate pulled on her shirt, almost pulling her down to the ground.

"I know, honey."

"Open, open."

Tina reluctantly opened the door. Jorge smiled as he looked at Tina, believing everything was all right between them. Kate bombarded Jorge with a tight hug around his waist as he held the pizza box.

"Why didn't you come for so long? I missed you," Kate said.

"Ah, Kate, Grandpa went on a long trip to Hungary. Do you know where that is?" he asked as he looked down at her.

Kate shook her head, thinking the word hungry only meant when your tummy needed food. She was a little confused by his question.

"Grandpa isn't going to be away that long anymore. I promise." Kate smiled.

"Hi, Christopher," Jorge said as he walked in from the garage.

"Oh, hi Jorge," Christopher said, surprised.

"Can you please take this to the kitchen?" Jorge asked while handing him the still-hot pizza box.

"Ok."

"Great, because I want to give my beautiful granddaughter a big hug and kiss. I miss you so much, my little girl."

He wore a big smile as he reached down and picked Kate up, kissing her until she could no longer take it anymore.

"Dad, I think she has had enough kisses to last her entire life," Tina said.

"What about you?" Jorge asked Tina.

Tina didn't say a word.

Christopher kept his eyes on Jorge going along with Jorge's game but was ready to interject if needed. Tina walked into the living room before he could kiss her.

"So, how have you been? Haven't seen you for a while," Tina asked.

"Good," Jorge said.

"That's good to hear."

"Let's eat. I'm starving."

Now, Tina could believe that line. Jorge looked thinner than usual, but she didn't feel sorry for him, because the last time she checked, he was at the track again.

"Me, hungry, too," Kate said.

"Oh, Kate, how I missed you," Jorge said, reaching to hold her hand, as they walked in the kitchen like best buddies.

Tina could admit it was bittersweet to see her father and Kate in a perfect moment, but she sadly realized that these little moments would end if he wouldn't stop gambling.

During dinner, Jorge did not mention Tina's letter, though he had plenty to say to Kate about his supposed travels, which he fabricated. Kate kept asking him question after question, which he had no problem answering. Even Tina started to believe that Jorge actually went to Hungary. His lies were so convincing that anyone who didn't know him would have thought he had just returned from Europe. Tina noticed what a seasoned manipulator he was, causing her to take a few deep breaths.

"All done, now let's go play," Jorge said.

Kate was still eating but suddenly became full when he said the magic words and was no longer interested in finishing the last few bites.

"Okay, Grandpa."

Tina watched Jorge follow Kate out of the kitchen into her room. She really wanted to talk to her father alone, but it didn't seem like that would happen tonight.

Lana was still sleeping, so Tina decided to take the laundry out of the dryer and put it away. She entered Kate's room with play dresses to hang in the closet.

Jorge and Kate were on the floor playing with Little People. At first, this didn't seem unusual, but this time she noticed an excitement in Kate's eyes that she had never seen before. Tina stopped as she watched Kate on her knees, bouncing up and down, as she watched

Grandpa move the horses around in a circle. Kate wildly clapped as her horse Buddy edged ahead of the other horses. Tina became breathless as she watched.

"Kate, honey, what are you and Grandpa playing? I've never seen you play this game before."

Kate didn't answer. She was only fixated at the track before her.

"Mommy, my horse won. I won money! Look, I won more," Kate said, proudly showing the quarters. The ones Jorge gave her. Jorge just smiled, not thinking there was anything wrong with the game.

"Wow, honey, that is great," Tina said, though she was fuming inside.

"Mom, do you want to play?" Kate asked, with such loving and innocent eyes.

"Ah, thank you for asking, but not now. But I know Daddy has a surprise for you in the garage."

"He does," Kate said, getting up from the floor and raising her arms to be picked up.

"Oh, sweetie, let's go and see Daddy."

"Grandpa, why don't you go to the back patio? I have something for you."

Jorge just looked at Tina as he was ready to leave; he could see in Tina's eyes that it was probably not true.

"Sure, I'll be in the back."

Christopher came in from the garage, and Kate ran to her father. "What's the surprise?"

He looked at Tina and knew that was the cue word for him to keep Kate occupied, so Tina could talk to Jorge.

"Oh, it is in the garage. Let's go look."

"What is it?"

"Now Kate, it wouldn't be a surprise if I told you. Now, would it?"

Kate took his hand and walked into the garage with him.

Tina looked at Jorge as he was still sitting on the floor.

"How could you ever think it was all right to introduce betting to Kate?" Tina demanded.

"What are you so worked up about? Kate loves it."

"What I'm so worked up about? What a dumb thing to say. You know how I feel about betting."

"Come on, Tina, it was harmless. Children love races."

"So you're saying that Kate should be a gambler like you?" Tina asked.

Jorge didn't answer; he didn't want to talk about his hobby. Jorge still had Tina's letter in his back pocket, wearing the same jeans.

"Did you get my letter?" Tina asked.

"Yes."

"And why haven't you said a word about it?"

"Why should I?" Jorge answered.

"So, you have nothing to say about it?"

"Nope. I'm going to pretend that I didn't get it. You're lucky that I'm forgetting about it, or you're the one that is going to be in a lot of trouble with the law. Who are you to tell me what to do? You should be ashamed of yourself. Hah, to evict me out of my own place. Now that is a joke."

Good job, let her have it!

"You mean *my place*. I meant every word I wrote in the letter. Every single word and every punctuation mark. Do you think pretending you didn't get the letter would change anything? How could you even think this way?"

"Girl, you are getting to be annoying like your mother," Jorge said.

"Dad, I have been more than patient and understanding. The villa is in horrible condition, and you don't seem to care. I was there."

"Don't exaggerate," Jorge said with a grin.

"I exaggerate. Are you kidding me? The place has mold growing in the master bedroom walls and ceiling, and you, too, must think it's bad because you don't even sleep in the room anymore. There's no water or electricity in the place either. It reeks of mold and cigarette smoke. If the health department got word of the horrible conditions, they'd deemed it uninhabitable."

"Again, you are exaggerating. A little bleach will take care of the mold."

Tina took a deep breath.

"Dad, you know I love you, but . . ." Tina said, as she started to feel herself become emotional. Her eyes were burning, and her throat felt like it was closing up.

"Yes, but sometimes you can be like your mother," Jorge said, as he was not going to admit to anything.

"But as I said, things cannot go on like this anymore. Your gambling is out of control, and it has gotten to where you can't admit it is pulling the carpet from under you. Please tell me why you still gamble?"

Jorge kept quiet.

Tina continued, "You've lost so much. You hardly work. You can't afford to pay basic bills like water and electricity. And I just got a letter from Bank of America saying the last two months haven't been paid, and this month's payment is due. Did you think Bank of America would forget about the payments if you ignored them?"

"I'll pay," Jorge said.

"When will that be?" Tina asked.

"When I can, that's when."

"When can you? What kind of answer is that? Or are you just waiting for the property to foreclosure at my expense? So, you won't have to pay."

Jorge felt the rage in him grow.

Don't listen to her! She is out of line.

"Dad, you have a gambling addiction. I will help you get the help you need, but first, you need to admit you have a problem. Otherwise, your life will spiral downward. Can't you see your gambling tearing you and our family apart? Think of Kate, me, and Lana. We all love you," Tina pleaded.

I'm the one who is always there for you. Nothing feels better than a win.

"What I do is my business. I don't need you to tell me what problem I have or don't have. You sure have a strange way of showing love," Jorge rebutted.

"Well, then, I will not sit and watch you lose whatever dignity you have left," Tina said.

Tell her to get lost.

"Get lost, Tina. I don't need you or anyone else to tell me how to run my life. I've done fine before you were born, and I'll do fine without you if you don't stop." Jorge said, looking straight at Tina with the cruelest of eyes.

Suddenly, Tina feared that her father was about to hit her. Goosebumps ran up her body as he looked at her with such hate and anger. But she wasn't going to back down. Tina wanted to say something that would leave him thinking and what she was fully prepared to follow through with.

Tina took a deep breath as she looked at her father, wrapped tight in the grips of denial and addiction. She walked to the sliding glass door where Christopher and Kate could see her. She wasn't going to take any chances with the monster raging inside her father.

"Well, then you have until July 21," Tina said.

"Yeah, right."

"Yeah, right, or you will be evicted."

"Bullshit! Who would ever believe you?" Jorge shouted.

"A judge would!" Tina shouted.

"I'm out of here. What kind of daughter are you?"

"I'm telling you, you have ten days, not a day more."

Jorge furiously opened the sliding glass door to find Kate playing on the floor with her new blocks.

"Grandpa, come play with me," Kate said.

"I have to go."

Kate got up and started to cry, "Where are you going, Grandpa? I set up the track."

"Ask your mother. She said Grandpa isn't good, so I have to go."

"Mom, Grandpa is good." Kate started to cry as she watched him leave the house, slamming the door behind him. Christopher went to Kate and carried her in his arms.

"Honey, it is all right."

"I want Grandpa. I want to play with him."

"I know, honey. He's sick. That is what Mommy meant, not that he is bad but sick."

"Sick, how?"

"In the head."

"Oh."

"See how upset he looked?"

"Yes," Kate said, nodding as she stopped crying.

"Mommy just didn't want you to get sick in the head either, so she asked him to leave."

"Is he going to get better?"

"Hopefully, that's if he wants to."

"Okay, Papa, will you play with me?"

Christopher hugged Kate with all his might, as he knew Kate loved her Grandpa, but he also knew that Tina was doing the right thing.

How Tina wished her father was responsible like the hundred million other dads in the world. How he would have taken care of the villa, paid the home equity, and not gambled every cent he had. It hurt her to know how she trusted him with her heart and money when others warned her, always giving him the benefit of the doubt. While all along he was gambling and placing himself in harm's way, Tina too, not caring if she could even handle the mess he created.

Tina knew now trying to help her father was pointless. He didn't want it, yet she knew she had to get help because she needed it.

After tossing and turning most of the night. Tina went to the living room and wrote her first online post. She was nervous, but she felt like she had already made a few friends and promised to post to Starlight. Instead, she noticed a twenty-four-hour chat room and joined, thinking it would be nice to chat with someone who could offer her support.

Palm Beach is now connected.
Starlight: Hi, you're up late.
Palm Beach: Hi, I didn't think anyone would be here.
Starlight: There is always someone here. So how are you tonight?
Palm Beach: Not so good. Dad stormed off tonight.
Starlight: Why?
Palm Beach: I had an intervention with him. For the life of him he will not admit he has a gambling problem, so I told him that I was not going to watch the addiction take him.
Starlight: The only way a compulsive gambler (cg, for short) will know you mean business is if you follow through with your words. If not, he will never take you seriously, and the addiction will gain more strength.
Palm Beach: I can see that I just believed him for many years. Now I have no other choice but to follow through, or my family will suffer.
Starlight: I will be here to support you. Estrangement is often necessary for a cg to hit rock bottom. Sadly, this doesn't guarantee that this will happen to your father. Many times it won't. They continue to gamble, getting deep into the addiction as they find enablement from others. As you know, they are very charming and have a knack for storytelling. As you know too well ☹
Palm Beach: I'm scared. It looks like I will have to involve the courts.
Starlight: Don't be. You'll make it. You took a big step by confronting your father. Don't let him take anymore from you.
Palm Beach: TY Starlight. Suddenly I'm tired, thanks to you, in a good way. I was restless after today.

Starlight: Monday, there is a Family and Friends group. I hope you will join us for cyber tea and pudding.

Palm Beach: See you then. I can now go to bed with a smile. TY 1000X

Starlight: You are welcomed 1000X

Palm Beach: Goodnight, Starlight.

Starlight: Sweet dreams

Palm Beach has signed off.

Finally, Tina was sleepy. She couldn't keep her eyes open anymore as she logged off the computer. Once her head hit the pillow, she was out.

The next morning, she was ready to write her first thread after she visited Uncle Fernando, hoping he could help.

CHAPTER 37

Stunned Fernando

"Hi, Uncle Fernando."
     "Hi, Tina."
"How are the girls? I hear they are beautiful."

"Good, and thank you," Tina said as she smiled, wondering if her uncle even knew their names.

"So, you want to talk about your father? What is it that you want to talk about?"

"Yes, I'm not sure what you know about what is happening between us."

Fernando was going to let Tina talk first. Jorge had been over earlier, complaining about Tina's letter. He knew about the planned eviction.

"I don't know much. I didn't even know there was anything wrong between you two."

Tina wasn't buying it, but she hoped that Uncle Fernando would help. Maybe he could talk with Jorge.

"Well, things have been bad between us . . . for months now, actually . . . years, and there's so much I have overlooked, but this time, I can't. I'm prepared to take him to court if need be."

"Is that really necessary? He's your father." Fernando acted surprised, though he already knew this.

Tina opened her purse and took out a set of pictures of the villa.

"Here, look at these," Tina said.

"Nice place. I heard your mother gave you the villa as a graduation gift, but your father also said he was supposed to get the villa in the divorce settlement, not you. And somehow, your mother illegally gave you the property," Fernando said, realizing he had said too much.

Tina knew Fernando knew more than he was letting on.

"Well, that's not true. If he had read the divorce papers he signed, he would clearly see it was never his. I have a copy if you would like to see for yourself."

"Oh, no, that's okay. I believe you," Fernando said as he shook his head.

"Now, going back to the reason why I'm here. Yes, the villa was a nice place."

"What do you mean...was?"

"There are no words to describe how it is now. I should never have let him move in because now it's completely destroyed," Tina said as she looked away to gather her bearings.

"Look at these pictures. This is how the place looks now."

Fernando's face dropped, speechless as he looked at the photos, each one worse. At first, he questioned if he was actually looking at the same villa, but when he saw the Mexican title he installed, he knew he was. Fernando couldn't get over the black mold growing in the master bedroom. This had to be from the roof leak. He had told Jorge that the patch-up work was only temporary until a roofer could properly fix it, but he could see that he never got anyone to fix it and let it go. *What an idiot,* he thought.

"How did this happen?" Fernando asked.

"Didn't you help him with the roof, or was that another lie of his?" Tina answered.

Fernando's heart dropped. He never thought his brother would involve him in a lie, but he did.

"Well, honestly, I just helped him patch it up until he could get a real roofer, and again I told him it was only a temporary fix lasting until the next heavy rain, which we have been having on and off for weeks," Fernando said.

"Uncle Fernando, I trusted Dad would keep up the place. I could have rented the villa but I didn't because he didn't have a place to live after the foreclosure. Of course, I only did this because he was my father. He also said he only needed a place until he could find one. But now it's trashed, and I'm left with this mess he created, yet he acts like he doesn't have a care in the world. And there hasn't been running water and electricity in the villa for months either," Tina said, feeling anxious.

"I don't know what to say. I'm lost for words. I had no idea how the place was inside. I told him that it was just a patch job," Fernando said.

"I had an intervention with him last night. I told him that as long as he kept gambling, I was closing the door on our relationship. I told him that I would not let him stay in the villa anymore, and that I would no longer help him with any of his money emergencies, and that I would stop paying for his cell phone. I basically told him he was on his own," Tina said.

"You were paying for his cell phone? I had no idea." Fernando said, now feeling like he had also been played as he had given him money to pay for the supposed cell phone bill.

"Yes, I have been for four years."

"If anything, he should be the one paying for yours."

Tina nodded in agreement, "He is a compulsive gambler."

"What does that mean?"

"He lives and breathes gambling, and the worst part is he's in denial of it. He thinks nothing of it, blaming everyone else for his misfortunes when he should be looking at his actions. And he thinks it's his right to gamble. Can you imagine?" Tina asked.

Fernando knew Jorge gambled as he did too, but he could never imagine it would spiral so out of control. He felt sorry for Tina. He could see the hurt and disappointment in her eyes. He could only imagine her heartaches, but Fernando also knew how strong she was.

"I'll talk to him, and I'll see what I can do. What do you want from him?" Fernando asked.

"I want him to stop gambling, fix the place, and return my fifty thousand."

"What fifty thousand?" Fernando asked.

"The fifty thousand he bullied me into signing, it's actually a home equity line of credit to pay off his high-interest car loan, which I just found out he still has. Instead of using the money, as he promised, he gambled it in one month. He also hasn't paid the loan in months, so now I have to come up with three months' payments by next week. I'm beyond stressed," Tina said.

"No! This can't be."

"He just cares about his Palm Springs Kennel Club VIP membership by gambling every chance he gets. I'm sure he's at the kennel club as we speak."

"You know, Tina, I'll see what I can do, but I know your father doesn't have any money. He just asked me for gas and food money. Unfortunately, your father has a mind of his own, and gambling doesn't help. So, whatever you do, just do it, and don't look back."

Fernando paused to gather his thoughts.

"No one should go through this, especially you, who has always been there for your father. I wish I could help you more."

"Actually, you did. Thank you...I will do what I have to do, and I won't look back," Tina said.

Fernando felt a shift in Tina's words. He knew now that Jorge had met his match, for his daughter would not back down, but he also knew that Jorge wasn't going to either. This sickened him because Tina was just doing the right thing.

What a fucking mess, he thought.

CHAPTER 38

Jorge goes for the jugular

Jorge was so upset that he went to Tim's apartment in a fit, letting him read Tina's letter.

"What? Your daughter needs a good whack in the head. I would call Mr. Baldwin if I were you."

"I need you to help me. Get a few of your friends and help me fix the villa, or she will kick me out."

"That's not what the letter said," Tim said.

"I don't care what the letter says."

"No, what you need is a good lawyer. He will have Tina making the repairs."

"What? I don't get what you are saying?" Jorge said.

"Did you sign anything saying you were responsible for fixing the place?"

"No, but I said I would," Jorge said.

"That doesn't mean shit in a court of law. You were never responsible if you didn't sign a paper that said you would fix the villa. It's that simple," Tim said.

Jorge smiled as he got Tim's logic. *Bingo,* he thought.

"Let her take you to court. It takes a while anyway, and the judge will throw the case out because they don't like to get between families, and afterward Tina will be feeding out of your hand," Tim said.

"Are you serious?"

"Yes, I should know. My ex took me to court many times. All you need to do is act stupid, be on your best behavior, and cry like a baby. Trust me, it worked for me every time, and I still owe the bitch twenty grand."

"Thanks, man, you saved me. What is the jackpot today?"

"Ten grand."

Jorge went and lost at the track. Then he drove to Tina's for one last effort to make peace. He felt confident about what Tim said to him, but he still wished the courts weren't involved.

Tina looked out of the peephole to see Jorge. She slightly opened the door but didn't invite him in.

"I told you everything I had to say last night. It's not a good idea for you to come here anymore."

"Listen, I've had about as much as I can take with you calling the shots and ruining my life," Jorge shouted.

"Bye," Tina said, feeling threatened by Jorge's tone.

"No, you listen to me. If you go through with the courts, your mother will know how you lied to her. How you took the home equity behind her back when it was the wrong thing to do. If you let me stay in the villa, she will never have to know. Do you want to lose your mother and me?" Jorge said.

"So, now you're threatening me again? How could you when I did everything for you? When you stole from me? How could you look at yourself in the mirror anymore and show up here after what you did? Who does this?"

"What will Christopher think about you taking a loan behind his back? He will be furious with you," Jorge said.

"What's the difference? You don't pay them now."

Tina's heart was racing so violently that she placed her right hand over it and found herself leaning against the door, feeling lightheaded.

"You're not my father. No father would do what you have done to me," Tina said, wiping away the tears through her hurt.

Jorge just looked at Tina, wanting to smack her. "Your mother will disown you for what you did. Borrowing against what she gave you. You will lose not only me but her. Do you want that?" Jorge threatened.

"No, that's where you are wrong. She hasn't."

"What?"

"Yes, Mom knows everything, and she is sorry that you are even my father. She also said you were a monster. I'm sure you can remember those exact words from when I was a little girl when you would come home threatening Mom for money. I heard you bully her," Tina said.

"I don't believe you. Your mother would have called me by now," Jorge said.

"No, she is done with you."

"We'll see about that." Jorge smiled like he had an agenda in mind.

"But I'm sure Christopher will divorce you after he finds out you lied to him. He will never ever be able to trust you again. Think about that!"

"I never lied to him."

"No, you just hid the truth from him, which is even worse. What kind of wife has secrets from her husband?" Jorge said.

"Stop twisting everything around…there is nothing you can say now that will ever hurt me as much as what you have done to me," Tina said.

"Bullshit! I did nothing to you."

"You did enough to last my lifetime, plus more. Just remember July 21. It's right around the corner. I not only want you out but all of your gambling friends. If I need to, I will call the police."

"They left already."

"I don't believe a word you say anymore. You lied so many times. I don't even think you know the difference anymore."

Jorge stormed off, cursing under his breath. He rushed back to Tim's stank apartment and told him Tina was still set on evicting him. Tim laughed it off and said Jorge was getting worked up for nothing.

"Like I told you, let her take you to court. Who are they going to believe? A heartless daughter kicking her father out, or a humble father who happens to be a senior citizen that tells the court how forgiving you are toward his daughter? By the time this goes through the court, they will dismiss the case. Trust me," Tim said.

"Thank you."

"Now, forget about it."

Jorge laughed it off and was glad he went to Tim for advice, as he was street-smart.

Tina returned to the house emotionally drained and shaky as she sat on the couch. Things with her father weren't improving, taking such a toll on her mental health. Her breathing was still labored, and her stomach was in knots like she'd just been punched. Now all she could do was cry as she replayed in her mind what had happened.

As she sat on the couch, she reached for her laptop on the end table and wondered if Starlight would be on chat.

PALM BEACH just logged on.

Gordy: Hi PB

Blue Bird: Hi PB

Palm Beach: Hi u all

Gordy: r u a cg?

Palm Beach: no, my dad is.

Gordy: Oh, I am a cg.

Palm Beach: For how long?

Gordy: For 25 years

Palm Beach: That is a long time. It is great that you are cured.

Gordy: Actually, one is never cured. Once a cg, always a cg.

Palm Beach: I didn't know this.

Gordy: It is an addiction; cg should never gamble. Just like an alcoholic should never drink alcohol or like a drug addict should never take drugs.

Palm Beach: So, when was your last bet?

Gordy: A year ago.

Palm Beach: Congratulations!

Gordy: Tell me about your dad.

Palm Beach: Well, he has been a cg for most of my life and the worst part is that he is in denial. He sees nothing wrong with it. We are not on good terms.

Gordy: Ah, that is the worst part. Unless he admits to his addiction, there is nothing you can do.

Palm Beach: I'm learning this, and it still doesn't make it easier.

Gordy: You'll be fine. Just stick around, post as much as you like, and come on chats.

Palm Beach: Yes, I am so thankful that I am here.

Jorge saw Mr. Baldwin at the track, though they weren't on the best of terms after Jorge strung him along during his foreclosure. Still, he saw no shame in approaching him.

"Hi," Jorge said like he was a lost-long friend expecting a warm welcome.

Mr. Baldwin smiled back and turned away, looking at the teller prompt. He wasn't going to entertain small talk with Jorge. Mr. Baldwin had seen him at the track a thousand times after the foreclosure but at a distance. He was good with keeping his distance, but now he knew Jorge was up to something. He thought about walking away, but he knew Jorge would follow.

"Um," Jorge said.

"I can't believe you have the balls to come over and talk to me. I only talk to paying customers," Mr. Baldwin said.

"I'm sorry. I just have one question and will be out of your way, and I won't bother you again," Jorge asked, looking sincere.

Mr. Baldwin thought it was worth answering just for him to leave.

"I will answer this one question as long as I never have to see your face again."

Jorge smiled as he was about to get what he wanted and didn't have to pay.

Well done, man!

"Well, then a question or two it is."

Mr. Baldwin shook his head as he placed his right hand under his chin. He felt whatever Jorge was about to tell him was going to be half true, but he would answer his question or two just to get rid of him.

"What is it?"

"I've been staying at my daughter's villa, and now she wants to evict me because we had a little fallout about repairs."

"She can, especially if there is no lease between you."

"But she is lying because I never agreed to the repairs. Won't the judge make her do the repairs and let me stay?" Jorge asked.

"If I were you, I would start making those repairs or try to work it out with your daughter. That is the best legal advice I can give you," Mr. Baldwin said.

He is lying, Jorge!

"Well, I don't know about that. I still believe she can't just have me thrown out. I'm almost a senior citizen too."

"Yes, she can, and I know the judge who handles eviction cases in the county, and she is by the books, and doesn't take any bullshit. I think you better start packing, buddy. Get ahead while you can."

"Well, I am tougher."

"Okay, Jorge, you seem to think you know more than me. Good luck."

Jorge smiled as he believed this to be true. He wasn't going to budge and make any house repairs, and he wasn't going to turn the water or electricity on either. He was going to let the place rot.

Let her have it!

He believed Tim over Mr. Baldwin and wondered if he would go with him to court.

A few hours later, Fernando stopped by the villa. He couldn't stand being in the place for a few seconds. His eyes burned just from the front door. He had no idea how Jorge tolerated it either.

"Have you talked to Tina?" Fernando asked, taking a drag from his cigarette, sitting on the back patio overlooking the lake.

"No, and I'm not going to. She is off her rocker like her mother," Jorge said.

"And I see you haven't made any repairs here. And are you planning to? You only have a few days. July 21 is right around the corner," Fernando asked.

Jorge was quiet as he looked out to the lake. He didn't want to hear another word about Tina.

"Why aren't you taking any of this seriously, brother?" Fernando asked.

"This is all bullshit! That's why…she should let me live my own life. I'm not going to do anything here. Let her do what she wants. Let her take me to court. The judge will see that I am right."

Fernando felt sad for his brother as he watched Jorge looking so confused by his own lies, deep in denial as Tina had said. He felt there was no point in trying to talk to him anymore.

"It seems like you're ready to lose your daughter and grandchildren. Now that is sad, my brother. Have you really thought about this?"

Fernando looked at Jorge, surprised, he didn't even care to acknowledge his question.

"I see you have made your choice. It's hard to see, but I see you have."

Jorge didn't acknowledge him again, just keeping his gaze out to the lake.

"Well, I'm with Tina. From now on, you are on your own, brother." Fernando got up, walked out the back patio door, and around to his car, feeling nauseated by the mold and Jorge's denial of what was actually happening to him.

Don't listen to him. He'll get over it.

Jorge just brushed it off, went into the villa, opened all the windows, and went to bed. He thought about how he could get some fast money.

He was planning to go to Fernando's house tomorrow morning to take a shower, but now he would have to take one using the neighbor's garden hose. He even thought about asking the neighbors if he could use their shower, telling some lies, but he couldn't remember their names.

Jorge still didn't think his life was that bad. He was just having bad luck.

CHAPTER 39

The courthouse

Palm Beach has connected.

Victoria: Hi PB.

Palm Beach: Hi Victoria.

Victoria: I read from your thread that tomorrow is the big day. How do you feel about it?

Palm Beach: Not good. I actually feel sick about going. I wish tomorrow would never come.

Victoria: That's normal. You're just doing what you have to do. The addiction has to know you mean business. There is no other way.

Palm Beach: I just thought the letter would be a wake-up call to him, but I was wrong. He is acting like he never received it. I even drove by the villa in hopes I would see repairs being done but nothing. It's still as it was. It just breaks my heart.

Victoria: His mind is full of addiction. He's only driven to gamble. There is nothing you can do but to move forward. Remember, you are not just doing this for you, but him. He will only get worse. He has to hit rock bottom and want help for any chance against the addiction.

Palm Beach: I see this more than ever. It just makes me sick thinking about it. The steps I need to take aren't going to be easy, and I hate that I have to do them.

Victoria: They never are, but you are strong PB.

Palm Beach: Sometimes, I don't feel so strong.

Palm Beach: You know Victoria. I would have gladly accepted his apology and put the past behind us, but he has done nothing.

Victoria: He is too deep in the addiction. He does what it tells him to do. I'm afraid you will never come close to it. He has to be the one who stops listening to it.

Palm Beach: :(

Victoria: You have been through a lot. The child of a cg is one of the hardest, as you have a past. Keep us posted.

Palm Beach: I will and thanks XXX

On July 21, Tina woke up at 6:00 a.m. after a restless night. She had the eviction papers completed. She took Kate and Lana to the courthouse as she didn't want her in-laws to know about her plan yet.

"Mommy, where are we going?" Kate asked.

"We are just going downtown. Mommy just needs to turn in some papers. It will be quick. I promise," Tina said as she wiped the plump, salty tears falling down her cheeks.

Thankfully, she wore her sunglasses, so Kate couldn't see how bloodshot and puffy her eyes were.

"Okay, Mommy."

Lana had fallen back to sleep.

Once inside the courthouse, Tina and the girls had to go through security, which scared them. Kate was afraid of going through the metal detector. Tina had to be checked by an officer with a wand while holding Lana as she was not allowed to stay in the stroller. Just being in the courthouse was overwhelming enough. Tina felt sick knowing she was about to file eviction papers.

Never in a million years did she ever think this would happen, and she knew like the sun would rise tomorrow, this would not be the first or last time coming to the courthouse, which shook her to the core.

"Good morning. How can I help you?" the clerk asked.

Tina handed the clerk the eviction papers. The lady flipped through each page to ensure they were signed and completed properly.

"The police will serve these eviction papers to Mr. Jorge Gabor in about four days."

Kate looked strangely at her mother, hearing her grandfather's name being said. It was like she had seen a ghost. Yet, she was still too young to know what was really happening.

Tina woke up before dawn feeling sick with worry. She drove to the villa and saw the same black beat-up Chrysler in the driveway. Her heart started to race, seeing that her father had not told whoever was still in the villa their last day was yesterday.

"911, what is your emergency?"

"There is someone in my villa who shouldn't be."

"Are you inside?"

"No, I'm outside."

"Stay outside. Don't try to confront the person. Officers are on their way."

Tina parked behind the car just in case whoever was inside wouldn't try to leave. No longer than five minutes, a cop car came cruising down and parked next to Tina's car.

"Hello, ma'am. I am Officer Joe. What is the problem?"

Tina explained the situation and provided the deed of the property and her driver's license.

"So, you are saying that your father allowed someone to live in your villa without your permission?"

"Yes, I never allowed him to have others move in. I wrote a letter to my father saying that he needed to tell anyone living here they needed to leave, or I would call the police." Tina said.

"Do you happen to know who this person is?"

"No, I have no idea. Probably one of his gambling buddies."

The officer looked at Tina oddly but remembered Tina had said her father had changed the locks.

Officer Joe knocked on the door. There was no answer. Then he shouted, "Police, open up. We know you are here." Still no answer, then Tina told the police the back sliding door could be opened.

Fabio tried calling Jorge, scared out of his mind, hearing the police outside, but he wasn't answering. He looked outside to see there were two policemen, and the only thought he had was that he didn't want to go to jail. Fabio realized he had no other option but to open the door and see what they wanted.

He finally opened the door, dressed only in his underwear. He saw Tina, and this made him feel uneasy.

"Sir, according to the owner, you have no right to be here."

"Well, I pay rent to her father, Jorge Gabor, who has allowed me to live here."

Tina's heart sank.

"How long have you been here?"

"About five days."

He was lying. She knew he had been there for a few months now, but she wasn't going to interrupt the officer from asking questions.

"Well, since you have only been here less than ten days, you must pack up your things and leave."

"You can't just throw me out. I can stay until I am evicted. I know my rights," Fabio said.

"Well, this would have been true if you had lived here for over two weeks, but you just said you have only been here for five days. So now you must pack up your things and be on your way, or you will be arrested for trespassing."

"I lied. I have been here for three months. I didn't want to say so because I didn't want to cause any problems between Jorge and his daughter. I was trying to be a good person here. Tina, I was here when you came by banging on the door. You were still pregnant. Your key wouldn't work, so you kept banging on the door. Remember Tina?"

Tina just shook her head, refusing to be a pawn in his game.

"Look at my driver's license; this is the address I have on it."

"Pack up your things, buddy. I'm going by what you said first. Your first mistake was lying, and your second was trying to cover it by involving an innocent person. Now leave, or I will arrest you."

"Come on, Tina, let's work something out. I've been paying your father three hundred dollars each month. I have nowhere else to go."

"There is nothing to work out. I want you out. I don't even know you."

"Everything I own is here. There is no way I can get everything out today."

"Well, you will have to. You can leave what you can't fit in your car by the curb and get it later."

Officer Joe and Tina followed Fabio inside the villa. She felt betrayed all over again, as it was just as abused as she was.

"Is this a rehab property?" Officer Joe asked as he covered his mouth.

"No, this place used to be beautiful. Here look at these," Tina said as she reached in her purse for the pictures she had shown Fernando earlier.

"Wow, you would never think this was the same place."

"Well, this is what happens when all you think about is betting."

"What a shame. So, your father is a gambler?"

"Yes, it is a sad story. I gave him so many chances, but all he wants to do is gamble."

"This must be hard for you. Actually, my brother is a gambler, and he lost everything too. What a tragedy. His wife left him, and the last I heard is that he is living in the woods somewhere around here. I try not to think about it. My parents tried to help him too, but he didn't want any. He used to call them every once in a while, but the calls have stopped. My parents ask me to check him in the system to see if he is in jail. To his credit, he has avoided it. Yet, it makes me sick thinking about how he lives and what he does to gamble," Officer Joe said.

"I'm sorry. Your brother sounds a lot like my father. Maybe they know each other. This has been the hardest thing I have had to deal with. I just pray he sees the addiction for what it is and gets the help he needs, or who knows what awful things will happen to him."

Officer Joe nodded as he walked into the kitchen. He didn't want to talk about his brother anymore or gambling.

"How could anyone actually live here?" Officer Joe asked as he looked at Fabio. He just kept quiet, like he didn't hear the question. A typical gambler's response when they didn't like the question.

"Buddy, she is actually doing you a favor. No one should be living here."

While Fabio continued to pack, Tina walked back to the master bedroom. The door was locked again, but she quickly opened it with her key, and to her horror, the ceiling had caved in. She quickly closed the door, fearing if Officer Joe saw the black walls, he would call the health department.

"We can only stay here for another thirty minutes, so pack as much as you can."

"All right, I'm trying to get in touch with Jorge," Fabio said as he stopped packing, praying Jorge would answer.

"Even if you get in touch with him, it doesn't matter—you still need to leave. He has no rights to the property."

Fabio hoped Jorge would answer, but he didn't. The call went to voicemail, and Fabio was madder than hell now. *He is going to pay for this,* he thought.

Thirty minutes later, Officer Joe said it was time to leave the premises. Tina had asked him if he could get the villa's key from Fabio, and he agreed, though he said he couldn't force Fabio to. Fabio took his keychain full of keys from his jeans pocket. It looked like he was a super tenant with thirty or more keys from all the places he used to live at.

"Sure, let me find it," Fabio asked.

Finally, he located the key and tried it on the lock to make sure it worked, and it did.

"Thank you," Tina said.

"How about letting me stay until later?"

Tina shook her head, though she did feel a little sorry for him, it was not her fault.

"Fabio, you now have an early start to find a real place," Officer Joe said as he looked at his watch. It was only 6:16 a.m.

There are shelters if you really need a place to stay. If not, you have some nice things you can sell for extra money."

Fabio knew he wouldn't be able to change Tina's mind with a police officer beside her, he wasn't going to waste any more time. He went in his car and left with the little gas he had.

"Now, you just have to deal with your father."

"Yes," Tina said as she took a deep breath. It wasn't going to be easy.

Jorge won a little money last night, and he rushed to Sheri with a bouquet of flowers and money hoping she would forgive him, which she did.

Four days later, after a blissful three nights of binge gambling, he came home to find the eviction papers in the mailbox.

So, she wants to play hardball. Let's see how hard she can play!

He looked at the envelope and tossed it on the kitchen counter, though he knew he had to open it this time. After all, it was from the courthouse.

He looked at his cell phone, wanting to call Tina, but he knew this would get him nowhere. This infuriated him. He wanted to drive over to Tina's house and end this on his own terms.

However, Jorge had given his daughter little credit as she was proving to be quite strong-willed, more than he ever thought possible. Finally, he opened the eviction papers; the hearing was in two weeks. He quickly felt his heart drop as he sat on the hard kitchen floor, depressed.

Jorge was scared now as this was getting serious. He still had a little money and wondered if he could still make the repairs.

Don't you dare start feeling sorry for yourself or her!

In a panic, he called Tim. He told him about the hearing.

"Well, you still have some time to live in the villa if the judge sides with Tina."

Tim was an experienced evictor, as he had been evicted many times in the last ten years.

"I thought you said the judge would side with me."

"You or anyone should know there is never a sure bet regardless of the odds. It's the luck of the draw," Tim said.

"I wish you would have reminded me of this earlier."

Jorge left the villa and drove by Tina's house, but she wasn't home.

He then drove to the dog track hoping to see Mr. Baldwin and ask him for advice.

He was there sitting in his usual seat, but when he saw Jorge come his way, he left and got lost in a crowd. Mr. Baldwin was done giving free legal advice to him. Jorge brushed it off. He would try him again later. He wasn't going to take no for an answer.

Palm Beach just connected.

Victoria: Glad to see you here PB.

Starlight: Hi PB.

Victoria: How was your week?

Palm Beach: Well, he got the eviction paper yesterday.

Starlight: You're alive, aren't you?

Palm Beach: Yes, LOL

Victoria: Watch out Starlight, though I know you mean well ☺

Palm Beach: I'm starting to feel depressed about this whole thing.

Starlight: Rightfully so, just know you are doing the right thing.

Palm Beach: I know it's the right thing, but it still hurts. I still can't believe he has yet to admit to his addiction.

Victoria: Have you read Starlight's posts? There are many similarities between you two.

Palm Beach: I've read them all :)

Victoria: Ah, then you know that everything will turn out for the best.

Palm Beach: Victoria, you always have a way with words. Star, you haven't posted in a while, though. Is everything okay?

Starlight: Just received some unexpected news about my father.

Palm Beach: I am sensing it isn't good. Hope I am wrong.

Starlight: It isn't, and I'm still in shock...

Victoria: It's ok if you don't want to share.

Starlight: I have to be someplace in thirty minutes. Don't want to show up at my appointment as a mess. I'll post later xxx.

Starlight has logged off.

Palm Beach: Do you know what happened?

Victoria: I'm not allowed to speak about members who aren't in the group anymore, but I know Starlight is good for her word and will post later.

Palm Beach: Did something happen to her dad?

Victoria: I'm not at liberty to say, but I can say it isn't good.

Palm Beach: I'm sorry to know this. See, this is why I'm afraid something will happen to my father and I'll regret all of this. He isn't street-smart and could never survive on the streets either. I'm more terrified of him than me.

Victoria: Ask yourself, are you prepared to go back with the addiction and him calling the shots? Do you want to continue the life you've been living?

Palm Beach: No, why can't he just snap out of this?

Victoria: He can't because he can't see the addiction for what it is. He has to hit rock bottom, and maybe then.

Palm Beach: How long does rock bottom usually take?

Victoria: I don't have the answer. No one knows. It could take years, or it could never happen.

Palm Beach: :(

Victoria: You just have to look for yourself and your family. Remember, the monster takes care of its own.

Palm Beach: The monster?

Victoria: As you come to know more about the addiction. It is often compared to the monster for good reason. It's malicious and heartless.

Palm Beach: That's what my mother calls it, and so do I.

Victoria: Because we have seen it...see yah PB. I have to wrap up. Time is up.

Starlight posted what had happened. It was worse than Tina imagined. Her father sold her identity to a female friend, who opened two credit cards and gambled over ten thousand dollars together.

Now Starlight had to be dragged in a legal suit against her father and this woman friend, or she would have to pay the money back.

The more Tina read about the great lengths compulsive gamblers went to gamble, the more she realized how she shouldn't back down. This ripped her heart as she never wanted any of this, hating that she cried for a father who cared more about gambling than her. How she longed for those days when she was naïve to his gambling, but then again, she realized that naivety did her no good. It brought her to where she was now.

CHAPTER 40

Face-to-face at court

Tomorrow I will see my father for the first time in six weeks. I'm shaking as I type this. My stomach is full of knots and butterflies. Is that even possible? Saying I'm nervous is an understatement. I'm sick with worry. Will I break down and cry when I see him, or will I be stone cold? I just wish this nightmare wasn't real. Keep me in your prayers, as tomorrow will be a very big day for me. Good night! Palm Beach

Gordy: PB, we all will be thinking of you :) You are and have been a wonderful daughter to your father. His head is just too full of addiction to know this. Stay strong! You cannot give in to your emotions. You are doing this for him too. He cannot do it for himself.
Starlight: I was hoping you would pop in and let us know how you are doing, though I cannot hold your hand. Just know that I will be there in spirit, standing next to you. If you cry tomorrow, it's ok. After all, you have a big heart. We will be waiting for your update. XXX Starlight

The next morning there were five other messages for Tina from Bello Boo, Millie May, Peace, Freedom, and Beautiful Day.
She was still a ball of nerves. Tina could not eat or drink as nothing would stay in her system. She was functioning on pure adrenaline.
Earlier in the morning, she could hardly handle a few sips of coffee, as it caused her stomach to go sour, and she couldn't stop going to the bathroom. Her stomach sunk in, rejecting anything in it.

Tina left the house with a five-inch, thick, red binder she prepared for the hearing, which included the deed to the property, before and after pictures of the villa, copies of bills, and notices from the electrical and water company for the last two years, showing how there were months when services for both were disconnected for nonpayment.

By the grace of God, Tina followed a hunch she had about there being a possible violation citation on the property. She went to the town center and was horrified to discover a ten thousand dollar lien. This lien opened doors to other issues with the property she had no knowledge of, as all notices were sent to the villa's address.

Tina also got documentation of this and was ready to provide what was necessary to the court. It seemed the more she dug, the more she found. Code enforcement knew Jorge and said he was difficult to deal with. First, they found him amicable, agreeing to repair damages to the property, but did nothing and ignored all notices. Naturally, code enforcement upped their notices to include fines and fees if repairs were not made by a certain date, and when inspectors arrived, he would ignore them.

Never once did he tell Tina about their visits or the letters. However, Tina had them now. Along with the inspector's detailed notes with the time and date of phone calls, letters, and visits. There was even a comment noted in the file where the inspector had written that the father had spoken with the daughter. Daughter agreed to the repairs. The file was sixty pages thick.

"All rise for Honorable Judge Marshall."

Tina rose, fearing her shaky legs would give out as she saw the shadow of her father stand up in the corner of her eye. The judge walked to the podium.

"You may be seated."

Tina looked straight ahead, not wanting to look at her father as she was terrified by him, the lies he told, and how he allowed it to get to this point of being in a courtroom, feeling hate towards him.

Jorge was happy to see the judge was a woman, believing he had the upper hand. He had years of experience being a charmer, cutting women's hair. He knew when to smile and say the right things, but Tina had the documents and evidence backing everything she would say.

"So, I see the Plaintiff is the daughter and the Defendant is the father," the judge said, looking down at the file in front of her.

"Yes, Judge," Tina said.

"This should be interesting," the judge said, looking through the papers without a smile.

"So, Ms. Gabor, you are asking the court to evict your father from your property. Is that correct?"

"Yes."

"Now, why would you want to do this? Your father says here, in his reply to the court, he has no other place to go if you evict him. Would you be okay if he were to be homeless?" Judge Marshall asked.

Tina fumbled for words, not expecting the judge to side with Jorge without knowing the story first.

"Well, he has destroyed my property." She then opened the red binder where she had three sets of copies, each photo numbered.

"I have photos of how the property currently looks and how inhabitable it is."

She now had the photos in her hand, thinking the police officer would come to take them, but he just stood next to the judge, waiting for her direction. Judge Marshall doubtfully looked at Tina, not liking her.

"The photos aren't necessary."

Score.

"Mrs. Gabor, is there a lease between you and your father?"

"No, Your Honor Marshall, but we agreed before he moved in he would maintain the villa, pay the property taxes, homeowner's insurance, and the home equity loan. He has done neither, except for randomly paying the home equity," Tina said.

"Do you have this in writing?"

"No, it was verbally agreed between us. I didn't think it was necessary at the time as I believed he would stay true to his promise. I didn't think he would go against his word to his own daughter."

"Ms. Gabor, your father says in his written response that it was your responsibility to repair the roof and other repairs. He tells the court he is sick now because of your negligence and is suffering from chest pains and asthma," Judge Marshall said, as she looked stone straight at Tina like she was a heartless person.

"He is lying. He was supposed to be the one to take care of the villa."

Tears streamed down her cheeks as she became flushed and dizzy, feeling the room close in. It was unimaginable how she was the one who the judge was hard on and not Jorge. She looked like the heartless daughter to the outside world, while Jorge stood a few feet away looking like the victim.

"Your Honor, I know it is hard to believe my father has done what I'm saying because I have a hard time believing it myself, but I'm telling the truth. The last place I want to be is in a courtroom, but my father would not listen. I had no other choice but to let the courts handle this serious matter," Tina said.

The judge had many family hearings in her ten-year career but felt this topped them all. She also felt she had been too hard on Tina and should listen and let her explain the situation.

Maybe it was because her father was always there for her. He had worked two jobs, so she could go to college and even helped pay for law school. She would now direct her questions to Jorge.

"Your daughter tells the court under oath there was a verbal agreement between you two, and one of the terms was you were responsible for the maintenance of the villa. Is this true, Mr. Gabor?"

"No, judge, there was no such thing. How could I do repairs like the roof? I'm not as young as you think," Jorge said, smiling, trying to charm Judge Marshall.

"I also see the electrical and water bills haven't been paid for three months. Has this changed?"

Jorge just looked at the judge like he didn't understand the question.

"Let me put it this way, Mr. Gabor. Is there any electricity and water at the villa now?"

Jorge just smiled and batted his eyelashes as he tried to laugh off what he was about to say.

"I'm working on it."

"So, your answer is no."

"Correct."

"Then please tell the court, how are you managing to live in the villa?"

Tina raised her hand, wanting to answer the question.

"Yes, Ms. Gabor. Do you have anything to add which would help the court?"

"I believe so. My father gambles. He would rather spend a hundred dollars on a bet than pay the water bill."

The judge looked at Jorge, seeing how she had him all wrong. She thought he was the victim, but it looked more like Tina was.

She then thought of her brother-in-law, who liked to gamble, and felt a chill thinking about her sister and how her husband's gambling got his family in a bind. Remembering now how once she helped her sister so the water wouldn't be shut off.

"So, Mr. Gabor, how are you living in the villa? I can't imagine not having water or power."

"Well, truthfully, I have been staying with my girlfriend."

"So, you really wouldn't be homeless. You would have a place to go to if needed."

All Jorge could do was smile and look down as he looked through useless papers, pretending to be searching for something to avoid eye contact with the judge.

"Ms. Gabor, I actually would like to see those pictures. I find them relevant now."

The bailiff walked over to Tina to get the photos. Jorge still smiled as Judge Marshall covered her mouth in horror as she flipped through the pictures. Tina was right when she said the place looked inhabitable because it was. The judge looked at Jorge seeing nothing more than a con artist who almost fooled her, and she didn't like that one bit.

"Mr. Gabor, you mean to tell me you had no part in how the villa stands now?"

"No," Jorge said.

"Sir, I don't believe you. Your daughter owns the property and has the right to say who can live or cannot live in her villa. Therefore, you must find other living arrangements. The court rules for the Plaintiff."

"Does that mean I get to stay?"

"No, Mr. Gabor, it actually means that you have three days to make arrangements to get your things and leave the villa."

"What? I shouldn't have to. I'm her father."

"And she's your daughter. Have you thought about this? Have you thought how awful it was for her to bring you here because you wouldn't listen? You should have listened to her and paid your bills, sir. Now have a good day."

Jorge just smiled as he shook his head in disbelief.

"Mr. Gabor, if you return to the villa after three days, you'll be arrested in violation of the court's ruling."

Jorge just stood there, this time without expression, as the judge walked to her chambers. He couldn't believe the verdict, believing Judge Marshall would rule in his favor, even with the mounting evidence against him. He became mad, as he thought there had to be a way that he could still stay in the villa. He wouldn't let Judge Marshall's ruling stop him from doing so either.

Tears of relief calmed Tina as she thought it was finally over and Jorge would follow the court's decision, but she was wrong. Her troubles with her father were only beginning as he got deeper and deeper into the addiction. If he didn't like what he heard, he ignored it, and this was exactly what he did.

The judge doesn't know who she is dealing with! Screw her.

Palm Beach signed on.

Victoria: How was court today? How was it seeing him?

Starlight: I must have logged on here about twenty times hoping you would be in chat.

Gordy: Hi, PB

Swagger: Hi, PB

Palm Beach: Hi, at first, I didn't think I would make it. It was surreal just being a few feet away from him. He wrote a letter full of lies to the judge. In the beginning, it seemed like she was going to dismiss the case, but once she saw discrepancies between what was true and what he said, she quickly changed her tone.

Gordy: So, he is out then?

Palm Beach: Yes, he is. I still feel ill about the whole thing. In a crazy way, I still love him. I just see a man very confused by the addiction, yet he doesn't see it that way.

Starlight: Your love for your father will always be there and should be. We cannot hate our cg because they have an addiction, but unfortunately, until they admit to their addiction, we cannot help them.

Palm Beach: I'm really afraid of the path he's on. In his eyes, he can't do any wrong. He blames everyone else for his misfortunes. He must really hate me as he tried to turn me into a monster today.

Victoria: You a monster? Hah, now that is a good one. XXXXX

Palm Beach: My father and I were strangers today. We did not show an ounce of love toward each other. It was like we were no longer daughter and father, and it broke my heart.

Gordy: I'm sorry.

Palm Beach: Our eyes met once, and I just had to turn away. I still get chills thinking about how he looked so coldly at me.

Starlight: I know the look. The dark, perching, *I hate you* look.

Palm Beach: Yes, I hate you more than anything. :(

Starlight: It's the addiction wanting to make its presence known.

Palm Beach: I was thinking along the same lines.

Gordy: Whether you realize it or not. You've done right by him. Remember, you cannot help him. He has to reach rock bottom first. He cannot do this if you go back on your word. Hold on PB.

Victoria: You'll still be standing tall when the storm passes.

Palm Beach: Never in my life could I have ever imagined this would be happening to me and my father.

Starlight: This addiction is ruthless and damages everything in its path.

Palm Beach: Thank you all for your support. Good night to you all across the sea.

Eviction day came and went. And Jorge didn't move a thing out of the villa. He left it as it was, not caring that the police posted a poster-size eviction notice on the front door. He just ripped it off like it was no big deal, even though it said it was police property and not to be removed. He wasn't going to pay it any attention.

A few days later, Tina and Eva went to the property, thinking it would be empty, but to their horror, Jorge's belongings were still in the villa untouched. The locksmith came to change the locks, and the neighbor's son, a handyman, boarded up the back patio where the sliding door was broken. Glass was everywhere, and feral cats were now living in the villa.

Tina and Eva couldn't stay too long in the villa because of the mold burning their eyes, even with the windows up and the front door open. It was intolerable to their health. The villa was in worse condition than she thought. As Tina and her mother started to close the villa, Jorge arrived with Tim. Tina just happened to be closing the front room window when she saw his car pull into the driveway.

"Mom, Dad is outside," Tina called.

"I can't believe him. He doesn't listen to anybody, even the law. Don't go outside. He's dangerous now, Tina," Eva said.

"I won't, but I'm not going to take any chances with him. I am going to call the police," Tina said, terrified Jorge and his friend would break into the villa.

"911. What is your emergency?"

Eva went on to explain the reason for the call. The dispatcher was a bit confused as she just received a similar call from a man who said he was locked out from his own home.

"The police are already on their way."

"Who called?" Tina asked.

"A man called, saying he was unlawfully locked out of his own place," the dispatcher said.

"Unbelievable, he has lost his mind. How could he be locked out when he was the one evicted? I have all the paperwork with me."

"I don't know what else to say other than to show the officer when he comes."

A few minutes later, Officer Joe was knocking on the door. When Tina saw him from the peephole, she immediately opened the door, feeling safe.

"Hi, Officer Joe."

"Hi Tina," he said, smiling. "When I got the call and was told of the address, I thought I might see you here. So now it is your father's turn to leave."

"Unfortunately, my father still thinks he can come to the property when he cannot. Here are the eviction papers."

He looked at them page by page and said, "Your father is delusional, and he is wasting police time. Hopefully, he will leave peacefully, or he will be arrested."

Though Officer Joe was right, Tina still didn't like when other people spoke unkindly about her father.

"Stay here while I go talk to him. He looks like he is about to bust a fuse. I had him stay by his car as he started to walk with me here. He said I needed to arrest you and let him back in the house."

"He did?"

Tina started to fear for her safety. Her father seemed to be getting worse by the moment.

Officer Joe was now inches away from Jorge.

"I went to the courthouse today and appealed the eviction. So here are my papers," Jorge said.

Officer Joe carefully looked at the papers.

"Well, this isn't an appeal form. This is just a letter you wrote about why you think the judge wasn't fair. Legally this doesn't mean anything."

Jorge kept pushing how he still had the right to return to the villa. Finally, Officer Joe said he would be cited for trespassing if he didn't leave.

"Well, this is not over. I will be back," Jorge said.

"If you do, you'll be arrested," Officer Joe said.

"Arrested. You gotta be kidding me. I'm not a criminal."

He got in his car and drove around the block twice, trying to intimidate Office Joe, aware he could drive on the road as many times as he wanted. He knew it was not deeded to anyone.

Officer Joe walked back to Tina and told her she better be careful as her father wasn't comprehending what he was saying or the court's ruling.

"In my experience, your father will be back. Just call the police when he does. Don't talk to him. I won't pass it by him to hurt you."

Days later, Jorge got arrested and was charged with trespassing and stalking.

Tina was sick of worry. Things were only getting worse.

CHAPTER 41

The deposition

"Mr. Gabor," Mrs. Jones said as she greeted him from across the table.

"Yes," Jorge smiled back as he leaned forward with handcuffs. "Did you talk to my daughter?"

"Yes, I spoke with Tina."

"Did she drop the charges?" Jorge asked.

He wanted out of jail. Two weeks was enough, though it wasn't that bad because he became friends with his cellmate. However, he missed the freedom of the outside world and the track.

"No, she did not, and she isn't planning to," Mrs. Jones said.

"Bring her to me! Let me settle this once and for all!" Jorge shouted as he banged his wrists on the table.

"No, Mr. Gabor, I don't think you understand the severity of the charges against you. You could go to jail for a year, if not longer," Mrs. Jones said.

"Get lost. I did nothing wrong! I told you she's just upset with me because she doesn't like my girlfriend, that's it. That's it! What is it with you girls? Don't you know how to talk, girl to girl? Couldn't you threaten her with jail time or something?" Jorge said.

Attorney Jones was starting to not like Jorge as she did in the beginning. Now she saw a man that was a far cry from the sweet, caring one she first met and believed him to be.

Initially, she had thought Tina was the hard, cold-ass daughter she couldn't wait to tear up in court, but now she felt sorry for her. Mrs. Jones had realized Jorge was everything Tina and Officer Joe had said in their depositions. Even when it sounded so far-fetched at the time.

It was hard to believe she was fooled by Jorge. His gentle blue eyes were just a ruse because deep down, they were manipulative and self-serving.

Here he was telling her how to do her job when she had years of experience as one of the top public defense attorneys in the area. Days like these, she wished she was on the prosecutor's side, so she could teach him a lesson on being responsible for owning up to one's actions.

If only she could tell the prosecutor how to play Jorge, she would have the last say. Jorge was easy to place in a corner after you caught him in a lie. His memory wasn't good because he couldn't separate the lies from the truth, having a hard time telling them apart. The lies were only good for the moment, and Jorge wasn't in the dark about this either.

Mrs. Jones' thoughts took her back to the deposition room, meeting Tina for the first time. She waited to pin her in a lie, but Tina could not be tricked because she was telling the truth. She remembered Tina being only a few inches away, how she kept shaking, holding her hands to calm her distress and anxiousness. Tina reminded her of a child that was somehow victimized, not wanting to relive past traumas.

"Hi, Tina, I'm Mrs. Jones."

"Hi," Tina said softly, almost unable to hear her.

Mrs. Jones was the one who sent Tina the deposition notice, and she was the one handling her father's case and signed all his paperwork.

Mrs. Jones was beautiful. She easily could have been a model. She was dressed in a classic beige Armani suit and wore real pearls her grandmother passed on to her when she died.

"Are we ready to start?" The court reporter asked.

"Are we?" Mrs. Jones asked Tina.

Tina shook her head, feeling her throat close in.

"Yes, I am," Tina said.

"What is your name?" The court reporter asked as she looked at Tina.

"Tina Gabor."

"Do you swear to tell the truth and nothing but the truth?"

"I do," Tina said, her voice cracking, thinking she would have to say her response again.

"Okay, we can start now," said the court reporter.

"Tina, tell me about Mr. Gabor, your father?"

When Tina didn't answer right away, Mrs. Jones restated the question as she felt it was too general.

"Rather, how is your relationship with him?"

Stay strong, Tina, don't let them do this to you. Show them who you are, she thought. This helped as she looked at Mrs. Jones, only imagining the lies Jorge told her, feeling like she was already at a disadvantage. Yet, she realized it wasn't her job to prove that he hardly told the truth but to be truthful herself as then the truth would come out.

"Well, there isn't one."

"Oh, I see, and why is that?" Mrs. Jones asked as she leaned towards Tina, looking at her brown eyes, waiting to hear the answer.

It was like the weight of the world was on her shoulder as Mrs. Jones wanted to know why their relationship was strained. Her mind was racing. How he lied, stole, and cheated from her. How he took advantage of her goodness and love. How he continued to lie, how it was because of him she was questioned by the court at a deposition, how he lifted his hand to hit her, shouting at the top of his lungs, "You are not my daughter." How he tormented her like a bully, threatening her family's financial well-being and future. Remembering different times he was out to hurt her made it hard for her to speak without crying.

Mrs. Jones passed a tissue to Tina.

"He did a lot of bad things to me because of his gambling."

"So, he likes to gamble. That is hardly a crime, Mrs. Gabor."

"I know, but he is a compulsive gambler. He will do anything to gamble. He is like a drug addict. If he doesn't gamble, he becomes hostile. Almost like having a withdrawal. He threatens, cheats, and lies, and he has done all of this to me regularly. I have had to deal with this for most of my life, and once I said no more, he turned against me. All the things attached to his gambling are crimes," Tina said.

She felt it was important the lawyers knew that he had a gambling addiction as it showed his character. It wasn't just one thing. It was years, decades, that he lied and lived the life of a gambler, only wanting support to gamble more.

Mrs. Jones didn't want to get into Jorge's gambling just yet. She needed to know what happened the day he got arrested.

"Tell me about the day in question. Describe the day you called the police on your father. The first day and night your father spent in prison."

Tina nodded, yet she did not want to relive that awful morning, but she was under oath and knew she had to answer any questions the defense had, or she would be in contempt of court. She would tell the truth; there was nothing to hide.

"On that morning, I was meeting the roofers at the villa. It was around 8:00 a.m. I parked my car down the street at a friend's driveway because the villa's driveway was full with the roofer's truck. As I was walking I saw my father's car parked next to the villa."

Tina placed her hand over her forehead, feeling anxious as she saw the images again play in her mind.

"I just couldn't believe that he would be at the villa again after the judge told him never to return again," Tina said.

Tina felt a terrible pain on the right side of her brow like she was just hit with a pellet.

"The last time he came, I told my father never to return again. Officer Joe even wrote him a citation, but he didn't listen."

"Yes, Officer Joe confirmed this as well. What else happened?"

Tina took a deep breath before continuing.

"The roofers said the man whose car was parked next to the villa was now in the villa. They said my father walked around the back trying to get in, but he saw that the sliding glass door was boarded up. He walked back to the front and walked in the opened front door. The roofers called to him, but he didn't listen. They kept their distance away from him. Seeing he was acting erratic and incoherent."

Mrs. Jones looked puzzled as Jorge's story was much different.

"Oh, I see, and what else happened?"

"I called him from outside and told him I would call the police if he didn't get out and leave. I was giving him a chance to leave, but he refused," Tina said as she took another deep breath, remembering how she stood in front of the villa, shouting, pleading for him to leave.

"He just told me to get lost!"

Mrs. Jones' heart dropped as Jorge had said the same line to her.

"It wasn't until after I called the police that he decided to leave. When he heard I was on the phone with a 911 dispatcher, he rushed to his car and drove off."

"What else happened?"

"Nothing."

Tina could see her father had added another lie to the story.

"Your father said you actually invited him back to the property, so he could get his things."

"Why would I do that when I never wanted him to return? And there was nothing in the villa anyway."

"According to your daughter, the roofers, and the police, you have been stalking and threatening Tina, Mr. Gabor."

"What? She said that?" Jorge said.

"Stalking is when you go by another person's house or work after they told you to stop, but you don't listen and continue to do so. You continued to go by Tina's villa and house. There are a few videos of you driving through the development's gates, and her neighbor from across the street will testify that you have actually stopped in front of her house. Seeing you walk up the walkway, and there's video footage too."

"I'm her father, not a stranger. I can see her if I want."

"No, you cannot. The law does not exclude families."

"Wait until I get out of here. Just wait!" Jorge shouted as he banged the table again, frustrated.

Calm down, or we will never get out of here. Remember the jackpot.

"Mr. Gabor, you are walking on thin ice. Everything you say is being recorded."

"I have to watch what I say? This is bullshit. How about Tina? How come she can say whatever she wants?" Jorge said, coldly staring at Mrs. Jones, causing her to feel threatened, looking like he was about to get physical.

"Well, I'm innocent," Jorge said.

"Mr. Gabor, you will have to stay in jail until the trial and prove your innocence."

"How long will that be?"

"Four to five weeks. The courts are backlogged, so I can even see the trial being as far as eight weeks away," Mrs. Jones said, hoping to add pressure on Jorge.

"What? This is bullshit. I need to get out of this paradise and work. It's criminal to lock up an innocent person. I swear, where is this country going?" Jorge said.

And gambling, Mrs. Jones thought.

"Well, if you post bail, you'll be free to leave jail until the trial, of course."

"Mrs. Jones," Jorge said, changing his tone, wanting to get out of prison more than anything.

Bingo!

Mrs. Jones just looked at him, like she did to all the guilty men she represented in the past, relieved that the meeting was about over, and soon the guard would come and say time was up. There wasn't much left to say.

"Do you know of anyone who could loan me ten thousand dollars?" Jorge asked.

"No, but I know a bondsman will."

"Can you help me? I just want out. I don't belong here."

Mrs. Jones just stared at Jorge like she didn't quite understand his question.

"Won't you help an innocent senior citizen get out of this hellhole?"

"I think you should take the plea and go on with your life. I have the papers with me. If you sign them, you'll be out by tomorrow morning."

"Not over my dead body. I thought you were on my side."

Bitch!

A week later, Jorge posted bail. He was able to get in touch with Tony. Gabby agreed to loan Jorge twenty thousand. Jorge would use ten grand for bail and gamble the other ten for a new life.

When you win the big one, you can buy a new, better place. Screw everyone else.

When Tina got the news that Jorge was out, she was terrified. She knew without a doubt he would come after her. This made many restless nights. Falling asleep was a challenge; some nights, she would just stare out the window.

It wasn't until two weeks later when Jorge called Tina from church. He kept on calling, leaving message after message, how he needed to meet with her and Christopher and "talk about things". Tina was too afraid to let Jorge back into her life.

However, the calls wouldn't stop, so she pulled the phone line from the phone jack. Tina felt the walls close in as she sat on the master bedroom floor in a panic, wanting out of her skin, screaming in the pillows to let her frustrations out, as Christopher was outside with the girls. Tina had nowhere to run or hide.

A half hour later, there were hard knocks at the door. It was Jorge. She told Christopher to make sure the girls stayed in, and she would go outside to see what he wanted, as she did not trust him to come inside.

"What are you doing here? I don't even think you are supposed to contact me," Tina said.

Yet, Jorge started to make his way into the house, but Tina shut the door before he could. He tried to hug her, but she pulled back.

"You can't expect to come here and act like everything is good between us, when it is not," Tina said.

"Girl, wait, I actually have nowhere to go. I'm sleeping in the car now." Jorge said as he looked at Tina.

"Weren't you staying at Sheri's?"

"Not anymore. She kicked me out when she found out you had evicted me. She was upset I didn't tell her about it. You know it's because of you she kicked me out. So you sort of owe me," Jorge said.

"How about your gambling friends? Where are they? After you gave them a place to sleep in my place, without permission, sleeping in sleeping bags, and pissing in empty cans, when there wasn't any water. Where are they now? Go find them…. they owe you big time, or rather me."

Let her talk.

"Look, I just need a place to sleep for a few days until Sheri cools off. Then I will be on my way back to her place, and you'll never see me again," Jorge said.

"There are plenty of places around town where you can rent a room."

"Yeah. Where?"

"Look in the classifieds."

Jorge reached into his right pants pocket and took out all he had. In his palm, he had wage tickets from the Palm Springs Kennel Club and useless business cards where he had phone numbers of people written on the back he hardly spoke to anymore.

"Still gambling? I thought you would have stopped by now."

Jorge smiled and said, "What is it to you?"

"It destroyed you and us. That's what it is to me!"

"Bullshit! You are being overdramatic like your mother again. When will you learn that what I do with my life is my business? Not yours!"

Tina's heart started racing, feeling threatened, but she was going to stand her ground, not letting her heartstrings get in the way.

"Please girl, just let me stay for a few days. I have no other place to go."

Tina kept quiet.

"No," Tina said, feeling hurt and resentment towards Jorge.

"Just a day, please, girl," Jorge asked again.

"No, anyway, there's nothing in the villa anymore," Tina said.

Tina was telling the truth, too.

"Where's the furniture? The couches, the chairs, and beds."

"Everything had to be thrown away because of the mold. Don't you remember how you had a towel rolled up against the locked master bedroom door because the stench was so bad?"

"It doesn't matter. I can just sleep on the floor. Any place is better than in the car. Please, girl. I am begging you to help your old man."

You're the man, Jorge.

Tina wasn't immune to her father's tugs at her heart, holding onto every piece of strength she had as she struggled to turn him away.

"There still isn't water or electricity," Tina said.

"Yes, there is," Jorge said.

"No, there isn't," Tina said firmly.

"When I was there earlier, I used the garden hose to shower quickly," Jorge said.

"What! You're not supposed to go back to the villa ever. It's part of the agreement and condition of your bail, or you'll be arrested again. Are you kidding me? Why would you risk that?"

"Bullshit. I swear if you don't let me in, I will break in and kill myself," Jorge threatened.

Tina felt the air being sucked from within, but she kept quiet.

Jorge saw he was getting nowhere, and it was getting darker by the minute. He had other people to visit. So, he tried one last time, and this time he was going to lay the guilt hard.

"May this always be on your conscience for the rest of your life that you let me kill myself and did nothing to help your father."

Tina couldn't believe how he was turning the tables on her like everything was her fault.

"That's on you, not me. How sick of you to even think I'm responsible for any of this. Look at the monster looking back at you in the mirror and see who is responsible," Tina said.

Don't listen to her!

Kate was behind the door crying as she heard every word exchanged between her mom and grandpa. When she saw the front door handle twist, she ran to her room, not wanting Tina to know she was listening.

Jorge rushed to his car.

Tina returned inside where Christopher was standing.

"You know Kate had her ear glued against the door, listening.

"Were we that loud?"

"No, I couldn't hear, but I was sitting on the couch."

"Why didn't you distract Kate or take her away? I didn't want her to hear anything. I always wanted to spare her from what I went through when my parents fought. This isn't good."

"I tried to, but she said she wanted to hear grandpa's voice to see if his head was better. You know how crazy she is for him."

"Yes, I do. But things are very difficult right now. I can't just tell her what is really happening," Tina said.

"What did he want?" Christopher asked.

"A place to stay."

"Always coming around when he wants something. Isn't it enough that we are paying the home equity now? Tina, I'm telling you he can never ever stay here," Christopher said.

"I know, but he has an addiction," Tina said.

Tina had a hard time sleeping, tossing and turning most of the night, struggling with Jorge's suicide threat. A few times, she got up to check her cell phone, thinking there would be a voicemail from the police or the hospital.

Palm Beach just logged on

Starlight: Hi PB

Palm Beach: Hi, I was hoping you would be online. My father showed up earlier. What a fiasco that was. After all I have been through. He wanted me to let him back into the villa. I don't understand how he even thought this was an option.

Starlight: He knows better. Remember, he will always listen to whatever the addiction tells him to do. So don't take this personally. He was going back to the person who was his greatest enabler. YOU.

Palm Beach: When I told him no, he said he would break in and kill himself. I'm scared for him and scared for me. I am just sick with worry that my insides hurt, having a hard time breathing. I honestly don't know what to do. This is getting too much to handle. What happens if he follows through?

Starlight: I'm so sorry. It sounds like the addiction has him by the throat. And he is trying to guilt you into giving him what he wants. Stay firm. You will get over this. I promise.

Palm Beach: It's been incredibly hard; my oldest daughter heard the whole thing. Why can't he see what is happening to him, me, and now his granddaughter?

Starlight: He's in a very dark place now. Please don't go there. He has to want help. Your hands are tied.

Palm Beach: I would give my life for him, but not the addiction.

Starlight: Don't you know that the addiction knows this? That is why it is using emotional blackmail on you. It wants to break you.

Palm Beach: It never will. XXXX

Tina still couldn't sleep, tossing and turning, worried Jorge was now dead. This frightened her so much that she snuck out of the house in the middle of the night and drove to the villa on pure adrenaline, feeling her world falling apart.

As she pulled into the driveway, she was relieved his car wasn't there but still wanted to check around the villa. She turned the ignition off and walked around to the back. There weren't any broken windows, and the patio sliding glass door was still boarded up. *So far, so good,* she thought. She then walked back to the front door and it was still locked.

The next day, the public defender called Tina. He had a question about when she actually arrived at the villa the day Jorge was arrested.

When she mentioned that Jorge had stopped by last night, he said she needed to go to the police station and file a police report, as one of the conditions of his bail was not to contact her. He said if she didn't, it would be used against her. How she wished she didn't say anything; she did not want her father to get in trouble with the law again, but why shouldn't he? He was doing what he shouldn't. He was the one breaking the law, not her. Still, it was not easy to go and file a police report.

A few days later, Jorge was picked up and arrested. He spent the next six weeks in jail. Still, Jorge would not admit to any wrongdoing, saying he only wanted to reconcile with his daughter.

Tina's neighbor from across the street saw the whole thing while watering the lawn and almost called 911 when she heard Jorge screaming at Tina. She also saw him raise his hand to her. When Tina heard this, she started to cry as she wanted to erase the painful memory.

CHAPTER 42

Jorge folds

Minutes before the trial started, Jorge accepted the plea.
Tina was anxiously waiting to be called. She was the prosecution's first witness.

Finally, the door opened, expecting to see the bailiff, but the state's attorney stood before her with a smile.

"Your father just agreed to the plea."

"What? I don't believe it."

"I can't either. He strung us along this long, so I didn't expect him to finally accept the plea, but he did."

Tina didn't believe anything was ever over with her father. Unfortunately, it was only over when he said it was over. This still frightened her, wondering what would happen next. She hated feeling doubtful, but she still did.

"In fifteen minutes, the judge will give him the plea conditions. Of course, this technically isn't closed until he signs on the line."

"I see," Tina said as she felt anxious again.

How she wished Jorge signed the plea, but this could still be part of the addiction's game, and she began to doubt if this was really good news.

"You are more than welcome to see your father in front of the judge."

"I don't know. I don't want him to change his mind."

"I think it would be good for you to hear what the judge has to say. Your father wouldn't have to see you. You could sit in the back of the courtroom and listen."

"Okay, maybe the judge's words will impact him."

"Follow me. I'll have the bailiff walk you to the back. Tina, you have been through so much. This may offer you the closure you need too."

Tina just smiled, got up from the seat, and followed John to the bailiff.

"Please call me if you need anything. Your father will be on probation. I'm certain of this, and if he breaks any of the conditions, he will face other charges and more jail time."

Hearing this only brought chills; she didn't want to be reminded of what bad could still happen to him. She had hoped he was done with jail and breaking the law.

"Mrs. Jones has stated to the court that you are prepared to enter a guilty plea."

"Yes, I am, judge," Jorge said.

Tina placed both hands over her head as she heard her father speak. Seeing her father before a judge was so surreal.

"You did the right thing, Mr. Gabor, as your daughter has suffered greatly."

Jorge wanted to shout, "Bullshit," but just kept quiet.

"As part of your plea, you should not contact your daughter for a year. This means no phone calls, no text messages, no email, and you must not drive by her house. The security tapes at the development where she resides will be randomly checked. This also means you cannot have someone else contact her on your behalf. If you do, Mr. Gabor, you will be arrested, and additional charges will be made against you. I will personally see that you will get the maximum punishment possible by the court," Judge John said.

Jorge just stood expressionless, keeping his eyes on the judge. He did not cry, nor did he dispute anything he said. He just wanted to sign the damn papers, so he could be released. He really didn't care to hear what the judge was saying.

"Do I make myself clear, or do I need to explain it again? I will if you would like me to."

Jorge smiled as he shook his head up and down, like a bobbing toy trying to keep his cool.

"Sir, I need you to state this verbally to the court. You have to say you understand."

"Yes, I promise not to contact my daughter though . . ."

The judge looked at Jorge coldly before he signed the plea papers. When he was done with all the signatures, he wanted to leave Jorge with a thought, hoping it would make him think twice about ever gambling again.

"Beware, Mr. Gabor, you are about to cross into dangerous waters, where you will eventually find no way back."

Jorge froze as he remembered the same warning many years ago when he snuck out of work to gamble.

"You are old enough to know what is right and wrong. I hope you take this opportunity to reflect on what you have done. How you are hurting yourself, your daughter, granddaughters, and others that love you. If you don't stop, the addiction will only become worse. It is a drug, too, just like alcohol and drugs. It will destroy you. I wish I could place you in a program, but unfortunately, I cannot. It is now up to you to get your life together. Only you can stop gambling. The greatest gift you can give your daughter, and yourself is for you to stop."

Don't listen!

Tina got the chills listening to the judge as he said what she had been telling her father all these years. His no-nonsense approach was what she believed her father needed. A sense of relief and thankfulness embraced her feeling his words would finally reach her father. Everyone in the courtroom deeply respected Judge John as he was a family man. He did what he could to keep families together. Eight out of ten cases he preceded involved an addiction.

"Now, Mr. Gabor, will you get help for your gambling addiction?"

"Yes, I will."

Tina cried as her prayers seemed to be answered. Hearing her father say he would get help was all she ever wanted to hear. *This was big,* she thought. He was finally listening to someone, and she didn't care if it wasn't her.

"Jorge, you didn't ask for this addiction, but now that you have it, it's your job to fight it, and not surround yourself with any type of its influences."

Jorge just smiled as he was half hearing Judge John.

You are almost done.

"I have signed the plea with the conditions outlined. All that is left is for your signature. Once the paperwork is processed, you can leave jail later today. I hope you stay away from the dangerous waters. They are not worth testing, for they are hard to get out, Mr. Gabor."

"Thank you, Your Honor."

He looked at Jorge again and finally spoke his last words as Jorge had just signed the plea papers.

"A wise man told me this, and I find it appropriate to pass it to you."

Jorge looked at him as if he did not expect the judge to say anything else.

"Luck never gives. It only lends. Think of this when you feel the urge to gamble, Mr. Gabor."

Jorge looked at Judge John, puzzled like he didn't know what the saying meant. The judge picked up on this and said, "It means don't rely on luck as it is temporary. A win never lasts. You will end up losing what you have won."

Jorge still didn't get it, and the addiction was glad.

It is just a stupid saying.

Jorge left the courtroom a free man, though he was holding out for the charges to be dropped. He didn't care anymore, as he'd had enough of being behind bars. On the bus ride back to jail, he thought about the thrill of the bet. Maybe he liked it too much and overdid it at times, but he still didn't think it was a huge problem, maybe a little one, but not a huge one. It made him feel alive, part of something that needed him and vice versa.

Once he arrived at the jail, he called Sheri, letting her know he would be released at five pm. He was already aching to go to the dog track. He still had his Social Security checks to bet with.

Jorge, you are the man!

Sheri picked Jorge up from the prison with a motive. She had his Social Security checks ready for him to cash. He still owed her a grand, and she was going to get it. If he objected, she wouldn't let him in the car, rip the checks, and not only would he be without money, he wouldn't have a place to stay. Sheri was tired of his games.

However, Jorge only paid her half with his slick, street-talking ways. He convinced her that his ex-cellmate sister, who worked at the kennel club, already gave him the picks for the jackpot race. In return, he would give the ex-cellmate sister a referral fee of 10% of the winnings. Of course, this was just part of Jorge's elaborate lie. There was no such ex-cellmate sister.

Sheri only agreed, because the last time Jorge said this, he won. But then lost it all when he couldn't stop betting. This time the only way she agreed was if she held the ticket, and afterward, they'd leave. Jorge agreed.

Tina left the courtroom smiling, feeling utter relief that the case was finally over and that she could finally bid this chapter of her life goodbye, thinking the worst was behind her.

Though the sensible part of her knew she could never underestimate her father or the addiction, and just this thought within, would never free her completely, she was thankful that the court part was over. Maybe time would heal everything, as she read about this happening, and this all would be a faint memory. She'd finally live a life of normalcy.

It was like Jorge taking it to the end, though, not giving in when he could have, just like when he gambled. He held onto the very end when he should have folded, but that was his style, and she should have known this from the start. Maybe she could have avoided many restless nights.

Instead of going home, she drove to Palm Beach to feel the ocean breeze. She parked on a side street next to renowned Worth Ave, admiring the estate properties, but nothing called to her like the ocean. Tina walked over to a bench and sat down, mesmerized by the waves. It was a perfect moment, much like a postcard.

Today was the start of a new chapter, a turning point in her life. Tina thought about the quote Judge John said as a parting gift to Jorge, realizing it couldn't be more perfect. Life was not about luck; it was about making your own way, and that was what she was doing. She kept staring out to the ocean, feeling that her life was going to change in ways she couldn't imagine yet.

"How did the trial go?" Christopher asked when she got home.

"At the last minute, my father took the plea deal, which was unexpected. Maybe, he's turning another leaf and wants to change. Maybe, he is starting to own up to his actions," Tina said.

She hoped Christopher would agree.

"Your father doesn't do something unless it benefits him. I think he knew he was going to lose. I'm sure his attorney scared him with more prison time if he didn't take the plea. Don't underestimate him."

Tina just looked at Christopher, disheartened by his response.

"Why are you being negative? Can't a person change?" Tina asked.

"I'm not being negative. I'm just being real. I have nothing else to go on other than what he has already done in the past. I'm sorry, but I just don't see him changing."

Tina sighed as Christopher was right, but it didn't sit well with her.

"I was at the back of the courtroom when the judge reviewed the plea. My father didn't know I was even there. Judge John had warned him about the dangers of gambling, and he was listening," Tina said.

"He did?"

"The whole courtroom was speechless as he spoke. And I even heard dad say he was going to get help. Now that's an accomplishment in itself, don't you think?" Tina asked.

"Okay, honey, I'll give Jorge the benefit of the doubt that he may get the help he needs. It would be nice if the girls had a grandfather again and for him to come over like he used to. I know Kate would be over the moon as she misses her grandpa."

Tina smiled, "Thank you, I just don't want anyone to lose hope. There are gamblers that do get help and recover. Maybe he will."

A month later, Tina saw Donna at the supermarket.

"Oh, hi, Tina. I almost didn't recognize you. Are you still working?"

"Yes, I'm now the managing editor."

"Congratulations. I always knew you would do something great."

"Thanks," Tina said, still feeling uncomfortable around Donna.

"How are you?" Donna asked.

"Good," Tina said, trying to keep her responses short.

"It is a shame what happened to your father."

Tina just smiled.

"I actually wasn't surprised. He ran behind your mother's back every chance he got to go to the track, even when you were a little girl. I'm just sorry it ended up happening to you too. I don't know how you managed," Donna said.

Tina just forced a smile.

"It was nice seeing you. I have to get back home."

"Oh, Tina, before you leave, I just want you to know in case you are wondering about your father. He's back at the salon. The owners gave him a second chance. And he isn't rushing off to track either," Donna said.

Tina smiled. This was way better news than she could've hoped for.

She took the sunglasses above her head, as she liked wearing them like a headband, and wore them, covering up her watery eyes, even though she was inside. It amazed Tina how any type of emotions she felt for her father was always heavy and twofold, always triggering tears and heart palpitations, for deep down, she loved him dearly. More than she should have. Something she would eventually have to go to therapy for.

"Oh, honey, don't cry."

"I'm fine. I just have something in my eye," Tina said, downplaying her emotions.

"I can't even imagine what you went through. You two were so close. He'd always say you were his girl, his eyes sparkling each time saying it. It must have ripped you apart taking the steps you did, but you did what was necessary. Your father was only headed for destruction. You saved his life."

Tina just smiled, fearing she couldn't say a word without triggering tears. So, she kept quiet. Donna sensed this and wanted to leave Tina with some good news about her father.

"Tina, it was so nice seeing you."

Tina smiled again and was about to walk away.

"Listen, your dad would be proud to know you're doing so well. Just don't give up on him. Just promise you'll keep the door open. He seems to be making a change. Many of us in the salon are praying for him. As you know, he's a good guy. He just got involved in something stronger than him," Donna said.

"Thank you," Tina said.

Tina left the supermarket elated. Everything that Donna said pointed out that Jorge had hit rock bottom and was on the road to some type of recovery. How she hoped it was true. She now couldn't wait for eleven more months to pass. It was the best news she had heard in a while. Things seemed to be looking up for her father. Maybe he had gotten serious about his recovery, though she would not know for almost a year. She now had solid proof that he was headed in the right direction, which was everything to her.

Thank you, God, she thought as she looked at a family picture of him hidden in her sock drawer. She believed he was finally on the right path to becoming the father she always wanted.

As the months passed, the hurt, anger, and resentment she had for him lessened, and she was able to forgive him.

Starlight: Hi, Palm Beach. You haven't been on chat for a while. Is everything ok? We've been worried here over the pond.

Victoria: If you hadn't been posting. I would have flown to Florida and used all of my frequent flier miles I was saving for a trip with hubby to Aruba to check on you.

Palm Beach: Now, I wouldn't want you to do that. I'm fine. I've been reading more and just thinking about my dad.

Victoria: The months seem to be flying along. Have you heard from him?

Palm Beach: No, he's still on probation. It's been hard dealing with a court-ordered separation for a year. I'll think of a memory, and I'll start crying. I just miss him.

Starlight: Of course, you do. You're only human. After all, he's your dad, and nothing will ever change that.

Palm Beach: I also forgive him. And this has opened a lot of bottled-up hurt.

Starlight: It is good you can because this is part of the healing process, but never forget what he has done to you.

Victoria: Yes, you must never forget. You know the saying, hurt me once, shame on you, hurt me twice, shame on me?

Starlight: It's so true, yet the second part is overlooked by many, including myself until I got it right. Thanks for the reminder, V.

Victoria: Anytime

Palm Beach: I agree I must never forget. I just feel sorry for him.

Victoria: Why? He should be the one feeling sorry.

Starlight: My thoughts exactly, sorry PB. Didn't he almost hit you in front of the girls?

Tina wiped the tears away as she typed. Realizing she had been missing the father she remembered and later wanted as a teenager, not the one who only months ago conned, lied, and threatened her.

But she promised herself that she wasn't going to hate him. She refused to live with hate in her heart, though she sometimes struggled with it. Hate would not overtake her.

Palm Beach: You all have helped me more than you'll ever know. Thank YOU.

Starlight: As you to us. Your perspective as a child of a compulsive gambler is invaluable. Stay strong. The addiction is still within your father. You really don't know what he has been doing these past months. Hopefully, he has been getting help for his addiction, but he could have very well been gambling. Just be on guard.

Victoria: Stay true to your recovery, Palm Beach. Let your father take care of him. Don't let the addiction play you anymore, as it will try.

Palm Beach: I will.

Tina signed off crying and did until she couldn't any longer. She was willing to give her father another chance, despite the past. Now the question remains, was he going to take it? Or was he going to only stay true to the addiction?

CHAPTER 43

Almost a year later

O n Tina's thirty-fifth birthday, Jorge did not call, though he could have, as his probation ended over a week ago.

Tina found this odd as she was certain he would. Could it be he simply forgot her birthday, or was he now shutting the door on her? Either way, she wasn't going to contact him.

When Tina was sitting in a staff meeting three days later, her phone vibrated. Startled, she looked down to see it was Jorge; he still had the same number.

Her heart started to race as she kept seeing his number until it went to voicemail. In less than a minute, she would know if he had left a voicemail or not. If he didn't, she wondered if he would call again, or would she just call him back?

A smile graced her, seeing he had left a message. Now she couldn't wait to listen to what Jorge said. The anticipation was leaving her lightheaded and absentminded. She could only think of her father and his voice message, not the meeting.

How much she wanted to excuse herself, but now that she was the managing editor, she couldn't just leave, as she was part of the team running the meeting. She was about to give a presentation about new feature stories she had planned for the next upcoming issues on addictions.

She wanted four addictions featured for each month, covering each in great detail: alcohol, drugs, compulsive eating, and compulsive gambling. The articles would include interviews of addicts, interviews of family and friends, statistics, and staff writers' personal incidents, if possible, information about local support groups, support websites, and recovery programs in the area and globally.

Tina wanted each staff writer to dig deep in their research, focusing on the addiction and answering how the addict could control their addiction if they really wanted to.

"I like it! Readers need to know as much as they can about these addictions," Mr. Jackson said, praising Tina.

He often sat on staff meetings, though he wasn't required to. He liked the way Tina handled them. She made his life easier. He was thinking of retiring soon as he was already asked who he would like to replace him.

"For compulsive gambling, I'd like Jill to cover this piece," Tina said.

Mr. Jackson looked at his daughter, Jill, sitting around the staff table, bright-eyed as she was probably not expecting to be chosen.

"Is that okay, Jill?" Tina asked.

"Wow, I'd love to, Ms. Gabor," Jill said with a smile.

"Well, you all have your assignments. At the next week's meeting, your research should be done. Here's a checklist of what should be in your writing. These feature stories need to blow people's minds about addictions. Don't be afraid to report what you find. Addiction is never pretty, and don't be too easy on it either."

Everyone rushed out of the office excited to start their assignments, except Mr. Jackson, who just sat at the back of the room waiting to speak to Tina.

Tina was startled, thinking she was alone.

"You seem to have a passion for this assignment. Is there a reason?"

"I do," Tina said, feeling emotional.

Mr. Jackson just looked at Tina feeling it may be personal. Suddenly she became sad and withdrawn.

"Are you all right?"

"A very ugly side to addiction has been kept under the wraps for far too long. It just doesn't affect the person with addiction but also family members."

"Seems like this is hitting home for you."

"Well, it does, or it actually did," Tina said.

Mr. Jackson thought for a second maybe Tina was a recovering addict of some kind. He certainly did not want to know if she was, feeling this was not his business. He knew he was a borderline alcoholic.

"I never said this to anyone, but my father is a compulsive gambler and has been for most of my life."

"Sorry, better him than you, though." Mr. Jackson said, trying to add a positive spin.

"Actually, it might have been me. I suffered years with this addiction as if it was my own, but I learned it wasn't. Still, it damaged me and took many good years away from me. And it still haunts me. I wish it never knew it existed."

Mr. Jackson hadn't seen it that way and was interested to know more.

"See, this addiction touches not only the addict but also their loved ones. It attaches itself firmly as it manipulates by playing with the loved ones' emotions, relentlessly pulling real hard at the heartstrings, laying the guilt thick until it gets what it wants. It will not back down. No matter what you do, it can be quite traumatizing. Feeling cornered in with no way out."

"What does it want?" Mr. Jackson asked.

"It wants to be enabled. It wants support to continue the addiction. It wants money to feed the monster addiction, twenty-four-seven."

"Unbelievable."

"Tina, I would have never known if you didn't just tell me. What a survivor you are. I'm so sorry," Mr. Jackson said, looking at Tina in awe at what she went through.

"Thank you, I like to keep it a secret for now. I just don't want to be known as the gambler's daughter. I want to be me, without gambling having any part of my life. It has already taken enough, and now I want it gone forever. You know what I mean?"

"Oh, don't worry, your secret's safe with me. Tina, I don't know how things are with your father now, but I want you to know you can always come to me. I know a few years back, I was a jerk, and I apologize. But now I have come to see you as a daughter," Mr. Jackson said.

Tina smiled, "Don't make me cry now, and yes, you were, but you are forgiven. You know your daughter is quite the writer. I picked her not because of you if you are wondering, but for her writing. I know she'll do a great job, and I know more writing jobs will follow," Tina said.

"I appreciate that, as I have always wanted Jill to make her own way. She is lucky to have you as a role model and mentor. You'll like the older sister she always wanted."

"Thanks. I always like to be fair."

Tina left for her office and sat on her chair for a few moments before she listened to her father's voicemail. She started feeling anxious again, as she didn't know if there would be a relationship with him anymore. She took a few deep breaths, breathing in and out, before playing the message, hoping for the best. Hoping he wasn't going to ask her for a favor.

"Girl, hi, it's Dad," Jorge said.

Tina couldn't help but feel the tears bunch up in her eyes, burning them as they streamed down, like many times before.

"My probation is over. I did what I was supposed to do. How are Kate and Lana? Tell them their grandpa loves them. Girl, I promise to be a better father. I'm going to be here for you like I should. I promise. Give me a call, please, girl. I love you."

Tina couldn't ignore her feelings for Jorge forever. Through her own recovery, and now with the knowledge of the addiction, she wasn't going to give up hope that he would recover too.

She listened to the voicemail again before calling him back. The call was brief. They agreed to meet at the park Saturday, next to the salon he still worked at. She couldn't wait to go home to tell Kate the good news. Hopefully, this would be the happy ending she had been praying for.

"Kate, honey," Tina said.

"Yes, Mommy?"

"Well, it looks like Grandpa's head is better, and guess what? We are going to see him this Saturday at the park. How does that sound?" Tina asked.

"Oh, Mom," Kate said, her eyes starting to water, quickly turning to tears.

Her prayers were answered. She was finally going to see her Grandpa. The one that always made her laugh with his funny faces and silly things they'd do together.

This broke Tina's heart; she knew how much Kate loved him. She was just too young to know why Grandpa wasn't around anymore.

"I miss him."

"I know, honey. I miss him too."

"Let's now be happy that we are going to see him in a couple of days. Ok?"

"Ok, Mommy."

The next morning Tina called Jorge to know of his true intentions for the Saturday meet-up. She felt like she was jumping ahead of herself if she didn't. She couldn't bear the thought of Kate being disappointed again. How she wished she would have spoken about this earlier with him before telling Kate about the meeting at the park.

However, Jorge reassured Tina that he only wanted to see her and the girls and nothing more. A huge weight was lifted after hearing this, but it was just temporary.

Tina was a ball of nerves on the day of the park meetup, whereas Kate couldn't stop smiling, asking every ten minutes what time it was. Tina wished the meetup, or reunion, as she thought of it, would have been earlier in the day than late afternoon, as they agreed.

The girls and Tina arrived at the park a half hour early. Tina wanted to get her bearings around the park. It was packed, which was good. The more people, the better; she still didn't know what to expect from her father. She found an empty bench, under a palm tree which not only offered shade but privacy. Yet it was close to the swings where Lana liked to play.

Nervousness overwhelmed Tina as she kept her eyes fixated on the park's entrance. Looking every so often, she glanced back down at the book, trying to give the impression that she was reading.

"Grandpa, Grandpa," Kate shouted, running to him with open arms, sprinting as fast as she could, almost falling over her feet.

Tina stood up from the bench, her book fell to the ground, and she ran after Kate. Lana was only a few feet trailing behind her sister.

"Oh, Kate."

"Oh, Grandpa, Grandpa,"

Kate hugged him as she cried. He held her tight as he swung her around in a circle. It was just like in the movies. Kate was in tears, resting against her chest against Jorge, as he held her tight, spinning around and around until he stopped to maintain his balance.

"Oh, Kate, you made my day. How have you been?"

"Good, I play the piano now, Grandpa," Kate said.

"You do. You know your mother used to play the piano too when she was your age."

"Hello, Lana, my girl, you've grown. Come to Grandpa," called Jorge.

Lana stayed behind Tina because she was a little intimidated by him. When the girls went to play, Tina and Jorge sat on the park bench, just looking at each other. Inches away, just smiling.

Tina wore her Jackie-O-type glasses to hide her eyes. Just sitting a few inches away from Jorge was emotional and surreal after all the ugly that transpired between them. She didn't know how to feel but was genuinely happy to see him.

He looked much better than when she saw him a year ago. He was wearing a clean, blue and white striped, long-sleeve oxford. His navy dress pants were cleaned and pressed. This brought tears to her eyes, seeing him looking so well, and wasn't showing signs of being homeless like she had feared.

"So, how are you, girl?" Jorge asked.

Tina smiled, believing Jorge was now a changed man. He never really asked that question before.

"Good, and you? Are you still gambling?" Tina asked, looking at him, hoping he would say no, but he just looked down at his phone. Not wanting to answer the question.

"I'm good."

Tina felt it wasn't a good sign that he didn't answer, but she would let it go. Maybe gambling was a trigger word for him, and he didn't want to acknowledge it for what it did to him, but then again, he could have said no and moved on.

"How is Christopher?" Jorge asked.

"He is doing well. You know, Dad, I love you. I always did and will."

Bingo!

Jorge just smiled and said, "And I love you."

Tina reached over and hugged her father, believing everything was going to be good between them from now on. And felt she was strong enough not to enable him anymore yet still have a relationship with him.

"Mom, Mom. The ice cream truck is here. Can we get some?" Kate asked.

"Sure, honey."

Tina grabbed her purse and gave Kate ten dollars. She thought Jorge might offer to pay for it, but he didn't.

Instead, he watched her take the money from her wallet, noticing the cash she had and feeling his heartbeat rise.

As the girls ran to the ice cream truck, Jorge looked at Tina and said, "Girl, I need a favor."

Tina's heart quickly dropped, feeling anxious, wanting out of her skin. It was not what she wanted to hear. She was sick of favors from him, but this one involved looking for his passport. Why would she have it?

After they said their good-byes, Jorge looked at Tina and said, "Just look for it. I am sure you have it... bring it the next time we meet," Jorge said.

He waited until the last moment to ask Tina to avoid questions. Tina had second thoughts about the meeting. It didn't seem genuine on her father's part.

On the way home, Kate surprised her with a bombshell.

"Mommy?"

"Yes, my love."

"I'm so happy we saw Grandpa today," Kate said as she looked out the car window into the traffic.

This tugged at Tina's heart more than anything. She wondered if she was setting Kate up for more heartache now.

Palm Beach just logged on.

Victoria: We've been waiting for you. How did today go?

Starlight: Was it all that you hoped for?

Palm Beach: At first, it was, but then I started to see the same patterns. I asked him if he was still gambling, and he didn't answer.

Victoria: Well, his silence was your answer.

Palm Beach: Yes, it was. My initial response was to retract, but it didn't feel right either. There has been enough estrangement between us for both of us to learn.

Starlight: Yes, you are a different person now, before, you didn't know how to separate the addiction from your father. But now you do.

Palm Beach: Yes, and I will never ever provide any enablement to him.

Victoria: You have come so far PB. You have shown others here that you can go against addiction and win.

Palm Beach: Yes, it's really the only way to go or be dragged down by its claws again. I swear his addiction gave me the evil eye a few times, and I had to look away.

Palm Beach: I have also learned never to give up hope on him either, though the past was full of betrayal, bitter moments, courts, police, and harassment. This was the addiction battling it out with me, doing what it could to get enablement.

Victoria: Being able to still have hope in your heart is good. Just remember that addiction is always looking for a way to get what it wants. You must remember that even when you think you don't have to anymore.

Palm Beach: Sad but true. I realized as I looked at my father today that it didn't matter that he gambled anymore. What mattered most was that I wouldn't be part of it anymore.

Starlight: Well, take it slow with your father. Think of Saturdays at the park with him as moments of daughter and father time.

Palm Beach: I like that. Oh, he did ask me for a favor.

Victoria: Oh, brother, what was it?

Palm Beach: He wanted me to look for his passport. He said he left it in the villa.

Starlight: Be careful. One favor leads to another.

Victoria: My thoughts exactly.

Palm Beach: I already told him there was nothing left in the villa, but of course, he kept pushing for me to look again.

Starlight: Don't be afraid of putting your foot down this soon.

Palm Beach: I'm not, thanks to you.

Starlight: LOL

Palm Beach: How are things with your father?

Starlight: Same old. He is in prison now after he involved me in an identity scam. The credit card company will not erase the debt if I don't press charges against him and his girlfriend.

Palm Beach: OMG, it is unbelievable how a cg can think this is ok.

Starlight: It is, and I still suffer from it. So please be careful of your father. He has an evil and relentless addiction that lives in him that he can't even acknowledge. He is a slave to this addiction and will do whatever it asks him to do.

Palm Beach: I'll be sticking to Saturdays at the park for the time being.

Starlight: Just remember, don't give the addiction any opportunity.

"So, how is the research going?" Tina asked Jill as she passed her on the way to get coffee to start the day.

"Good, really good. I'll actually never ever see gambling in the same light again. I think people need to be monitored when going to the track or casinos. My eyes have been forever opened to the ugly of this addiction," Jill said.

"I see you have done your research," Tina said, sitting down beside Jill.

"Well, when you gave me this assignment about gambling addiction. I was worried I wouldn't find enough support or statistics, but I found plenty. I was actually floored with the amount that is readily out there, but no one is talking about it."

Jill took out her research file, ready to show Tina her findings, hoping she would think it was good enough for the article.

"Great, the Internet is a wonderful tool. Just remember to make sure you are getting information from reputable sources." Tina said.

"Do you have a moment? I found some mind-blowing statistics about compulsive gambling. It's terrifying how the gambler's mind works."

"Sure, what did you find?" Tina asked.

"Did you know that sixty-five percent of pathological gamblers commit crimes to support their gambling habit?" Jill said.

"Wow, that is mind-blowing."

"Also, in a Florida study, one in five inmates is a problem gambler," "Jill said.

"That is another mind-blowing statistic."

Tina had personal knowledge of that already with her father.

"I have tons more. Did you know the average divorce rates for problem gamblers are nearly double that of non-gamblers?" Jill said.

"Wow! Another eye-awakening statistic, great job, Jill."

"The saddest part is that one study found that fifty percent of the children of pathological gamblers were also pathological gamblers. I just can't imagine the hell these children went through and still do with a compulsive gambler as a parent. Some leave their children in cars when they go, abandon their families and gamble. Some even died. It is a vicious cycle."

"I think these statistics would do well in a text box next to your article. They speak volumes. What is your next step?"

"I'd like to interview a few compulsive gamblers."

"That's a great idea. Check out Gamblers Anonymous."

"Thanks, Mrs. Gabor," Tina said.

CHAPTER 44

Father and daughter moments

Tina's meetings with her father were still limited to thirty minutes on Saturdays at the park.

Jorge would say one thing and do another. Tina learned not to take anything he said seriously. All signs pointed that he was slipping deeper and deeper into his addiction.

Now he didn't even lie about gambling. He'd openly said he was still betting, but only with his tips. This didn't impress Tina as he thought it would. If anything, she felt the urge to detach from him.

Still, this saddened Tina, realizing he never hit rock bottom as she thought, but she decided to continue having a relationship with him until she could. She'd test the waters, and hopefully, they'd work.

They'd meet at the park, not too far from the salon he still worked at, and they'd have their moments. Some Saturdays were better than others. Sometimes there wasn't much to say other than a hello.

This particular Saturday meeting almost didn't happen, as Tina was still on the edge from their last phone call. It was upsetting that she really didn't want to see him, but she did.

As she waited for Jorge on the park bench, she thought about the last call they had. It still troubled her, and the only thing she could do was block it from her memory which she perfected from doing so in her life.

Tina and Kate had spent the day together at the beach. Lana had a playdate, and as they were on their way to pick her up, Jorge called, and instead of slowly easing his demand, he came right out and said it, cutting to the chase.

"Listen, I need a favor."

"Not now. I'm in the car with Kate."

"It can't wait," Jorge said.

"What is it?" Tina asked.

Tina listened, her heart pounding in panic, feeling overwhelmed and lightheaded, as Kate sat a few inches behind, sipping on a Slurpee and looking out the window.

"See, things are not worrying out with Sheri. I need to leave her place by Saturday, or she will call the cops, and I have nowhere else to go."

"What happened? I thought you both were doing well," Tina said.

"She wants this and that, and I'm tired of it. No money, no love," Jorge complained.

The first thing that came to Tina's mind was that Sheri was kicking him out because he wasn't paying his share of the bills.

"Well, call your brother or your sister."

"I have to be in the area. I have clients."

Really, she thought.

"Well, Kate and I had a wonderful day at the beach. Talk to you later," Tina said.

Tina hoped Jorge would realize when she said the second time that Kate was inches away, listening to the conversation, he'd stop with asking for a favor, but it didn't. It was like he didn't hear anything or didn't care.

"Ask your mother then if I can stay with her," Jorge said.

"No, that isn't possible. What about your brother?" Tina asked.

"I can't," Jorge said.

"Why not?" Tina asked.

"Why can't I stay with your mother? After all, we were married, and she still owes me."

"What? I got to go!"

"Don't you dare. If you hang-up. I'm going to show up at her place. I don't care if she calls the cops and I go to prison. She is lucky

I didn't take her to court. Tell her that. Tell her I will, if she doesn't let me stay with her."

"If you show up at her place, I will never speak to you again, and you'll never see me, Kate, Lana, and Christopher again. Is that what you want?"

Tina became so upset that she had to pull over. *The nerve of him,* she thought. *What a monster! How dare he drag her mother in his threats again?*

"Mom, are you talking to Grandpa? Is his mind sick again?" Kate asked. She turned away and cried, hating how upset her mother was and how it was because of Grandpa again.

"You will go to prison. You'll be arrested for stalking again. Do you want that? Not only are you upsetting me, but you are upsetting Kate now, and you know how much she loves you."

"Let me talk to her," Jorge shouted.

"No, she has had enough already. How could you?"

"You used to love me. What happened?"

"You don't need me to tell you. You know the answer."

Now she wished she didn't agree to meet him at the park. She felt sick all over again. The vicious cycle was happening again.

"Hi, girl. Where is Kate?"

"Oh, she couldn't make it. She's at a birthday party."

"Oh, well. I remember when you went to birthday parties."

"So, how are you doing?" Tina asked, feeling like a hypocrite.

She didn't really want to know. It often led him to voice how hard things were in his life and how he needed a favor.

"Good, but my car broke down," Jorge said.

Tina's heart rate started to pick up; she didn't want to hear this. She didn't care about his car. It wouldn't have broken down if he'd taken care of it in the first place.

"Don't you have a friend who is a mechanic?" Tina asked, trying to direct him in finding help elsewhere.

"Yes, but he doesn't fix electrical problems."

Tina tried changing the subject, but Jorge would go back to his car troubles.

"Girl, I just need six hundred dollars, please, girl," Jorge said.

"Well, I don't have it. I'm still paying the home equity each month, and it's been financially draining. Something I shouldn't even be doing."

Jorge just smiled, thinking it would erase his wrongs. How wrong he was.

"What about your mother? She has money. Doesn't she have a rich boyfriend now?" Jorge asked.

Tina looked at him stone-faced, "If you don't stop, I will leave."

Jorge just looked down at his lap, the same reaction, when he didn't like what was said to him.

"You're gonna have to figure this out for yourself. Just like how I figured out how to pay the home equity. There is no other way," Tina said.

Again, Jorge was quiet.

"If you'd stop gambling, you would be able to save enough for your car to be fixed. I guarantee you this."

"Well, that's how I pay my bills."

"Is that so? Then how come you can't pay for your car?"

"Can you just drive me to church then? Otherwise, I have to walk, and I'll be late."

"I can do that," Tina said, feeling that was an acceptable request.

Tina dropped Jorge at the church parking lot. He sat quietly for the hour-long service, and afterward he would stay until the church cleared out. He was friendly with the priest who sometimes gave him money, giving him a twenty here and there. Jorge even asked if the church could help him pay for his car, and the priest said they couldn't. But he promised Jorge that God would somehow provide what he needed. He just needed to pray.

Tina was interrupted by a knock at her office door. It was Jill with a big smile, excited to share her findings about compulsive gambling.

"Nice to see someone smiling around here," Tina said, as the office atmosphere was a bit tense now with numerous deadlines approaching.

"I was able to interview five compulsive gamblers after I sat in a Gamblers Anonymous meeting. I have to tell you; their stories are downright sad. Their lives are so messed up because of their gambling that you almost feel sorry for them," Jill said.

"What was so sad about them?" Tina asked.

"Well, they have literally lost everything in their world. Not only are they broke financially, but emotionally and spiritually. Three of the men I interviewed are estranged from their families. One hasn't spoken to his daughter for over ten years, and they live in the same town. It's so sad."

"I'd say so."

"Did they tell you why they gambled?"

"Mostly for the high, the thrill, or to be in the zone, as some say. The feel of euphoria," Jill said.

" I hear it's intense."

"Exactly, the intense pleasure seems to get them all the time. They chase after it like a drug."

"Sad but true. I think at the end of the article, we'll be able to agree that addictions are the same in ways. As you will see when you interview loved ones of compulsive gamblers."

"Tony, one of the men I interviewed, said he gambled to escape his problems, but then it became a major problem."

Tina's heart dropped hearing the name Tony and she wondered if it was Alex's father.

Later she would check on the message boards to see if Swagger posted. It would be nice to read that it was Alex's father. Though they knew each other in life, they always kept their distance on the boards to protect each other's identity.

"Actually, I have spoken to the daughter of a compulsive gambler."

"Really, what did she have to say?"

"Well, not only did her father gamble her college fund away, but he borrowed a hundred thousand dollars for this so-called new business. Later it was discovered that he never used the money for the business. He actually gambled it away, and she eventually lost her house because she could not afford to repay the loan, and neither could her father. How awful!"

"What a monster!" Tina said.

"I know. I can't even imagine how awful my life would be if I were that daughter."

Five days later, Jorge called.

"Hello," Tina said, smiling.

"Hi, girl. I'm walking to church. Can you come by and take me there?"

He still didn't have his car. It was still at the dealership though it was already fixed; he just didn't have the money to take it off the lot. The dealership was getting impatient with the car taking up space. However, Jorge had managed to gain the manager's sympathy by saying he was out of a job, and when he'd receive his Social Security check, he could pay for the car repairs.

"I'll be there in a few."

Tina rushed out of the house with a bottle of cold water, a bag of chips, and a few cheese sticks if he was hungry. Tina had no real expectations from him other than to be her father at that moment. She wondered if this was even possible anymore.

Tina was driving on the opposite side of the road as she saw him walking in the other direction. She made a U-turn and beeped the horn as she got closer, thinking he would hear, but he didn't. He kept walking, not stopping to look, so she beeped again. Again, he didn't stop. It wasn't until she beeped the third time, coasting next to him, that he stopped and realized it was her. Finally, he snapped out of the addiction's trance.

"Hey, girl."

"Hi, Dad. Here is some water and a few snacks."

"Ah, thanks."

She glanced at him. He was a mess, his shirt wrinkled with dirty rings around the collar and the sleeves. His once-nice khaki pants had stains. She wanted to take him home so he could shower, and wash his clothes, but she knew the addiction would take it the wrong way and start giving commands again, and Tina did not want this.

"So, how was your day?"

"Good, I was busy. I made a hundred dollars."

"Great."

She was happy for her father if that was the truth, but if it wasn't, it didn't bother her either. She dropped him off at church, and that was the last time she saw him for a while.

CHAPTER 45

Emotional blackmail

Another month had passed, and still not a word from Jorge. Tina couldn't help but wonder how he was doing. A few weeks back, she had called him twice on his cell phone but only got voicemail, and he never returned her calls.

A wave of worry flushed over Tina when she called again, and this time the call did not ring or go to voicemail; instead, a recording that said, "The person you are trying to reach is not accepting calls at this time." His phone was disconnected.

Things must really be going bad for him, as the cellphone was his lifeline, and for him not to have it anymore was alarming. It was the only real form of communication between Tina and Jorge.

Tina felt like she did as a teenager, worried sick of where he was, remembering when she called the hospital. Regardless of the time she spent online getting support, she couldn't shake the panic feeling consuming her that something bad happened to Jorge.

Palm Beach just logged on.

Victoria: Hi Palm Beach

Palm Beach: I am scared. I really think something bad has happened to my dad. It has been over a month since I last heard from him, and now his cell phone is disconnected. My mom thinks he is fine, gambling and being inconsiderate, not calling.

Victoria: You know bad news is the fastest news to travel. I'd listen to your mom. His addiction is inconsiderate and selfish, and you know that.

Palm Beach: You're right. Sometimes I feel it would be better if I just cut ties with him. Having him halfway in my life still causes me unnecessary anxiety. The little Saturday moments are now far and in between. I feel myself slipping, living in fear of what could happen to him and the sad part is that he probably doesn't care.

Victoria: This is most probably true as he hasn't controlled his addiction. Look after you, your daughters, and hubby. You cannot help him. No one can help him but him.

Palm Beach: I know this. Thank you for reminding me, but it is still so hard. What has become of me?

Victoria: You are who you are, a loving daughter who gave him another chance. However, he hasn't taken the chance because he is wrapped up in his addiction.

Palm Beach: I have to let go.

Victoria: I would agree. He is still standing, somewhere, still fighting to feed his addiction. He is still standing and doing without you, and he will continue to do so.

Palm Beach: I just want to be happy again.

Victoria: You will.

Five days later, Jorge called Tina from his ex-girlfriend's house as he lost her number, but Sheri had it. They agreed to meet next Saturday afternoon at three thirty.

Tina arrived at the park feeling anxious and nervous. She could not help but think he was not doing well as he was still gambling.

Twenty minutes later, Tina saw him walking through the park's gates. Even from afar, she could see he was not well. He wore the same outfit she saw him in the last time, a pair of red-stained khaki pants and a white and blue oxford. It was also the same shirt he wore for his last mug shot. What happened to his other clothes?

Tina sat on a bench in the south corner of the park, close to the monkey bars where Lana had mastered swinging back and forth. She watched him as he stopped by each bench to see if it was her. He smiled at each person.

Watching her father looking so off was surreal; he seemed like a different person, not the father she remembered. His hair was now white instead of gray and much longer, almost wild looking. He could have easily pulled it back in a ponytail if he wanted to.

As he got closer, Tina turned her attention to her book on her lap, half reading while looking from the corner of her eye at his whereabouts as he continued to walk in the park, as she did so many times before.

"There you are," Jorge said.

"Oh, hi," Tina said as she got up from the bench to hug him.

"I don't know if you tried calling me but I don't have a cell phone anymore."

"Oh, and why?"

"Well, I didn't know when I made calls to Miami I would be charged. I hate cell phones anyway. They can keep the phone if they think they can charge one hundred and ninety dollars from me now. That's an outrage. I'm not Mr. Rockefeller," Jorge complained.

Tina didn't say anything as there was nothing to say. He never once said he hated cell phones until today.

Suddenly, Lana ran up to him and gave him a hug. A voice inside of Tina said to take a picture of him as it would be the last time, she would see him. At first, she fought the feeling but listened and took a quick snap of him from her phone as Lana broke away from his arms. The picture wasn't complimentary at all. Jorge's eyes were wide open, his crazy hair sticking out, and his once-white teeth were yellowed and chipped.

"Where is Kate? She hasn't been around for a while." Jorge asked.

"She is at her friend's birthday party," Tina said.

"Okay, tell her grandpa loves her very much."

Lana took off, going up and down the slides.

"Girl, last night I slept in the car."

Make her feel guilty!

"Oh, I thought you lived with a friend in Fort Lauderdale. What happened?" Tina asked.

"Well, when I moved in, I was only supposed to pay for the water bill, but once I moved in, he said I also had to pay a hundred dollars a week for rent. He lied to me."

"It still sounds like a good deal."

"Well, not when there isn't hot water. I just left, and I need to find another place to live. Can I stay with your mother? She has an extra room."

"How can you even ask after what you did?"

"Well . . ."

"If you don't stop, I'm leaving. I did not come here to get stressed out by you," Tina voiced.

"All right, but I still need a place to live."

"How about living in public housing? There must be some type of government assistant for senior citizens, especially now with the economy so tough. I could see you qualifying for this," Tina said, offering to help Jorge.

Years ago, Jorge would have never considered this, but here he was, now jumping on the opportunity. He would if he could move in one of the units regardless of the area. It was better than sleeping in the places he has.

"Where do I go? Can you take me there?" Jorge asked.

"Um, let's see . . ."

Jorge kept his desperate gaze on her, not looking away until she committed to a time and place.

"Well, I could take off next Tuesday."

"Let's say we meet back here at the park at 1:00 p.m."

"Dad, don't expect miracles. I'm sure the process takes time, and there may even be a waiting list. I will help with the paperwork, though," Tina said.

"Well, you better help more than just filling out papers. I'm your father. Don't you ever forget it, and you'll always owe me. I'm tired of your bullshit Tina."

Yes, you are here, father. She will always owe you.

She looked straight at him and said, "Never mind! You can go by yourself."

"Tina, you better listen real hard. You are the reason why my life is the way it is."

"No, you're living your awful life because you gamble, not because of me. The gambling devil lives in you."

"You don't know what you are talking about. The devil isn't real."

"Yes, he is. Just look at yourself in the mirror. Look at your eyes. They are full of addiction."

"Get lost!"

"Oh, your favorite line whenever you don't want to deal with the truth."

Lana was just a few inches hiding behind Tina, afraid of her grandfather now.

"So, I'll see you Tuesday afternoon at 1:00."

"No, you're on your own." Tina turned around and picked up Lana. Though old enough to walk alone, she wanted to leave the park in a hurry.

Jorge stayed and sat on the park bench with his head down.

You had to blow it again.

He quickly forgot what had just happened and believed Tina would show up Tuesday.

In the meantime, he would tell all his gambling buddies his daughter was going to help him find an apartment so they'd think highly of him again. They were relieved to think they'd now have a place to stay if they didn't already have one.

He got up from the park bench, people staring or turning their heads whenever he looked their way. He arrived at his car, where all his belongings were piled high, touching the roof. Whatever he still owned was destroyed, dirty, yellow-stained, and ripped. He only had one pair of shoes left—he sold all the expensive Italian ones for a fraction of their value so he could bet—but he still didn't think he had a problem. He only wished he had more shoes to sell.

Tuesday came and went, and Jorge had long forgotten his plans to meet Tina.

Tina still felt sick days after the meeting. The queasiness in her stomach just wouldn't go away when she thought of him. The only thing she was certain of was he would stay away for a while, possibly a few months after this last stunt. This was his usual pattern. He would hide for however long he felt necessary to clear the air between them, and then he would call, for neither he nor the addiction would ever let go of Tina.

But amid this chaos, fate had created a lifetime opportunity for Tina, which would create the distance she needed from the addiction.

"Tina, when you have a chance, can you please come to my office for a moment?" Mr. Jackson asked as he stood in the doorway of her office.

Tina looked up surprised, thinking why he couldn't just say what he wanted to say.

"Sure, but I haven't finished editing Julia's Super Eats."

"No rush. Come by my office when you can, but I would like to see you before the end of the day. It is sort of important," he said as he smiled, adding a little mystery to his request.

"Now is good. I know you are dying to tell me. I see it in your eyes," Tina said, following him to his office.

"Ha, ha, sometimes you are too real for me. I don't know anyone else who can bust out a laugh from me like you. Please take a seat. Now onto something serious."

Tina sat down, and the tone turned professional.

"You know how much I value you. You're a superb writer, editor, speaker, and person."

Tina smiled, and her eyes started to water, feeling something big was about to happen.

"I was asked to recommend a Chief Managing Editor for a new office."

Tina smiled, feeling like a hundred eyes on her, trying not to fall out of her chair. Feeling the opportunity of a lifetime was about to happen. The one she dreamt about. Then she took a deep breath, not wanting to jinx herself.

"Are you interested?"

"Of course, yes, I would. This is a dream come true."

"Good, but . . . you will have to move. Are you prepared to do so?"

"Yes," Tina said, thinking the move would be somewhere else in Florida.

"It's far away. Are you still interested?"

"Of course, I am," Tina said, thinking now of New York or maybe California.

"Well, how does London sound?"

Tina's jaw dropped as she heard her dream city, but she never connected it to her dream job.

"Do you still want the job?"

"Yes, I'm just lost for words," Tina said, tears of joy rolling down her cheeks.

"You earned it, kid."

"Thank you."

"You'll love *The London Express*."

"I can't wait."

Three days later, during an interview, she received a call from a number she didn't recognize. Ten minutes later, she received another call from the same number, but the interview was still not done, so it went to voicemail.

Once alone, she Googled the number—a cell number from the Weston area. Finally, she was able to listen to the two voicemails.

The first one was from her father, saying he was calling just to say hello, and to see how Kate and Lana were doing. The second voicemail was from Sheri.

"Out of the goodness of your heart, please call us back."

Tina's heart dropped, fearing what they wanted.

How pathetic, she thought.

Tina returned the call, hoping to end further calls. Sheri answered after the first ring. Tina could hear her father asking, "Did she pick up? Are you talking to Tina?"

Sheri finally said, "You know your father does not live with me anymore, but out of the goodness of my heart, your father still has his mail sent here."

Tina rolled her eyes, thinking," *Who says something so stupid, thinking it is going to work?*

"Anyway, Tina, I was going through the mail and opened a letter from Honda because I drive a Honda. Anyway, it wasn't for me."

Tina kept listening, wishing this lady would get to the punch line.

"It was for your father."

Tina found this strange; he didn't drive a Honda.

"Well, apparently, your father signed a twenty thousand dollar note so a friend could buy a car for his daughter."

Tina did not believe a word she said. It was no secret that her father had bad credit, probably in the 300s. It didn't seem plausible he could borrow any money, especially not for a car.

"Anyway, his friend is in prison now and has stopped paying, and the car has been repossessed."

"What did she say? Is she going to help?" Jorge said, yelling in the background.

"So, Tina, how are you going to handle this?"

"I'm not. If my father did this, he has to deal with it, not me. I have nothing to do with it."

"So, who else can I call to handle this?"

"I don't know. How about you?"

"Hold on," Sheri said to Tina, covering the phone receiver as she told Jorge that Tina wouldn't help. He got upset and left the room. Afraid of Sheri's wrath.

"Honey, your father is your responsibility. No matter what anybody tells you or what you believe. He is your blood."

"No, he isn't my responsibility."

"He is as long as he is alive."

"No, he's not. My two children are my responsibility. He is old enough to take care of himself."

"I cannot help him," Sheri said, wanting to stir fear in Tina.

"I can't either," Tina said, thinking *I've done it all my life but not anymore.*

"How can you say he is not your responsibility? He is your father, and he is your responsibility," Sheri said, again like a broken record.

"Sheri, don't call anymore; if you do, I will call the police," Tina said.

"Oh, okay, that won't be necessary," Sheri said.

She hung up the phone and started throwing Jorge's clothes out of the condo. "Your daughter can't be played, and neither can I, so get the hell out!"

Tina hung up feeling free. There would be no more Saturdays at the park or phone calls. No more drive-bys to see if her father's car was parked behind the hair salon and if he was alive. Now she would avoid the shopping plaza at all costs.

Soon afterward, she left for London and looked forward to her new life without her father and his addiction.

CHAPTER 46

An ocean away

Four months later, Jorge drove by Tina's house with a pizza on a Friday night.

He kept on driving by the house. The flowers in the front garden had been replaced by rocks and boulders. He ended up eating the pizza alone in the church parking lot.

The next day, he went to the park, feeling it was the best place to see her, but she never came.

Jorge walked up to an older lady he recognized with her grandchildren. They occasionally exchanged small talk when Kate, Lana, and her grandchildren played on the monkey bars. Jorge believed she would remember him.

"Sorry to bother you. My grandchildren would sometimes play with your grandkids. My daughter, Tina, was always with them. Do you remember?"

"Yes, I remember."

"Oh, that is great."

"I'm actually looking for my daughter, Tina. Have you seen her?"

"I have, but it's been about five months now."

"Has it really been that long?" Jorge questioned.

"Yes, I'm afraid so. Time really goes by. I have been coming to this park with my grandchildren every Saturday for years now. They love it here," Mrs. Howard said as she looked at Jorge.

"Oh, do you know where she may be?" Jorge asked.

"Oh, she's a thousand miles away. Tina lives in London now. She got a big promotion at the newspaper she was working at."

"London?" Jorge said, stammering slightly. "Are you sure? She never said this to me."

"Yes, I'm quite sure."

Jorge was lost for words. He just knew he reached another dead end.

"However, she did leave me a letter to give to you if you ever stopped and asked. I almost threw it away last week when months went by, and you never showed, but something told me to keep it, and I'm glad I did."

Mrs. Howard reached into her purse and took the letter out.

He looked at the envelope. His name Jorge Gabor was written in Tina's handwriting. Jorge couldn't bring himself to read the letter. Instead, he placed the letter inside the breast pocket of his worn and dirty blazer.

"Aren't you going to read it? Don't you want to know what she wrote?" Mrs. Howard asked.

"Some other time, you see, my daughter has a way with words. And I don't know if I could handle it right now, especially when she's in London. Well, thank you. I don't want to be late for church," Jorge said.

"Oh, okay," Mrs. Howard said, feeling bad for Jorge.

Don't read it!

Jorge got up, and on his way out of the park, he took the letter out of his blazer. He held it between his shaky fingers and could only imagine what his dear Tina had written. For a brief moment, he thought about his daughter, how she had grown up, how she always made his life so difficult. But deep down, he knew she loved him, just as she did as a little girl, and was always there for him.

As his finger glided over the back of the envelope, he was tempted to tear it, to pull out the piece of paper and hold onto the last words he knew he would ever hear from his daughter, his Tina, his Please Girl.

Another part of him wanted to rip it into a million pieces but didn't. Instead, he put Tina's letter back in his blazer, close to his heart, and walked off to church crying.

Acknowledgments

I want to thank God for always guiding me, especially during the toughest times, with love, grace, compassion and strength.

Many thanks to the enormous support I received from the Family and Friends Group of Gambling Therapy (Gordon Moody) as a person whose family member is a problem gambler. I found this community as I searched the internet, and it became the place where I started my recovery.

The support from one particular member, Velvet, has been paramount to not just my recovery but to many members of the Family and Friends Group and the My Journal Group of gamblers in recovery.

The inspiration of Please Girl came from learning about others' experiences and my own with a problem gambler. Hoping to bring more awareness to the struggles of loving a compulsive gambler. However, there is no right way to handle being in the situation; there is much to learn to cope with it. Thankfully, there is hope at the end of the tunnel for everyone involved once you know about gambling addiction.

Many thanks to my mom, dad, husband, and daughters, who knew how hard writing this book was, yet with their encouragement, Please Girl was possible. Thank you, love you.

About The Author

Jeannie Kraft constructed Please Girl based on true-life experiences. She is an educator and lives in South Florida with her family. Visit Jeannie at jeannie_kraft_the_writer on Instagram and Facebook.

If you would like to contact Jeannie, you may do so at JeannieKraft.thewriter@gmail.com.

www.ingramcontent.com/pod-product-compliance
Lightning Source LLC
Chambersburg PA
CBHW051446260626

47162CB00001B/274